LEGEND OF AHN

KING'S DARK TIDINGS

BOOK 3

KEL KADE

Written by Kel Kade
Edited by Leslie Watts
Interior Illustrations by Kel Kade
Cover art by Chris McGrath

ACKNOWLEDGMENTS

I would like to thank my daughter, who has more patience and understanding than should be expected from a child. She is never hesitant to express how proud she is of me.

The wonderful people at Podium Publishing have provided not only fantastic audiobooks but also encouragement, support, advice, and belief in my abilities.

My editor, Leslie Watts, excels in making me feel great about my writing, even while correcting my mistakes and offering suggestions. I appreciate her professionalism, positive outlook, and enthusiasm.

BOOKS BY KEL KADE

King's Dark Tidings Series

Free the Darkness

Reign of Madness

Legends of Ahn

Kingdoms and Chaos

Shroud of Prophecy Series

Fate of the Fallen

Visit www.kelkade.com

Available in audiobook

Sign up for Kel Kade's newsletter for updates!

PROLOGUE

R hesh stalked through the corridor with a sense of purpose that could
only be bred of deep-seated anger and hatred. The white marble walls
were strung with elegant tapestries, floors were adorned with lush carpets, and
brightly lit windows were embellished with rich draperies. It was all a charade.
Within these walls lay nothing but festering evil wrought of greed and ambition. This house existed for a singular purpose, and that was to *consume*.

He rapped on the chamber door without concern for anyone hearing. His
father had set him to the task, after all. The door opened a crack, just enough
for two large doe eyes to peer out from the shadows. The eyes were filled with
fear and distrust and for good reason. Naught but terror sought this boy once
having had the misfortune to join the *fallen*. That is what Rhesh had taken to
calling the hostages his father kept, for none of these young ones would ever
rise again from the depths of their despair. Rhesh, himself, would have
succumbed to the piteous darkness long ago had it not been for his dear mother
and her cunning ways. Of course, it helped that he had developed a far greater
power than either his father or brother could ever hope to bear.

"You will come with me," he intoned, and the boy jumped back in fright.
The Gerrand boy always shied away from him. One look at Rhesh's grey robes
with red panels, and the boy looked as if he would bolt. Rhesh could not blame
him. Most people feared fire mages—not as much as true battle mages, but
fear was fear, and still they cringed.

The boy bent and grabbed the pack lain by the door. Nothing in the pack had great value, but it was all the boy would probably ever have again, if Rhesh's father, Lord Carinen, took notice. Luckily for the boy, Gresh Carinen had been busy this past month and had not had time to spend on his pet projects. The boy's luck had just run out, though. Gresh had sent for the ten-year-old, and Rhesh was beholden to deliver.

The two walked out to the stables where two horses were saddled and a third was loaded with packs and travel supplies. Rhesh's horse, Winter, was a beautiful white mare gifted to him by Duke Darning, his mother's cousin, with whom he had stayed for the past few years—until his father called him home just before the King's Tournament. That debacle had been a terrible nightmare in itself. Rhesh had finished fourth in the fourth tier finals of the competition; but, of course, his father had not been satisfied. Rhesh had told his father that Swordmaster Moroven had not taught him to duel, but rather to *fight*—as in the methods used in real battles. His father had many colorful things to say about Moroven, and Rhesh had simply been glad his instructor had not been present to hear them. Then again, if Moroven *had* been present, maybe his father would no longer be a problem.

In the end, it would not matter, because Dynen would just take the old man's place. Rhesh's older brother was just as bad or worse than his father. He was sick and demented—the kind of man who enjoyed witnessing and inflicting pain on others. It had only gotten worse since the infamous Dark Tidings had easily whipped the arrogant Swordmaster in front of thousands of spectators. Of course, Dark Tidings had prevailed over every one of his foes, but Dynen's crass words had elicited the wraith's anger. The shadowed man had made Dynen look the fool.

Rhesh's brother would do anything he could to bring down everyone around him, and he reveled in tarnishing anything that was pure. Alon Gerrand was an innocent boy from a good House with good people. Rhesh's father and brother would make it their purpose to corrupt the boy into becoming just as sick and sordid as they were.

It was for this reason Rhesh was to bring the boy to their northern holdings near Braeby. Gresh was now a member of the Council of Lords and held the title of duke, even if he did not have actual possession of the duchy. The old dukes held their lands with the strength of arms and righteous indignation. According to the laws of Ashai, King Caydean did not have the right to displace the dukes without a significant reason and the vote of the Council, the rightful Council, not Caydean's construction; but Caydean was not playing by the rules. He made his own rules. Fortunately for the dukes, Caydean had alienated General Marcum and replaced the highly decorated war veteran with the idiot Lord Abrigan, whose older brother was also newly raised to the rank of duke. Lord Abrigan had no military training or experience, and his campaign against the three remaining rightful dukes was completely ineffective. The army had made no headway in claiming any of the dukes' heads or their lands.

The fire mage led the boy out of the Carinen estate and through the city of Kaibain. They left the city through the Northern Gate and then continued north. The journey to Braeby would take several weeks and the road would be rife with bandits and other hazards. No one had questioned Rhesh when he claimed no need for an escort, though. The bandits would have to be idiots to mess with a fire mage. In truth, Rhesh was not so confident. He was not a fully trained mage. He was not even a journeyman. He was just an apprentice who probably would never get the chance to complete his training under Caydean's rule and his father's machinations.

The horses plodded north until the city walls had disappeared. To get to Braeby, they would head northwest straight up the Lorelis Trade Route through Cheswick and beyond. With this in mind, Rhesh turned the horses east. Their true destination was a very, *very* long way.

1

The ship lurched, throwing Rezkin to the tilted planks. He twisted to the side, just missing a blade that sank deeply into the wood where his chest had been. His opponent released the trapped blade, choosing instead to attack him with fists and feet.

With a malicious growl, Malcius threw himself onto the downed wraith, taking advantage of the swordmaster's misfortune, a stroke of luck he would probably never have again. Straddling the younger man's torso, Malcius reached for Rezkin's throat, but the warrior was undaunted. Rezkin thrust his hips upward and grasped Malcius's arm, twisting it as the man tumbled from atop him. Malcius struck the deck with his face, his arm wrenched behind him. He could not move unless he was willing to break, or at least dislocate, his own arm.

"I concede," he muttered into the grimy, salty boards.

Rezkin released his hold and stepped back, allowing his friend to regain his feet on his own. Malcius scowled as he rose, shaking his arm to loosen the tension.

"I thought I might have had you when you fell," he grumbled.

Rezkin shook his head and said, "It is true the fates occasionally deal us an unfortunate hand, but we must learn to combat it with speed and focus."

"Yes, yes, speed and focus. So you have said," Malcius spat as he retrieved his sword. "Palis was fast and focused, and it did not save *him*."

Rezkin's gaze turned to the deep blue and grey waves bobbing and rolling over the distance. Smaller ripples danced across their surfaces, reminding him of the breeze blowing over the hills of golden grasses back in the land he called home. Distance-wise, Ashai was not so far from their present location, only a few weeks by ship. He would not be returning anytime soon, though, and it felt so very far from where he had last fought beside Palis. Rezkin realized, now, that Palis had been his *friend* and was the first one Rezkin had lost. When he thought of the fallen hero, he felt a tightening in his chest and his stomach soured. He told himself the feelings resulted from having failed in his duty to protect his friend, but he was concerned that he was failing in other respects. He needed to be more diligent in avoiding emotional attachments.

Turning back to Malcius, he said, "Palis was not fast enough. You will become faster. Then you and I, together, will reclaim our home and bring justice to Palis's killer."

Accusation was heavy in his voice as Malcius said, "You told me that Palis's killer was dead."

"I was speaking of Caydean, of course," Rezkin replied. "It was by his orders that our Ashaiian brethren attacked us. They sought only to do their king's bidding."

The two men were interrupted by a soft voice at the steps to the lower deck. "If you gentlemen are ready, lunch is served."

"Thank you, Frisha," Rezkin replied, turning to the young woman. Frisha nodded and then walked away without a backward glance.

Noticing the awkward exchange, Malcius remarked, "She is still upset over Palis's death."

"It is more than that," Rezkin observed. "She barely speaks to me, and when she does, it is always formal and distant. She has not smiled or laughed since that day, at least not with *me*."

"Perhaps she blames you," Malcius suggested, the edge returning to his voice. "I admit that I blamed you at first. Sometimes I still do." He sighed and begrudgingly added, "I do realize, however, that it was my brother's choice to do what he did. He was his own man, not a child to be coddled."

Rezkin knew that Frisha's behavior was due to more than just Palis's death, though. "She does not blame me for killing Palis. She blames me for killing *Rezkin*."

Malcius viewed Rezkin askance. "What do you mean?"

"The Rezkin she knew," he clarified. "Or *thought* she knew."

After two weeks of confinement on the ship, Frisha still had not confronted Rezkin about the revelation that *he* was Dark Tidings and the one referred to as the True King. Considering her generally amicable nature, her aloofness was disconcerting.

"Yes, it came as a shock to all of us," Malcius snapped. "Even I continue to have feelings of betrayal for your deception." His eyes momentarily flashed with fury.

"I have explained my reasoning," Rezkin replied as he wiped the sweat from his face and neck.

"I know, and I accept it. It does not soothe the sting, though."

"And for that, I am truly sorry, Malcius. I have endeavored to honor my friends, but I must also protect you. Sometimes the two goals are at odds," Rezkin said.

"I have never met a man who worked so hard to do either," Malcius replied. "In truth, I never really think about how I treat my friends. Perhaps you take yourself too seriously."

Rezkin turned with surprise. "It is *Rule 1*, Malcius. It is my purpose for being."

"Maybe you should just be yourself," Malcius said.

Malcius's statement frustrated Rezkin more than he thought it should have. Every day of his life had been spent in training to play a role, to be *someone else* when the need arose. He was everyone and no one. That *was* his role in life, yet people were constantly trying to push him into only one. It served as more proof that he needed to keep the lives of his individual personas separate.

After meandering through the maze of ropes and pulleys piled on the lower deck, they ducked into the shady dining area. The mood in the mess was subdued, as usual. People sat around several tables finishing the midday meal. Frisha steadfastly ignored Rezkin as she sat beside her lifelong friend Tam. Malcius took a seat next to his sister, Shiela, across from Tieran Nirius. The reluctant beginner apprentice healer, Reaylin, had been chatting quietly with Journeyman Wesson. Baron Drom Nasque and his son Waylen occupied one end of a second table. Captain Jimson, Second Lieutenant Drascon, and Sergeant Millins from the King's Army were gathered around the opposite end.

Though not currently present, most of the baron's guards had opted to stay with Rezkin's entourage since they were now considered fugitives, although a couple of them had decided to return to Ashai in hopes of saving their families knowing it was probably a lost cause. Nirius and Jebai house guards were also concerned for their families, but since their houses had been declared traitors, they felt they had no hope of saving their loved ones until they took back Ashai.

Three strikers were gathered at another table, and Kai could be heard grumbling about the fact that there was no ale to be found anywhere on the vessel. Shezar Olnag and Roark Genring now also claimed Rezkin as their king. He was fairly certain of Kai's loyalty since it was largely by *his* influence that Rezkin had landed in his current predicament. The man had ambitions, though, and Rezkin was not certain they were in line with his own. Shezar and Roark had switched sides only after Rezkin had defeated five of their brethren, so they were at the top of his list of immediate, potential threats. Rezkin's relationship with the strikers was tenuous as far as he was concerned. There had to have been a reason he was ordered to kill so many of them. While he now considered those orders to be suspect, the fact that he had followed through would not incite loyalty from the rest.

Rezkin's friends also would not be pleased to hear of his clandestine activities. The fact that he was the undefeated champion of the King's Tournament and a rival for the throne had been hard enough for his friends to accept. Tensions were already high. He would probably lose their support altogether if they found out he was the leader of the Ashaiian underworld. Rezkin felt no regret for his actions, though. He was doing what he was trained to do. The others' opinions were irrelevant.

Besides the possible enemies in his own camp, there were many others to concern him. If history was an indication of what was in store for the future, it would not be long before the simple state of being Ashaiian was cause for mistrust and even hatred. Every kingdom near the Souelian Sea was after Caydean's head, but they would not hesitate to punish anyone they could get their hands on in lieu of the king. It would not matter that Rezkin was in opposition to Caydean. Any Ashaiian would be a target and especially one with a claim to the throne. Now he had not only to defeat the mad mage king, but also prevent the other kingdoms from laying waste to his homeland.

A shout sounded from outside, followed by thundering footsteps across the deck. A few moments later, *Stargazer*'s Captain Merk Estadd entered the mess and announced, "Lord Rezkin, we have reached the cove."

"Thank you, Captain. Are you certain it is unoccupied?" Rezkin asked.

"No, my lord, we will have to send a scout to know for sure."

"Very well. Have one of your men row ashore with Striker Kai." He turned to the striker and said, "Scout the cove and surrounding forest. I want to know if so much as a trapper has been nearby recently."

Kai nodded and stood from his bench. The captain and Kai left the mess, and Rezkin surveyed the curious faces of his companions. The *Stargazer* was one of the largest merchant ships that made port in Ashai, and he and his comrades had been able to rescue many people from Caydean's hostile forces. When the city had erupted in chaos and Striker Shezar's explanation of the mad king's plan reached the ears of every tournament spectator, people had flocked to the tournament champion for protection. Most of the refugees were foreigners, but a good number of Ashaiian citizens had ridden his wake as well. In the end, over a hundred refugees had crammed into the ship, in addition to the cadaverous slaves found in Duke Ytrevius's subterranean cavern.

The ship's mess was the largest room on the ship besides the hold that was filled with refugees and supplies, and it had been reserved for use by Rezkin's companions. It was now his command center as well as a place for those in his confidence to take their meals.

"What's going on?" Tam asked. "I thought we were going to Serret."

"Serret is less than a day from our current position, but we are taking a short respite," Rezkin answered.

"A *respite*? Where and why?" Tieran asked. "Have we not spent enough time aboard this miserable ship?"

Tieran had been highly vocal about his disdain for the traveling conditions. While the voyage from Kaibain to Skutton had not been pleasant by any of the nobles' standards, traveling on a ship crammed full of angry, resentful, and mournful refugees had been far worse.

Rezkin said, "The ship does not possess a certified manifest, trading certificate, or port visa, all of which should have been acquired in Skutton per the trade agreements enforced by the Interkingdom Trading Authority."

Tieran said, "Right. The ITA. I was not thinking of them. We are refugees." He sniffed disdainfully. "Surely they will make an exception. Once they know who we are ..."

Rezkin shook his head. "This ship is carrying more than a hundred undocumented people. Most of these refugees have no proof of identity, and we *all* lack the necessary travelling papers. From Channería's perspective, and pretty much everyone else's, our port of origin is in a hostile kingdom. We made our escape from what could rightfully be called a warzone. While Channería may be willing to assist other foreigners in returning to their own lands, I doubt they will look kindly on a swarm of refugees invading their largest port. They will see many of us as enemies and potential spies."

"So what are we supposed to do?" Tam asked. "How do we get what we need?"

Rezkin did not say it, but he had already made the documents. Without access to a mage relay, though, he could not file the record with the ITA office in Serret.

"I will take care of that. In the meantime, I need you all to perform a task."

The others looked at Rezkin skeptically, but Tam seemed eager to do something useful.

"Right. What is it?" he said with a little too much enthusiasm.

"I need you to convince the other passengers and ship's crew of the importance of concealing their identities—*all* of our identities. It would be best for no one to discover who we really are so long as the port authority and Channerian navy have the ability to capture us or prevent our escape. As far as the ITA is concerned, we are a passenger ship from Torrel. We were unable to resupply in Skutton due to the turmoil, so we were forced to make for Serret, arriving a week ahead of schedule."

Malcius said, "But we were not scheduled to be there at all."

"They will not know that. To prevent exposure, only the few I authorize will be permitted to disembark while we are at port. Anyone wishing to leave the ship will have to wait until we are ready to depart."

"But there are over a hundred people on board! It will seem suspicious if a passenger ship arrives and no one gets off," said Tieran.

"Not if we are under quarantine," Rezkin said. At their confused expressions he explained, "Any ship carrying a communicable disease, no matter how minor, is placed under quarantine for a minimum of three days or until all on board are cleared as healthy by an ITA healer. The ship may, however, take on supplies and new passengers, assuming any desire to board a quarantined vessel. After examination by the healer, a maximum of two crewmen are permitted to leave the ship to organize such affairs. Kai and Roark will pose as the crewmen."

"So you will be staying aboard," Tam said, appearing both disappointed and relieved.

Rezkin smiled indulgently and replied, "No, I will not be aboard at all. I will rejoin you before the ship leaves port."

"Where will *you* be?" Malcius asked.

"I go by land. I told you, I must to arrange the necessary documentation."

Malcius huffed. "But if you are getting the documents, then how will *we* get them before we arrive in Serret?"

"Do not worry, Malcius. The captain already has them," Rezkin answered.

"But—"

"The problem is not acquiring the documents," Rezkin explained. "It is that they must be recorded with the ITA. Maritime trade is highly regulated and costly. If the officials cannot find a record of the vessel and its occupants, *Stargazer* will not be permitted to dock and will likely be seized."

Frisha surprised Rezkin when, from where she sat sulking in the corner, she snapped, "You've been on the ship with us the whole time. How did *you* get the documents?"

Rezkin looked at the estranged young woman. Since leaving Skutton, she had generally been cool and distant, but her current tone could only be described as hostile.

"That is not important, Frisha. Suffice it to say that we have them."

His tone lacked emotion, but an uncomfortable silence ensued as Frisha continued to glare at him. The others chose to stay out of what appeared to be a battle of wills between would-be lovers. At least, *most* of them possessed such tact.

"I do not *want* to stay on the ship," Shiela whined. "It is filthy and smelly and full of undesirables. If we are not to stay in Serret, then where will we go? I want to go home."

"I will not discuss future destinations, and, at present, you do not have a home."

Shiela buried her face in her hands and released a mournful wail.

Frisha stood and placed her arms around her *beloved* cousin. "Rezkin, how can you be so insensitive?" she asked.

"What would be the point of lying, Frisha? It is simple fact—one that she must accept, and the sooner the better." His gaze roved over the others. "It is one you will all have to accept for now."

Without waiting for a reply, Rezkin turned and ducked through the doorway. It was time for Dark Tidings to make an appearance. While he had revealed that persona to those closest to him and to the strikers, everyone else aboard was oblivious. He strode about the ship in full costume once or twice a day. On occasion, one of the strikers donned the guise so that others would not become suspicious of him. He would make a show of reporting to the True King and receiving orders. The ruse might have been unnecessary, but the less information others had about him the better. Eventually the truth would get out, but he hoped it did not become common knowledge until after they left Channería. Besides that, it gave him something to do on what was otherwise a tedious journey.

Dark Tidings trod across the deck, and some people openly gawked, as they always did, while others avoided looking at him altogether. After about an hour, Kai returned with news that the cove was indeed unoccupied, and there were signs that a patrol had passed through recently. It had been a gamble, but this was good news. The cove was deep enough for a ship but was hidden from view by high banks and dense forest. According to the captain, it was used by a few of the more unscrupulous smugglers and slavers who felt it was their civic duty to prevent others from discovering the hideout. Estadd did not mention how it was that *he* knew about it. Far from any settlements and steeped in superstition, it was rare for an honest man to visit the cove. The Channerían army was aware of the haven's existence, however, and patrols were sent to check for visitors every few weeks. The fact that a patrol had been there recently meant it was unlikely another would pass through in the short time *Stargazer* would be there.

Dark Tidings listened to the striker's report, issued a few unnecessary orders, and then announced loud enough for those closest to hear that he would be sending Lord Rezkin on an errand. Then, Kai followed him to his berth. Rezkin knew the man had some protest on his tongue by the stubborn set of his jaw.

"You cannot go alone," Kai huffed as soon as the door was shut.

Rezkin pulled the mask from his face and began unclipping braids from his hair. If he had known he would need to keep up the ruse for longer than the duration of the tournament, he might have come up with a simpler disguise.

"I am capable of conducting the mission without assistance. What is the problem?"

Kai slammed his fist on the stout table along one wall. "You are the king! You cannot go gallivanting through hostile kingdoms without an escort. At the very least, you should take some strikers. It is our duty to protect you."

"I need you here to make sure things go as planned," Rezkin replied. "Do you think these refugees will stay in line without a strong leader? Many of them are not used to taking orders. They are nobles, accomplished swordsmen, warriors, and mages from nearly every kingdom, and we have barely avoided serious bloodshed from the cultural conflicts alone."

"One striker"—Kai held up a finger—"could handle those issues, especially since they will believe Dark Tidings is still aboard. You have two more strikers to accompany you. There is no reason for you to go alone."

Except that there *were* reasons. Rezkin just did not want Kai to know about them. He shook his head and said, "When the ship reaches Serret, we will need one striker to stay aboard and maintain order while the other two go into the city."

"We need only one in the city," Kai argued. "Anyone trustworthy can fill the other role. We can send Lord Tieran or Malcius. That would free one striker to go with you."

"It will be easier for a single man to slip through the kingdom unseen," Rezkin replied.

Kai grumbled something unintelligible and then said, "I know I was not at my best when we met, and I admit that age has slowed me a bit, but I am still more than capable of accomplishing what you propose. If that does not satisfy you, then take Shezar. He is younger and has mastered both day and night stealth skills."

"We do not know how far we can trust him," Rezkin said. It was hardly necessary to point that out, but it was a good excuse.

"It is better for him to stay with you, then, so you can keep an eye on him. You are the True King. People who would otherwise decry rebellion will follow you. What if you are killed or captured?"

Rezkin rolled Dark Tiding's cloak into a bundle and stuffed it into a trunk. He sat on a bunk to shuck his boots. "I will not be captured," he said with resolve. "If I die, then you will go on without me. The people know that Dark Tidings is the True King. He is no more than a mask, a persona. Anyone with a decent amount of skill can play the role. You, Shezar, and Roark can trade off if necessary. No one but those in our confidence will know of the deception, and they likely will not care."

"But you, *Rezkin* the Swordbearer, are the one with the claim to the throne. Without that, Dark Tidings is nothing but an illegitimate figurehead."

When Rezkin finally turned on the man, his expression was one that insisted he would brook no further argument. "Kai, this is not up for debate. I go alone."

By the time he emerged from the cabin, the ship was secure in the cove. He had already discussed the plan with the strikers and Jimson, so he had only one task left to do.

Frisha, Tam, and Wesson were at the deck rail eyeing the forest beyond the banks.

"They say it is haunted," Wesson remarked as Rezkin approached from behind.

Tam laughed. "Who says?"

The mage shrugged. "Before I joined you, I spent some time in the villages of Fendendril. The people there are very poor and a bit odd, if you ask me. They are highly superstitious. It is common belief that the Fendendril Forest is haunted. The locals never go east of Banton. I had a mind to see for myself, but to the Fendens, returning is worse than going. They believe that anyone coming from the eastern woods must be possessed. Village law requires that they take *preventative* measures."

"Like what?" Tam asked.

Wesson looked at him sideways. "Anyone who survives the eastern woods does not survive the return." Turning his gaze back to the dark forest, he said, "According to the Fendens, the haunting does not stop at the break. The forest in Channería is supposed to be inhabited by the spirits as well. Even the sailors have said as much."

"Do you believe it?" Tam asked.

Frisha elbowed Tam and said, "Don't be silly. There's no such thing as spirits."

"How do *you* know? Mages can do all kinds of things," Tam said with a nod toward Wesson. "How do you know that some of them haven't figured out how to walk around without their bodies?"

Wesson turned toward Tam with wide eyes. "I have never heard of anything like that, but there are other *things* that remain unexplained. You have surely heard the tales of people being possessed by demons, and there are untold numbers of forest creatures, both magical and mundane. *I* am not ready to discount the idea of spirits."

Rezkin cleared his throat and all three jumped. The railing beneath Wesson's hand split with a resounding *crack*. Rezkin lifted a brow at the mage.

"Oops," Wesson said as he rubbed his hand and looked at Rezkin with chagrin. "Perhaps you should not sneak up on a battle mage."

"Perhaps the battle mage should pay more attention to his surroundings,"

Rezkin said. He glanced at Tam and Frisha. "I must attend to an errand. I am leaving, but I will meet you in Serret."

"Wait, you're leaving us?" Frisha exclaimed. "You can't leave us. What if something happens?"

"The strikers are capable of handling any problems that arise." He glanced around to make sure no one else was within hearing range and said, "Everyone else will be under the impression that Dark Tidings is still aboard. It is doubtful they will cause many problems."

Frisha's expression sobered at the mention of the infamous dark warrior. Rezkin saw the change in Frisha's eyes, but there was nothing he could say in that moment.

"The strikers aren't going with you?" Tam asked. "But you're the—"

"Tam," Rezkin said.

Tam's gaze darted around anxiously. "Right. You know what I'm saying. You can't go alone."

"I should go with you," Wesson interjected.

"Why is that, Journeyman?" Rezkin asked.

Wesson nodded over his shoulder. "The forest is not safe. Who knows what kind of trouble you might encounter. I could help you. Besides, I have a feeling it is going to be difficult for Ashaiians in Channería right now. You should not be traveling alone."

Rezkin frowned. Everyone was so concerned about keeping him safe. Did they not recognize that he was a trained warrior? He had already proven himself to them at the tournament. Did they think he could not fend for himself in the wild? No, they knew he was capable. He looked into Tam and Frisha's anxious eyes and realized they were not so concerned for him as they were for themselves. They worried about what might happen to them if he perished.

"I am capable of performing this task on my own. I must make arrangements so that you will all be safe upon arrival," Rezkin said.

"So you're going to find us a place to stay?" Tam asked.

"Yes. Some of the foreigners will be able to return to their homes, but many more of us have no place to go."

Tam shook his head. "That's considerate of you, but I really don't think that's your responsibility, Rez. Besides, there's no reason you have to do it alone."

Rezkin was tired of discussing the subject. Perhaps next time he would skip the courtesy of a farewell and leave a note.

"I will see you all in Serret. If you have any problems, talk to one of the strikers. Frisha, please remember to stay near Malcius. He is your escort, and with the selection of international nobility on board, it would be best for you to observe an acceptable level of propriety."

Frisha huffed and crossed her arms, her anxious thoughts overshadowed by anger. How dare he lecture her about propriety. Did he think she would make him look the fool? Was he worried that others would think her a disgrace? She opened her mouth to respond, but Rezkin staved her retort with a raised hand.

"I know you have misgivings about me, and it is obvious you have reconsidered the prospect of betrothal. No matter what your future holds—*whoever* —I only desire your safety and happiness. A perceived misstep now could render that difficult or impossible, no matter your innocence."

Frisha flushed. She was resentful of so many things, and she knew she had been acting petulant, but she had not realized how obvious her feelings were. Rezkin took it in stride, though, appearing unfazed. Before, she might have thought him putting on a brave face, reserving his emotions both for her sake and for appearances. Now she wondered if he had any feelings. She shrugged and looked away.

Rezkin said farewell to Tam and then turned to the mage. Wesson was distracted again. He stared into the forest, his gaze distant. Rezkin thought perhaps the journeyman wanted to avoid the discomfort of a farewell, so he left it at that.

After collecting his travel gear, one of the crewmen rowed him the short distance across the water. He tossed the pack onto the high bank and then clung to thick tree roots to pull himself up the slick mud. It would have been nice to have Pride for the journey, but it was not practical. This would be a long run. He estimated it would take at least two days to run the distance to Serret if he stopped for only a few hours rest. He had to get there in time to take care of his business before the ship arrived. Otherwise, the trip would be pointless and his friends would be in greater danger.

After a short distance into the forest, it grew dark. The trees were straight and tall, and the canopy blocked most of the sunlight. Very little grew on the forest floor, but his passage was hardly eased. The terrain was rough, marred by thick tangles of roots and crumbling outcrops relieved only by steep, briar-filled crevices through which icy streams swept across slick, moss-covered detritus. He briefly wondered if he might make better time leaping through the canopy, but after peering into the darkness above, he realized the branches were much too thin to hold his weight.

While he saw no sign that anyone had been in the vicinity, he was careful to step lightly and leave little evidence of his own passing. His pants, hooded tunic, and armor were of varying shades of green and brown, and his pack lay over his swords, which were strapped across his back. The hilts were pointed down where he could still access them if necessary, but they would not be obvious to anyone with whom he might cross paths.

Less than an hour into his journey, Rezkin felt the hairs on the back of his neck stand on end. He spun, drawing the dagger at his belt, and caught sight of a shadowy figure just as it stepped around a tree. The silhouette froze and then steadily strode forward as if conceding the game.

Rezkin's eyes widened. He had not expected this. "What are you doing here?"

"I need to come with you," Wesson said.

"I told you to stay with the ship. Why do you defy my orders?"

Wesson looked up as a soft breeze blew through the canopy. He tilted his head as if listening and then shrugged. "You should not be traveling alone. I must accompany you."

"That was not for you to decide. You cannot come with me," Rezkin replied.

The mage nodded patiently and then said, "How will you stop me?"

Rezkin narrowed his eyes. Wesson had never been so impertinent. The journeyman had always been eager to please, so long as what Rezkin asked of him did not violate their agreement. He looked past the mage, but it was too dark to see the evidence of his passing.

"You will slow me down. I must move quickly," Rezkin said. "If you insist on following me, you will be left behind."

Wesson's boyish smile belied the seriousness of the situation. "I will keep up. Do not worry about me."

"Where is your pack?" Rezkin asked.

Wesson's smile fell, and he appeared embarrassed. "I was in a hurry. I forgot. But, I am a mage, am I not?" He spread his hands and said, "I will find what I need." The mage did not appear the least bit concerned.

Rezkin did not have time to argue with the journeyman. Something was amiss, but he decided he would have to let it play out and see.

Frisha sat on her bunk staring out the porthole. The still water around the ship was nearly black, and the dark forest seemed to loom closer every time she spied it. She wrung soft fabric between her fingers and then tossed it to the floor. She stared at the sinuous creature, its green scales glinting in the fading light. She huffed and snatched the silky scarf from the grimy floorboards. Her mind and heart were a jumbled mess, and it was all his fault.

When she imagined Rezkin dressed in his embroidered silk doublet and polished boots, it was easy to forget that he was also the undefeated, demonic executioner of the tournament. His soft voice and reassuring demeanor lulled her into forgetting that he was a brutal killer, a weapon of bloodshed. His impeccable manners and chivalrous honor had blinded her to the cold indifference that lay beneath the surface.

Rezkin was not at all the man she thought he was. It seemed absurd now that she looked back on the past few months. Who had she thought he was? Had she ever truly considered? None of that time made sense anymore. He was not an average young man traveling alone. Why had she ever thought he appeared normal? Even at the time, his mannerisms and dress had been better than any commoner, and the swords and assortment of other weapons should have been a dead giveaway that he was not so simple.

Rezkin always had too much money and not enough … well, just not *enough*. Her uncle had been right. Rezkin was a man with no name from a place with no name. He never discussed his past in the slightest detail. He had no home and no family, and yet he had never shown any concern for the lack. In their society, a man was judged by the family that reared him and the station to which he was born. By that regard, Rezkin was no one. He had once said, though, that a person should be defined by the sum of his experiences and the choices he made. If this was true, then he had never been a person—not to *her*, since she had known none of his either. Even now, the only details she had learned about him had to do with fighting and killing. Was that all he was?

No, that was not quite true. She knew how he had treated *her*. She knew how he had treated Tam and Reaylin and Jimson and Wesson. He had saved Kai from a noose around his neck. It seemed so altruistic. The depth of Rezkin's deception, though, had shown her that he was cunning. What was his motive? *Why* had he attached himself to Tam and her? She was nothing special, not unless you considered her relationship with the general of the army. What a fantastic coincidence that the contender for the throne would chose *her.* She understood, now, why Kai had been so excited to learn her uncle's identity.

She felt so stupid. She had just accepted it all—accepted *him.* Even Tam had tried to warn her, and she had berated him for it. Tam had told her that Rezkin had killed people, but she had imagined a young man carrying out his duty for the king with a heavy heart. That was not at all who Rezkin was.

She had seen him kill the bandit who attacked Reaylin. She remembered being terrified, and then her savior swooped in and rescued Reaylin. But she would never forget that cold, empty gaze as he stood over the defeated man and ran him through. Afterward, she had told herself that the dreaded look had all been in her head, a result of the trauma and an overactive imagination. Then, Dark Tidings killed the sandman. He had not just killed him. He had chopped him to pieces in front of thousands of people. While part of her applauded the justice he wrought, the display had been gruesome and disturbing. It was an act expected of a king, a leader burdened by the weight of difficult decisions. But she did not know if she could call the same man her lover. Once upon a time, she looked into Rezkin's eyes and saw beautiful crystal pools. Now, all she saw was frozen ice, empty and cold, and somehow the bright, clear blue was filled with darkness.

Rezkin was a warrior king—at least he could be one day. Wesson had confirmed that Rezkin was closely related to Tieran, which meant he was also of relation to the royal family. He was someone important even without his mysterious claim to the throne. Although he had exposed himself as Dark Tidings, he had not divulged the evidence of said claim. She had little idea of who Rezkin was, and she was starting to wonder if she really wanted to know.

The thought alone stoked her anger. Rezkin was supposed to be *hers.* He was supposed to be the handsome, young man who spoke with eloquence and enchanted her with his cool gaze and dazzling smiles.

Frisha frowned. Was that it? Wesson had explained that a spell lay over Rezkin that allowed him to influence people's perceptions. Had he used the spell on *her*? Had Rezkin truly enchanted her?

2

Rezkin could not see through trees, the darkness having finally swallowed the forest whole. He continued east toward Serret stepping silently where he could. The small stone he carried in his palm was successful only in lighting the forest for a few feet in front of him. He glanced back every so often to see that the mage was still with him. Wesson strolled through the entangled forest as though it were a mere walk in a city garden. When Rezkin stopped to survey his surroundings, Wesson stood patiently waiting. Rezkin could not see him in the darkness, but he had the sense that Wesson was studying him.

The mage finally spoke the first words either had said in hours. "How do you find your way?"

"What do you mean?" Rezkin asked. Their voices sounded like explosions in the stillness of the night.

"You seem to be using many of your senses, but it appears that you depend primarily on sight. The forest is dark, yet you consistently travel east. How do you know which way to go?"

Rezkin eyed the mage a moment and then turned and continued walking. He pointed to a tree trunk and said, "It is the moss. Very little light reaches down here, but it is enough. The moss prefers the shade, so it primarily grows on the side of the trunks that face north."

"But I see moss all over. There seems to be no pattern," Wesson argued.

Rezkin shook his head. "It is not that consistent. The moss will grow wherever it finds shade, but if you look closely, the densest coverings are on the northern side. That is not the only indication, though. There is also the breeze. When it was lighter, I could see the leaves in the canopy. At this time of year, the wind tends to blow from the southwest. Now that it is dark, I must depend on the sound and brief sensations when the wind reaches this far down."

"That also does not seem dependable," Wesson said. "A weather disturbance or the shape of the land could disrupt the flow."

Rezkin hopped down from an outcrop landing in the talus below with an unavoidable crunch. As he righted himself, he asked, "How do *you* know we are continuing east?"

Wesson's voice was much closer than Rezkin was expecting when he replied. "Because it is the direction you wish to go."

Suddenly feeling the need to put more distance between himself and the mage, he quickened his stride and then barely caught hold of a struggling sapling before he plummeted into a rocky crevice. The mage light slipped from his fingers, its glow extinguished the moment it left his hand. A few long seconds later, he heard a crack against the rocks below, followed by a plunk into water.

Rezkin pulled his foot back from the empty void over which it hovered and then turned to peer at the mage in the darkness. Wesson was naught but a shadow, and he stood much farther away than he should have given the close proximity of his voice a moment ago. The mage had not moved to assist Rezkin when he nearly fell to what might have been an untimely death, nor did he seem surprised or concerned.

"Perhaps you would care to produce a light for us, Journeyman," Rezkin calmly remarked.

Wesson did not create his usual glowing blue orb. Instead, hundreds of tiny lights danced forth from the trees to gather in their vicinity. The lights flashed on and off, a gradual ebb and flow of illumination. One passed only inches from Rezkin's face, and he realized the radiance emanated from miniscule flying insects.

"Will this suffice?" Wesson asked.

Rezkin surveyed the forest that was now illuminated in a subtle, golden glow that reached much farther than had the light of his mage stone.

"Will they stay with us?" he asked.

Wesson tilted his head and said, "If I wish it to be so."

Rezkin eyed the mage suspiciously. "One of those life mage skills you were working on?"

Wesson smiled pleasantly and shrugged.

~

Tam was getting on her nerves. It was unfair to take her frustrations out on him, but she could not take a single minute more of his constant chattering about Rezkin.

"You don't know that," she snapped. "You don't know anything about him. For all you know, he could be in favor of ritual bonding."

"I don't think Rezkin is in favor of doing anything he doesn't want to do," Tam replied with a chuckle as he pushed his plate away.

Frisha scowled at her friend. "Of course. Rezkin does what Rezkin wants. Doesn't matter what anyone *else* wants. I'm just saying, you don't know that he would reject the bond if it suited him."

Malcius's cup hit the table with a clunk. "Why would Rezkin possibly want to bond with a Pruari?" he asked in dismay.

"I didn't say he would," she exclaimed. "You were the one that brought it up."

"It was a hypothetical situation, and it was not specifically about Rezkin!" Malcius said as he threw his hands in the air.

Frisha huffed, "Tam brought up Rezkin, just like he always does."

Tam's eyes widened, and he sputtered. "There was a time when that's all we ever heard from *you*!"

"Well, grow up! He's not so perfect," she said.

Tam brushed the hair from his eyes in frustration. It had grown too long, and he needed it cut. Frisha had been doing it for him, but he was not sure he wanted her near his head with shears.

"What is your problem, Frisha? You've been surly this entire voyage. I understand, I do. Your family has suffered a great loss, and Rezkin's revelation was no small matter, especially for you. But you've been positively unbearable since Rez left. I don't get it. You weren't even talking to him before. Why does it matter that he'll be gone for a few days?"

Frisha groaned and buried her face in her hands. "I'm sorry, Tam, Malcius. It's just ... when I was sent to Uncle Marcum's to find a husband, I expected that I would have to marry a stranger. I was sick with worry. Would he be young or old? Would he be handsome or … *not*. Would he be kind or cruel? I know Uncle Marcum and Aunt Adelina would do their best for me, but we've all heard the stories about people not being who you think they are when behind closed doors."

"I had no idea you were so concerned," Tam said. "You never talked about it."

"I didn't want to worry you, and I didn't want to think about it. It's not like there was anything you could do."

Tam flushed and glanced away. The only thing he could have done was to marry her himself, and he really did not want to marry Frisha. Still, if she had allowed him to see how upset she was, he might have considered it.

Frisha peered at the table in the dim lighting of the mess and said, "Rezkin was like a dream come true. He was so handsome and courteous, and he always treated me like a lady. He was young and self-assured, and he made me feel safe. I always felt like he could handle anything, like everything would be okay."

Tam understood. Slowly, he said, "I felt that way with Rez, too. I still do, and that's the only reason I can function with any sense of normalcy everyday while my family is potentially suffering in Ashai. We have no home, no haven. We are all adrift, our foundations ripped from beneath us, but I feel secure because Rezkin is holding us up."

Frisha nodded. "In my heart, he was always a prince, and he wanted *me*." She looked up with unshed tears. "But now I know it was all a lie."

"Oh, Frisha. It wasn't *all* a lie. I am sure of it," Tam replied.

Malcius added, "Just because he is more than you thought he was doesn't mean his feelings are any less."

Frisha blinked and the tears trailed down her face, which hardened again with anger. "More? You think he is *more*? You've only seen him kill from afar or in the heat of battle during our escape. I've seen close up the death in his eyes. I didn't want to admit it before, but I see it now. He was untouchable in the tournament. How do you think he got so good, Malcius?" She paused and then looked back to her friend. "I'm sorry, Tam. You were right before, when you said that he was a killer. You told me I shouldn't marry him. I should have listened to you then."

Tam shook his head. "I don't know, Frisha. I think that maybe you are overreacting."

"Wesson said that Rezkin could influence our thoughts and feelings. Do you think he did that to me? Do you think he made me want him?"

"Why would he do that?" Tam asked doubtfully.

"Because of Uncle Marcum," Frisha answered.

Tam and Malcius shared a look. It was not completely unfathomable, nor was it the first time the prospect had been considered.

"Perhaps we should ask an expert," Malcius suggested. He raised his voice and called to a table on the other side of the small room. "Journeyman, would you join us?"

Wesson looked up from his meal and smiled pleasantly. "Of course, Lord Malcius."

Rezkin and Wesson trudged through the forest throughout the night. They stopped only for a few hours of rest. The mage had still been awake when Rezkin entered his meditation. When he awoke, Wesson was sitting on the same stone.

"You were keeping watch?" Rezkin asked.

The journeyman shrugged. He bore no signs of fatigue, though. The midmorning light that was finally making its way through the filter of boughs revealed a fresh-faced young man unruffled by an entire night of rough travel through difficult terrain.

"Do you wish to continue now?" Wesson asked.

Rezkin retied his hair in a queue at his nape and said, "You have not slept."

The mage tilted his head curiously. "I am well. We may go."

A breakfast of dried fish, fried potato sticks, and hard flatbread was not particularly appetizing, but it was not the worst thing Rezkin had ever eaten. He offered as much to Wesson, but the mage declined. Rezkin filled his water skin several times at the intermittent streams, but the journeyman had apparently discovered a way to stay hydrated without drinking.

Rezkin had just climbed atop a fallen tree when an ear-splitting scream emanated from somewhere beneath him. He crouched low with his dagger in hand, searching for the source of the wail. Growls and angry hisses drew him to a pile of rocks where the tree lay nestled. Wesson stood back and watched, his hands casually clasped behind him.

"What is it?" the mage asked.

Rezkin glanced up from where he was bent examining the creature. "It is a young keurg. This tree is freshly fallen. The keurg is trapped between the tree and the rocks."

Wesson nodded. "Will you kill it?"

"No," he replied. "*We* are going to free it."

Wesson's expression was inscrutable. "Why would we do that?"

Rezkin considered the best way to release the animal as he said, "Because it cannot free itself. I have never tried it, but I was told keurgs are inedible. The quills that protrude from their bodies form deep in the flesh beneath. The meat is riddled with tiny spines in various stages of formation. Killing it would serve no purpose."

"Keurgs are known for violence," Wesson said. "Some say they kill for sport. You said we are in a hurry. Perhaps we should leave it be."

"If we leave it here, it will die," Rezkin said as he stood and closed the distance between them. He pointed and said, "I need you to *gently* destroy those rocks closest to the trunk. The others will hold the weight of the tree, and the keurg will be able to escape."

"Perhaps it would be better to put it out of its misery," the mage replied. Wesson's placid face was indifferent, if slightly curious.

Rezkin's expression hardened. "Like the donkey?"

"What donkey?" Wesson asked, glancing around as though such a beast might be found hiding in the trees.

Rezkin raised a brow and said, "The one with the broken leg."

"Oh, right. Sad business that, but it had to be done."

Rezkin straightened. One hand rested on his dagger while the other hovered near his sword hilt. "Enough of this. Who are you?"

Wesson's gaze was steady as he tilted his head. He again appeared to be listening to something that Rezkin could not hear.

"How long have you known?" Wesson finally asked.

"I suspected something was amiss when first you emerged from the woods. It did not take long to realize you are not who you say you are. Journeyman Wesson is not particularly strong in woodcraft. Your steps make no sound or mark, and you have not fallen once ... among other things." He paused but received no response. "Is he in there somewhere?" Rezkin asked, tilting his chin toward the mage. "Have you possessed him?"

Wesson smiled. "You misunderstand. I am not him at all. I have only taken this form."

If that was true, Rezkin could find no fault in the reproduction. He asked, "Why him? He does not tend to disobey my orders. It would have been more convincing had you chosen Striker Kai."

Wesson calmly nodded, and his smile and tone were congenial. "I am capable of taking on the shape of any living being for short periods. Magical creatures are the easiest to mimic, the stronger the better. The warrior was close to you, but not ... what do the humans call it ... *talented*. This one was much easier, and I think I did well." He said the last with a prideful smile as he patted his body like one would a new set of clothes.

Rezkin had never met a being of another race, much less a magical creature. The teachings of the Maker largely ignored the other races, but the old religions had much to say about them. One thing they all agreed upon was that magical creatures could be temperamental. They were referred to as the fae, but there were many separate races. Some races, such as pixies, were said to be vast, numbering in the tens of thousands, while others were relegated to singular beings. Rezkin could not imagine being the only one of his kind. At times, though, among the outworlders, he felt as such. Whatever this thing was, it seemed pleasant enough for the moment. He did not wish to garner its animosity so he maintained the casual conversation.

"Why are magical beings easier?" he asked.

The creature wearing Wesson shrugged and said, "A magical aura is easier to copy since I am a magical being. I study the desired form, produce a nearly flawless replica of an individual's aura"—he rocked on his feet with pride— "and then pull it into myself. The better the copy, the more information I receive—mannerisms, speech, even recent memories. I *could* appear as anyone —a human, a keurg, a tree."

"You could mimic my aura?" Rezkin asked. He did not like the idea of someone impersonating him, but he could see the advantage to such an arrangement *if* he could gain the creature's cooperation.

The Wesson-creature grimaced. His gaze flicked over Rezkin again, and it did not appear to like what it saw.

"No, I would never desire to become *you*." His voice held a note of pity, but then it shifted to irritation. "Why do you ask such questions? I should think you would be more interested in *why* I am here."

Rezkin was surprised by the sudden shift in disposition but decided he should have expected it from the infamously fickle fae. "You would speak truth? I think you will tell me only what you want me to hear."

"True," the creature said, "but that does not mean you would not benefit from hearing it."

"Nor am I guaranteed no harm. The fae are not known for generosity. There is always a price," Rezkin retorted. "I have read of men being told their futures with disastrous consequences."

The creature shrugged. "Shall we continue then?" He flicked his fingers toward the forest. "I believe you are on a deadline."

"The keurg ..." Rezkin said as he glanced back toward the beast. It was gone. He turned to the Wesson-creature and asked, "What did you do with it?"

"It was no longer needed," the creature replied.

This was beginning to feel like one of the training scenarios that he had been required to complete without being informed of the rules. "This was some kind of test?"

"You are a warrior, a killer. I did not expect mercy or compassion," the Wesson-creature said.

Rezkin shook his head. "It was not a matter of mercy *or* compassion. I was simply following the *Rules*."

"Oh, you have rules. How endearing. What are they?" it asked with child-like curiosity.

Rezkin frowned. At times, it seemed the creature could read his mind, while at others, it was completely at a loss. Either way, the thing could benefit from the *Rules*. At least if it did, Rezkin would understand its behavior.

"*Rule 102 – Do not kill without cause, Rule 188 – Do not engage in combat unless you must*, and possibly *Rule 2 – Kill with conscience*."

"Possibly?" it asked.

"I admit that I still do not understand that one. I would ask if you have any insight, but I fear what it would cost me." Rezkin thought he saw a flash of golden light behind the green-blue of Wesson's eyes.

"So you *do* feel fear?" it asked.

For a moment, Rezkin felt as though he were facing one of his former masters. He said, "Emotional fear is a hindrance without purpose. Instinctual fear breeds caution and knowledge of one's surroundings. One would be at a disadvantage without it."

The Wesson-creature strolled around him as it said, "A being with such discipline and practiced introspection. I shall enjoy our time together. But I think you underestimate yourself and your motives."

"What are you?" Rezkin finally asked.

A shadow fell over the mage, and when it passed, where Wesson once stood was a new being. The creature was about five feet tall, and its build was slight, like that of an adolescent human. It had two arms and legs and a mouth, nose, eyes, and ears, but that was where its likeness to a human ended. Its brown skin was smooth but textured like driftwood that had not yet been bleached by the sun. From its crown grew what looked like thin twigs, on the ends of which fluttered leaves or possibly feathers—maybe both. The twigs drooped toward its shoulders like the branches of a willow tree. The creature's mouth was but a slit in its face beneath a dainty nose. Its overly large eyes were golden-orange disks, like two small suns set into a bronze mask. It wore no clothes and possessed no features to indicate its gender.

The sounds of wind and rain surged past sharp, pointed teeth as it spoke.

The katerghen be me.

The creature crouched and scurried across the ground.

In human tongue,

In lyrics sung,

It clambered up the loose rocks—

Nymph they hail,

Of wood and vale,

—and scurried across the downed tree.

Devil of tor,

In Daem'Ahn lore,

It twisted its head and torso to peer at Rezkin upside down—

But among the we,

—then dropped to the ground to stand in front of him.

Katerghen be me.

Rezkin stared at the wondrous creature as he processed the sing-song speech. "*Katerghen*," he repeated. He had never heard the term, but the creature's words echoed in his mind. "You are a wood nymph."

It blinked and smiled. "So they say, the human way."

"Your speech is strange. It was not so earlier," he observed.

The feathery leaves on its head abruptly trembled and then ceased. "Mine aura I be. I speak as the we," it replied.

Rezkin was fascinated by the being, but he was pressed for time. He had to move this along. "What is your name?"

It tilted its head to rest on its shoulder. "Bilior, you may say."

"Bilior, I do not desire to minimize this encounter, but as you said, I must hurry. I have wasted enough time as it is."

"Your haste is waste," Bilior replied.

Rezkin thought the sound of rustling leaves rushing from the katerghen's throat might have been a giggle. He frowned. He might have been annoyed, but Bilior appeared quite confident in his assertion. While the nymph looked like an adolescent, his eyes held the depth of ages. Rezkin shook his head and stepped around the creature.

"I do not have time for this. I must go."

Bilior followed silently as Rezkin made his way through the forest. Trees and rocks fell behind in perpetual rest, water gurgled as it rushed toward distant adventures, and the random squawk of birds and buzz of insects reminded Rezkin that he was not alone. Three hours later, he stopped in a relatively open space and dropped his pack. With a promise of violence in his eyes, he turned to face the unsuspecting katerghen and drew Kingslayer. Bilior looked at the Sheyalin longsword, blinked, and then met Rezkin's gaze. He did not appear concerned.

"I have no wish to harm you, creature, but I will if you do not cease your meddling."

Bilior tilted his head, assessing Rezkin critically with large gold-orange orbs. "Perhaps you could, but methinks you know not how." Again, he chittered, a rustle of leaves.

"We have passed this tree at least three times today," Rezkin stated. "I marked it."

The creature tilted his head to the side to study the slight score on the trunk. "This is sure?" He pointed to the mark on the tree and then gestured to several others around them. "Not there nor yon nor fore?"

Rezkin's gaze passed over every tree in sight. All of them, dozens, bore the mark, all in the same location. "Why are you doing this?"

"Because I can. Because you won't. Because I must. Because you are."

"You speak in riddles," Rezkin growled.

"Riddles? I speak answers to questions unasked."

Rezkin was frustrated. He had read the folklore and legends of the fae, but none of his training had prepared him for such irrational behavior. "What questions? What do you want?"

Bilior raised his arms out to the side and swayed like a sapling bending in the breeze. "He begins to see with open eyes. Greetings from the Ahn'an."

Rezkin sighed and sheathed Kingslayer. It seemed the katerghen wanted to talk. He took a seat on a stump that had not been present moments ago and resolved himself to a break of unspecified length. One lesson he had gleaned from the legends was that if he were ever to encounter the fae, he should show respect but no weakness. To attempt to fight this creature would be a violation of so many *Rules* that he did not care to count. It was obvious by the subtle, yet effortless, displays of the creature's power that he could not win.

The katerghen's stare was disconcerting, but Rezkin could not tell his thoughts by his mannerisms. "What?" Rezkin asked.

"What are you?" Bilior asked. The creature's confusion was evidenced by its sudden clarity and directness.

"You have certainly seen humans before. I know the patrols pass through here every few weeks. I am a man," Rezkin said.

The katerghen chittered as his twigs rustled. "Tromp and scuff over leaves and logs, humans pass, a clomp, a whump, a snort, and thud. I see these men, but what are *you*?"

Rezkin had no idea what the creature was talking about, so he remained silent.

Bilior moved closer, much closer than Rezkin would have preferred. The golden gaze swept over him several times, and then the creature stared into his eyes for a long moment. "I sensed it, felt it, but could not see. Oh, the damage done. Long they passed, but you are one."

"Listen, katerghen. I must arrive in Serret before dusk on the morrow. I know not how long you have kept me walking in circles, but if I do not arrive on time, the consequences could be dire. More than a hundred people's lives are on the line."

Bilior sat cross-legged on the ground and placed his elbows on his knees with his face in his hands. "Wh-h-h-y?" he asked, appearing as the small-men did when listening to their tutors' stories.

"Why *what*?" Rezkin asked in frustration.

"Why must you save them?" it asked.

"Because it is the responsibility I accepted," Rezkin answered.

"It is in your rules to save people?" the katerghen asked.

"No, but I am to honor and protect my friends."

The katerghen sat up with overly dramatic cheerfulness. "They are *all* your friends?"

Rezkin sighed. "No, only a few."

"Then why did you save the others?" Bilior asked.

Rezkin paused. Why had he taken it upon himself to save the others? If he was supposed to be their king, he might have been meant to save some of the Ashaiians, but most of the refugees were foreigners. Perhaps, as king, he was simply trying to preserve Ashaiian honor. No, the reason had to be much simpler. He had not thought much about it at the time. It had been an instinctual response.

Finally, he settled on an answer. "King Caydean's orders were not consistent with the *Rules*, so I intervened."

"So, you are to ensure that *others* follow these rules?" Bilior asked.

Rezkin was discomfited and uncertain. "No, I am only accountable for my own actions. Whether others follow the *Rules* is not my responsibility."

Bilior uncoiled, gracefully gaining his feet. He chittered and danced, seemingly pleased to have made the point. Rezkin also knew a point had been made, one that was causing him uncharacteristic distress over his own actions. The problem was, he could not figure out what the point actually was. Why *had* he saved the others?

"It matters not," Rezkin barked. "I accepted the responsibility of their safety, and I will see it done. Now I must reach Serret as quickly as possible and figure out how to undo whatever damage you have caused by postponing my arrival."

"To where will you take them?" Bilior abruptly asked as though Rezkin had not just been chiding him for the delay.

"What makes you think I trust you with such information?" Rezkin snapped.

He was frustrated and concerned that the fae creature had managed to get into his head, figuratively if not literally.

Bilior tilted his head and chittered. "Methinks you do not know."

Rezkin scowled at the fae creature. He had ideas, and he had ways of influencing people. If one possible haven did not work out, he would find another. The longer it took, though, the longer it would be before he could apply himself to other matters. Unfortunately, without certain *diplomatic* persuasions, they were just as likely to end up in someone's prison as they were a sanctuary. Perhaps more so.

Bilior said, "Humans lost in a human world—unwanted, undesired, unwelcome. They be criminals or contemptibles? Nay. But lesser in the eyes of neighbors, lesser as are rats and curs."

The creature blinked and tilted his head, as though waiting for Rezkin to deny it. He could not, so it continued. "But you are not as they, and they will follow thee"—a snicker of rustling leaves—"and Bilior can send thee safely, assured a haven be—for a fee."

The creature's entire body trembled, his leafy feathers flittered, and sounds of wind and thunder echoed off the trees.

"You know of a place? Somewhere I can take them where they will be safe?" Rezkin asked in surprise.

The tales claimed the fae were often conniving, masters of equivocal speech and trickery. Men were enticed into agreeing to more than they understood. One of the older Adianaik texts claimed, though, that if a fae failed to deliver on a promise, he would be bound to the service of the other party until one or the other died or he was released by his master. The text did not specify, however, what prevented the fae from simply killing the master.

Bilior chittered cheerfully. "A king you be, in mage's mind I see. Your kingdom I find, if you pay me in kind."

Rezkin sighed and shook his head. "We sailed *from* Ashai. We cannot return lest we risk imprisonment and death."

"Ashai, Ashai, a human abode," the creature spat as it crouched on the ground and turned away. It obviously was not a fan. It turned its head back to peer at Rezkin over its shoulder. "Not right for *your* kind." He paused, and his demeanor shifted once again. Bilior strode slowly toward Rezkin like a predator stalking its prey. "Your humans are sinking in a human well. Of sanctuary, of haven, of asylum I tell."

Rezkin had already realized he was caught in the creature's web. Bilior would not allow him to leave the forest labyrinth until he got what he wanted. The creature seemed to want him to go to this mysterious place.

"How do I know we will not be heading to our deaths?" he asked.

Bilior's countenance became serious for the first time since he had revealed himself. "The need is great, the need of the we. The price be high, the price is for thee. A fortress, a palace, a kingdom grand. You sail on your ship, far from this land. But in time come to pass, your kingdom grows bold. Your forces you bring, to save we of old."

As Bilior's words settled in his mind, Rezkin could not sit still. He stood and paced the clearing while surveying the dark recesses of the forest. When he turned back, the fae creature was sitting on the ground with his knees pulled up to his chest, his arms wrapped around them. He peered at Rezkin with pleading gold-orange eyes.

"You have an enemy? You wish for me to create an army to defend your kind?" he said.

The creature lurched to its feet and began pacing rapidly across the forest floor. His feet made no mark or shuffle, but his limbs and twigs creaked and rustled as feathery leaves fluttered. "Mine and thine! None will be spared."

Rezkin said, "The fae are far more powerful than any human threat."

In a flurry of crackling branches and wind, the creature was suddenly hanging from a tree limb directly in front of Rezkin's face. "We are not so easily dismayed. 'Tis not the human army vast, nor mages born of Eihelvanan cast." The next words were uttered in a harsh whisper as though Bilior feared speaking them would draw the enemy's attention. "'Tis the rise of the *underlings* we fear."

Rezkin narrowed his eyes. "What *underlings*?"

"H'khajnak," Bilior said in a hiss.

Rezkin stared at the fae creature. He thought the katerghen must be toying with him. Bilior's concern appeared sincere, but how could one tell with a being so foreign? Was he playing a joke on a hapless human who wandered into his domain? Knowing nothing more of the creature than what was passed among the bards and fairytales of the ancients, Rezkin could not fathom the katerghen's motives. Would he so blithely invoke *that* name?

"The demon realm? I am supposed to believe that demons will cross into our world?"

Bilior dropped, placed a palm on the ground, and then perched on one arm as if clinging to a tree trunk. "Not will ... *have*."

Rezkin had seen and heard tales of demons that abounded in both historic and recent folklore. Plenty of people, it seemed, believed *him* to be a demon. The katerghen obviously knew better, but now he wished for Rezkin to believe that demons were real. He had never given much thought to the prospect, but then he had never been inclined to believe in the superstition. Having a fae woodland nymph make the assertion was going a long way in convincing him, though.

"These demons, where are they?" Rezkin asked.

The katerghen jumped up and down and sang, "The west, the west, already they infest, the west." The song and dance felt cheerful, but the crackling and thunderous booms emanating from the small creature sounded furious.

The west.

"You mean Ashai?" Rezkin asked with a growing sense of alarm.

"Ashai, Ashai, the Daem'Ahn nest," the katerghen sang.

"You know I came from Ashai. Is that why you chose me?" Rezkin asked. He was both apprehensive and suspicious at once. "Creature, if this is some jest or plot to impede my journey, it must cease."

Bilior scurried around him and chittered. "Yes, yes, haste is waste no more. We must be gone, the power fades." The katerghen abruptly stopped and took up a tree-like stance once more. "But first, a deal we make. Safety, a haven, a kingdom ... for an army."

In all the tales Rezkin had read, deals with the fae rarely ever worked in the human's favor. In fact, many of the tales were meant to serve as warnings against making such a foolish mistake. For Rezkin, though, the answer was simple. If Ashai was infested with demons, then he would eventually have to fight them anyway. He might as well claim this so-called kingdom. Even as he spoke, he knew he would likely regret it.

"Very well, Bilior the katerghen. I accept your terms."

Sounds of rustling leaves and rain erupted as the creature spun. "Come, you delay too long, too long you wait."

"*I* delay?" Rezkin asked in dismay.

"Yes, yes, now hurry. Bilior must better your blunder."

Rezkin did not want to argue the point. Perhaps if he had listened to the creature in the first place, he would not have gotten so far behind. Still, he did not appreciate being detained against his will. This was a lesson sorely learned. If ever he were approached by a fae in the future, he would make it a point to listen to what it had to say.

He followed Bilior into the thick forest. The katerghen scurried ahead and then turned to wait. As Rezkin approached, the creature pointed through the trees. The shadows of the forest bled away, and beyond the hill upon which they stood was the coastline. The sound of waves lashing against the shore reached his ears while a salty breeze slapped against his face. Considering he had presumably been trailing the coastline during his trek through the forest, the scene should not have been all that impressive. What astounded him was the presence of the sprawling port city with its famously invulnerable, high walls and the docks and shipyards that sat on floating platforms stretching far into the surf.

"How is this possible?" Rezkin asked in awe as he crouched at the tree line. Below sat the city of Serret, and he was more than a day ahead of schedule. While he worked hard to analyze each situation for every perceivable outcome, he knew there would always be those he could not anticipate. He had trained to be prepared for such events so that he would not be overly surprised and would be ready to react. Nothing could have prepared him for this. He could not remember being so overcome with wonder.

Rezkin was shaken from his thoughts when he realized the katerghen had not answered. He turned his head, and his cheek brushed against the smooth, wood-like skin of the creature's face. Rezkin braced himself but avoided an instinctual overreaction. The creature was leaning over his shoulder staring at the scene as if trying to see through Rezkin's eyes. Bilior turned his head, and the two stared at each other, their noses nearly touching. The katerghen grinned, displaying its tiny, sharp teeth, and when he spoke, his breath smelled of musky earth.

"To Caellurum you go."

Rezkin eased back to a more comfortable distance, although not quite far enough from the creature for his taste.

"The mythical city?" he said with skepticism.

"Your myth, mine memory. Upon the island your kingdom be," Bilior said. "'Tis hidden from human sight, but with your power 'twill alight."

"Power? I am not a mage," Rezkin replied with only slightly less certainty than he had possessed in the past. His discussions about mage power and the revelation of his relationship to Tieran had him questioning whether he possessed the *talent*. All the tests had been conclusive, though. He was not a mage.

The katerghen released a surge of crackling limbs and stuttering gusts. Rezkin thought it might have been a scoff. "You be no feeble mage. Power derived from another age. By your *will* you will find, the city long left behind. You knew this, did you not? Has been a while." He pointed a long, twiggy finger toward the open ocean. "You sail to the isle."

Rezkin was not surprised that the creature knew their destination. At the very least, he had gleaned some of Wesson's recent thoughts and memories. Upon consideration of where he might find refuge, his first instinct had been to go to the Yeltin Isles. Such were his orders to the ship's captain. He had justified his decision based on a number of points, not the least of which was that it was the farthest from Ashai that they could sail upon the Souelian. He knew Uthrel could not be their final destination, though, since the *talent* was outlawed in Gendishen and many of his companions were mages. King Privoth was also unlikely to accept any refugees. Rezkin had hoped to form a plan during the voyage based on whatever resources he could acquire.

"You are saying that *I* can find Caellurum when, for more than a millennium, others could not?" Rezkin said as he drew his eyes away from the ocean. Orange orbs stared at him expectantly. Rezkin blinked, and then Bilior was no longer there. He spun and searched the boughs of the trees. The katerghen had disappeared right before his eyes.

3

"You are intentionally delaying our arrival," Lord Gerresy huffed.

Tieran straightened and looked down his nose at the flustered Torreli ambassador. Brendam LuDou, captain of the Torreli Royal Guard, had informed him that Lord Gerresy's ambassadorial powers had been strictly limited to a supervisorial role at the tournament. According to the captain, Lord Gerresy was a middling noble of minor importance who had been an irritation at court. He had been sent to the tournament for no other reason than to relieve said court of his presence. Tieran wondered if Lord Gerresy was aware of the slight but decided it was unlikely considering the man's exaggerated sense of self-importance.

Tieran sniffed. Gerresy lacked sufficient position to warrant his oversized ego. "Lord Gerresy, we are most certainly delaying our arrival."

Gerresy blubbered a few incomprehensible sounds and said, "Then you admit it!"

The man continued sputtering, but Tieran could not take his eyes off the throbbing vein in the center of the man's forehead. It almost looked to have a life of its own as it wiggled up and down, the purple of its sinuous form complemented by the ruddy hue of the lord's flushed face.

Interrupting whatever drivel was spilling from the man's lips, Tieran said, "The king has given orders to wait, so we wait. We will resume our journey tomorrow eve and arrive in Serret by midday on the next."

"I do not understand why we must wait in this swamp when we could already be in decent, if not optimal, accommodations in the Channerían capital city," Gerresy said, tugging at the collar of his sweat-stained doublet.

Tieran unnecessarily straightened his own doublet, which was pristine since he had finally succumbed to his own stench and deigned to learn a cleansing spell. He was grateful that he had humbled himself to the menial task that *should* have been carried out by Colton, his manservant. Colton was not *talented*, though, and getting anything clean on a refugee ship was next to impossible. Actually, Colton should feel so grateful to have such a discerning master.

To Gerresy, Tieran said, "If you had bothered to learn anything about maritime trade and travel regulations, then you would understand."

"And it is hardly a swamp," LuDou added. "The water is quite clear if you care to take a swim."

Tieran thought the word *bath* would have been more apt, but it was admittedly less appropriate.

Gerresy scowled at the captain of his kingdom's royal guard. "I was not speaking to you, LuDou. Mind your tongue."

LuDou raised a brow but no objection. Tieran admired the man's self-restraint in allowing Gerresy to speak to him in such a way, although he felt the restraint unnecessary. The captain of the royal guard was generally afforded no small amount of respect, particularly since it was well known that he was also a close friend of King Desbian. The king would probably commend LuDou for putting Gerresy in his place. Gerresy seemed to be overlooking the fact that LuDou was also a Fifth Tier champion of the King's Tournament and would be entirely capable of doing so.

"Lord Gerresy, you will return to your quarters in the hold," Tieran said.

"*Quarters*? You mean the miniscule allotment of musty floorboards that would hardly be fit for a scullery maid? I demand to speak to this king of yours!"

Tieran said, "The king does not care to speak with *you*. Now return to your quarters, or I will have the strikers drag you there."

Kai grinned and cracked his knuckles, appearing eager for the chance.

Gerresy clenched his jaw, and his nostrils flared with every heaving breath. "It is to your kingdom's benefit, Lord Tieran, that you bow to a lesser man, for you are surely lesser than he."

Tieran could not understand the man's next words over Kai's booming laughter and the spurting blood that was pouring from Gerresy's nose and mouth. Flexing his fingers, Tieran marveled at his own lack of injury. He was now more appreciative of the training he endured daily with Rezkin and the strikers.

"Y-you struck me!" Gerresy sputtered. "LuDou, do something!"

LuDou shrugged and said, "I think it best to mind my words."

Tieran grabbed Gerresy by the collar and said, "I *am* lesser than he, but only because his greatness is beyond compare." He shoved the smaller man toward Kai and said, "Take him to the hold and make sure he does not leave." He straightened and wiped the blood from his knuckles with a kerchief. Belatedly, he added, "I suppose you may see if any of the healers are willing to treat him."

Tieran turned to pour a cup of wine while LuDou followed the pair out of the command center. In truth, the wine had been reserved for the *king*, but Rezkin claimed to prefer water. Tieran decided not to question such an absurdity when his cousin's loss was his gain. He glanced up to see Striker Shezar staring at him. While Tieran felt some modicum of comfort with Striker Kai, who had been training him, he was still anxious around the other strikers. The two had only joined their party upon their flight from Skutton, and Tieran did not yet trust them.

"What is it? Why do you stare at me so?" he asked.

Shezar smirked and replied, "I never expected to hear the *great* Lord Tieran Nirius sing the praises of another human being—except perhaps of his own father when social or political niceties required it."

Tieran inhaled quickly but held his breath. His first inclination was to berate the man for his insolence. Shezar was a striker, though, and only answerable to the king. He knew Kai had been so accommodating with Lord Gerresy only because it had suited him to do so. Tieran also liked to think that he had developed a working relationship with the striker if nothing else. Their goals were the same at least.

He released his breath and then sunk into an uncomfortable chair in a very un-*lord*-like manner. The crimson liquid swirled in his cup as he considered the striker's words. "Rezkin can hardly be described as such," he said with acceptance.

"What? Human?" Shezar asked.

It was the first time in his life that Tieran truly knew what it was to feel inferior. It was not a perception born of self-pity, drama, or political status, but a simple truth. Rezkin was intelligent, educated, cunning, and a favorite with the ladies. Tieran thought *he* had been all of those things until he had seen it for truth in Rezkin. He had not even known to which house Rezkin belonged, and he had not questioned him in his claims to power. The truth was, when first they met, Tieran had been terrified of the man. He knew, now, that he had been right to be frightened.

Tieran barely heard his own words over his thoughts. "We may be related by blood, but I think that is where our similarities end." How could one hope to compete with such a man?

⌒

Rezkin spied the city from beyond the outer bulwark. The city's greatest defense was the overlapping series of walls that stretched around its perimeter. One could not travel from the outskirts to the city center without trudging down the outer corridors and switchbacks. City workers kept the corridors clean of loiterers and debris, and the inner walls were lined with arrow chutes. The port side had the extra security of several manned gates topped with cauldrons that would be filled with boiling oil during a siege.

Passage into and out of the city was open at the moment, though, and no one questioned him or any of the dozens of people entering the northern gate with him. The guards leaned against the walls as they chatted or occupied themselves with other diversions, like whittling or even reading. Every once in a while, one would bark at a pedestrian to keep moving or pick up a discarded object. Otherwise, the travelers were ignored.

Rezkin shuffled along with the rest, his pack and swords hidden beneath a stack of animal hides he had procured from a trader who was only too happy to part with his goods before even arriving at market. Rezkin's black hair was tied atop his head in a messy Channerían-style knot, and his face held a few days' worth of growth. He maintained a perpetual squint to hide the light of his eyes and slouched as he adopted a loping gait. It was unlikely that someone would be looking for him, but wanted to ensure that no one would remember him.

An inn with a comfortable bed would have been preferable, but he knew he would not be making much use of it. While the wall guards were without a doubt the worst he had seen, the city's investigative unit was supposed to be unparalleled. It was almost as if they were encouraging discord so they would have something to investigate and someone to prosecute. Staying at an inn might leave him vulnerable to discovery if his actions came under scrutiny, which they surely would.

Once he finally entered the city proper, he circuited the outer lane to the seedier parish. The symbol of a sinuous fish with a slash through it, like an embellished *x*, was sloppily painted or scored onto many of the walls and posts. Rezkin had studied several historical accounts of nations in which the military, law enforcement, or religious orders had gained too much unchecked power, and these civilizations ultimately ended in disaster. Such were the beginnings in this city. The zealous determination of the investigators and the high-handedness of the Temple led to the rise of an underground organization of vigilante protesters, called Fishers, who sought not to destabilize the government, but to expose corruption among those with power. They apparently felt it necessary to leave their mark wherever they could.

The buildings and streets looked much like those in Ashaiian cities, except for the multitude of temples that Rezkin passed on the way. A number of men and some women went about their business dressed in the traditional garb of the priesthood. They wore loose black pants with a belted, thigh-length tunic in shades varying from white to dark grey, depending on the priest or priestess's rank. Only the *collectiare*, as the temples' leader, wore black. Upon each of their breasts was a golden, eight-point star, the top and bottom spikes longer than the others. At the center of the star was a hollow eye, the sign of the all-seeing Maker.

Channería was officially a kingdom, but the balance of power between the king and the collectiare was debatable. While the king had authority over the governance, laws, and military of Channería, the Temple of the Maker ruled the people's hearts and souls, including those of the king. Rezkin knew much about the collectiare's official acts and teachings, but he had very little personal information about the man.

Like all big cities, Serret had its share of *deplorables*, as the Serretians called them. The teachings of the Maker professed equality and compassion for all people, but men were capricious and corruptible. People chose to interpret the teachings of the Maker how they saw fit. Some claimed that everyone had the *potential* for equality, but it had to be earned. Others claimed that equality applied only to the soul and not to its living embodiment. The interpretations were limitless, but one thing remained the same. People existed in this society, like in every other, whose value was deemed to be *less*.

It was all beyond Rezkin's control, so he did not care much either way. Actually, their hypocrisy was of benefit to him. Those who were castigated by society tended to look the other way when others engaged in questionable or offensive behavior. They also had a general dislike of officials and were less inclined to provide information to investigators.

He followed his nose to accommodations that might suit him. He studied the aged wooden building for only a moment before rapping on the door. In this parish, people would be watching always, either looking for an easy target or hoping to out an investigator in disguise. He did not want to appear as either.

A scantily clad, middle-aged woman opened the door and leaned against the frame as she studied him. "What do ya want?"

Her Channerían was accented with the burr of the slums. She wore a wig that might have been expensive at one time with thick black ringlets that hung past her virtually bare bosom. Her makeup was smudged and looked to have been applied several days past.

Rezkin hung his head and shuffled his feet. He looked up with a squint and avoided eye contact. Mimicking the woman's style of speech, he mumbled, "I need a place ta stay."

The woman huffed a husky chuckle. "We ain't no boarding house." She reached out and lifted his chin, turning his face from side to side. "Ya might clean up nice. Could give ya some work. Plenty of folks lookin' for a pretty man."

"Don't think I'm wantin' that kinda work, thank ya nicely," he replied. "Couldn't help but smell yer stables though. Don't think they been cared fer much. Only need a few days. Could take care of them stalls and sleep in 'em too."

The woman sniffed and grimaced. "Yeah, I guess we're needin' that too. Ya ain't gonna cause no trouble, 'cause if ya is, Brendish'll have yer hide."

"No ma'am. Don't want no trouble. Don't wanna meet Brendish. Jus' wanna sleep under a roof."

"Don't we all," the madam muttered as she led him through the house toward the back.

The front rooms were decorated in aged velvet and lace that had been mended with care. Pictures of lewd scenes decorated the walls, and faded, musty drapes covered the bubbled glass windows. A couple of cats lounged in the sunlight sprawled across plush chairs. Rezkin and the madam passed through the kitchen that had been added to the back of the abode. A heavily spiced meal boiled over a hearth set into a stone wall. Finally, they exited the back door and trudged through an overgrown courtyard toward the stables. It looked and smelled like they had not been cleaned for months.

Rezkin dropped his pack and the stack of furs at the edge of the stables, taking care to ensure his swords remained hidden. Several cats scurried out of the structure, startled by the noise. Only one horse was tied to a rail, but Rezkin knew it would not be there for long. Most likely, the owner of the horse was expected to arrive home by dark, and he certainly would not wish to be in *this* parish so late.

Just as he had the thought, a man strode out of the rear door, slamming it behind him. He was hastily buckling his belt as he snapped, "Your whores smell as bad as your stables."

The madam crossed her arms and said, "Didn't seem ta bother ya much a few minutes ago."

Rezkin snickered as he thought a man might under the circumstances.

The man scowled at him and said, "What are you laughing at?"

He kicked Rezkin in the stomach, knocking him back so that his foot lodged in a pail. His other foot caught under a pitch fork, sweeping it into the air to whack the man in the back of the head. The man turned with an angry shout just as the pail sailed off Rezkin's other foot and caught him in the mouth. The man fell to the ground clutching his face.

Rezkin rushed forward and crouched over the injured patron. "I'm sorry, sir, so sorry. Please let me help ya sir."

The man shoved Rezkin away, and this time his foot came down on the man's other hand with an audible crunch. The man wailed and jerked at his flattened hand, causing Rezkin to lose his balance once again. He fell with a *whomp*, all his weight landing on his elbow, which was luckily cushioned by the man's crotch. The man's continuous tirade was finally silenced as he curled into a ball, gasping for air. Rezkin untangled himself and got to his feet to the sound of unbridled laughter.

"Oh, by the Maker, that was the funniest thing I ever seen, and don't think the tellin'll do it justice," the woman said between gales of laughter. "Here, help me get 'im in the saddle. Don't think he'll be comin' back here ... or anywhere," she said with a cackle.

The man whimpered and groaned as they draped him over the saddle. The madam led the horse to the gate and set it free. Rezkin doubted the man would arrive at his destination with whatever was left in his purse.

When the madam returned, Rezkin was staring at the ground, shuffling his feet.

"What's yer name?" she asked.

"M-my name is Royance, but people jus' call me Roy," he said. "I'm surely sorry 'bout the master."

"A'right Roy. I'm Grebella, and don't ya worry 'bout that lout. We don't need his kind hangin' 'round here causin' trouble no how."

"Thank ya ma'am. I'll be no trouble fer ya. I can start cleanin' the stalls now, if'n ya like."

Grebella smiled, and through her sincerity, Rezkin could see the genuine person beneath the harsh but sensual veneer. "Sure, there's a bit of fresh hay in the loft. I'll send fer some more ta be delivered in the morn. Come ta the kitchen in an hour an' we'll get ya somethin' ta eat."

"That'd be mighty kind of ya ma'am," he said with a duck of his head.

Grebella shook her head and returned to the house.

Rezkin did as he said and got to work on the stables, mostly because he did not wish to sleep in manure that night. He did not plan to sleep much, though, and he had planning to do after a bit of reconnaissance. Unfortunately, most of his information related to Channería was several months old at this point. The more recent information had been gleaned from the strikers and the few Channerían refugees who were willing to share. None of his strikers had recently been assigned to Channería, though.

After cleaning the stalls, an act protested by a number of cats that had taken up residence in the stables, he joined the women of the house in the kitchen for a meal. The stew left much to be desired, but after two days of dried fish and hard flat bread, it was a feast. The vegetables were limp and wilted, but they had been seasoned well enough to mostly cover the bitter taste. He was not sure if it contained any actual meat, but he thought he might have identified a few chunks. He did not wish to consider what else they might have been. It was served from a community pot, and he doubted anyone would desire to poison a stranger who spent his time mucking their stables. Regardless, he kept quiet and ate with the enthusiasm of a young man who had not had a hot meal in some time.

"So are we gonna be gettin' some fresh meat again?" a woman named Tiani asked.

"Suras ain't been slippin' us nothin' since Tak left," Urmel added. She lifted her chin in Rezkin's direction and asked, "He gonna take Tak's place?"

Rezkin forced a flush to his face. The outworlders often reddened in the face when they were embarrassed, and he had come to understand that anything of an intimate nature tended to have that effect on most of them. He buried his head in his bowl and shoveled another bite into his mouth.

"Girls, leave 'im be. He ain't lookin' fer that kind of work," Grebella said. She looked at him with fondness and added, "Don't think he's got the heart fer it no ways."

"Did any of us?" said Tiani.

Grebella reached over and stroked Rezkin's scruffy cheek with a finger. "Let's get ya cleaned up. Ain't no need fer ya ta be walkin' 'round like ya are. I see ya done mucked the stables, so ya won't be gettin' too dirty no more."

Rezkin shifted uncomfortably, and it was only partly feigned. The attention she was giving him seemed excessive, especially for someone who had no intention of paying for her services. He picked up his pack, which lay at his feet, and followed her to a small room behind the kitchen. It contained a wall-length hearth, an extension of the kitchen hearth, over which rested several cauldrons of scented water. Steam rose from a couple of the cauldrons, and she instructed him to pour those into an empty basin that sat in the middle of the room. Meanwhile, Grebella poured buckets of tepid water from a barrel into the tub. Rezkin refilled the cauldrons from the barrel and set them back over the fire.

"I don't s'pose you'll be needin' help?" she asked with a teasing smirk. Her smile grew when she saw the flush on Rezkin's face. "Didn't think so. Take yer time an' empty the tub when yer done. We don't share water here. D'spite what that lout said, we keep things clean."

"Yes ma'am. I'll do jus' that. Don't worry. Won't cause no trouble," Rezkin said as he slouched in on himself.

Grebella's expression appeared sad, and her eyes were distant as she murmured, "I'm not so sure of that." The woman left the room, pulling a curtain closed behind her.

Rezkin cleaned and shaved as quickly as possible. He had no desire to remain unarmed and un*clothed* for any length of time in this house. There was no telling what ideas might get into these women's heads. It was their business, after all. He emptied the tub and slipped out unseen.

Rezkin slept in the hay loft for a few hours and found that at least one of the stable cats had forgiven his intrusion. The scrawny thing with mottled black and brown fur had apparently decided he was more comfortable than the hay and had elected to sleep on Rezkin's chest. He was not sure why he had allowed it, except that he had appreciated the animal's warmth and the vibration of its soft purr on his chest. He was not worried that it would harm him. If anything, he was more concerned about inadvertently crushing the tiny creature. He scolded himself for the ridiculous thought. It was nothing more than a feral animal.

Rezkin shooed the cat away and then donned his night stealth gear. The Sheyalins were strapped across his back, and his dark hood pulled over his head. The buildings in this part of the city were close together, but they were poorly constructed and unstable. Rooftop passage was ill advised in most places, so he padded through alleys and ducked behind empty stalls. The city guard was more active at night, and he saw far fewer *deplorables* going about than was typical for an area such as this. Besides the guards and a few unscrupulous characters who were doing a fine job of staying in the darkest shadows, only the priests of the Maker were free to walk the streets at night, and they were. The Temple preached that the Maker never rested, and so their members could be found in training, at worship, or serving the community at any time.

Rezkin's first order of business was to breach the Interkingdom Trading Authority office, which was located within the city walls on the port side, not far from where he was staying. The ITA was the only official entity that was contained within its own building in Serret. All other government and guild offices were maintained within the estates of the nobles to whom the responsibilities were assigned.

In Ashai, most of the stations would be considered positions of civil service, beneath any high standing noble. Positions were granted to minor lords and even commoners, and those serving in the roles tended to change regularly with the political and social climate. In Channería, however, it was a matter of personal and family honor to be granted the authority over an office. Anyone failing in that duty would also lose his or her family estate, which would be granted to the party's successor.

The ITA, however, was an interkingdom organization, not subject to Channerían authority. To avoid bias, each office was governed by a board of multi-kingdom representatives who were elected and approved by the ITA Council. Such was the same in all kingdoms that had adopted the ITA. According to

Serretian law, all legitimate trading was to occur only during daylight hours. Therefore, the ITA office was closed when Rezkin arrived. The doors were locked, the windows were latched, and the wards had been activated.

Wesson had explained to Rezkin that Duke Ytrevius's wards felt different from those of the surrounding community and military buildings because Ytrevius had been a Wardmaster, and his wards had been linked to his own aura in a very personal way. Although Rezkin had been concerned that Ytrevius would sense the breach if he had attempted to enter, Wesson had not been certain of that outcome given Rezkin's ability to walk through other wards unhindered and undetected. Unlike those at Ytrevius's estate, though, the wards on the ITA office were designed to be maintained by multiple individuals. This meant they were not linked to any one individual's aura, so Rezkin had no trouble with them.

The building's façade was a combination of stone and plaster and was as stark as the rest of the city, save for the temples, but the interior was both functional and designed for comfort. It was obvious that many people spent a great deal of time here. The front half of the room was furnished with cushioned seating that stretched around tables separated from each other by opaque screens painted with scenes from nature. The area was separated from the back of the room by a long counter that stretched the width of the room. One end of the counter held an assortment of empty trays, pitchers and goblets, and the area behind it was filled with desks, shelves, and cabinets containing office materials.

Rezkin vaulted over the counter, undeterred by the thin chain and lock that sealed the wooden gate at one end. He had just found the logbook in the administrator's desk, when the front door rattled. He tested the strength of the shelving unit behind him to see if it would collapse under his weight. It was a bit wobbly, but he felt it a minor risk with careful weight distribution. He scurried to the top just as moonlight spilled through the cracked door. Although he was at an awkward angle and height, the battle energy coursing through his veins gave him the confidence to propel through the air to the rafter that was just barely within his reach. The door finally swung open as he lay along the rafter carefully keeping all his parts hidden.

"I'm telling you, I felt something in the ward," a guard said as he drew closer.

"Which was it?" a second, more nasally guard asked.

"The stacks," said the first.

Rezkin frowned. He had not gone into the back room that held the archives, or stacks, as the guard had called them. He could not have triggered the ward.

The two guards moved to the counter with careful steps. He could no longer see them below, but their attempts at subtlety were foiled by the rattle of the chain and creak of the gate as they entered the enclave behind the counter. Just as they came back into Rezkin's view, a dark figure sailed out of the back room. One guard was shoved into the counter, the impact knocking him unconscious. The intruder kicked backward into the second guard's stomach. He doubled over gasping for breath, and the black clad woman slammed his face into her knee. Before the guard fell over, the woman spun around and kicked him in the temple. When she was certain the man was unconscious, she checked the other guard. Rezkin was too far away to tell for sure, but he thought they both lived.

The woman cautiously padded around the room, checking under desks and counters. She even surveyed the rafters but did not appear to have seen him. Finally, she spoke in a conversational voice.

"I know you're in here. Show yourself."

Well, this is going to be interesting, Rezkin thought. The woman seemed to be here specifically for him, and she certainly did not work for the ITA. He could leave and come back later, but now he was curious. He unfurled his body as he clung to the rafter and then dropped to the ground. The soft muffle of his stealth boots alerted the woman to his presence. She spun around, simultaneously launching a throwing star and drawing the sword from her back. She came at him on swift feet. Rezkin wanted to avoid loud sounds that might attract more guards, so he did not draw his own weapons.

She slashed at his head, and he ducked behind her. He caught her foot and swept her legs out from under her. She rolled as she struck the ground and immediately attacked as she regained her feet. He caught her arm, and she caught his other. They twisted around each other, until he spun her away, carefully steering her farther from a ward. She was fast and agile, but he was too, and he had the advantage of greater strength and reach. She ran at him and then swiped her blade at his legs as she came out of a forward roll. He dove over her, dropping into a roll of his own. As his shoulders struck the ground, he reached back and grabbed the woman's shoulders. By the time his back hit the floor, the woman was sailing over him. He used her momentum to pull himself to his feet before he released her. She did not manage to get her legs under her properly, and she tumbled to the floor on the other side of the counter. The clattering of her sword was muffled by the thick carpet that cushioned her landing. Rezkin followed her over the divider.

The woman lurched to her feet looking slightly more ragged than when they began. The black cloth that covered her head had come loose, and a braided tail of long brown locks swung like a pendulum behind her as she moved. He turned to the side, preparing himself for another projectile, but otherwise holding his ground. She crossed the carpet, sweeping her sword up as she came at him again. This time, he waited until she was close and then turned, ducking under her guard and reaching for her wrist. The assassin was prepared for the move, though, and she twisted around him, rolling over his back. He was nearly wrenched from his feet when her sheath caught on his own, but both of them managed to recover in time to meet their opponent's next move.

The woman slashed and jabbed at him several times before he finally grabbed her free hand, pulling her into him. He twisted to the side so that she slipped under his arm. He leveraged her against his body and grabbed at her hips with both hands. He then bent low and sprung upward, launching her backward over his shoulder. She flipped over in the air, and her chest struck the ground hard. Rezkin heard the crack of broken bones, most likely her ribs if his own experience with the move was anything to go by. The wind had been knocked out of her, and she struggled to fill her lungs while her cheek was pressed into the stone. No carpet was present to cushion the impact this time.

Rezkin plucked the sword from the ground and leaned back against the counter waiting for her to recover. After several minutes, she managed to sit up while doing an admirable job of hiding her pain.

"What are you doing here?" he asked.

The woman spat a bit of phlegm and croaked, "What do you think? I was following you."

Her words were strained but clear. She took a deep breath, and even in the dark, he could see the pain in her dark brown eyes. She pushed to her feet despite the discomfort and then shuffled to the counter, careful to maintain a few paces between them. Rezkin slid the sword across the wooden surface, returning it to its owner.

"How?" he asked.

She almost laughed but stopped herself with a grimace. "You walked in the front door. Kind of obvious, don't you think?"

"It was the easiest method of entry, and none of the guards were paying it any attention."

The woman smirked and said, "You're a formidable fighter, but the stories of your cunning were exaggerated, I think. Anyone could've seen you."

Rezkin shrugged and said, "Perhaps, but they did not. Only you, and *you* were the one to trip the ward."

She scowled at him and huffed, "It was an uncommon failure on my part. I was in a hurry to keep up with you now that we'd finally found you."

Rezkin nodded. "Which leads us to my original question. How?"

For any other, it might have been difficult to tell that the woman was still using the counter to hold herself upright. She plucked a dagger from her sleeve and used it to casually scrape at her fingernails. Rezkin felt it a weakly concealed attempt to secure a weapon in hand.

"We are watching all of the major ports that you could have reached in this time. If you did land in Serret, we figured you would come here eventually. We've been keeping eyes on the buildings you were likely to attend. Looks like I was the lucky one." She winced and pressed a hand to her ribs. She spied him suspiciously from the corner of her eye. "We might have found you sooner but, for some reason, my brothers and sisters could not remember anything specific about you. Average height, average build, average coloration ... except to look at you now, I can see nothing average about you."

Rezkin ignored the observation and asked, "How did you know to look for me at the ports?" The last he had seen of the Adana'Ro was at the Black Hall, long before the tournament and his subsequent escape.

The woman rolled her eyes. "Oh, please. Mysterious dark warrior defeats *everyone* without acquiring so much as a scratch. Raven, meet *Dark Tidings*. It doesn't take a genius to figure out."

Rezkin raised a brow. "You would be surprised."

She tilted her head and looked at him appraisingly. "Your claim to the throne—is that real? Are you trying to take over Ashai?"

"*I* am merely a weapon, one of many in an arsenal to be used in saving it," Rezkin said.

Silence ensued as the woman looked upon him uncertainly. It appeared as though she had something to say but, in the end, resolved not to. She finally asked, "Are you going to kill me?"

Rezkin turned and held her firmly in his gaze. "Do I have cause to?"

Her expression was one of surprise and confusion as she shifted. "I am Adana'Ro."

Rezkin affected a look of boredom and leaned back against the counter again. "And?"

"You're just going to let me go?"

"What else am I supposed to do? Killing you would serve no purpose. I could torture you for information, but I doubt you would provide something of use, only misinformation. I might conscript your services, but I could not trust you to carry out the tasks—"

"You insult my honor?" she snapped with fire in her eyes.

He smirked and said, "I had no idea you felt it would be an honor to serve me."

The woman's nostrils flared with indignation. "I serve the Adana'Ro."

He nodded with a patronizing smile. "As I was saying, I cannot trust you to carry out my orders, so short of dragging you around by a leash to no end, the only remaining option is to let you go."

"Perhaps you not only lack intelligence, but sanity as well. You would just let your enemies free …"

"*Are* we enemies?" he asked with a hardened gaze.

She snapped her mouth shut.

Rezkin sighed dramatically and said, "I have much to do and little time. Thus far, neither you nor the Adana'Ro have done anything to garner my ire. So long as you stay out of my way, do not interfere, and do not threaten anyone in my charge, I am content to let you be."

"But I attacked you," she huffed with disbelief.

He shrugged and replied, "It is effectual to practice one's skills with a well-trained opponent."

The woman scowled. "I don't know whether to be flattered that you consider me well trained or insulted that you found our *practice* to be of such little threat."

Rezkin shrugged but said nothing. Before the woman could walk away, he asked, "Why did you attack me?"

"It was a preemptive strike," she said, but her tone carried a hint of embarrassment.

Rezkin cocked his head. "You regularly attack people for no cause?"

The woman hissed. "No, I was afraid you might attack first and gain the upper hand. Besides, I had to know it was you."

"So you attacked me," he said with a nod, as though that made sense. "You believed you could defeat me?"

"No,"—she hesitated—"not from what I've heard of you."

"So you fought a battle you could not win. You expected to die."

She shifted and replied, "Well, I didn't *want* to die, but if I did, at least my sisters would know I found you."

Rezkin nodded again. As she started to walk away, he added, "The ship has not yet arrived."

The woman turned. "What?"

He slipped back over the counter and went to the desk that held the logbook. He spoke as he flipped through several pages.

"The ship upon which Dark Tidings sails has not yet arrived."

"Impossible," she hissed. "You are he."

He opened an inkwell and began making notations. "I am marking the plans as we speak. It was my purpose in coming here tonight. I need to smooth the way for the ship's arrival."

"But ..."

Rezkin finished entering the information in the log and blotted the ink. Rather than entering the ship's arrival for two days hence, when it would actually sail to port, he added it for the following week. It would be consistent with their story that they had arrived early due to the unrest in Ashai, and it was unlikely that anyone would notice the new addition so far in advance. An entry for arrival in two days would be suspicious since the log had surely been checked by multiple officials and no orders had been sent to the dock master.

After closing the logbook, he glanced around for something someone might think worth stealing. He grabbed a few invoices, some letters of correspondence, and an official seal. He found no money box, so he assumed the funds were deposited at the bank after closing. The only object he truly appreciated was a small mage stone he found in one of the drawers.

"What are you doing?" the Adana'Ro asked.

Rezkin glanced up and said, "You *did* take out two guards. I need an excuse for their distress that will steer people away from my true purpose. Do you see anything you want?"

He waved his hand over the room. He spied some kind of award displayed on a small pedestal on a desk. It appeared to have been dipped in gold, so he took that too. Surely a thief would not leave something like that behind.

The woman huffed, "I am not a common thief ... but I do see your point."

She rolled her eyes then grabbed a few random objects that probably had value to someone and stuffed them into a sack she found under the counter.

Rezkin strode toward the door while keeping an eye on the Adana'Ro.

"Wait," she called, "the ward!"

Rezkin smiled back at her from the other side of the ward and reached out to her. She looked at his hand doubtfully, and then her gaze followed the length of the ward, the tingle of mage power vibrating through his flesh as she did so.

"Give me your hand," he said. "We would not want you setting off another ward."

She looked at him with distrust, and he raised a brow sardonically. He had already defeated her. It would have been ludicrous to attack her now. Of course, if he *did* kill her, he could leave her body nearby. He could make it look like one of the guards had managed to stab her before being rendered unconscious, thereby redirecting all the investigators' attention on to *her*. But, no. An Adana'Ro was worth more than a mere distraction. He briefly wondered if he should find another *distraction* on whom he could blame the intrusion. One of the night stalkers hiding in the shadows perhaps. He pushed the idea aside deciding it was too much effort for little effect. He felt that their thieving efforts would be sufficient, especially since no one had been killed.

Finally, the woman took his hand, and he pulled her through the ward. They slipped out the door without bothering to lock it behind them. The guards were still in there, after all.

"You have not asked my name," she said.

Rezkin released her hand and replied, "I do not care." Following her look of displeasure, he asked, "Were you looking for the Raven or Dark Tidings?"

"We believed you to be the same," she whispered back. He could tell she was uncertain and not yet willing to accept that they might have been wrong.

"Well, you found the Raven," he said with a grin. "Perhaps in a few days you will meet Dark Tidings."

Rezkin slipped into the shadow of the building and spent half a mark of extra effort making sure she could not follow. He had not spied her in pursuit, but if she was to be believed, the Adana'Ro were committing substantial resources to finding him. It certainly would not end with the confirmation that he was here. Her people would find him again; therefore, he had little reason to follow *her*. When he was certain he had lost the woman, he made his way toward the nearest councilor's estate. Having completed his original task to clear the way for the ship's arrival, it was time to secure the resources he needed for his new objective—Caellurum.

The councilor's estate was not the elegant home with sprawling gardens of an Ashaiian lord of the council. It was an austere, four-story building surrounded by a cobbled yard suitable for holding multiple carriages and wagons. The yard was bordered by a short, waist-high wall that served little purpose except to define the boundaries of the estate, and beyond that were roads and shops for craftsmen and merchants of high end goods. As was customary in Channería, a temple lay directly across the street to remind the counselor that the Maker was always watching.

Several guards patrolled the perimeter, and two more were on the roof watching the surrounding streets and buildings. The windows on the first, second, and fourth levels were closed, possibly sealed, and most likely warded. The majority of those on the third level were open to the flow of the fresh sea breeze. That, combined with the fact that the third floor was the least accessible from the outside, indicated that the level probably contained the sleeping quarters.

Rezkin doubted he could enter through one of the two doors on the first level. Each probably had a guard stationed inside the building. He did not want anyone knowing of his contact with the councilor, so he could not disable any of the guards. Actually … now that he thought about it, he probably could. A plan came together in his mind that would make things simultaneously easier and more complicated.

Reaching into the sack tied at his waist, Rezkin shuffled through the papers he had procured from the ITA office. He hoped he had picked up something of use, even though he had not been particularly discerning at the time. He used the sack and one wall of the alley to hide his mage stone as he held it over the papers. One of the ship manifests claimed some questionable cargo. Although not completely absurd, it was a little odd that anyone would be trading in Walcuttin Golden Ale at this time of year, especially in such large quantities. That particular variety from Verril was supposed to be served fresh and did not age well. A few months ago, it would have fetched twice the price at market. It was strange that anyone would hold on to so many barrels of the ale past its prime. He did not find it strange, however, that the army would be the beneficiary of the foul brew. For what he had planned, the questionable trade alone *might* be enough to arouse the investigators' suspicions. Still, it would be better if he had something more consequential.

He examined several pages of correspondence and finally settled on one letter to the ITA administrator from Count Mestison, Minister of Agricultural Affairs. Mestison was petitioning the ITA for a temporary increase in permissible trade limits for grains and grain products. In addition, he cited his prior acquisition of an import tax reduction for such goods throughout the season. Both seemed reasonable since Channería was likely preparing for a military campaign against Ashai. He doubted their efforts to acquire more military rations would be successful, though, since every other kingdom was also preparing to carve out their own pieces of his homeland.

Rezkin stashed the sack in the alley and then flitted across the road. With a nearly full moon, the night was not dark enough to hide his presence. There were no trees or decorative structures in this area, so the shadows were few. It meant he could also see the guards fairly well, so he was extra vigilant to move only when they were out of view or their backs were turned. He approached one guard from the side yard and rendered him unconscious before the man knew he had been struck. Rezkin dragged the man to the side of the building, hoping the body would be hidden by the eave, at least for a while.

None of this was in his original plan, and he wished he had more time to do things properly. Wishing never made anything happen, though, so he worked with what he had. The building's outer wall was plastered and would not provide footholds. He drew the mage rope from one of the pouches at his belt. The thin line would be strong enough to hold two or three times his weight, but true mage rope was a rare find. It did not last forever and lost strength with each use, so he used it sparingly. He was a bit piqued that he would have to use it now, but once he had an idea of what these buildings held in store, the others would be easier to infiltrate.

He plucked a palm-sized, three-pronged hook from another of his belt pouches and tied it to one end of the rope. After a quick survey of the yard, he stepped away from the wall and launched the grappling hook at the third-story window. One prong sunk into the inner corner of the sill, and he tugged to make sure it held strong. His masters would have punished him severely had he failed in such a simple task. Rezkin shrugged the thought away as he began scaling the wall. He did not know why the errant thought had crossed his mind, but now was not the time for reminiscing. He doubted there was *ever* a need for such things unless the historical account could be of use.

Since no one sounded an alarm, Rezkin felt it unlikely his entrance had been noticed. He drew up the rope behind him as he surveyed the dark room.

He felt no sense of anyone's presence, besides the small animal that streaked out the door upon his arrival. He thought it might have been a cat, and based on the smell, there were likely several more in the vicinity. Outworlders in Ashai often chose to share their living spaces with animals. Although he appreciated the practical reasons for keeping animals, it seemed some people developed emotional attachments to the beasts. He saw no advantage to such sentiments.

The councilor apparently had an affinity for cats, as did many Channeríans. In fact, the kingdom was overrun with the little beasts since the present king's great-grandfather had enacted a law preventing anyone from harming felines. The law had made sense at the time. Channería was deficient in life mages, and the capital city of Serret had been infested with rats due to its proximity to water and the large number of ships and food storehouses.

The presence of the beasts was advantageous for Rezkin, though, because it was unlikely there would be any strong wards on this level or any of the floors on which the cats were permitted. If the wards were too strong, the cats would set them off, and no one would get any sleep. In fact, he had barely had to try when he slipped through the ward on the window. His goal was to find the councilor, but the room in which he presently crouched was not a bedchamber. Dark silhouettes lead him to believe it a study.

Sounds of the hurried but cautious footsteps of multiple people could be heard ascending wooden stairs not far from the room's entrance. He hid behind the doorframe where he could see into the corridor though not in the direction of the stairwell. A small white cat with one blue eye and one green sat staring at him from across the hall. Rezkin frowned, and the cat slowly blinked unconcernedly. The cat's attention was suddenly captured by the source of the heavy footsteps that were approaching his doorway. It turned and scurried away.

"It has to be this room," one man whispered. "Their strange behavior seems to be focused here."

"The wards weren't activated," a second said.

"Maybe not, but the cats know," the first replied.

The rush of footsteps on the stairs preceded a sudden announcement. "Captain! Hedly was just found unconscious in the yard."

Rezkin was impressed. He had barely made it into the room and already he had been exposed by the furry little beasts. The sounds of shuffling bodies and the drawing of weapons reached his ears. This had not quite gone to plan. He had intended to draw the guards' attention, just not so quickly.

"Alright!" the first man, presumably the captain, announced. "We know you're in there! You might as well come out. Don't make any sudden moves. We have three crossbows aimed your way."

Rezkin thought it considerate of the man to provide him the number of crossbows with which he would have to contend. He ensured his features were hidden beneath his hood and then stuck his arm out into the hall to wave at the guards. A crossbow bolt shot past the doorway, and he jerked his hand back. Luckily for him, the man had poor aim.

"Hold your fire!" called the captain, and then Rezkin heard a thump that sounded much like someone being struck on the helmet. In a quieter yet irritated voice, the captain said, "He won't come out if you're shooting at him, you idiot." He raised his voice again and announced, "We won't fire if you come out peaceably."

Rezkin stuck his hand out into the hallway again. When it was not fired upon, the rest of his body followed. He stepped with large strides so that he stood closer to the far wall than the center of the corridor. It was to his good fortune, because two more crossbow bolts whizzed through the air where the guards had apparently expected him to stop.

He tisked and said, "Captain, you and your men lack honor or discipline. Either way, it is unbecoming for members of the councilor's guard."

The three crouching crossbowmen were hurriedly attempting to reload. The captain and two additional swordsmen stood behind the crossbowmen with weapons drawn. Their swords were short and designed for jabbing, and thus effective for indoor combat.

Before the crossbowmen could release their bolts, he said, "I had no intention of killing any of you, but if you continue to shoot at me, I will. Consider that your only warning."

The crossbowmen paused and glanced back at their captain. The man scowled and pointed his sword at Rezkin. "You are an intruder on these premises, in the councilor's estate. You are not entitled to honor."

Rezkin grinned so that they could hear it in his voice. "I did not claim to have any, but it is not *my* honor in question. The only reason I am even speaking to you is because it is more convenient for you to bring the councilor to me."

"You do not make demands, intruder. You will surrender or die," said the captain.

Rezkin tilted his head. "No."

The captain blinked. "What? You can't just say no. Surrender now."

"A less skilled opponent might be intimidated into accepting your offer, but it does not accurately represent the options available to me given the circumstances. I am confident in my ability to prevail. There are only six of you after all."

"What is going on here?" a man hollered as he came around the corner at the end of the hallway.

Rezkin could now see that the building was arranged so that a corridor circled the level with the rooms arranged extending from its outer perimeter. A sturdy wooden stairwell occupied the center.

"Ah, I see the councilor has graciously agreed to meet with me," Rezkin said.

He was a bit surprised to see what followed in the councilor's wake, though. Cats. Many, many cats. Perhaps twenty of them.

"Who are you and why have you broken into my home in the middle of the night?" the councilor shouted from behind the wall of guards.

"Greetings, Councilor. I bring information on behalf of the Fishers."

"The Fishers have grown bold, breaking into the estate of a councilor." The man snatched the cap from his head, gripping it tightly as he pointed at Rezkin. "You are not welcome here, Fisher. If you have evidence of a crime, you may bring it before the magistrate, and he will determine if it is worthy of the council's attention." He tugged at his bedclothes and ran a hand through his unruly hair. "Your breaking in is not only a crime in itself, it is highly disrespectful." He continued muttering beneath his breath as he surveyed the feline hoard. "Breaking into a man's home in the middle of the night … disturbing his rest … dragging him from his bed."

Rezkin surreptitiously palmed two throwing daggers as he interrupted the man's rambling. "Councilor, you may either dismiss your guards and speak to me privately, or I will dispatch them for you."

"By the Hells I will! Guards, capture this man. Kill him if you must!"

Rezkin immediately fell backward to the ground, just in time to avoid three crossbow bolts that became lodged in the wall behind where he had been standing. As he rolled to his feet, he launched the daggers at two of the men, striking and disabling one of the crossbows and sinking a blade in the other man's hand. From his sleeve, he slipped one of the throwing stars he had confiscated from the Adana'Ro and hurled it at the third crossbowman. Before any had time to react, Rezkin was upon them. He ducked under the captain's thrust aimed at his chest and smashed the man in the side of his knee. The man crumpled with a shout, but swung his sword mightily at Rezkin's head. He dodged and punched the captain in the temple, spinning him around and leaving him dazed. Rezkin kicked him in the back sending him spilling into the other guards.

It was to his advantage that there were so many guards in the cramped hall. As he was positioned, only perhaps two could reach him at a time, and the others were making it difficult for them to maneuver effectively. While it was apparent that they had a fair amount of indoor combat training, their methods were better suited for either a larger invading force or apprehension of a lesser-experienced, singular opponent.

Rezkin had just elbowed one of the guards in the throat when his feet suddenly became tangled and a screeching yowl resounded through the corridor. He managed to recover just in time to dodge a sword thrust that deflected off his chest plate scoring the leather. He dodged a swing at his head and smashed another man in the face with his elbow just before his foot came down with a crunch on a squirming rope. His leg gained an extra ten pounds when the cat latched onto his boot. It was absurd. The cats were actually running *into* the fray and attacking him. He was forced to shift awkwardly to avoid stepping on a black-and-white shorthair, and a yellow tabby was suddenly flying at his face as it leaped off a guard's back. Rezkin ducked and turned, leaving his side exposed just long enough for one of the guards to tackle him.

The two struck the ground, and Rezkin immediately wrapped his legs around the man's middle. He grabbed the guard by the collar, lifted his own hips and twisted his body, wresting control as he gained the upper position. With a powerful fist to the jaw, the man was rendered unconscious, but Rezkin got no reprieve as tiny claws sunk into his neck. He reached over his shoulder, snatched the calico from his back, and tossed it down the corridor. It slid across the floor bowling into the feline ranks.

Never had Rezkin thought he would endure such an attack. In his experience, cats tended to run *away* from such chaos. It was then he realized the truth that had been eluding him since the onset of the battle. The tingle of mage power was effusive but definitely present. The councilor was keeping his distance, but the intensity of his gaze was telling.

As the final guard fell, and Rezkin blocked attacks by three more cats, he said, "Councilor Rebek, thus far I have avoided killing any of your guards or cats, but if you do not cease this assault, I will be forced to change my methods. You do not wish to lose all of your precious cats, do you?"

The councilor did not let up, though. Rezkin did not care for the idea of killing the cats. They were animals, beasts without contempt. The masters had not included much in his training regarding the killing of animals except for the purpose of acquiring food or rendering them disabled or dead in battle. That usually applied to horses or other beasts of burden, though. He had never been attacked by a larger predatory species such as lions or wolves, but personal defense would also be an acceptable cause. These were not lions. They were common house cats, and he was not in danger of being killed, though mutilation was a possibility. Still, he did not feel right about killing the little creatures. These were under the control of a man, and Rezkin would much prefer to contend with the source.

He seized a long-haired, cream-colored fur ball that tried to scale his leg and tossed it at the mage. The councilor cringed and covered his face as the cat plummeted into him, clawing at his scalp for purchase and then leaping away. The buzz of mage power ceased, and the cats scattered, disappearing through doorways and around corners in a matter of seconds.

"You lost your focus, Councilor. You should practice more, or perhaps you are not strong enough," Rezkin observed.

The older man jumped when he realized that Rezkin had closed the distance between them. Rebek wiped at the trickle of blood running down his forehead and shot Rezkin an angry glare. The man looked as if he would bolt, but Rezkin shook his head slightly and tapped the dagger at his waist.

"What do you want?" Rebek asked.

"We will discuss that in private," Rezkin answered with a tilt of his head toward the guards. "Lead the way, Councilor."

Rebek's study was functional and without embellishment. The papers on the desk were neatly stacked in a short, wooden box, next to which sat the inkwell, pen, wax, and seal, all in perfect alignment. The room would have lacked any character whatsoever if not for the cushions and pillows that occupied nearly every flat surface besides the desk. Several of them were currently occupied by the furry fiends. They blinked and stared at Rezkin with intelligent eyes.

"Now what is this about?" Rebek asked as he rounded his desk. He did not sit, so Rezkin wondered if the man had only moved there because he felt more comfortable with the furniture between them.

Rezkin drew the folded papers from the pouch at his belt and placed them on the desk. The councilor snatched them up with a huff and surveyed their contents.

"What is this? I see nothing of interest."

"The invoice for importation of the ale and the receipt for payment for the goods by the military to agricultural affairs were both dated prior to the letter from the count. The delivery of said goods to the military storehouses was dated *after* the count's letter. By regulation, import taxes were paid upon acquisition of the goods, which in this case was paid by agricultural affairs upon delivery to the military storehouses. Therefore, the military paid significantly more for the goods than agricultural affairs."

The councilor tugged at his nightclothes and sat with a huff. "This is nothing—nothing worth this trouble, anyway."

Rezkin would have agreed if that had been his only purpose in coming. It was best he had to work with on such short notice, though. He did not really believe the incidents were related, and truly it was a stretch. Most likely, the circumstantial disparity would be resolved between the parties without incident. It was not difficult to plant ideas of conspiracies in already suspicious minds, though. An investigator *might* be inclined to believe the excess payment had gone into the count's purse. At the very least, it appeared to be a legitimate reason for the Fishers to be involved. Even if the investigators did not believe the conspiracy, they would accept that the Fishers did.

"Make of it what you will. *That* is what you will give to the investigators and is the official reason for this visit. It is not, however, my true purpose in coming here tonight."

Rebek wiped a hand down his fatigued face and frowned when it came away bloody. He drew a kerchief from one of the desk drawers and blotted his forehead. "More of this fisher business?" he asked with disdain.

"No," Rezkin answered. "I never said I was a fisher. I am here for an altogether different reason. I require a vote."

"A vote? You mean a council vote?" He chuckled with derision. "No one makes demands of the council except the king."

"Exactly," Rezkin said. "In a few days, a ship will arrive at port carrying refugees. A man will petition the king for asylum."

"Never," Rebek said. "King Ionius will never accept Ashaiian deplorables."

"They are hardly *deplorables*," Rezkin replied. "Many of them are nobles of influential houses."

"*Were* nobles. Now they are nothing. Spies, most likely, and fugitives. We would be better off sending them back and claiming the reward!"

It was Rezkin's turn to laugh, and he did—for effect. He actually found nothing humorous about the situation. "You truly believe Caydean would part with even an ounce of copper or that he would give it to Channería? The only payment you would receive would be a dagger through your back."

Rebek grunted but did not disagree.

Rezkin's voice hardened again. "The king will make a proposal to the council, and you will vote in favor."

"How do you know what the king will do?" Rebek asked.

"That is not your concern," Rezkin answered.

"What will be the proposal?"

"To give the petitioner Cael."

The councilor laughed again. "Of course, if the king were to allow refugees to live anywhere, it would be there. It is useless, a virtually barren rock."

"You misunderstand. He will not *allow* them to live there. He is going to *give* it to them. He will recognize it as its own kingdom independent of Channería."

"That is absurd. It requires a two-thirds majority vote of the council for the king to concede land."

Rezkin nodded. "Which is my purpose for being here."

"Why would they even want it? The island is uninhabitable, and it may not even be ours to give. I am sure you know that Gendishen lays claim to all of the Yeltin Isles. It is my opinion that Channería has maintained its own claim to the northernmost island only out of spite."

"Then you will feel no loss in releasing that claim," Rezkin said.

"I did not say that," Rebek snapped. "A kingdom's success is measured by its growth. We do not *give away* land, even contested, useless land. What is this man going to offer in compensation?"

"Nothing," Rezkin answered.

Rebek scoffed. "Who is this man to whom the king wishes to *give* land?"

"I am sure you have heard of the warrior known as Dark Tidings?"

"The tournament champion? Of course I have heard. *Everyone* has heard. We have also heard that he lays claim to the Ashaiian throne."

Rezkin nodded. "He does."

Rebek's face turned dark, and a fresh trickle of blood spilled down his forehead. "Then we are to give land to Ashai? To a kingdom that has declared war?"

"No. You will recognize the independent Kingdom of Cael."

"Ha! He cannot have one kingdom, so he will make another. The tiniest kingdom in the world," he muttered.

"It requires only a seed. As you said—*growth*."

"Do you work for the king then or this Dark Tidings?" Rebek asked with suspicion.

"Neither. I am … say … an independent. I am merely assisting in securing an outcome of mutual interest."

Rebek pondered the assertion and then said, "You assert that the king will make the offer. Does that mean this Dark Tidings does not know of your involvement?"

Rezkin shrugged but did not answer.

"What is my incentive to do as you ask?"

"Besides the king's appreciation of your support? The simple assurance that I will involve myself in your affairs no further. I *can* make your life very difficult."

Rebek's face flushed again as he gripped his kerchief so tightly that tiny droplets of blood dripped from his hand onto his desk. "Who are you to make such threats?"

Rezkin lifted his chin and said, "I am someone else of whom you may have heard tell. They call me the Raven."

The councilor's eyes widened, and his throat bobbed as he swallowed hard. "Impossible. Every day we receive reports from the mage relay of the Raven's activities in Ashai."

"Is that so? Where in Ashai?" Rezkin asked with genuine curiosity.

"Well, almost everywhere."

Rezkin laughed. "I cannot possibly be everywhere at once—or can I?"

The councilor's face was now pale as he leaned back in his chair.

"I am here now," Rezkin said. "Perhaps I will stay awhile. At least as long as it takes to get what I want." He leaned forward and held the councilor's gaze. "Longer even, if I find *projects* of particular interest."

Rebek inhaled sharply through his nose and said, "You cannot go around making demands and getting what you want. You must be stopped."

Rezkin leaned back casually and said, "You may be right, but that does not have to be *your* fight. You give your king what he wants, and I go on my way. Leave it to someone more qualified to fight me. We both know you are a weak mage, and I doubt you have any martial skill. Do not make things harder on yourself than they need to be."

The man anxiously drummed his fingers on the desk, most likely pondering the alternative. With a heavy breath he said, "The king wants this?"

Rezkin grinned. "Of course he does. As I said, it will be his proposal."

4

R ezkin was glad to be away from the house of cats. His first undertaking was to clean the wounds on his neck and administer an antiseptic. Due to the breadth of his training, he had thought he could anticipate nearly any threat. He was now reminded of something Jaiardun was fond of saying, particularly when Rezkin was injured. *Experience is the greatest teacher.* He would not underestimate the presence of small, seemingly innocuous creatures ever again.

His visit with the second councilor went more smoothly since he was now familiar with the layout of the interior of the councilors' estates, for they were all the same. That and the fact that Councilor Harid did not keep any pets. Rezkin had successfully avoided the notice of the guards, so he did not require an excuse for the councilor to give to investigators. With any luck, no one but the councilor would know he had been there. Harid had been more than happy to garner the Raven's favor. Rezkin had but to imply he might be indebted to the man to gain his agreement. The fire in the councilor's eyes had been almost fanatical, and Rezkin wondered just how many people the man intended him to murder. For his part, Rezkin had no intention of giving Councilor Harid anything, though Harid had given him one particularly useful bit of information regarding another councilor.

Councilor Onelle was a self-proclaimed altruist. She had been appointed to the position only upon the death of her predecessor a few weeks past, and she was leading an initiative to reform the deplorables of the kingdom. In her mind, the best way to do that was with a tough stance against illegal and immoral activities, strong penalties, and harsh punishment. Harid's observation had been meant as a warning against attempting to coerce her.

Less than two hours remained before dawn by the time Rezkin reached Onelle's estate. For her sake, he had made a few modifications to his appearance. With a flesh-toned putty that he made from ingredients procured from an apothecary's shop, he extended his nose and added a hook. He also blackened a few of his teeth, created a convincing scar along his cheek, and powdered his lips to make them appear dry and cracked. His loose hair hung from beneath his hood and was streaked with oil and dirt. If Onelle was to meet the Raven, he would be exactly the kind of man she expected.

Councilor Onelle's estate appeared to be in a state of transition. Some of the rooms were dark and minimalistic, while others were brightened with colorful paintings and tapestries. One entire sitting room was filled with packing crates, and objects yet without homes cluttered the floor and surfaces. The wards on the property were stronger than those at Rebek's, but they felt impersonal, and he figured that Onelle had not yet gotten around to creating her own, if she was capable.

He let himself into her bedchamber and was glad to see that the woman kept with the custom of high society Channerians in which husbands and wives slept in separate rooms. Rezkin approved of this particular Channerianism and thought that if he ever did marry, he would enact it in his own household. The woman's bed was a large four-posted structure, and the bed curtains were pulled back to permit the night's cool breeze into the otherwise stuffy room.

Rezkin lit the lamp on her bedside table and then grabbed the woman's throat, squeezing just hard enough that she could not scream. Onelle's eyes shot open in alarm, and she clawed at his hand as she kicked and struggled.

He raised a finger to his lips. "Shh." Lowering his voice an octave, he spoke in Channerian with a raspy Ashaiian accent. "You will not live long enough to shout if you try. Do you understand?"

The woman struggled to breathe, and by the blaze in her eyes and stubborn set of her jaw, he could tell that she would berate him if she could. He squeezed a little harder, and her obstinacy was replaced with fear.

"Good," he said as he released her and stepped back a pace.

The woman rose quickly and scurried to her feet on the other side of the bed. Two braids of greying hair hung to her waist, which was hidden beneath a loose night rail. She looked as if she might dart toward the door, so Rezkin drew his curved, serrated dagger from his belt and casually spun it in his hand for effect. Onelle froze in place, but her gaze darted around looking for something. She snatched a book from the other bedtable and held it before her. Rezkin wondered what the woman thought she could do with the book. He could think of several uses for it as a weapon, but he doubted she was capable of performing any of them. Perhaps she hoped to use it as a shield or to bludgeon him.

"Who are you? What do you want?" she asked.

It was always the same two questions, but he rarely answered them the same way.

"How many men do you know who could breach your security?" he flippantly asked.

Rezkin had known several, but they were gone now. Such thoughts always led to Farson, and he felt a spike of anger regarding the way his old trainer had treated him that day on the rooftop in Skutton. Rezkin rejected the emotion with a swift mental shove. He needed all his attention in the here and now, and he would not betray his training for counterproductive emotional entanglements.

Onelle raised her chin and said, "*I*, of course, do not know any. I would not associate with such people."

Her words were clipped, and her face was soured by a stern expression, but Rezkin still thought her quite attractive for a woman of her age. Then he wondered why he had just experienced such a thought.

"Now you can say you've had the *privilege* of meeting the Raven," he said with a poorly executed flourish.

"You mean that reprobate who has managed to take over the Ashaiian underworld?" Pursing her lips, she appraised his disguise with a condescending gaze. "You are exactly as I expected. It is no wonder that *Ashai* would spawn one such as you—a land where the king is no better than the criminals."

"You're candid for someone facing death," Rezkin rasped.

"You do not want to kill me or I would be dead already. You want something," she said. Her confidence was belied by her white knuckled grip.

Rezkin grinned. "I'm glad to hear that we're now on the same page. We'll get right to business. The king is going to make a proposal to the council. He'll wish to give the island of Cael to the Ashaiian traitors led by the so-called *Dark Tidings*." His voice held naught but disgust and loathing.

The woman glared at him. "It is rumored that the man who goes by Dark Tidings has a legitimate claim to the Ashaiian throne."

"Rebel scum," he spat. "We'll make it worth your while to have him captured the moment he steps foot in Channería."

"*We?*" she said with suspicion. "You're working with Caydean."

Rezkin cackled. "No one works with a madman. I work for myself, but in this, our interests are the same. His chaos is my fortune."

He grinned maliciously as he stabbed the dagger into its sheath at his belt and then drew a throwing dagger. The blade flashed in the lamp light as it rolled across his fingers, between them and around and then began its circuit over again.

Onelle scowled and pointed her book at him. "You seek to profit from the terror he inflicts upon his own people, *your* people. You are disgusting."

He grunted. "I've been accused of worse. Let's get back to *your* role. You're going to vote against the king's proposal and denounce Dark Tidings and all who follow him as traitors."

"When first I heard of Dark Tidings, he sounded like no more than a rebel terror. The very fact that both Caydean and a fiend of your ill repute oppose him makes me reconsider. For years, rebel factions have lurked within your borders, and Caydean has done nothing. For *him*, though, you go to great lengths. You believe his claim is legitimate. He is a true threat."

Rezkin stabbed the knife into the bedtable and growled, "That is not important."

She lifted her chin and said, "If King Ionius wants to give that useless island to Dark Tidings, then I am sure he has his reasons, which will be explained in detail to the council."

He spun on his heel and stomped toward the open window. Before making his exit, he turned back and said, "It doesn't matter. You will vote against it. I'm sure I don't need to tell you what can happen if you defy me."

By the time the alarm had been raised, Rezkin was already across the street and scaling the temple. The buildings in this area were strong and close enough together that he could travel by rooftop. When he got closer to the slums, he dropped to the ground. He dashed through the alleys back toward the stables. After scrubbing his hair, face, and teeth in a rain barrel, he lay down in the hay for a few hours of sleep.

Rezkin awoke to the stroke of wet sandstone at his temple. The repetitive lapping continued into his hair. A furry paw came to rest on his cheek, gently kneading at his flesh. His eye popped open to find the little beast nearly wrapped around his head. Its yellow eyes stared back at him. A rumbling began in its chest, and then it butted him with its forehead. When he did not respond, it butted him again and then pawed at his nose. Rezkin frowned at the thing. His attention was then diverted by the soft crunch of footsteps outside the stable door. Grebella appeared a moment later. She leaned on the frame and crossed her arms over her chest.

"Well, seems ya've made a friend," she said with a smile.

The cat twisted and pawed at Rezkin's face once more before it resumed licking his hair.

Grebella's laugh was husky. "I think that little tortie's gone and adopted ya. She's a sweet thing. Had a litter a few months ago—jus' one kitten. Poor thing died. She was too young to be a mamma, anyhow, only a kitten 'erself." The woman's thoughtful gaze sought the house behind her, and the smile slipped from her lips. "Too much of that 'round here."

Rezkin awkwardly drew himself to his feet, slouching and stumbling as he made a show of rubbing sleep from his eyes. The long, black hair that hung about his face was flecked through with golden hay, as were his rumpled, ill-fitted clothes. He shuffled toward the door and squinted down at the woman.

"What's 'er name?" he asked. He did not actually care if the cat had a name, but outworlders seemed to think those things were important.

Grebella gazed up at him, but her expression was sad and searching. It was not the kind of look he was used to receiving from women. "Who?"

"The cat," he said, pointing down at the small fur ball that was rubbing against his legs.

"Oh, um, don't think she's got one," Grebella answered. "Got too many of them 'round here to keep track." She pulled her gaze away and started to walk back toward the house. "The hay's gonna be delivered soon. Ya can come get somethin' to eat after yer done."

When Rezkin was finished refreshing the hay in the stalls, he went to the house for a meal. He had not anticipated being fed, but it would have been rude and suspicious for him to refuse. Only Grebella was in the kitchen when he arrived. She poured him a cup of tea and placed a bowl of plain porridge on the table. Rezkin dug in immediately, as befitted a young wanderer such as he. In truth, he was starving and intended to stop in the market for a larger meal. For the past several weeks, his appetite had been growing, despite the fact that his training regimen was significantly reduced since leaving the northern fortress. He wondered if perhaps his body was preparing for additional growth. He hoped not. It would be highly inconvenient to have to replace all his armor, and he was already taller than most of the outworlders.

A soft, manicured finger stroked his cheek, and he glanced up to see Grebella staring at him with that enigmatic smile of hers. He shifted awkwardly and leaned away, hoping she would think he was bashful and not that he was preparing to defend himself against an unprovoked attack.

"I'm sorry," she said softly. "Didn't mean to embarrass ya. Ya don't care much fer bein' touched, do ya?"

"Not much, no ma'am," he mumbled.

"Strange that you'd come to a place like this then," she said with a grin. "I ain't gonna hurt ya, darlin'. It's jus' that ya remind me of someone."

He ducked his head and forced a flush to his cheeks. He had been practicing the effect, but he was not sure of his success.

Grebella smirked. "Oh, not like that, sugar. Not exactly." She went about scrubbing the pots and counters as she spoke. "Was a long time ago. Pa was a city guard. Didn't have much money, but we had a nice home—safe as could be. Was jus' him and me, since ma died when I was little. Well, ya know, there was a boy. His name was Sim. Ya remind me of 'im. Not in the way ya look— no, not like that—but the way ya act. He was sweet and kind and didn't talk much ... and *shy*."

She smiled when he glanced away. He was doing his best to imitate the way Waylen acted whenever the ladies paid him attention. It seemed to be working. Her eyes were sad as she continued.

"I got pregnant. Sim was happy. Asked me to marry 'im. We told Pa, and I ain't never seen 'im like that. Pa and me, we'd always been good together— called me 'is princess. But that day—he said I broke 'is heart." She looked down at the counter and scrubbed extra hard at a nonexistent spot. "He kicked me out. Never did see my Sim again. He weren't the kind to take off, ya know. I know Pa did somethin'—called his guard friends mayhap." She shrugged dismissively, but the heave of her chest spoke of her distress. "Didn't 'ave no place to go. Came here broken. They gave me a job and food, a place to stay."

She paused, clenching the rag in her fist, and then looked up at him through unshed tears. "Always wondered what he was like—the babe. Took 'im to the temple o'course, like we all do here. You look the right age, and I was thinkin' … maybe he'd be 'bout like *you*."

Rezkin was not exactly sure why the woman was telling him all of this, except perhaps it had something to do with his *will*. Ever since he came here, he had been focusing to make her feel that he was not a threat, to feel familiar and comfortable with him.

He met her gaze with squinty eyes and muttered, "I'm awful sorry, ma'am, but ya know I'm not yer boy."

She smiled and tossed the rag at him with a chuckle that sounded forced. "I know that. Can't fault a grieving mother from seein' her lost boy in a handsome young man who come knockin' at her door … especially the kind that ain't wantin' our services."

Rezkin thought he understood now. The woman was already inclined to look for her lost son in the young men she met, an inclination that was magnified by the spell that lay over him.

"Well," she said, abruptly changing the tone, "the place is mine now, and I've got to keep things runnin' so as we can keep takin' in the ones that need us. Best be seein' the girls are gettin' up. Got chores to do before the gents come callin' this eve."

Grebella left the kitchen, already hollering to the women before she had reached the stairs. Rezkin returned to the stable to collect his supplies while pondering the woman's story. It made little sense to him. If the father of the baby wanted to marry Grebella, why would her own father react the way he had? Sim was likely dead, the baby had grown up in an orphanage, and Grebella worked in a brothel. It seemed that Grebella's father had been angry at the perceived loss of his daughter. Instead of growing his family to include a son-in-law and grandson, he ended up with nobody.

Upon leaving the slums, Rezkin skirted the docks and wove through the crowds that flowed like water toward and away from the market. As he walked, the story continued to churn through his mind. He had read dramatic tales with similar premises. One or more of the characters become angry and ultimately destroy everything and everyone for whom they cared. Based on historical and fictional accounts, Rezkin knew that outworlders did such things, but he could not summon the intensity of emotion to truly understand why. It was a madness, born of emotion, that consumed them, further evidence of the need for *Rule 37*.

The street vendors at the market were ready to serve the midday meal, and he chose two savory pies that were filled with meat and vegetables. He was not fully satisfied but did not wish to embark on a mission with a heavy stomach. Rezkin still did not care for the crowds in the cities, and he left the main thoroughfare as soon as possible. In the high society district, smartly dressed men in floppy, feathered hats strutted beside women as they strolled along the boulevard under cover of decorative parasols that even Lady Shiela would envy. Both men and women could be seen carrying intricately woven baskets, in which lounged tiny, fluffy cats that were adorned nearly as ostentatiously as their owners. Most of the pedestrians ignored Rezkin. Those who did not gave him reproving looks and clutched at their purses as though he might lunge at them in broad daylight to steal their belongings in front of so many witnesses.

He passed a busy social house, which was the refined way of saying tavern and found two carts parked in the alley. Workmen were unloading goods from the carts, while a woman stood in the rear stable yard scolding the stable boy. With all the commotion, nobody noticed Rezkin grab a sack of turnips from one of the carts. He carried it into the store room at the back of the tavern, and none of the busy kitchen staff acknowledged his presence except to skitter around him in their frenzy.

Rezkin emerged from the storeroom hidden beneath the same tattered cloak in which he had entered. Once he reached the entrance to the parlor, though, he slipped the cloak from his shoulders and stuffed it into the bag from which he had drawn the Channerían finery he now wore. Some of the inn's patrons smiled and bobbed their heads as he passed, and he returned the gesture. As he exited the social house, he slapped a floppy hat on his head, sans feather, since one would have been crushed in the bag. The people he passed were courteous and treated him as amicably as had those in the parlor.

His first order of business was to gain access to the mage relay. In the two weeks since leaving Skutton, he had not had any contact with his agents in Ashai. Those two weeks had also been the most tumultuous for the kingdom. His personnel were either frantically awaiting his orders or, most likely, plotting ways to overthrow him. Luckily, he had accounted for the latter, but it would not hurt to remind the Black Hall of their duty.

The mage relay was housed in a conical spire in the middle of a busy square surrounded by wealthy merchant and guild houses, the Golden Trust Bank, and a Temple of the Maker. A sign on the building situated between the temple and the bank identified it as *the number one breeder of purebred cats of the highest bloodlines.* Rezkin mentally shook his head. He could not fathom these outworlders' fascination with the little beasts.

The relay building's façade was ornately decorated with magical symbols, but since Rezkin's training had been deficient in that area, he did not know what they meant. He knew the building's construct had to be important, though, since all the mage relays he had visited in Ashai had been the same. He considered that it might be worth his while to obtain a few books on mage power and symbols if he could find them. With much to accomplish, though, he doubted he would have the time. Magical tomes were usually archived in the secure libraries of the mage academies and guilds. He would appreciate the challenge of such an endeavor, but it would be time consuming.

Rezkin entered the building with a swagger, smiling and nodding to its occupants, which included the two mages operating the relay and half a dozen administrators all vying for the chance to send their missives on behalf of important persons or offices. The administrators waited in the seating area at the front of the room as they fussed about their duties. Rezkin strode to the desk and was greeted by a harried blonde mage who had not yet grown into his ears.

"Greetings. What can I do for you, sir?" the young mage asked.

Rezkin pulled a stack of notes from the sack that he carried like a messenger's satchel and said, "I have several letters to be sent on behalf of Councilor Harid. Confidential, of course."

The mage's eyes widened. "Oh! The councilor! We will send them straight away. Do you have the letter of authorization?"

Rezkin smiled congenially. "Certainly."

This time, his letter was genuine. The greedy Councilor Harid had been most accommodating with the Raven. To the mages, the messages appeared as business correspondence to various officials and nobles in several of the Ashaiian capital cities. Each of the letters was from a fictitious noble or merchant, with whom the councilor presumably had investments, and some of them were addressed to equally fictitious recipients. In a few cases, the actual recipients would be confounded about their presumed *business,* of which they had no knowledge, but Rezkin's spies would be watching for the messages and would understand their meaning. The benign correspondence contained coded instructions that mages and anyone intercepting them should not find suspicious since nothing in them was of political significance.

The blonde mage took the papers and scurried over to the second mage, a young woman who wore her auburn locks braided in the shape of a butterfly on top of her head. The two communicated in harsh whispers as they surveyed the messages and shook their heads while pointing animatedly at the relay.

Rezkin leaned across the counter and kept his voice low as he asked, "Is there a problem?"

The two glanced at each other and then looked back at Rezkin with embarrassment. The man returned and nervously said, "Well, sir, Mage Calderson was suddenly called away on official business, and his replacement has not arrived." With a nod toward the other mage, he said, "We are both apprentices, and neither of us has sent anything to these relays before."

"I see. Perhaps if you tell me the problem, I might be able to assist you," Rezkin suggested.

"Are you a mage?" the young man asked hopefully.

Rezkin smiled and said, "No, but I have seen it done before, so I might possess whatever bit of information you are missing."

Rezkin had never actually operated a relay, but his masters had insisted he memorize the rune arrangements for each of the relays in Ashai. He learned the pattern of motions required to activate the pathways that would have allowed him to send messages had he been a mage. He had not questioned his masters and had learned everything they asked of him, even though it made little sense to him at the time. He had not understood why he should learn the actions for something he was incapable of performing, but now it made sense. He could show these mages how to do their job.

The blonde mage looked at him doubtfully. "It is a little more complicated than that."

"Of course," Rezkin said. "Then we will have to wait until the next mage arrives." He motioned to the female mage who was busy sending a message for one of the other patrons and said, "Since she is busy with the relay, would you mind explaining to me how it works? I have always been curious."

The young mage brightened and appeared eager to share his knowledge, explaining as he pointed to the different components of the relay. He even invited Rezkin to walk around the device after securing a promise that he would not touch anything. Like the other relays he had seen, it had a wide, cylindrical base approximately two meters in diameter. At waist height, it became conical, rising nearly to the woman's shoulders where the vertex appeared to have been sheared away, leaving the top flat. From the ceiling hung an identical form pointing downward so that only a handspan gap lay

74

between them. The rune engraved into the flat surface of the top section was the final rune that identified this particular relay. Dozens of other runes decorated both the top and bottom conical sections.

The mage explained that the runes did not actually hold any power. Rather, they identified the necessary spells and how to form them. Each rune represented a collection of spells, and the shape of the rune designated the shape and order in which the spells were to be layered upon each other. If a mage could memorize the order of dozens of spell sets, each containing dozens of spells, and the shapes in which they were layered with unerring precision, he or she could potentially use the mage relay without the runes.

The shape of the relay, and in fact the entire building, was designed to magnify and focus the mage's spells so that the messages could be transmitted and received by other relays. Each relay had rune configurations representing only the relays within its transmission range, which partly depended on the strength and capability of the mages powering it. Even if a mage could somehow manage to shape the spells without assistance from the runes, he or she could not possibly have the power or focus to transmit the spells without the relay.

The mage's explanation was fascinating and not at all what Rezkin had been taught. Aside from the healings, he had never witnessed the use of *talent* by his masters. The strikers with *talent* or other *visitors* had been called upon anytime he was required to train with *talent* wielders. Still, he had never found fault in his masters' teachings, so he thought perhaps there was more than one way to accomplish the task.

Eventually, the senior mage's replacement arrived and was able to send Rezkin's missives. The man became quite flustered when he found out that the councilor's administrator had been delayed for so long, and he did not stop to ask questions or read the messages.

Rezkin was finally free to complete the remainder of his tasks. By the time night fell, he had visited four more of the councilors. He had dropped in on the last while the man was using the privy. The councilor had been extremely uncomfortable during the entire exchange and agreed to do whatever the Raven asked if he would just leave him in peace with all his extremities intact. Some of the councilors had held their positions for many years, and Rezkin felt reasonably sure they would vote in favor of the king's proposal without the Raven's influence. A few, like Councilor Onelle, were more likely to vote in his favor to spite the Raven when he encouraged them to do otherwise. He needed seven of the ten votes, but outworlders were fickle. If they did not vote in his favor, he would resort to other methods.

The darkness enveloped him as he bounded across rooftops in the heart of the city. He crossed to the lower end where the average commoners drank and socialized. His stomach grumbled expressing its displeasure at being starved for the past few hours. This surprised him since he had eaten more than usual throughout the day. Crouching on the rooftop of a tavern, he changed his appearance once again. He stuffed his doublet into his sack, untucked his undershirt, and buckled his belt on the outside. He reversed the tattered cloak so that the worn spots were on the inside with the outer part being of average quality for a respectable commoner. The floppy hat went into the bag, and his loose hair was pulled back into the usual queue.

Rezkin did not dally in the tavern, only staying long enough to consume two meals, a pint of ale, for the sake of appearances, and a pitcher of water. When he left, he still was not satisfied, and he began to wonder if he was ill. When he returned to the ship, he would have one of the healers examine him. Then he wondered if he would be better off seeing one of the healers in the city. A regular healer in Serret would be no more concerned for his weakness than for any other stranger, but exposing the potential weakness to the mages on the ship might have severe consequences. He decided to consider the problem later. For now, he had to exact an entire island from a kingdom. At least it was a worthless island.

The palace gates were open when Rezkin arrived. Unfortunately, they were manned by well-armed guards, and a line of carriages surrounded by a forest of torches was rolling through. Had he arrived earlier, he might have been able to hide himself among the carriages, but it would be difficult now with so many alert guards and coachmen. Even the bedecked passengers were peeking out to witness their grand entry onto the palace grounds.

King Ionius was throwing a ball to celebrate his daughter's engagement, although the princess was only sixteen and would not actually marry for another year or two, depending on the terms of the arrangement. Such was the custom in Channería *unless* she was found to possess the *talent*, in which case she could put off marrying for another ten years to ensure the best matching of mage power. Channerians believed they could influence the development of certain *talents* through proper breeding.

So long as so many eyes were on the front of the palace, fewer would be watching other possible entrances. Rezkin slinked along the wall perimeter in the moon-cast shadow. Guards paced the wall walk beyond the torch-lit battlement. He pressed himself against the stone and waited for the two guards above to finish their conversation and move in opposite directions. As he began climbing, his fingers and soft boots finding purchase in the cracks between stones, he felt a surge of battle energy. His masters had told him the energy was the body's way of preparing a warrior for difficult physical and mental tasks. He usually did not feel its familiar heat until he was about to engage an enemy, and sometimes even then it was delayed or never came at all. Tonight, it was preemptive, and he hoped it was not a sign of difficulty to come.

The castle had only one curtain wall, a front bailey, a rear bailey, and a keep in between. The rear bailey contained the guard barracks, smithy, and small training grounds. The front bailey had been cleared of anything useful and was presently drowning in decorative frivolities. Rezkin was over the wall without incident. He dropped into the darkness below and then stole across the practice grounds using a low fence and hedges to hide his progress. He rounded the corner of the barracks just as a guard exited. The guard squinted in the darkness, and Rezkin knew he could not be seen clearly, but he was definitely exposed. He grabbed the ladle hanging from a water barrel and dunked it noisily into the water before raising it to his lips.

"Got any root?" the guard asked, referring to the crass root that some outworlders chewed for its slightly intoxicating effects.

Mimicking the guard's guttural drawl, Rezkin said, "Ran out hours ago."

The guard spit off to the side. "Bloody balls. Hate 'em. Been on duty near on two days straight." The man was still grumbling to himself as he tromped away.

Rezkin hurried past the barracks. After surveying the area for guards, he began climbing the keep wall. The window was at least thirty feet above the ground, and he had to scale the wall before anyone glanced his way. He chose this wall because it was likely to be under the least amount of scrutiny. Who would attempt to steal into the castle from the guards' barracks?

The window was small and heavily warded, but he did not think he had set off any alarms when he squeezed through. It was a little difficult to tell since there appeared to be several wards created by different mages that were layered on top of each other. The room was musty, despite the open window, and held a table in the center with a workbench along one wall. Books, mixing bowls, several bottles of ingredients, and other alchemy essentials were scattered across the workbench. A candle burned beside an open book, and one of the bowls held a steeping mixture, so he knew someone had been there recently. He peeked at the title of the recipe, which indicated it was to be used to cure headaches. After reading the list of ingredients, he decided the author must have meant a metaphorical headache, since the brew was sure to kill anyone who drank it.

The door creaked as it opened, and Rezkin ducked under the center table. Two pairs of soft, brown slippers padded by the table beneath swishing grey robes. Both mages wore brown panels indicating a primary affinity for earth, and each had a white stripe denoting a secondary air affinity. One had an additional blue stripe indicating a third affinity for water. According to Wesson, most mages had only one or two affinities in which they were strong enough to earn stripes. Three was unusual, so it was likely this was the king's mage and the other was his assistant or a visiting mage scholar.

"Is it ready?" the triple-striped mage asked. His voice was slightly raspy with age.

"Yes, I just need to transfer it to the bottle," the younger man said.

They were now standing away from Rezkin's hiding place and were turned in profile. He peered around the edge of the table and saw that they were both hunched over the workbench examining the concoction. The younger mage transferred the contents of the bowl into a bit of cloth, wrapped it tightly, and then squeezed it so that the liquid streamed into a cup. He then emptied the cup into a small green vial with a cork stopper. After tossing the cloth and its contents into the hearth, he scrubbed at his hands furiously in a basin of water. The room quickly filled with the stench of a fetid corpse. Rezkin felt the tingle of mage power and then a gust swept through the room carrying the malodorous vapors out the window.

The older mage gathered the book and ingredients into a sack and then knelt on the floor near the window. He swept away a section of rushes and then pried at the timber with an iron rod. A piece of the floor tilted upward, and the old man stuffed the sack into a hole beneath. When he was finished, he covered over the area and turned as he struggled to his feet. If he had raised his eyes, he would have seen Rezkin. The two men turned and left the chamber, locking the door and creating a ward as they departed.

Rezkin shuffled over to the hideaway and retrieved the burlap sack. He surveyed the other books but found only one on alchemy that might be of interest and was also small enough to fit into the sack. The others were mundane apothecary tomes, several of which he had already studied. Two of the ingredients on the shelf were unfamiliar to him, so he stuffed those in the sack as well. He bundled the sack tighter with the black strips of fabric he had wound about his limbs and then secured it to his belt. He slipped through door, relocked it, and then followed the retreating shuffle of distant footsteps. The two mages were up to something, and it would likely lead him to the king. Whether they were working for or against the king, Rezkin did not know, but one thing was certain. Someone was going to die.

The Channerían king's castle, like the other castles and palaces of foreign monarchs, had been among the floorplans he memorized when he was young. He remembered learning this one when he was fourteen. Strikers Baen and Ridney had collectively spent nearly four years in service at the castle and had provided him with firsthand accounts of its structure and workings. They had also helped him to design the best strategy for infiltration, one which he was now implementing.

The mages turned down the corridor that led to the king's chambers but stopped short, only halfway. The younger mage rapped lightly on what Rezkin knew to be the princess's door. A portly woman slipped into the corridor and pulled the door closed behind her. Rezkin could hear most of what they were saying from his hiding place. He was crouched behind a decorative suit of armor, but he knew he could not stay long. Thus far, this part of the castle had been relatively clear. Regular servants were not permitted to use the main corridors, being relegated to the hidden servants' passages behind the walls, and most of the guards and other staff were attending to the ball.

"Has the gift arrived yet?" the older mage asked the woman.

The woman was dressed as a nursemaid, and her wide eyes, tense stance, and constant wringing of the hands indicated that she was expecting trouble.

"Yes, only just. Are ... are you sure this is necessary?" She spoke in a loud whisper that carried farther down the passage than the man's gruff voice. Her gaze darted back to the closed door, and she bit her lip. "She is just a child. What if we get caught? Surely there is another way."

"It is not your place to question the king's orders ... nor is it mine," the old mage snapped.

The nursemaid curtsied deeply and bowed her head. "Of course, Archmage. My apologies. I do not doubt the king." Her voice turned contemptuous as she said, "I admit I will not mourn her. She is a horrid, petulant girl."

The younger mage handed the green vial to the woman, and she took it with shaking hands. He said, "If you fail, you will not survive the consequences."

Rezkin doubted the woman would survive the night. He was now in a quandary. It seemed the king wanted to kill his own daughter on her engagement night, and he had to decide whether to intercede. The girl was not his *friend*, nor was she one of his subjects. He was under no obligation to assist. Getting involved would make this mission far more complicated than necessary. If he did nothing, the princess would die, and he would go about his business as planned. It seemed the logical choice.

The mages continued down the passage toward the king's chambers, and Rezkin wondered again why no guards were posted. Perhaps the king had called them into his chambers or they were dismissed to prevent additional witnesses. Rezkin was about to follow the mages when he observed the woman returning to the princess's rooms, the green vial clasped tightly in her palm. A chill slithered up his spine, and he was assailed by an emotion. It felt something like a mixture of anger and fear. His stomach dropped, and his blood was cold. The buzz of battle energy seeped into his system unsummoned. He had no explanation for the reaction. He tried to push it down, to separate himself from the emotion per *Rule 37*, but it would not yield.

He took a step to follow the mages and had another thought. Perhaps his instincts were trying to tell him something. Somewhere in his mind, he may have already deduced the benefits of saving the princess, but he had not yet come to realize them consciously. *Rule 41—heed your instincts*. It was good enough. He could worry about his reasoning later. If he did not act soon, the princess would be dead, and that could not be undone.

Rezkin checked the corridors around him and then sprinted toward the princess's chambers. It was unlocked, so he let himself in without notice. The sitting room was comfortably appointed with two lilac settees and two high-back chairs, each dotted with small pillows embroidered with flowers. A tea set occupied one sideboard, and dinnerware containing a partially eaten meal was abandoned on the dining table by the window. Hot air from the hearth mixed with the cool night breeze to produce an eddy of shifting temperatures.

The princess could be heard squabbling with the nursemaid in the next room.

"I told you I do not want any wine," the girl huffed. "I can barely fit into this dress as it is, and it is too hot in here. Why is it so hot in here? No, I cannot go. Tell them I am unwell. Better yet, tell them I have contracted some fatal illness."

The young woman's distress was clear. She did not sound like a lovestruck bride-to-be, and her words were disturbingly prophetic.

"You should not be so overly dramatic, Ilanet," said the nursemaid. "The prince is not so bad. You have barely spoken to him. I am sure you will grow to care for him in time. Here, drink this and all will be well."

Rezkin peered through the open doorway and saw that the two women were preoccupied on the far side of the room. The princess turned from the window and dropped inelegantly onto the seat at the vanity along the far wall.

"How is *that* going to make anything better?" she whined.

Padding silently into the room, Rezkin took a seat in a chair on the opposite wall and lounged casually as if he had been there all night.

"It was a gift from the prince. It will help you relax," the older woman said as she settled the goblet on the vanity directly in front of her young charge.

The princess sighed heavily and reached for the wine.

Rezkin said, "I would not drink that if I were you."

5

I lanet squealed upon hearing the unexpected male voice. She spun as she rose from her seat, causing her skirts to become tangled in the legs of the vanity bench, and she tumbled to the ground. Nurse Mables shouted in alarm and flung her arms out to the side, upsetting a vase that she somehow managed to rescue, despite fumbling it. Mables held the vase before her as a shield.

"Who are you? What are you doing here?" Mables shouted. "Guards!"

"You know as well as I that there are no guards to be summoned," the intruder said.

Ilanet battled her ball gown as she regained her feet. "What? No guards? Why are there no guards?" she asked, directing the question to Mables.

Before Mables could answer, Ilanet grabbed the vase from the woman's hands and threw it at the intruder. He did not bother to move, and the vase fell short. It had been a bit heavier than she expected. She turned to the window to shout for help, but she was suddenly wrenched from her feet. She cried out as she was tossed into the air and then landed with a thump on the bed. The nurse's blubbering ceased with the sound of a smack, and then Ilanet was being pulled by the ankles. She grabbed at the bedcovers and kicked, but the intruder was twisting her own skirts about her legs so that she could not move. She hollered and grabbed the first thing that fell into her hands. She swung the pillow at the massive man, but he snatched it from her hand. He flipped her over and used the bedcovers to bind her arms to her sides. She opened her mouth to scream, but her efforts were foiled when he stuffed the linens between her teeth.

Ilanet was completely immobilized in seconds, and her ineffectual screams fell on deaf ears. She stared angrily up at the intruder while blinking away tears. If she had not been so terrified, she might have thought him handsome. The lines of his face were harsh in the lamplight, and his icy gaze was haunting. He appeared empty, devoid of heart and soul. She began to panic all over again when she saw the sword hilts at his back, the blackened armor, and the sheaths and hilts of multiple knives strapped to his body. She screamed again, the sound muffled by the linens, and her chest heaved as the tears began to flow.

To her minimal relief, the menacing intruder stepped away. He bowed slightly, a courtly bow, and said, "Greetings, Princess Ilanet. Once I have your attention, I will explain to you my presence."

A refined killer, she thought. An assassin. She cried harder and struggled with her bonds to no avail. This was so much worse. A professional assassin could not be reasoned with and would likely not be influenced by her position or wealth. The fact that he had not yet killed her gave her some small amount of solace. It meant he wanted something, and hopefully he would not kill her once he had it. She swallowed her sobs, nearly choking on the linens, and tried to temper her terror as she peered back at him.

"I have no intention of harming you," he said. "Quite the opposite."

She did not believe him, but hearing the words brought her an inordinate amount of joy. She might have laughed if she could, sure that her fear had driven her mad. A groan from the floor reached her ears, and she was relieved that Mables was not dead. Not yet, at least. Her nurse whimpered, and Ilanet could finally see the woman as she leveraged herself into a chair holding her head.

The intruder turned, presumably so that he could keep both in his sights. "You are smarter than most of the people I deal with, Princess. Most are cowards overcome with fear. Their arrogance betrays them when they try to hide behind their wealth and perception of power. You at least tried to fight for your life and freedom before I overcame you. Had you been faced with a lesser opponent, you might have succeeded. Though, your nurse must die."

Ilanet screamed and shook her head violently as Mables sobbed and begged for her life.

"Silence," ordered the intruder.

Mables continued to blather, even sliding to her knees as she pleaded for mercy. The intruder backhanded the woman, and Ilanet could just barely see Mables's head as she cowered against the chair. She would not give the intruder credit for withholding, but she knew from experience that her father struck much harder when angry. She shivered when he turned his attention back to her.

"This woman tried to poison you," the intruder said.

Ilanet screamed and shook her head. She tried to tell him that Mables would never do such a thing. The woman had raised her since infancy. If she had not been a servant, she might even feel like family.

"No, you are correct, Princess," the intruder said, somehow interpreting her meaning. "Your nursemaid does not have the constitution to carry out such a deed on her own. She merely served you the poison. The archmage and his colleague produced it. Can you guess who might have arranged this assassination?"

She stared into the stranger's icy blue eyes as the dread struck. Only one man in the kingdom had influenced with the archmage. No, it was preposterous. The stranger was lying. There probably was no poison. She scowled at the intruder attempting to convey her disbelief.

"No? You do not believe me." The stranger nodded as if this was to be expected. "Perhaps your nursemaid still carries the poison on her. Woman,"— he turned his attention to Mables—"empty your pockets."

Mables got to her feet and backed into the wall. "What? No, of course, I have nothing like that."

The intruder drew a knife from his belt. It was long and curved and had wicked serrations across the back. Mables's eyes widened, and she whimpered as she pulled a green vial from her skirt. After collecting the vial, the intruder held the empty vessel close for her to see. She glanced at Mables, who was sobbing against the wall. *Surely not.* Ilanet shook her head uncertainly.

The stranger cocked his head curiously. "I will remove the gag if you agree not to scream. If, by the end of this investigation, you remain unconvinced, I will leave you to your fate in peace."

Ilanet searched the man's face for deceit, but he was unreadable. She had difficulty believing he would go to all this trouble and then leave, but really, what other choice did she have? She nodded her agreement, and he pulled the linen from her mouth.

She swallowed several times to wet the dryness and then said, "That vial could have contained anything."

He studied the bottle and then looked back at her. "Look at the woman. Do you really believe that?"

Ilanet did look to Mables, and her nurse *did* appear quite guilty. Ilanet squirmed and said, "Unbind me."

The intruder shook his head. "If I do that, then you will try to run away, and we have not yet concluded our business. What will convince you of the truth?"

"How about *you* drink the wine, and we will see if it kills you," she snapped. She immediately regretted her tone and cringed in expectation of a blow that never landed. Her eyes opened slightly to see him staring at her, his face implacable.

"Woman," he barked, and Mables jumped. "Drink the wine."

Mables's panic was obvious as her gaze darted between them and the wine. "N-no, no, no. If it is poisoned, then I shall not drink it."

Ilanet scowled at her nurse. "Mables, drink the wine. Show him it is not poisoned. You would not do that to me!"

"But, Princess ..."—her eyes widened—"It was the prince! The prince is trying to kill you."

Ilanet heard the edge in her own voice when she said, "Mables, drink the wine." She still clung to the faint hope that none of this was real, that it was all a mistake.

"No, Princess, I cannot," the woman cried.

The intruder shook the knife in the air before Mables's eyes. The razor edge and jagged serrations glinted menacingly in the lamplight. "The wine ... or the knife," he said.

Mables stared at the silvery omen of her fate with a quivering lip. She slid stutteringly along the wall and then reached for the goblet with a shaking hand. Sobbing, she put the cup to her lips and drank. The knife flashed again in the light, and she drank more deeply. She sputtered. Wine poured from her lips and dribbled down her chin. The goblet struck the floor with a *clunk*, and to Ilanet's dismay, the woman doubled over and retched on the rushes. Ilanet shifted and rolled to the side of the bed so she could see the horror unfolding. After the initial upset, the red liquid that continued to spill forth was much too dark and voluminous to be wine. Ilanet cried as she witnessed the terror that might have befallen her. She continued to cry when Mables collapsed and then throughout the jostling of being unwrapped.

Then the intruder was moving away. He was heading for the door.

"Wait! Where are you going? You cannot just leave!"

He turned, and she thought she saw a flash of surprise on his otherwise impassive face.

He said, "A moment ago, you sought my death, and now you do not wish for me to leave?"

"That was before. Please, tell me what is happening. Why did she try to kill me? Tell me"—she choked up, and then in a whisper—"was it my father?"

"I think you know," he said.

"But why? And why are you here? Did someone send you here to save me?" she asked.

Her questions burst forth in a rush, and even so, they were only a small portion of the turmoil that flooded her mind.

Rezkin stared down at the small-woman. She was distraught and desiring of solace, but he did not have time for such things. She would have to find comfort elsewhere.

"I do not bear the answers you seek, Princess. I came here on other business. My involvement with you was merely happenstance. I became aware of the plot against you and decided to intercede for reasons of my own."

Rezkin admitted to himself that he was not certain of what those reasons were at that moment.

To her, he said, "I suggest you seek someone you can trust, or at the very least, someone who has an interest in your survival—your intended perhaps."

"No! I cannot marry him!" she shouted and threw herself at him. Rezkin held her hands against his chest so she could not access any of his weapons. The princess looked up at him with eyes the color of sapphires. Her caramel hair was mussed, and her cheeks were stained salty with tears. "My father chose him. If my father wants me dead, then Prince Nyan could be in on it."

Rezkin surveyed the body on the floor. The blood had poured not just from the woman's mouth, but also from her nose and ears. It spread through the rushes turning them varying shades of red and pink.

He looked back to the small-woman, not quite grown, and tried to soften his tone. "This was not a simple poison to put you to sleep, not one to be hidden. It was meant to appear a gruesome death, a death that would naturally incite outrage in the castle. The poison was placed in the wine sent to you as a gift from your betrothed. I believe your father intended to blame the murder on the prince, probably with the intention of receiving some recompense or ransom from his father, King Vergos, for the deed."

The small-woman seemed to age before his eyes as her face sobered.

"I knew he would marry me off to get what he wanted, but to take my *life*?"

She pulled away from him and paced as she wiped at her tear-streaked face.

"Nyan has been here for months trying to convince my father to accept his proposal. He is a second son, though, and Father was holding out. He wanted a better match—a crown prince or king. Initially, I was supposed to marry King Caydean of Ashai ... but then last week, Father suddenly accepted Nyan's offer." Her face turned petulant, and once again he saw her for the small-woman she was. "He is *thirty-seven* years old. *Ancient*! And, I do not love him."

"From what I know of such things, love has nothing to do with royal marriages, or almost any marriage, for that matter. You should go to Nyan. He has the means and resources to see you safe, provided you both leave the city immediately." He turned toward the door. "I must go."

She grabbed his arm. "Please, you cannot leave me here. People want to kill me! Now that I know, he most certainly will finish it. You decided to help me once. Please do so again. I will pay you. I have gold and jewelry. Please. I cannot go with Nyan, and if I stay here I will die."

Rezkin shook his head at the absurdity. He did have the resources to help her, or at least he would in a few days, but she did not know that. To her, he was only a stranger who, while obviously up to nefarious business in the castle, decided to break into her bedchamber, toss her around, and kill her nursemaid.

"What do you expect me to do with you, Princess? Where would I take you?"

"It does not matter. You look like a man of means. Take me anywhere but here—a cave if you must."

His eyes followed the sweep of her gown and then trailed back up to the jewels dangling from her ears. "You would not care to live in a cave."

She lifted her chin and said, "I would be alive. From there I would find some way, some*where*."

At least she was not the blubbering mess he had expected of the *horrid, petulant girl* the nursemaid had described. With another look into her pleading, sapphire eyes, Rezkin knew he would concede. He could not say why, but it was useless to argue with himself when he already knew the result.

"Very well. Stay here and lock the door. Do not open it for *anyone*. Change into something travel worthy, pants if you have them. A servant's clothes would be best. And cover your hair. You may pack *one* bag, and you must be capable of carrying it long distances on your own. If you attempt to bring too much, whatever you cannot carry will be left behind." He pulled the sack of alchemical materials from his belt and said, "Take this. I will retrieve it when I return. This will be easier if I do not have to carry it with me."

Ilanet hesitantly took the small, bulbous sack. "What is in it?"

"The materials and references needed to make the poison that killed your nursemaid," he said. Upon seeing the alarm on her face, he added, "I happened upon the mages when they were storing these away, so I took them."

Her eyes were once again fearful as she asked, "How do I know you did not make the poison?"

Rezkin shrugged. "Do you wish to stay?"

"No!" she blurted. "I mean, no, I will go with you. You *will* come back for me?"

"I will return when I am finished with my other business."

The princess's eyes held questions, but she did not voice them. Rezkin opened the door a crack and searched the corridor. A guard was retreating around a corner, and two servants shuffled into the servants' passage. Rezkin slipped into the hall and closed the door behind him. He waited only a moment before he heard the click of the bolt, and then he rushed down the corridor to the king's chambers. He was not sure what he would find once he entered. The guards could be manning the door from the inside, or the mages could still be in attendance. He did not care to test his *Skills* against an archmage.

Rezkin rapped lightly on the door as he listened carefully for sounds of motion inside. No guards immediately answered. He sensed a ward around the door, and it felt personal. The king had likely set it once the mages had left. The assumption was not worth the risk, though, so he drew Kingslayer from its sheath. He gathered his focus in preparation for a battle with the mages and felt the answering thrill of battle energy as it surged through him.

The door opened smoothly without a hiss, but the anteroom was dark save for a small fire in the hearth. His instincts spoke to him of more than one presence in the rooms. His roving gaze searched the dancing shadows as he barred the door behind him. The firelight did not reach the far side of the room where the door to the king's bedchamber stood open. A black figure was silhouetted by the moonlight streaming in through the large window behind him. He stood tall and still as Rezkin's gaze searched out the other presence.

"I knew you would come," said the shadowed figure. "You did not think you could threaten a councilor without my knowledge, did you?"

Councilor. Only one—certainly Onelle. Rezkin had counted on her reporting their meeting, though. He did not answer the distraction. Energy probed at him from two sides, sensing, seeking, grasping for knowledge.

"My ward remains undisturbed, and yet I see you here, in this room. You obviously hold unusual power to simply walk through such wards, though I feel nothing from you—only the emptiness of a *mundane.*"

Rezkin was surprised at the scorn the king showed for those who comprised the vast majority of his people.

Rezkin had his answer regarding the personal ward. The king had not sensed the breach, or so he said. It was something he would need to test further with his own mages when he had the time. He crept to his left, farther from the flames, into the darker recesses of the room. He could feel the foreign *vimara* emanating from its source, and he would rather be the hunter than the prey. The source shifted, and Rezkin understood. He was in the center of the web.

Strands of power suddenly wrapped around him from all directions just as a lithe figure dropped from the rafters. Rezkin shifted and slashed at the strings, but his sword was useless against them. In the dark, without his eyes to tell him otherwise, the strands of vimara almost felt solid, tangible. A flush of air warned him of an attack, and he ducked in time to avoid his opponent's blade. A second slashed at him from the other side and was met with the swift stroke of Kingslayer. The strands of power wound more tightly and he could feel them pressing against him. They abruptly cinched as his opponent muttered a verbal spell, but to the man's dismay, they did not hinder Rezkin's movement.

Rezkin drove forward, and the man backed into a table knocking its contents to the floor with a crash. The man dodged a thrust and then jumped atop the table as Rezkin followed through with an upward swing. The man parried, throwing Rezkin's sword wide, and then he kicked at Rezkin's head. He caught the leg and yanked it forward, causing the man to crash onto the table. The strands of power tugged at Rezkin from all sides like a strong wind ripping at his clothes. Without thinking about what he was doing, he grabbed at the strands with his free hand and was surprised when his fingers seemed to meet with solid substance. He gripped the strands tightly, winding them around his hand for leverage, and heaved. The opponent shouted as he was dragged from the table. When the man struck the floor, the spell unraveled. Rezkin stood poised to deliver the final blow when the man suddenly bellowed.

"I yield to the Riel'gesh! Fealty to the Raven!"

Rezkin was abruptly rocked by a powerful gust of wind. He redirected his focus shield to protect himself from the king's assault, but it did not shelter him from the turbulent debris that soared through the air. Papers, books, pillows, candle sticks, and dinner ware—pretty much anything smaller than his head that was not secured to the walls was flying at him. He dodged and blocked most of what came at him, but he did receive his share of minor injuries. A sudden painful stab to the back of his leg did not feel so minor. He reached down and pulled the small projectile from his hamstring—a metal-tipped quill. It was fitting, he thought. He could write of the king's death in blood.

Unfortunately, killing the king was not part of his plan. In fact, aside from infiltrating the castle, nothing that had happened that night had been part of the plan. The king backed away into his bedchamber as Rezkin advanced. The man raised the longsword he held at his side, but it quickly became obvious that the king was not used to fighting in the dark or in close quarters. His first swing became lodged in the bedpost. He pulled it out and tried again. Rezkin sheathed Kingslayer and drew Bladesunder. It would give him less reach but more maneuverability in the densely furnished room. Ionius was a skilled swordsman but no master, and it seemed his age and lavish lifestyle had reduced his speed and endurance.

Rezkin allowed the king a few moments of false hope before smashing it completely by disarming him and leaving him in the precarious position of remaining on his tiptoes against the wall. It was either that or be impaled by a sword through the throat.

"Do you yield?" he asked.

"You will never take the throne," Ionius spat.

Rezkin could not see the man well in the dark, but he imagined the king was red with anger. He was the kind who would rather lose his head than bow to another for any reason.

"I did not ask for the throne, only that you stop fighting me and concede to a few simple demands."

"You think to make demands of *me*! I am the king, and you are naught but a common criminal."

"I am anything but common," Rezkin said, and he knew it to be true.

Whether it was due to his training, his mysterious birth, or the supposedly undetectable power he might possess, he knew now that he was not like these outworlders. He called to the man in the other room. He had not heard him shuffling about, and Rezkin wondered if he had even left his place of defeat. The man moved silently in the dark, undetectable until his figure became visible in the moonlight. He stood a respectable distance from Rezkin and bowed deeply.

"I am at your command, Riel'gesh," he said.

"I am the king!" Ionius shouted. "You serve me!"

The man chuckled mirthlessly. "I serve the Order. You know this."

"So, you heard tell that I was coming for you, and you called upon the Order," Rezkin said. "I am disappointed in you, Ionius. You must know that the Order is of the Riel'sheng. They will serve the Riel'gesh."

"The *Riel'gesh*," Ionius spat, "is an absurd myth. I am not surprised the *Black Hall* fell for it."

"The Black Hall should not be dismissed," the assassin said. "They too are Riel'sheng. They carry the sacred right, same as we."

"No one is undefeatable," Ionius argued. To Rezkin he said, "You are a charlatan. This one has obviously fallen for your ruse. I will see that the Order punishes him for his treachery after they are finished with *you*."

Rezkin did not need to respond since his newest devotee was quick to his defense.

"You should choose your words carefully, King Ionius. You can see from where you stand that your life is forfeit. The Reil'gesh bestows life by his will alone, and you are not giving him reason."

"My life is not his to bestow. That was a privilege of the Maker," Ionius said.

"A blessing granted unto the Riel'gesh," the assassin argued.

The king scoffed. "You think the Maker would grant the power of life to an *assassin*?"

"We are assassins because it is the service we are best suited to provide. The Riel'sheng have trained for hundreds of years, preserving and improving upon our skills so that we may one day serve the Riel'gesh."

"You think he is this man?" Ionius asked in disbelief. "Just because he defeated you? How many men have defeated you in the past? You did not declare them *Riel'gesh*."

"It has been long since any but the Ong'ri has defeated me, and never so succinctly." The assassin's colorless features were awash with silvery moonlight as he turned to Rezkin. "You move silently and surely, and your skill is unmatched. Not for these reasons do I bow to you. Never has anyone arrested my power as you did. I was helpless under your *will*, and yet I sense nothing from you. You are naught but darkness, moving freely, a *will* of its own. I fear your wake."

Rezkin was discomfited by the assassin's impassioned speech. He did not care for the praise and felt that the title of Riel'gesh had been misplaced. When the Black Hall had declared him so, he had thought it convenient, a simple way of obtaining their loyalty. The Riel'sheng were not exclusive to Ashai, though, and news of the Raven's influence had spread with far-reaching consequences. The Ong'ri was the leader of the Order. From what the assassin had said, he had to be the Jeng'ri, the second of the Order. For him to recognize Rezkin as the Riel'gesh was significant, but not an official sanction on behalf of the Order.

Rezkin could think of nothing to say that was worthy of such a speech, so he chose not to respond. Instead, he turned to Ionius and said, "Are you ready to grant my demands?"

The man actually growled. "Lower your sword, and I shall hear what you have to say."

Rezkin lowered his sword and stepped back a few paces. The Jeng'ri held his position, presumably out of respect for the Riel'gesh, although he might have been more concerned that Rezkin would see him as a threat and end him. Ionius did not seem to have the same fears. He shuffled to a side table and fumbled in the dark for a decanter.

Flustered, he said, "Must we stand around in the dark? Let us at least light a lamp or candle."

"There is no need," Rezkin said. "I am perfectly comfortable in the dark." He turned to the Jeng'ri and asked, "You?"

"I am as well, Riel'gesh," he replied.

As Ionius lifted the goblet to his lips, he muttered, "Bloody assassins and their bloody night vision." He seated himself in a high-back chair, only stubbing his toe once in the process, and said, "What is it you want?"

"It is not a matter of what I *want* but what I am taking," Rezkin said. "I am taking two things from you, Ionius, and I think you will only protest one with any spirit."

"Besides my life and my throne, what of mine would you take for yourself?"

"I do not take it for myself but for another." Rezkin spread his hands and said, "I am the Raven, a thief, an assassin, a criminal. Surely I am unworthy of anything you hold dear. No, I do not take for myself. The one I intend to profit for my efforts is a savior, a champion, a leader of men, and a king by right."

Ionius huffed. "What is this nonsense? Of whom do you speak?"

"Soon, a man will set foot upon your shore, a man both glorified and vilified. He seeks to save his people and defeat the evil that has infested his land. You may know him as Dark Tidings."

"This is absurd!" said Ionius. "Caydean's filth is spilling into Channería in all forms. I will not have it! Neither you nor Dark Tidings are welcome here … and neither are any of those people he took with him. Yes, I know he left the tournament with a crowd of people who escaped Caydean's madness. Significant rewards have been proffered for their heads. It is surprising that none have been offered for yours."

Rezkin found that to be surprising as well. From the Ashaiian king's perspective, of all the people deserving of a warrant, the Raven should have been at the top of the list.

"Unless you really work for Caydean," Ionius added.

Rezkin chuckled. "Why would I work for Caydean when I already possess his people? Leave the endless court and council meetings to him. I will govern from the dark. With each of his destructive whims, my power grows. Upon the death of civilization, the strongest and fiercest prevail. Do you know who those people are, Ionius? *My* people."

Ionius said, "You are just as mad as he."

"Then you had best hope my madness does not spread within your land more than it already has," Rezkin replied with a nod toward the Jeng'ri.

Ionius nearly emptied his cup. "Tell me. What is it that will see you gone?"

"The first is your daughter," Rezkin said.

"What? What do you want with Ilanet?"

"That is not your concern. You will send Princess Ilanet with Dark Tidings. You may pose the arrangement however you like, a diplomatic mission if you will. In the end, she will go with him when he leaves your land."

"Impossible. I cannot give what you ask," Ionius said.

"And why is that?"

"Because Ilanet is de- ... betrothed. You must know that a ball is being held in the hall at this very moment in celebration of the engagement."

"Hmm, yes. It does seem strange, though, that neither the father of the bride nor the lady, herself, are in attendance," Rezkin said.

"What do you mean? Of course Ilanet is there. Where else would she be?" Ionius asked in a rush.

"Oh, perhaps in a bloody heap on her bedchamber floor."

Ionius surged to his feet. The moonlight spilled over his features to reveal a guilty man hiding behind righteous anger. "What have you done?"

Rezkin laughed. "What have *I* done? You cannot carry out an assassination of such significance and not expect to summon the Riel'gesh."

The king's eyes opened wide, and his face drained so that even in the dark he appeared ghostly. "H-how could you know? Impossible. The nurse ... the nursemaid must have told you. But, no, she only found out a few hours ago."

The king's muttering was desperate as he contemplated the alternatives. Rezkin felt the penetrating stare of the Jeng'ri and considered that perhaps his overly dramatic, mystical claim, intended for the benefit of the king, had fallen heavily on the wrong ears.

Ionius abruptly asked, "So she is dead, then? No, you said you wanted her. She cannot be dead. Unless ... do you hear the dead? Did she call to you?"

Rezkin had not expected the king to come to *that* conclusion. He glanced at the Jeng'ri, who was still staring at him with unsettling intensity. Maybe the assassin had somehow arrived at the same ridiculous conclusion. Rezkin could already imagine the stories that would spawn from this moment—a legend in which the spirits of the dead call to the Riel'gesh from the Afterlife and his vengeful answer.

The Jeng'ri finally pulled his attention away from Rezkin and directed it at the king. "You plotted to kill your daughter and did not call upon the Order?"

"I did not need a trained assassin to kill a stupid girl," Ionius snapped.

"You were wrong," Rezkin said. As interesting as the prospect of being a mystical creature summoned by the dead was, it did not fit into his plans. "A nursemaid, mage, and archmage were insufficient to get the job done. Your daughter lives."

"You granted her life," the Jeng'ri said with reverence.

Rezkin mentally sighed. It seemed the legend would not die here. To

Ionius, he said, "I claim her this night. She will be delivered when Dark Tidings arrives."

"What am I to tell Nyan?" Ionus asked.

Rezkin said, "You may tell him that you tried to frame him for her murder, if you like."

Ionius groaned. "Does nothing escape you? You do not understand. Vergos would not be swayed. I told him that I needed more iron, more weapons, more rations. I need his army. Caydean is mad, and Ashai is in turmoil. He spits on our longstanding alliance, and already I have Gendishen and the Eastern Mountains tribes threatening to invade my lands to get at Ashai. We must strike now."

The king abruptly paused and glanced up, appearing to have just realized to whom he was speaking. The Raven might not look kindly on an invasion of his homeland. Rezkin was perfectly willing to allow the king to rant about his plans.

Ionius cleared his throat and asked, "Are you working with *him*, then? This *Dark Tidings*?

Rezkin had to consider the relationship between the Raven and Dark Tidings carefully. He did not want anyone to know they were the same person, nor did he want them thinking that one was working for the other. Neither would benefit from the stigmas associated with the other within their respective communities of influence.

"You are aware that Dark Tidings bears claim to the Ashaiian throne?"

Ionius grunted. "Naught but rubbish. Caydean is Bordran's first born. No one denies it. Beyond that, there is a clear line of succession. Some might think it suspicious that Prince Thresson goes missing just before Dark Tidings declares himself Bordran's rightful heir. Some might believe the two are the same, but I have met Thresson on several occasions. I am quite certain he is *not* the untouchable tournament champion of whom I have heard tell."

It was an interesting point. Rezkin had not considered that people might think Prince Thresson had something to do with Dark Tidings.

He ignored that consideration for the moment and said, "Dark Tidings intends to bring war down on Caydean but with as little negative impact on the people of Ashai as possible. This means the least impact to *my* people. That is something that neither you nor any of the other kingdoms will offer."

"But I thought you wanted Caydean on the throne. What about that whole *chaos is good for business* speech?" Ionius said.

"There is such a thing as too much chaos. Caydean's insanity makes him unpredictable, and I recently received information that his strength and madness may be worse than you or I could have foreseen. No, his reign is not a sound long-term investment. At this point in time, what is good for Dark Tidings is good for me, which means it is also best for *you*." He finished with a feral grin that he hoped the king could see through the darkness.

"You are a cunning man, and you are without conscience. I can see now how it might have been possible for you to organize the takeover of so much of the Ashaiian criminal element. You might have made a good king except that I do not believe *you* altogether sane." More softly he muttered, "Then again, maybe none of us are."

The king managed to cross in the dark to the side table and pour himself another drink without incident. Once he had returned to his chair, he asked, "What do you ask, this second boon?"

Rezkin tilted his head and said, "I think you know. Did your counselor not say?"

"She said that I desired to grant the island of Cael to Dark Tidings and that you wanted her to oppose the proposition. Since I have no intention of doing anything of the sort, I do not see the need for your threats."

"I want you to give it to him."

"But you told her to vote against it!" Ionius said with frustration.

"Which nearly guarantees that she will vote in its favor when you make the proposal."

The room was silent as the king stared at him in the moonlit shadows. "And the others? Did you get to them as well?" he asked.

"I believe I have secured a majority vote. It is up to you to ensure that it passes," Rezkin said.

"So you have covered everything *except* the fact that I will not be making such a proposal," Ionius firmly stated.

Rezkin filled his voice with condescension. "Do not let your obstinacy get in the way of your kingship, Ionius. This is best for us all. Cael is useless land, uninhabitable. Your ongoing rivalry over the isle, simply for the sake of spite, ensures that an ember burns between you and Gendishen—a spark to be stoked on a whim. You give Cael to the Ashaiian refugees, and your people love you —Ionius, the merciful, the generous patron. You may even reach a profitable trade agreement. Release your claim altogether, and you are exculpated from any wrongdoing. No one can accuse you of harboring rebel traitors in your lands. Allow Gendishen to take the blame."

"And what of Gendishen? How will you contend with Privoth?"

Rezkin scoffed. "Let Dark Tidings deal with Privoth. He is not our concern."

Ionius replied with incredulity. "What makes you think Dark Tidings even wants Cael?"

"What does it matter?" Rezkin asked. "Give land to a homeless man, and he will take it. If he is destined to be a great king, then he can figure a way to keep his people on the rock. He may consider it a test of fortitude if he likes. I care not."

"And if I chose not to grant this request?" Ionius asked.

Rezkin was tired of arguing over what was, by all accounts, a tiny, useless, uninhabitable chunk of rock in the Souelian Sea. Ionius had protested the gift of his daughter only because he thought she was dead, and now he had spent significantly more time inciting the Raven's ire over a worthless island.

He said, "I am sure Dark Tidings will find *other* ways to acquire what he needs. I *had* intended to leave this kingdom, but perhaps I should expand my empire. I see so much potential for Serret, and I think it might be nice to visit the other cities. I am quite successful in my business, you know." With exaggerated disgust, he added, "Perhaps I can even assist you with your cat problem. Your country is completely infested."

"You are a ruthless creature," the king muttered. "I could have you killed!"

"By whom? *Him*?" Rezkin said, motioning in the dark toward the Jeng'ri who had remained silent and still throughout their exchange. He might have been easily forgotten if not for the constant threat.

"There are others," Ionius snapped. "I have an entire kingdom of guards, soldiers, and mages."

"And I could put my sword through you right now," Rezkin said as he began backing toward the door to the outer chamber. "I am through here, Ionius. I am not your friend, but I need not be your foe. Make the proposal, see that it passes, and I shall have little reason to remain in your kingdom ... for now."

Rezkin ducked through the doorway as the king stood by his chair boisterously berating him for his insolence and audacity. The Jeng'ri did not immediately follow but held back a respectful distance. When Rezkin was nearly to the exit, his instincts alerted him to danger. He ducked and dodged to the side.

A throwing dagger struck the door with a thud. Rezkin launched one of his own daggers at the assassin. The man was quick and used his whip-like threads of *talent* to dash the dagger from the air. He stooped to collect Rezkin's dagger and then bowed as he slipped the item up his sleeve. Rezkin collected the dagger from the door and nodded to the Jeng'ri as he exited the king's chambers.

He strode down the corridor to the princess's rooms, and the Jeng'ri followed a moment later. When Rezkin reached the door, he waited. Now that they were in the lit corridor, he could see the Jeng'ri clearly. He was several inches shorter than Rezkin and had a slim build beneath armor that was not unlike his own. His slick black hair was drawn into a topknot, and his chiseled features were unusual with high cheekbones and dark eyes. Although he looked to be in his early thirties, he could probably appear much younger or older with little effort. Rezkin had only once seen a similar looking man, a mercenary from a far eastern land who had been captured and forced to train Rezkin in the use of several odd weapons.

"What do you want?" Rezkin asked, deepening his voice so it would not carry.

"I will assist you in securing the princess," the Jeng'ri answered. "Your retreat will be more difficult with an untrained woman in tow."

Rezkin's first thought was to reject the Jeng'ri's offer, but the man was right. He had no idea how the young lady would behave during their escape. If the women he knew were any indication, she would be difficult. In addition, the Riel'sheng possessed a particularly strange sense of honor. If Rezkin refused the Jeng'ri's assistance, the man and his order might believe that Rezkin did not have confidence in his abilities. That could have serious consequences for the man's station as Jeng'ri. Since Rezkin presumably held this man's fealty already, it would be to his benefit for this man to retain his position as the second of the Order.

Rezkin finally said, "Very well, but if you stab me in the back, I will make your death painful beyond even *your* ability to cope."

The Jeng'ri smiled and said, "That will mean little if you are dead."

Rezkin caught the man's gaze and said, "What makes you think I can die?"

The man's smile was replaced with a fervent fire in his gaze. Rezkin decided that the man's zeal could be used to his advantage. If his bluff ever came to the fore, then it would no longer matter to him anyway.

The assassin bowed low and said, "My name is Ikaxayim, but most call me

Xa Jeng'ri. I serve the Raven Riel'gesh."

"And the Order?"

Uncertainty and doubt flashed through Xa's eyes before he regained his resolve. "They will come to recognize your might."

Rezkin thought that was a bit dramatic, but he was not going to argue the point.

"If they do not?"

Xa did not attempt to hide his grief over the potential loss when he said, "Then the Ong'ri will kill me for my betrayal or he will accept that I believe I serve the Riel'gesh, and I will be excommunicated."

"You are prepared to make that sacrifice?" Rezkin asked.

Xa tilted his head. "It is already done."

It was a clever ploy if the Order wanted to plant a spy in his midst. Although he did not trust the Jeng'ri, the benefits of gaining the Order's allegiance outweighed the risk at this point. He did not think that Xa would interfere with his current mission, but he would likely be looking for any weaknesses he could exploit or other useful information he could take back to the Order.

Rezkin listened at the door to the princess's outer chamber and then opened it carefully. Xa followed at a respectful distance as he crossed through the sitting room. The bedchamber door was closed and bolted. In less than a breath, Rezkin had the door unlocked. He tried pushing it open, but something heavy blocked the path. He leaned his weight into it, prepared to compensate in case someone suddenly pulled the door from the other side. Once it was open enough for him to see the blockage, he realized it was the body of a guard surrounded by pieces of broken pottery. He ducked just in time to avoid a similar fate, catching the princess's arms mid-swing. Xa managed to intercept the heavy urn before it struck the ground and potentially alerted anyone nearby.

The two men shuffled into the room and locked the door behind them. Rezkin glanced around and noticed that the body of the nursemaid had been covered with bed linen. A small bag filled to nearly bursting at the seams sat on the bed. The princess had retreated to the other side of the room, beside the dressing table, where her hand lingered near the lamp. She wore clothes that would suit a stable boy, and her hair was drawn back and hidden beneath a floppy cap of the traditional Channerían style. Rezkin was impressed with the young woman's resourcefulness.

"I worried that you would not come back," she said. Her eyes found Xa who was peeking under the linen covering the nursemaid.

Xa looked up at Rezkin, and for some reason seemed surprised. "You killed the maid," he said.

Rezkin frowned. "She killed herself." He ignored Xa's doubtful look.

"Who is he?" Ilanet asked. "You did not say that you had a partner."

"I do not."

Xa stood and bowed to the princess. "I am Xa." He grinned playfully and added, "I am an assassin."

Ilanet's eyes widened, and she looked in alarm to the stranger who had not introduced himself. "He was sent to kill me?"

The stranger who had saved her shook his head as he rifled through the guard's pockets. "No, Princess. He was to kill *me*."

Ilanet glanced between the two men. She was utterly confused. "But, you are both here … together."

The one named Xa smiled again, a sweet, boyish smile. He nodded toward the stranger and said, "He won."

She swallowed her fear and said, "I do not understand. You are assassins. If you fought, then one or both of you should be dead. That is how it works. You kill people!"

She could not help that her words came out in a rush or that her voice had peaked at the end in hysteria. She had a dead person … or maybe two dead people, and two assassins in her bedchamber, and she was locked in with them.

Xa said, "*He* cannot be killed"—with a nod toward the stranger—"and the Riel'gesh has thus far granted me life."

"What is the Riel'gesh? Is that like your god or something?" she asked as the stranger moved about the room searching for who-knows-what.

Tilting his again toward the stranger again he said, "He is the Riel'gesh."

The stranger turned to Xa and said, "*Rule 3—reveal nothing.* Learn it."

Xa said, "Yes, Riel'gesh, but it seems unnecessary since I never leave anyone alive."

"Until you do …" the stranger muttered as he went back to searching.

Ilanet held her tongue. Apparently, the short assassin was crazy and thought that the tall one was an immortal patron god of assassins. The tall stranger did have the *look* of a dark warrior god. She frowned when he tossed the rest of the bed covers onto the floor.

"For what do you search?" she asked.

He paused where he knelt by the bed and looked at her with pale blue eyes that glittered like topaz. "The backup plan." His gaze turned to the guard on the floor, and he asked, "Who is he? Did he say anything to you?"

She said, "He is one of my guards. He was supposed to be watching my chambers tonight. He came to the door claiming he was worried when I did not show up for the ball. I thought he might be in on the plot to kill me, so I struck him with the vase when he entered the room. I do hope he is not dead."

The unnamed stranger shook his head and rose. "If the king and his mages had planned this properly, there would have been a contingency plan in place in case you did not succumb to the poison. It might have been the guard, but I think not. I believe they did not consider the possibility that you might not die on the first attempt. They planned for the ball to be thrown into chaos when you were found murdered, which means someone had to find your body. That may have been this guard's role or perhaps it was the nursemaid's. The guards and most of the staff were sent away until the alarm was sounded to prevent witnesses and interference. This means it will be easier for us to depart without being seen."

Ilanet began to shake where she stood. The stranger was talking about a plot to murder her as though it were a game of strategy. These people she had known her entire life, people with whom she ate dinner and walked the gardens and laughed about inconsequential things, and they had been plotting to kill her for how long?

She looked to the stranger and begged, "Please, may we go now? I wish to be gone from this place."

Rezkin nodded and retrieved the small black bundle that he had given to her for safekeeping. He checked its contents and then directed the princess to collect her own pack. They took a winding route through the castle, ducking into servants' passages and through empty rooms whenever anyone came near. Rezkin and Xa rendered two unlucky passersby unconscious and locked a maid in a pantry, but they made it as far as the kitchen without further incident.

He turned to Xa and asked, "Can you use your power to upend that cauldron into the fire without being detected?"

Xa looked at him curiously and then nodded. The kitchen was a large room, but it was filled with sacks, barrels, tables, and other cooking necessities. It was also filled with people who were constantly running in and out of the door to provide fresh fare for the guests. The massive open hearth that ran the length of one wall would produce much of the castle's heat in the winter months, but in this season, the room was sweltering. As a result, the servant's entrance on the far wall had been left open to the night air.

Rezkin looked at the princess, contemplating whether she could be successful with the plan he had in mind. She glared back at him with such stubborn confidence that she appeared to know what he was thinking.

He said, "Xa is going to overturn that cauldron as a distraction. The room will fill with steam, and everybody's attention will be on the fire. When that happens, I want you to walk quickly across the room and grab those two empty buckets. You are then going to walk out the door and casually make your way to the well. Fill the buckets and then take them to the stables.

"What about you?" she asked.

"We will meet you there," he said.

Ilanet did as the stranger bade. The kitchen erupted into chaos, and she passed through without anyone noting her presence. She grabbed the buckets and then darted out the door. She had to remind herself that she was supposed to be *casual*. It was difficult when she knew that guards were probably watching. She tried to take solace in the fact that they would not be able to recognize her dressed as she was in the dark. The alarm had not yet sounded, and she wondered why her father had not called for help, especially if he knew assassins were in the castle.

Once the buckets were filled with water, she trudged toward the stables. Water buckets were much heavier than she had realized, and by the time she made it to the stables, she felt a bit sorry for the maids. She placed the buckets on the ground and rubbed at her sore hands. Just as she reached for the latch on the stable door, she heard a thump to her right. She jumped and then glanced over to see the stranger motioning to her. She hurried into the dark and found him and Xa standing next to a rope that had somehow been tied to the top of the wall.

"Can you climb the rope?" the stranger asked.

Ilanet looked up at it doubtfully. She had never climbed a rope before. She wrapped her fingers around the thin line and tried to pull herself upward. She lacked the strength to even get her feet off the ground for more than a moment, and her hands were already chaffed.

Conceding defeat, she said, "I cannot."

Xa said, "We could climb and then pull her up."

The stranger said, "No, it will be faster if I carry her." To her, he said, "Give your pack to Xa. Climb on my back. Wrap your legs around my waist, and try not to choke me."

Ilanet's heart raced. This strange man, *assassin*, was going to carry her up the rope, a very thin rope, to the top of a very high wall. It did not sound like a good idea to her, but she was afraid that if she protested too much he would leave her behind. She did as he instructed and wrapped herself around him. It was awkward for more than one reason, not the least of which was the numerous weapons he carried. A couple of knives and ... an *axe?* ... dug into her thighs. The swords that crisscrossed his back and pressed into her chest were frightening reminders that she was running away with a killer. She supposed that seeking refuge with a killer who had saved you was better than living with killers who wanted you dead. It did not hurt that he was actually quite handsome ... and *strong*. She looked down and immediately regretted it. The ground was far below, hidden in darkness, and her arms and legs were aching. She gripped the stranger more tightly as she squeezed her eyes shut. A tap on her forearm reminded her that she should *not* choke the life out of the man carrying her up the castle wall.

When they finally reached the top, she collapsed from his back and groped at the ground, happy to feel a solid surface beneath her. Then she noticed the unconscious guard and remembered that they were not yet safe. She also realized that they would have to somehow make it down the other side of the wall.

Rezkin led the young lady through the dark streets, cognizant of the assassin that followed by rooftop. The city guard patrols and priests were making their rounds, and he had to be careful to avoid detection. A pebble bounced off the ground in front of him, and he glanced up to see Xa motioning toward the end of the lane. It was the signal that a patrol was heading their way. He pulled the princess into a dark alley and shielded her with his body since his darker clothing would make detection more difficult. When he was satisfied with their location, Rezkin motioned to Xa to descend.

"It is time for us to part ways, Xa."

"Riel'gesh, you must come with me to the Order. They will not be swayed by my confidence alone."

"I do not have time to placate the Order, nor do I care for their acceptance as I have little need of them at this time."

Xa's face screwed up in irritation. "But they will not serve without proof."

Rezkin knew that Xa's frustration was not just for the sake of the Order. If the Ong'ri did not accept the Raven as the Riel'gesh, then Xa would, at best, be exiled.

"Then I will not call upon them," Rezkin said.

Xa's face fell. "No, you must! The Order has trained for hundreds of years to serve the Riel'gesh, to serve *you*. If you do not call upon us, then we exist for nothing."

Rezkin met the assassin's pleading eyes with an icy stare. "That is not my problem. I do not heed the call of the Order." He figured that so long as someone was willing to believe it, he might as well play the part of the indomitable demigod.

Xa bowed and said, "I will report to the Ong'ri. How will I find you again?"

Rezkin did not want the assassins to find him, but if he was to gain their service, they would need a way to contact him. He could send messages to his people via mage relay, but without one of his own, it was difficult for them to send any in return. He needed a mage relay.

"I will be keeping an eye on Dark Tidings. If you cannot find me, then find him."

After Xa disappeared into the darkness, Rezkin took the princess by the arm and led her in the opposite direction.

"Where are we going?" she whispered. "We just came this way."

"I did not desire for the assassin to know where we are going," he said.

"So you are saying that we have *more* walking to do?"

"Sorry, Princess, but we are not yet to your cave."

The princess said nothing more until they reached the brothel. From the outside, they could see that the lamps were lit, and shouts and laughter echoed into the night. A few men came stumbling out of the front door, and it did not take Ilanet long to realize where they were.

"You brought me to a … brothel?" she asked incredulously.

"I am surprised you know what one is," Rezkin replied.

Ilanet crossed her arms. "I am perfectly aware of the existence of *deplorables*. My brothers have spoken of such places often enough. You cannot expect me to become one of these ... these ... you know ..." she said with a wave of her hand as her face flushed.

"Whores?" Rezkin prodded. "Princess, you ran away alone with a complete stranger who broke into your bedchamber, killed your maid, and then escaped the castle in the company of an admitted assassin after conducting clandestine *business* with your father, the king. Few would be surprised if a man in my position chose to auction you at the slave market to be some rich man's play thing. I imagine a princess would fetch a high price, especially one with no hope of rescue."

"Is that what you intend to do with me, then?" she asked.

Ilanet was all too aware of the predicament in which she now found herself. This man, though, had saved her, while those at the castle had tried to kill her. This seemed like the fairer deal. She doubted he intended to sell her at a slave market. While he was cold and calculating, she had the feeling that he actually held some concern for her well-being. After all, he did not *have* to interfere with the assassination.

The stranger did not answer but instead said, "Come. We go to the stables in the back."

Ilanet was momentarily relieved. Perhaps he was retrieving a horse and they could leave. Her hopes were dashed when she discovered none were in the stables, only a few cats oddly cuddled together in a mound in the hay. The stranger appeared surprised as he stared at the cats and seemed to hesitate in his approach. It was an odd look on the man who had been completely in control since the moment she met him.

Rezkin stared at the mound of cats. He had seen cats sleep curled together before but never so many. Particularly odd, though, was that they were sleeping directly atop the hay stack he had used to cover his pack. He shook his head, deciding that most likely the little tortoiseshell cat had chosen that spot because it had smelled his scent on the pack. This led him to ponder whether it was to his advantage or disadvantage that the cats positioned themselves so in his absence. Would their presence deter others from inspecting the area, or would it attract attention? He decided that he did not understand the outworlders' interactions with the animals well enough to make a determination.

He padded across the hay and shooed the cats away. The others scattered with hisses and yowls, but the little tortie just stretched languidly and then sat blinking up at him. He knelt and pushed her aside while he dug for his pack. The animal took the opportunity to climb onto his back and perform some strange kneading ritual.

"You have a strong bond with your cat," Ilanet said. "I would not have expected that."

Rezkin frowned at the small-woman. He was not certain if she was insulting him, but her face seemed earnest. "It is not my cat. I only just met it."

"Oh!" she said. "It is an omen."

"An omen?" he asked with skepticism.

She nodded vigorously and said, "Oh, yes. An instantaneous bond with a feral is considered to be a harbinger of change."

Rezkin began removing his armor and more obvious weapons so that he could change into the drab traveler's disguise.

"What kind of change?" he asked. He really did not care about omens, but this seemed to be a significant precept of Channerían culture.

"Well, it depends on how you met. For example, if it attacked you at first and then bonded with you, then you will soon find yourself in good fortune." Her eyes sought the ceiling as she tapped at her bottom lip. "Um, if it ran across your path and then followed you home, it means someone you know will fall ill or die. Oh, I hope that was not it."

"No, when I awoke, it was sleeping on my chest," Rezkin said as he finished adjusting his clothes and pulled the floppy hat over his head.

Ilanet smiled brightly and said, "Oh, that is so sweet. But, I am not sure … um … if it was at your feet, it would mean you are going on a journey; if it was at your side, it would mean you are going to lose something dear or valuable; and if it was at your head, it would mean you are going to endure a challenge." Rezkin could tell by the crinkle of her brow and the way she chewed at her lip that she was taking this very seriously. "I think … well, I think that sleeping on your chest would either mean that you will soon find love *or* you are about to die."

Rezkin grunted. "I am fairly certain that the first would quickly lead to the second, so your anxiety over the appropriate interpretation is unnecessary."

Ilanet huffed. "I should have expected an assassin to say such a thing. Have you never been in love?"

"No," Rezkin said.

In truth, he did not know what love was supposed to feel like. If the dramatic plays and prose of poets were to be trusted, then he had never experienced the sensation.

She furrowed her brow. "Have you ever loved *anyone*?"

"No."

"That is truly sad," said the small-woman.

She had the soft doe eyes of a young girl dreaming of her prince. He had seen those eyes often enough on Frisha and now understood what it meant. Perhaps Ilanet was not dreaming of *her* prince, though, since she had run away from him. Maybe *her* dream was of a knight in shining armor. Rezkin pondered if he knew of any such men within a reasonable distance. It would be well enough if he could be rid of her quickly.

She was looking at him expectantly, so he said, "Love is an emotion that will divest you of reason and cause you to make mistakes and become self-destructive."

"You are a heartless pessimist," she said.

"Have you ever loved anyone?" Rezkin asked.

"Of course. I love my family."

"The family who just tried to kill you?"

The princess paused and looked away. After a moment, she said, "Their treachery does not negate the value of my love. If I allow them to change me, to destroy that part of me that cares and feels for others, then they will have succeeded in killing me."

Rezkin strode toward the door where she stood. He turned to her and said, "Let us hope, then, that your future path permits you such luxuries. Come. We will go to the house and see if we can find you somewhat better accommodations than the stable."

Dainty fingers gripped his arm, and he turned back to the young woman and her pleading eyes.

She asked, "What about my father?"

Rezkin tilted his head as he attempted to surreptitiously pull his arm away. "What about him?"

"He will send the guard after us," she said, dropping her hand.

"That is doubtful," Rezkin replied.

Hesitantly, she asked, "Then he is dead? Is that what you had to do?"

"No, he was not dead when I left his chambers," Rezkin said.

"Then someone else? One of my brothers?"

Rezkin frowned. "No, I did not kill anyone this night—unless you count the nursemaid, but I rather feel that was her own doing."

Ilanet eyes were sad as she said, "Quite. I still cannot believe she is gone … or that I am here … with you. Who *are* you?"

He still had not decided how to introduce himself to the princess. The assassin had referred to him as the Riel'gesh but not the Raven. It was unlikely the princess knew of the Riel'gesh, so if she did not repeat the term to anyone who did, his identity could remain secret. Still, she had seen far more of that persona than anyone else he knew, so he would need to make his desire for anonymity clear.

"The women of this house call me Roy," he said.

Her eyes roved over him in suspicious observation. "You have disguised yourself. That is not your real name."

"No, but it is the one you may use for now. When we go in there, you will not speak of anything you have witnessed tonight. You will not tell them who you are. Are you capable of speaking like an uneducated commoner?" he asked.

"I do not know," she said uncertainly. "I have never truly spoken to any."

"Then we will tell them that you were a lady's maid who was unfairly let go for theft but that you are innocent. You have interacted with ladies' maids before?"

"Of course. They tend to titter about and pretend to be of higher station than they are. When you are young, they condescend to you only because they fail to realize that you will remember it when you grow older. When you become older, they pander and flatter you with unsolicited praise while their eyes speak of resentment."

Rezkin raised a brow. "That is quite observant of you, Princess, and not at all what I expected of the romantic optimist I had judged you to be."

Ilanet lifted her chin and said, "I do not consider myself to be an optimist. A romantic, yes, but also a realist." She narrowed her eyes. "You are not from Channería, are you?" He looked at her questioningly. "By your speech, I would not have guessed it—you bear no foreign accent, but you lack certain knowledge that is distinctive of Channerian culture. The significance of an

instantaneous bond with a feral cat, for example, and the omen it represents
…"

"Superstition," he interjected.

Without acknowledging the interruption, she said, "And my earlier comment about the value of love and staying true to myself were quite obviously references to the teachings of Collectiare Malalea, a woman who was one of the most influential collectiares in Temple history. You did not seem to make the connection."

"You are much more intuitive than the typical outworlder *child*," he said. He had to remind himself that outworlders were often confused when he called them small-women.

Ilanet protested. "I am not a child! I will be of age next year."

"Which means that you are not yet an adult, but that was not the point."

She crossed her arms and frowned at him. "My father and brothers underestimate me. Everyone does. To them I am nothing more than a possession to be auctioned to the highest bidder. I refuse to be so inconsequential! When I was eight, I decided that if I were to become some foreign monarch's queen, as my father intends, then I would be a representative of my people. I would insist on participating in the governance, whether my future husband desired it or not.

"I told my father that I needed to learn if I was going to sound interesting to potential suitors. He said I did not need to be interesting, only pretty. By the time I was ten, he got tired of my *incessant pestering*, as he put it, and relented. I was able to retain the tutor long enough to learn my letters and numbers at least, and since then, I have taught myself as much as I could from the castle library."

Rezkin stared at the young woman as the motives and methods for her unusual behavior became clear. The princess's apparent privilege was a façade. While she had been decorated with frills and jewels, she had been denied much that even many commoners were encouraged to pursue.

He said, "Perhaps, through your pursuit of knowledge, you have developed faster than your years suggest by outworlder standards, but you are not yet grown."

He glanced at the house that was still busy with patrons. Many would stay the night in the common room to avoid trouble with the guards for being out past curfew. He turned back to the princess.

"No, I am not Channerían. I am familiar with Collectiare Malalea, but I have read few of her teachings. Such concerns were not liable to arise in my circles. If I were to infiltrate a community in which the knowledge was pertinent, I would spend the required time learning them. My present mission has considerable time constraints, and had I not met you, Malalea's teachings would not have been an issue. None of this is important, though. Right now, we need to consider *your* cover. The women of the house will suspect we are hiding something."

"Why would they?" Ilanet asked.

"Everyone in this district is hiding something, especially people seeking refuge in seedy brothels. These women are used to seeing all types, and they will peg you as a noble at the least. They will either accept that you are a high-born lady's maid but believe that you are lying about your innocence in the theft, or they will think you a noble lady running away from her family, probably to escape an arranged marriage. They may not pry. As I said, everyone here has secrets. If they do question you, then adamantly deny the first but concede the second. They may kick you out if they think you might steal from them, but they will probably treat you with compassion for the latter."

"Why are we going with the story that I got caught for stealing in the first place, then? Why not just tell them I am running away from a marriage, which is partially true?"

"Because if they care to expose your secret, then having another prepared for them to discover will deter them from learning the truth," Rezkin said.

"That is absurd," Ilanet exclaimed. "Why make it so complicated? I have been told that if you want to lie about something, then keep it simple."

Rezkin shook his head. "The *story* is simple. Its execution is complicated. Once they discover the false secret, they will stop digging. They would never consider that you would contrive multiple layers of deceit."

Ilanet narrowed her eyes again and said, "How many layers of deceit do *you* possess?"

Rezkin tilted his head in thought. Almost nothing he did was deceitful in and of itself. Since he had no sense of self or station of his own, every role he played was who he was in that moment. His only deceit was in keeping knowledge of each independent role from the people who associated him with one of the others.

"Quite plainly, Princess, I am everything I claim to be. At this moment,"— he gestured to his clothes—"I am a harmless traveler, a simpleton, who you convinced to escort you to wherever it is I am going next."

"*You—harmless*? No one will believe that," she said.

"I can be very convincing," he replied.

He tugged her arm to guide her to the back of the house. The door was ajar to permit the cool night breeze, but Tiani and another woman were preparing a meal in the kitchen. Rezkin rapped on the doorframe to catch their attention without startling them.

He slouched and squinted at Tiani as he awkwardly shuffled his feet. "Um, ma'am, is Madam Grebella 'vailable?"

Tiani laughed and shook her mixing spoon at him as she said, "Oh, did ya hear that, Rella? Called her a right proper *madam*, he did. You come on in here, darlin', and get some of this here stew. Suras—he's the butcher—he came in fer a treat tonight. Brought us some chicken an' pork trimmings."

Rezkin shuffled his feet and looked anxiously behind him, earning the woman's full attention.

"What ya got? You got someone back there?" she asked as she tried to peer over his shoulder into the dark.

He ducked his head and said, "I, ah, got a woman. I mean, no, *I* don't got a woman. I mean she's a woman, and I got 'er. No, I mean she's 'ere with me, ya know. I mean she ain't *my* woman ..."

The two women cackled boisterously at his awkward explanation, and Tiani came forward. "Well, move outta the way, then. Let's see what ya done dragged in. By the Maker, ya take in one stray an' next thing ya know, ya got yerself a whole litter."

"Ah, her name's Arissa," Rezkin said as he turned to the side so that Ilanet could enter. As she slid by, she looked up at him with surprise in her eyes. He ducked his head and forced a flush to his face for Tiani's sake.

"Oh, look at this. She's just a girl," Tiani said as she took Ilanet's hand and led her into the kitchen.

Ilanet bristled but thankfully held her tongue.

Rella smiled and paused in her kneading of the dough. "She's a pretty thing. Could make a bag jus' ta break 'er in."

"No!" Rezkin blurted, shuffling his feet and wringing his hands frantically. He paused and ducked his head. "I mean, no ma'am. She ain't lookin' fer work. She's got family waitin' fer her. Gonna take 'er there when we leave 'ere. Jus' was wonderin' if'n maybe she could sleep in the 'ouse tonight. Ain't right fer her ta stay in the stables with me, ya know?"

Tiani snickered and leaned in to whisper loudly in the Ilanet's ear. "The boy's sweet on ya, I see. I'm Tiani and that's Rella. As far as ya stayin', we'll have ta see what Grebella's got ta say. Between you an' me, though, I think she's kinda sweet on the boy 'erself."

Ilanet was nearly overwhelmed by these people. Not only did they seem to speak a different language, but their inappropriate discussions, dress, and living conditions were appalling. She had heard stories, mostly told by her brothers, about these kinds of places. She was now discovering the truth of the adage that knowledge and experience were two very different things.

The woman named Tiani left her standing beside the counter where Rella was working to make ... something. Ilanet had never spent more than a fleeting moment in the castle kitchens. It was not considered proper for the princess to spend time with, well, anyone not approved by her father. The bouncing of Rella's almost completely exposed bosom was a distraction she preferred to avoid. She glanced back to the stranger by the door. Now that she had run away with him, she did not care to think of him as the *stranger*. She refused to think of him as *Roy*, though, since she knew it was not his name. His speech and mannerisms were such that she would never have believed he was the same man who stole her away from the king. It seemed that this act was accepted by the people as truth, and they did not appear to suspect that anything was amiss where he was concerned.

Roy glanced up at her, and then his gaze quickly darted away as though he feared to be caught looking. Rella chuckled beside her, having apparently witnessed the silent exchange. What fascinated Ilanet the most was that those same eyes that earlier had flashed with intensity and intelligence now appeared dim and without thought or sense. She would have thought herself mad if it were not for the disturbing reality that surrounded her.

A few moments later, a middle-aged woman wearing naught but a blood-red skirt and black corset entered the kitchen. Her hair was pulled up to expose her neck, and dark ringlets fell over her shoulders. The woman's face was painted to emphasize her large brown eyes and plump lips. Somehow this woman, by her mere existence, left Ilanet feeling both disgusted and deficient. The woman smiled like a cat in an open larder. Her eyes traveled up and down Ilanet's body as she sashayed through the room to stand next to the stranger. She reached up and stroked his face, which was hidden beneath a cloak of bashful innocence.

"Oh, Roy, what *have* you brought home?"

Rella chuckled again and said, "It's hardly 'is home. He ain't been 'ere but a day."

The woman, whom Ilanet assumed was Grebella, shrugged and turned to inspect her again. "Hmm, those clothes don't suit you, dear, and if ya try and tell me yer anythin' but some rich, runaway youngin', I ain't buyin' it."

Ilanet's gaze darted to the stranger, but he was playing the dimwit. He had all these grand plans, but suddenly *she* was on the spot. It made her want to slap him. Then she remembered the ice in his deadly gaze when he had captured her in the bedchamber, and any thoughts of reprisal slithered away.

She lifted her chin and said, "My name is Arissa. I am a lady's maid … *was* a lady's maid. I was let go when something went missing. They thought I stole it."

With a quirk of her brow, the woman said, "Did you?"

"No, of course not," Ilanet said earnestly.

Grebella smirked and then turned to study the stranger. Her eyes remained on him while she spoke to Ilanet. "You may be a decent liar, girl, but Roy here ain't. He's a sweet boy," she said as she patted his cheek, "and he's got guilt written all over him."

Ilanet frowned when she looked at the stranger. He *did* look guilty. He glanced up at her and flushed as he looked away. Why was he doing that? Why he was intentionally compromising the story?

The woman looked back at Ilanet through narrowed eyes and said to the stranger, "Roy, be a dear, and go fetch us some water."

Ilanet glanced around and saw no use for water at that moment, but the stranger ducked out of the door in a hurry. Grebella sauntered toward her, and Ilanet was frustrated that she had to look up at the woman. At the castle, no woman would dare stand over her in such a way.

"What is it? Yer runnin' away from someone? Don't like the rules at home and thought ya'd make it better out here? Yer better off goin' back to yer daddy's table if ya want handouts."

"No, I cannot," she pleaded.

The thought of going back to the castle and facing her father or even Prince Nyan terrified her. It must have shown in her eyes because Grebella's gaze softened.

"No, I see that ya can't. But I'll say this. That boy's smitten with you, an' we both know a girl like you ain't interested in a sweet, homely boy like him.

He's handsome enough, but he ain't never gonna give ya the kinda life yer daddy did."

With a shudder, Ilanet said, "He has already given me the life my father tried to take."

Grebella shook her head. "You see him as some kinda savior now, but you'll jus' be stringin' him along 'til ya find someone ya think is better. A boy like that don't deserve to get his heart broken, and he don't deserve whatever yer daddy'll be sendin' after ya. You get him hurt or killed, and I'll be sendin' my own people after ya."

Ilanet shook her head vigorously. "No, I do not believe my father is sending anyone after me. Besides, no one saw us together." *Except the assassin*, she thought but felt it better to exclude that bit. She had to trust that the stranger had, in fact, somehow come to an agreement with her father. Now, she wondered at the details of that agreement. "Just ... tell no one that I am here, and there will be no problems," she said, trying to sound nonchalant.

Grebella was about to respond when the stranger reappeared at the door with a pail of water. He placed it by the door and then stared at Ilanet longingly, so much so that she felt herself flush. He glanced toward Grebella for only a second and then dropped his gaze to the floor. The depth of communication in that silence had even Ilanet feeling a strange need to comfort him.

Grebella's stern exterior fell away, and she said softly, "Oh, Roy, you said ya wouldn't be bringin' me no trouble."

He stuffed his hands in his pockets and glanced up with squinty eyes, "Ain't no trouble, ma'am. Just a girl."

The woman tisked. "That's the worst kinda trouble fer a boy like you." With a heavy sigh, she said, "Alright, Roy. Jus' fer you, though. I know you'll be leavin' soon, and you'll be takin' her with ya."

The stranger glanced at Grebella and said, "Yes, ma'am, if'n she wants. I got some money I can give ya ta keep her fer now."

Grebella smiled. It was a genuine smile that Ilanet thought made the woman appear ten years younger. "You keep yer money. I think ye'll be needin' it. We got a spare room ain't bein' used right now. I'll see it's cleaned."

The madam left, and a moment later Tiani reappeared looking quite ruffled. Ilanet blushed at the implication.

"What was that all about?" she asked. "Took long enough."

Rella stopped in her work and said, "I'm tellin' ya, I ain't never seen that woman so protective of nobody. She about stuffed that one"—she motioned with a flour-dusted hand at *Roy*—"into her nest and aint' never gonna let him out!"

Tiani's eyes roved over the stranger, and she said lasciviously, "If I had him in *my* nest, I wouldn't let him out neither." The women burst into hearty laughter as the stranger flushed and ducked out the door. Tiani called after him, "Come on, Roy, I's jus' playin' with ya!"

Ilanet's eyes widened in surprise. She had never heard *women* make such lewd remarks. They both smiled and looked at her teasingly as they went about their business in the kitchen. Ilanet tentatively waved after the stranger and asked, "Have you … um …"

Tiani giggled and said, "I think maybe yer likin' him a bit, ain't ya?"

Ilanet lifted her chin and denied it, as was proper. "No. He and I, we are not involved in that way."

"Mmhmm," Tiani hummed. "Sweetheart, ya ain't gotta worry 'bout that. When he came here, he made it clear he ain't wantin' of our wares, if ya know what I mean," she said with a wink.

Rella added, "Ya ask me, it ain't healthy fer a young man like that to be keepin' it to himself."

Tiani said, "Could be he has a wife. Ya know some men don't stray like the others."

"Nah," said Rella. "I seen the way he was lookin' at Sweetie here. He wouldn't be turnin' none of that down if she was offerin'."

Tiani nodded. "I ain't gonna argue with that."

Ilanet was at a loss for words. This whole conversation was beyond anything in her experience. Worse yet, she knew that everything she had witnessed of the stranger had been an act, so these women were leading her thoughts astray for naught. She was saved from further humiliation when Grebella returned, beckoning her toward the stairs.

The madam led Ilanet to an unoccupied bedroom while she tried to close her ears to the sounds emanating from the others. The room was small and most of it was occupied by the bed. She tried harder not to think of the things that happened in that bed.

Grebella smiled knowingly and said, "Ya ain't been with a man yet, have ya?"

Ilanet looked away and said, "No, I am only sixteen and not yet wed."

The woman laughed. "I knew ya was highborn. Commoners be marryin' at fifteen, sixteen. Girls' folks are wantin' them gone—less mouths to feed."

"But what if you are not ready?" Ilanet asked, unable to hide her fear.

Grebella shrugged. "What's there to be ready fer? Ya cook, ya clean, ya make babies. Unless ya got some special skill or the *talent,* don't nobody care if ya can do nothin' else."

Ilanet was appalled, but in truth, it did not sound that different from what her father expected of her ... except for the cooking and cleaning.

"Ya don't got the *talent,* do ya?" Grebella asked hopefully.

"No, not yet, at least," Ilanet admitted with longing.

"I s'pose at yer age you've still got time to hope. We all did. Ain't no other way to get outta this life anyhow. Still, we've got somthin' the married women ain't got. We got our independence. Ain't no men 'round to tell us what we should do or when to do it. Ain't nobody tellin' us what to spend our money on or how to dress. Course we gotta keep with the business." She said the last with a wink and a tug at her corset.

"But you have to ... you know ... with strange men," Ilanet said with trepidation.

"I'd be givin' it to a man anyhow, be it a husband or a caller. Besides, what if the one yer stuck with ain't no good?" she asked.

"I do not understand," Ilanet said hesitantly. "It is just ... what it is. You ... um ... do it, and then you are done."

Grebella laughed. "Oh, my sweet, no. Don't ya be fooled by those men with the money and power. If yer man ain't pleasin' ya, ain't no reason to keep with him—unless yer like me and he's payin' ya, I s'pose. No, *you* want a sweet one like Roy." The woman's gaze turned sad and distant. Her next words were barely above a whisper. "A boy like that wants nothin' more than to keep his girl happy."

Ilanet was sure that Grebella knew what she was talking about, since she seemed to be an expert on the subject. The problem was that Grebella did not know who *Roy* really was. For that matter, neither did Ilanet. She *did* know that he was anything but a *sweet boy.*

The woman misinterpreted Ilanet's doubtful look. "Now, I ain't sayin' ya should be like us. Ain't nobody want this kinda life. I was jus' lookin' fer an upside." She laughed again. "That's one thing 'bout bein' at the bottom. There's always upsides all around ya."

Ilanet smiled. The woman was crude and vulgar, but she liked her anyway. She placed the single bag she had been permitted on the small dressing table opposite the foot of the bed. She eyed the bed with concern, and Grebella took notice.

"Don't you worry, Sweetie. The straw's been replaced, and the linens are clean. Ya ain't gonna catch nothin' here. We ain't got much, but we try to keep nice the things we do. Don't have none of those fancy indoor privies, so you'll have to use the chamber pot. And, ya know Roy was nice enough to bring ya in a pail of water fer your pitcher." Grebella finished with a wink.

The woman stepped closer, her expression earnest. "Now, I got one last thing to say 'bout that boy, and then I'm done with it." She reached out and stroked a caramel lock that had fallen from beneath Ilanet's hat. "Yer a pretty girl from a wealthy family. Truth is, yer far above his station, and he knows it. Shy boys like him, they don't tell ya when they love ya, 'specially if they think yer too good fer 'em. Take my advice. If you want that boy, you tell him and don't let him make excuses. Sometimes a woman's got to do the pursuin'."

Grebella bid her goodnight and then left, closing the door behind her. Ilanet hurried to place the bar, and then she closed her eyes and leaned her forehead against the sturdy wood.

"Are you well?" a deep voice sounded from behind her.

She jumped and nearly screamed but managed to restrain herself before she lashed out at the stranger. He was in the room with her, and she was certain he had not been there when she had arrived. She realized he must have come in through the open window, a reminder that he was not the simpleton he pretended to be.

"Yes, but you nearly frightened me unto death," she said as she held a hand over her racing heart.

The stranger stood at the other side of the small room with the bed between them, and still it felt too close.

He bowed, and said, "I apologize for any distress I have caused you. I only meant to see to your well-being and inform you of my plans for the morrow."

Now she was even more confused. He was still dressed as the dimwitted traveler, but he was not acting like the ruthless assassin she had met earlier. His mannerisms and speech were gracious and possessed a familiarity of courtliness that put her at ease but was incongruent with the present setting.

"I am a bit overwhelmed, but I will manage. It is better than the alternative," she said.

He stared at her as she tried to hold her emotions together. Throughout the night, she had been reacting to the threat of death, struggling to survive and making quick judgments and decisions. Now that she had a place to sleep and was no longer in immediate danger, her body and mind both felt as if they would collapse.

The stranger's voice was calm, as though he were attempting to soothe a frightened animal. "I will be gone when you wake." Her heart abruptly battered her chest. He was going to leave her there, in a *brothel*. He must have seen the panic on her face, for he added, "Do not fret. I will return for you. The women of the house sleep late, and so should you. It would be best for you to remain in this room as much as possible, and avoid encountering any of the callers. You should dress as you are so as not to draw attention."

Ilanet shook her head vigorously but found no words.

"You are afraid," he observed.

Again, she shook her head, but she was afraid that if she tried to speak, the tears would begin to flow. She did not want this stranger to see her tears. If he saw her weakness, she would be more vulnerable.

"Is it this place or my presence?" he asked.

She swallowed and answered, "I have never been alone with a man before tonight. Even on the rare occasion when I met with my father or brothers, Mables was with me. Having you *here*"—she eyed the bed and wrapped her arms around herself—"in this place ..."

The man nodded and said, "I understand. I intend you no harm, and I will destroy any who dare." He backed slowly toward the window, and she could not help the step she took to stop him. He tilted his head and looked at her curiously. "You do not wish for me to leave?"

"I-I am afraid with you here, and I am afraid to be alone," she said, and to her dismay, her voice wavered at the end.

The stranger graced her with a beatific smile, and it felt as though a calming wave emanated from his very being. "You are not alone. I will be right out there"—he motioned with a thumb over his shoulder—"until dawn. You have but to call for me if you must."

"But, what do I call you?" she asked.

"I told you. You may call me Roy." He winked at her and then jumped out of the second-floor window.

She found herself smiling as she lay down to sleep.

6

B ilior stepped up to the sacred stone that lay just within the mouth of the cave. The stone had not always been there. The ancients could only postpone human expansion for so long before they were forced to move. Most of the Ahn'an had accepted that this was the age of the humans. The human civilizations would live and grow and then fade into memory just like every other Ahn'tep race. So it had been with the eihelvenan and the darwaven and the argonts, and so it would be with the humans. The human civilizations had grown vast, though, their numbers greater than all the Ahn'tep who preceded them. Some of the Ahn'an had begun to fear.

He sent his roots into the rubbly earth of the cave floor and sought the focus of power. To him, this place was not as good as the last where the ground had been soft and welcoming. Here, his connection did not run as deep, and he could not feel the earth's soothing cadence wrap around him so completely. Suitable convergences beyond human reach were becoming more difficult to find, though.

He shed a pile of dried leaves and twigs onto the stone and waited. A breeze swept into the cave, and as it passed, he felt Hvelia's welcoming caress. The dust in her draught permitted him to see her form, and he smiled. Always, he was happy to see her, to feel her, for she was the loveliest of her kind. Upon her current rode the vapor of Uspiul, who dotted the floor with his moistening presence. A trickle of water from the fall at the cave mouth began to flow inward past the sacred stone. It swirled into a pool over the wet spots on the ground until it grew into a form that only vaguely represented one of the walking races.

Hvelia's breeze rustled the twigs and leaves he had left on the stone, shuffling them together in quickening vibration until eventually a thin braid of smoke emerged. A small inferno ignited upon the stone in an instant and then was abruptly drawn into the forms of Liti and Itli. The tiny figures of flame, no larger than sparrows, danced across the stone, twirling as their arms and legs flickered about gracefully.

Ripples chased each other over Uspial's surface as the ground shook and lurched while a pillar grew from the cave floor. The grinding stone shifted and twisted until clumps formed extremities. The clumps elongated into lustrous crystal appendages, while the head remained a bulbous mass. Two large vesicles lined with blue and white crystals composed the eyes. Goragana grinned as glimmering white and grey sickles filled the cavity of his mouth.

Many other Ahn'an swept into the depths of the cave. Far above, a large portion of the ceiling was missing, leaving the chamber open to the sparkling stars that dotted the midnight sky. Towering trees grew right up to the edge of the opening, and vines and branches reached into the cave toward the ground. A few of the hardier plants had already managed to take root in the center, where the sun occasionally shone. Some of Bilior's own were among those trees, peering down upon the gathering. He could hear their chattering and whispers, but none would approach the sacred stone. This was reserved for the ancients. Bilior's twigs trembled with excitement.

The rush of wind, the spray of water, tremors of stone, flickers of flame, and rustles of branches and leaves filled the cavern as the colloquy commenced. The ancient Ahn'an had passed from one epoch to the next, gradually learning each other's languages. In fact, the Hadá, who were possessed of the power of wind and air, and the Setee, who lived amongst the flames, had developed their language together and communicated most efficiently when speaking in concert.

"*What news, what portent do you bring, Bilior? Will they come?*" rumbled Goragana's tremors.

The breeze and the crackling of the flames together said, "*Let him speak. His chittering brings good tidings.*"

Bilior bobbed up and down, his limbs creaking with anticipation. "*The powers of the Ahn'tep be not as strong as once they were, but they be many.*"

A flurry of commotion ensued with excitement from all. A gust and flicker said, *"Gale of power lack. Spring renewal in question. Their numbers consume."*

Bilior hissed and creaked. He knew it was Hvelia's optimism that balanced Liti and Itli's doubts. *"Conferred with the one, a deal is made. He has agreed."*

Uspial trickled and spurt. *"Your message is bright. Best not be in jest, Bilior. You are ever vexing on our rivulets."*

His twigs snapped. *"Nay! An army he brings, when Daem'Ahn blood sings. In turn for a fee, the defense of the we."*

Goragana rumbled. *"Build first the mountain, he must, a great orogeny. Only then may the enemy fall under tromp of bounding boulders bearing sharpened ore."*

Bilior agreed it would be difficult to build such an army, but he had hope, no, *confidence*, that the young king could prevail. *"Even now, his forest he gathers. His trees be the strongest, his creatures the most vicious. The darkness of the west may be defeated only by one darker still."*

Hvelia dominated the wind and fire when she whooshed. *"Bilior, such tempest comes with cost. What, my breath, have you promised?"*

He stood tall and held his limbs out proudly. *"The price for the we is none. Gave words of knowledge in the human tongue. His price, a haven, safety for his human foundlings."*

"Convergence?" Liti and Itli crackled, the message barely formed in flame.

Bilior conceded. *"Of the greatest, but not of our possession. A peak, a cyclone, a tide of the Ahn'tep. 'Twas belonging to his kind, yet but a corpse, an unfilled vessel. Caellurum!"* he sang.

Their response was not what he had anticipated. Angry groans, fervent flames, harsh wind lashed through his limbs as he was soaked in a salty spray.

"The unfilled vessel be not as vacant as you claim!" Hvelia, Liti, and Itli moaned.

"Promise of safety beyond Nihko's gate," Goragana grumbled.

Bilior angrily chattered back at them in a flurry of trembling cracks and gales. *"Not a threat unto him. Of the great Blessed he be, to even threaten the we. To breach the walls and take the halls, alert he sounds and calls them down! His army, to him they come."*

Goragana was not convinced. *"You gamble with grains for cobbles and draw down boulders. Your pillar may live, but his conglomerates will tumble under the fault. Then where will we be?"*

"*Bilior spoke on behalf of the Ahn'an,*" the wind and flames hissed. "*Through us his promise must be paid. Safety, you say? You cannot guarantee! And in Caellurum is likely not to be!*"

Uspial burbled. "*Your river is tied to ours, a tributary to the whole. You speak in human ripples, an agreement for all. If harm befalls the human minions, the ancients must serve this Ahn'tep master.*"

The nature of the other ancients' distress was not a surprise to Bilior. He had made a bargain on behalf of all the Ahn'an. He had promised the young king safety, a haven for his chosen people. If he and his people failed to reach Caellurum safely, or if the young king did not overcome the perils of the ancient fortress, the Ahn'an would be in his debt. The ancients, themselves, and all Ahn'an would be forced to serve the young Ahn'tep king. Bilior did not believe that would happen. He had stood in the Ahn'tep's presence, had tested him. He had confidence in the young one's strength. The others could not see it through their fear. They could not see it because they did not yet know him.

A cacophony of wails and groans suffused Bilior's being. The others were upset and drawn into a panic. The conversation had surpassed him, and he shuddered in the sudden silence that followed. Hvelia blew forward, and Itli and Liti were swept into her currents. Her shape was filled with swirling flame, and if the circumstances had not been so severe, Bilior would have enjoyed the watching.

"*Bilior,*" they said in the chorus of their combined speech. "*You have made a deal that affects us all. To this Ahn'tep king you must go. Ensure our promise is paid! We cannot serve in his wake should you fail. No single being may wield such power, and you know his kind are prone to madness.*"

Bilior was angered by their pessimism and contempt, and Hvelia, especially, he felt had betrayed him. He knew he was the youngest of the ancients, but still ancient was he.

"*Your regard for me—a green sapling! I know the cost. Believe you I did not think this through? Without* him *to lead the army, not the forest or human city, but ALL will be in peril, Ahn'an and Ahn'tep alike! When last the Daem'Ahns spawned, saved were we by the grace of the eihelvanan and by Knights of Nihko, Rheina, Mikayal! But none be nigh! Through* him *we beg our existence.*

"*The king was suspicious. Not wanting of a deal, not even answers to whet his appetite. Only one promise desired he, in return for protection of the we.*

Chosen was I to carry the message. I alone who understand. My connection with life, upon this you depend. Trust in my judgment. 'Twas my promise to spend."

The slightest breeze rustled his leaves. He felt the burn of Hvelia's caress as Liti and Itli lapped at him. "*My breath, you are right. In you we placed our faith, in your branches we entrusted our fate. But 'tis the greatest price you ask, and only for the making of the deal. Still no guarantee that he is capable, that he may build his army, or that it will suffice. Our decision stands. You must go to him for no more reason than to secure our promise.*"

"That's Serret? The king's seat of Channería? It doesn't look like much from here," Tam said. From what he could see, it was dull and smelled of fish. He wanted to wind through the labyrinth of walls and explore the grand temples that a few of the passengers had described.

"You are seeing a lower district, a working one," Kai said. "It is not the worst, not even close, but it is nothing to look at either. Most of the city is hidden behind the walls. You cannot see the castle from here. Brilliant design, really. The keep has never been breached."

"But we won't see any of it," Frisha remarked. "We have to stay on the ship."

"It is not safe for you to go about right now, Lady Frisha," Kai said. "But surely you will be happy to see your betrothed."

Frisha glanced at the striker sideways, and Tam was disheartened to see her distaste. "He is not my betrothed," she said.

Kai looked at her questioningly. "Your unease has not escaped my notice. You have taken issue with Lord Rezkin?"

Frisha held a hand over her eyes to block out the brightening midmorning sunlight as her gaze took in the sprawling port. "Maybe. I don't know. After what Wesson told me about the spell on Rezkin, I'm not sure how to feel. Part of me wants to keep wanting him. Another part wants to beat him to a pulp for manipulating me."

Tam scowled at her. "Frisha, you are being completely unfair. You don't know that Rezkin did anything to you."

Without turning, she said, "I'm so embarrassed. How I was falling all over myself for him, even getting into fights with Reaylin. And, maybe she was being influenced the same way. You know it's not like me, Tam. The other girls in Cheswick were throwing themselves at men, but I never fell for them."

Torn by his divided loyalties, Tam tried to stay true to his longtime friend. He thought she was being overly dramatic, and even that was not like her. Frisha was intelligent and sensible, *except* when it came to Rezkin. He said, "I think it *is* like you, Frisha. It's exactly like you. You have been saving up all your attention for the one man who could steal your heart away in an instant. How many times did you tell me how romantic it was to fall in love at first sight? It was what you wanted all along."

Frisha flushed and glanced between him and the striker. "I don't know that it is love, Tam. I feel like I don't know him at all."

"You're angry, Frisha. Anger means you care," Tam said.

"But *how* do I care? Am I just hurt by the deception? Am I repulsed, no longer wanting him?"

Tam looked at her doubtfully. She was overthinking things, and now she had his own mind muddled.

"Sometimes I wish I could just start over," she said.

"Perhaps the testing is in the second first sight," Kai mused. Tam and Frisha both looked at him questioningly. "You said you fell for him at first sight. You knew nothing about him, nothing of the kind of man he was. Now, you know something more, and you are uncertain. You question your judgment. You are approaching the subject with more sense. When first you see him again, you will know. What do you feel first, and what do you feel most? Love, anger, or rejection?"

Frisha blinked up at the older man. "That—that's quite good."

Tam grinned. "You're a romantic. I didn't expect that from the hardened striker."

"Bah!" Kai grumbled. "I have been around far longer than you two. I know something about women, but what it is I could not say." He laughed at his own jest and then said, "Tell no one, though. I have a reputation to uphold. This stays between you, me, and my wife."

"You're married?" said Frisha.

Tam recalled that Kai had said as much when Rezkin had interrogated him not long after they met. It was a fact he had forgotten. He wondered what had happened to the man's family since he had never heard Kai speak of them again.

"Well, that is a sad story that should not be told on a day like this," he said, motioning to the clear blue sky.

Seabirds circled the ship and dipped into the placid waters. A soft breeze ruffled Tam's long hair, and he was reminded once again that he needed to get it cut. He had never liked wearing it long like so many of the other young men he knew who preened and pretended to be more important than they were. At first, he had used a piece of twine to tie it back, but the rough material kept tangling in his hair. Now he was wearing one of the ridiculous ribbons Rezkin kept in his stash. He did not think his friend would mind, and it was only temporary until he could find someone to cut the frustrating locks. Frisha had told him it almost made him look dashing. The compliment was soured by the fact that she had added the *almost*, but then again, sincere words of that sort from Frisha would be uncomfortable.

Lord Tieran approached the deck rail on the other side of Striker Kai. "Do you think he is already here and ready to board? How long might we wait?"

Kai chuckled. "Are you so eager to be divested of your responsibilities, Lord Tieran?"

"Of course," Tieran said. "Why should I wish to work so hard at something that someone else can do?"

"I believe it was that attitude that landed you on this ship in the first place," Kai said.

"What do you mean?" Tieran asked.

Kai said, "Was it not a fateful run-in with Rezkin that prompted him to manipulate your travel arrangements so that he could teach you a lesson?"

"Must we revisit that?" Tieran snapped. "Consider it a lesson learned and let us move on."

Kai grinned patronizingly. "What lesson was it that you learned, Lord Tieran?"

Tieran lifted his chin and sniffed. "I am more cognizant of the social responsibilities for a man of my station."

"Is that so?" Kai said, his voice heavy with skepticism.

"What say you, Striker? You think I have not changed? I believe I am more … respectful … of my peers. Before, I did not even see them as peers since they are all beneath me. With Rezkin's encouragement, I have even accepted Lady Frisha into my cadre of personal friends."

"A cadre is it? You have so many," Kai remarked, and Tam was forced to swallow his laughter. It was not so funny when the striker turned his focus on *him*. "And what of Rezkin and Frisha's friend, Tamarin, here?"

Lord Tieran's passing glance slid away so quickly Tam was not sure he had endured it at all.

"What of him?" Tieran said.

Kai gripped Tam's shoulder and said, "He is a close friend of *your* close friends, your cousin even. Would you not consider making a friend of him as well? Have you even spoken to him?"

Tieran did not look Tam's way as he answered. "I am sure we have had an exchange of some sort in the weeks since we have joined parties."

Tam was unsure. He could not remember having a direct conversation with Lord Tieran, only when they were invested in group discussions to which Tam had been invited. He generally did not feel comfortable joining in unless Rezkin was involved, or sometimes Frisha. He otherwise tried to keep to himself when he was left alone with the nobles outside of training.

Kai grumbled, "You have not changed as much as you think, Lord Tieran. You would shirk your duties at the first opportunity, and the commoners are still too far beneath your notice for even the simplest conversation. You cannot even look at him."

The motion appeared forced as the noble turned his gaze. Tam did not care for the consideration, and he felt himself withering under the scrutiny. Lord Tieran frowned, and Tam ducked his head, averting his eyes.

"What is wrong with you?" Tieran asked.

"I'm sorry, my lord, I don't know what you mean," Tam muttered nervously as he stared at the salty deck planks.

"You look like a beaten dog. Why do you cower so?" Lord Tieran asked.

"Ah, because you are Lord Tieran Nirius," Tam said.

He glanced up to see Lord Tieran in silent communication with the striker. Kai nodded toward him, and Tam dropped his eyes quickly.

"Master Tamarin ... *Tam* ... look at me," ordered Lord Tieran.

Tam's eyes shot up, and he held the lord's gaze. He did not want to, but he dared not look away. No matter the point that Kai was trying to make, and despite Rezkin's idealistic speeches, he was still a commoner, and Tieran was still a high lord.

"I have seen you openly berate Lord Rezkin,"—he glanced around and lowered his voice—"your *king*. You converse with Striker Kai and Lord Malcius, practice with Lord Brandt and Lord Waylen, train with the army officers, and you seem to have no issue with spending time in the company of Journeyman Battle Mage Wesson; yet, you cannot look at *me*."

Tam chewed on his lower lip. Was that a question? What was he supposed to say? He chose to say nothing.

Lord Tieran huffed and said, "You are the apprentice to the greatest swordmaster any of us has ever seen. Your skills grow each day, and I am fairly certain you could best me in a fight, assuming you employ those underhanded tactics my cousin has been teaching you."

Tam said nothing again. Lord Tieran seemed to be talking *at* him more than *with* him, and he could not find words to bridge the gap. He did note that the lord appeared to enjoy referring to Rezkin as his cousin.

"Well?" Lord Tieran asked. "Could you?"

Tam's mouth wagged, and he eloquently replied, "Ah …"

Lord Tieran raised a brow impatiently.

Tam finally managed to say, "I suppose anything is possible, my lord."

He took a moment to direct an angry scowl at the striker. Why had Kai put him in this position? What had he ever done to the man to deserve this? Kai had never liked him, but he had thought the two of them had gotten past their differences. When he looked back, Lord Tieran's face bore a look of amazement. Tam wondered what he had done and worried over the potential consequences.

To his surprise, Lord Tieran chuckled. "You would challenge the striker but not *me*? I know you are no coward. We have been in close quarters for long, and I have seen your confidence. I have not treated you unfairly. Why do you cower before me? Tell me now."

Tam wrung his hands, an anxious habit he had picked up somewhere in their travels that he was trying to break. "Well, my lord, ah, if I managed to score on the striker, he would probably congratulate me for the accomplishment," he said with a glance at Kai, who nodded with a grin. "Then he would lay me out flat to remind me that I got lucky." Kai's bellow of laughter caught the attention of a few deckhands who quickly returned to their work. "But, ah, you know, if a commoner were to seriously injure a lord outside of the tournament, especially a high lord, even in fair and just combat, well, he would be flogged and likely hanged. It's not so appealing when the reward for winning is death."

Lord Tieran's expression was impassive, and he seemed to be waiting for more. Tam swallowed his anxiety and added, "You have never invited me into your company or indicated that I was welcome. If I were to speak out of turn or offend you in some way, you could equally have me flogged. I wouldn't care to endure such punishment; nor would I desire my friends to witness it."

"You do not fear punishment from Malcius or Brandt?" Lord Tieran asked.

Tam had been training with Malcius and Brandt for weeks now, and he felt a small sense of comradery with them, so he answered honestly. "I think that it would take some great offense to incur that kind of wrath from either of them."

Tieran scoffed. "So you are saying that I have thin skin?"

Tam's eyes widened, and he worried that he had overstepped.

Frisha gasped, a feigned expression, Tam knew. He likewise knew that Frisha was fully aware of the potential consequences for upsetting the nobles since they had engaged in more than a few discussions on the subject. "Tieran wouldn't have you flogged or hanged! You wouldn't, would you, Tieran?"

Tam was amazed by Frisha's transition into the nobles' circle. Where weeks before she had been begging for the slightest acceptance, she was now looking down on the high lord in judgment, and Lord Tieran appeared chastised. Tieran glanced from Frisha to Kai. Tam saw that he was no longer the center of attention and relaxed his shoulders. After another extended, silent exchange between the striker and Lord Tieran, during which Kai appeared to be saying *I told you so*, the lord's eyes fell on Tam again.

Lord Tieran inhaled deeply, and his nostrils flared before he spoke. "Tam," he said with a certain finality. "You will be my friend. You will no longer cower in my presence, and you will speak your mind." The lord glanced at Frisha and then added, "I will not have you flogged or hanged." After another deep breath, he said, "You should treat me with the same informal familiarity as you do my cousin."

Tam was shocked. This was not the result he expected. He had imagined himself scrubbing the decks while his tattered shirt rubbed at the welts on his back. It was considerate of Lord Tieran to add that part about not flogging or hanging him.

"Y-yes, my lord," he murmured.

Lord Tieran frowned at him. "Is that how you would address Rezkin?"

"Ah, no, my lord."

"Then do not do so with me," Lord Tieran turned to the striker and said, "See? I have changed."

Kai rolled his eyes and said, "Yes, Lord Tieran. Now that you have *ordered* a young man to be your token commoner friend, I can see my error."

Tieran lifted his chin, seemingly pleased with himself, and then strutted away.

Tam turned on Kai and blurted, "Why do you hate me?"

Rezkin watched *Stargazer* from atop a dockside warehouse. The ship flew three standards in addition to the traditional merchant vessel flag. The first was silver to indicate that the ship's passengers and crew were under the care of certified healers. The second was green, indicating that, while the ailment affecting the passengers and crew was communicable, it was not fatal. The third was yellow, which informed authorities that the ship was under voluntary quarantine. Rezkin appreciated the efficiency with which so many concepts could be communicated by a few pieces of fabric.

The ship's deck was cleared of people except for the few crew members who had to carry out their duties. The captain stood at the end of the gangplank speaking with the dock master and his assistant, and a healer employed by the ITA, as indicated by the man's white and red cap, was waiting to inspect any who disembarked. Rezkin could not hear the exchange from his vantage, but he could see Captain Estadd discussing the papers that he handed to the dock master. The dock master's assistant flipped through the logbook into which Rezkin had added *Stargazer*'s arrival for the next week. Serret was a busy port that received up to a dozen ships throughout the day. Some of them remained for a day or two, while others departed shortly after unloading and resupplying. After a long discussion, the dock master and his assistant finally moved on to the next ship while the healer remained behind.

Estadd returned to the ship, and a few minutes later Dark Tidings and Striker Roark came tromping down the gangplank. The healer took a step back when he saw the now infamous warrior. After a quick exchange, the healer hesitantly performed several motions over the two men, and then he handed Roark a paper onto which he had scrawled what was presumably permission to disembark. The healer quickly made his way back along the pier and disappeared into the ITA office. On the way, he nearly tripped over a few small-men who had been hired to scrub off the symbol of the Fishers that had been added to the façade at some point since Rezkin had last visited.

As Roark and Dark Tidings trod down the peer, travelers, dock workers, and sailors gawked, and the small-men who had been scrubbing at the ITA office ran over to get a better look. Rezkin crossed to the rear of the building and leapt from the roof, bounding off crates and equipment on the way down. He skulked to the end of the alley and waited. They had only a few minutes before the guards would arrive. Roark and Dark Tidings rounded the corner and then wove through the multitude of stacked crates, sacks, and barrels that lined the street behind the warehouses. Once they had lost the prying eyes of the crowd, Dark Tidings slipped into the alley.

Shezar began to undress while Striker Roark kept watch. The three said nothing as Rezkin and Shezar quickly exchanged clothes. Rezkin moved his Sheyalins to hang at his hips and strapped the black blade to his back where most of the scabbard was concealed by his cloak. He clipped the multitude of braids into his own braided hair and donned the mask just as he heard the tromp of boots speeding up the lane. Roark gave him the signal, and Rezkin stepped out of the alley to stand beside him in wait. When the guards arrived, he nodded courteously.

"It's him!" one of the guards in the back said in a harsh whisper.

"Shut up! We don't know that," said a second.

"But who else would dress like that?" the first said.

"I said shut up!"

The commander shot the two a withering glare and then turned back to Dark Tidings. "Are you the one known as Dark Tidings?"

"I am," came his discordant reply.

"I am Commander Cosp. We have orders to escort you to the castle," the man said hesitantly.

Dark Tidings tilted his head and said, "We appreciate your service, Commander."

The commander appeared surprised. He nodded once and then ordered his men to resume. This time Rezkin entered the castle through the front gate. The bailey was lined with rows of soldiers ready to react to his apparent threat. No doubt they were expecting a much larger entourage. They had not anticipated the ship arriving under quarantine. The plan was efficient, however, and Rezkin preferred it this way. Kai could stay behind and maintain security of the ship, Shezar was positioned to provide backup from afar, and Roark kept watch at his back. Rezkin did not know Shezar and Roark well, and he was ever cognizant of the possibility that they would betray him, regardless of their oaths. They could be members of Caydean's select, and those strikers seemed to have shed their honor. It was doubtful, however, that either would choose this moment to enact the deed.

They were led into the grand entry room of the keep and then beyond to the great hall. Rezkin's footsteps thundered about the chamber as he intentionally announced his presence. The courtiers and councilors had not yet separated themselves into their respective coteries, which told him they had likely assembled in haste upon hearing of his arrival. Ionius was dressed in splendor, draped in a crimson cape of crushed velvet lined with the fur of the Channerían woodland fox. Encircling his head was a crown mottled with jewels, and he sat upon a throne of intricately carved white driftwood that was as smooth as silk and inlaid with mother-of-pearl. His hair and beard were streaked with more grey than brown, but he was fit of form, and his gaze was sharp. Dark Tidings performed a shallow bow toward the king, the kind executed between men of equal station.

Ionius scowled and said in accented Ashaiian, "You are the so-called *Dark Tidings*, the King's Tournament Champion?"

The voice that answered was not Rezkin's own but the unnerving projection of Wesson's spell, designed not just to disguise it but to prevent anyone from committing it to memory. "I am. You seem to have been expecting me," he replied in perfect Channerían.

After an initial involuntary shudder, Ionius grinned smugly and continued in Channerían. "I was forewarned of your coming."

"Oh? I should like to know your informant so that I may thank him for clearing the way."

The king's scowl returned, and he barked, "Tell me, what is your name?"

Dark Tidings rumbled, "The people of Ashai are in peril, the same peril that I foresee will soon be testing your own borders. In the chaos that has ensued, and that which is to come, my name is of little significance. Dark Tidings will suffice, for that is all I have brought."

The gaggle of courtiers and councilors filled the room with their mutterings and whispers. He was being overly dramatic, but their reactions revealed that he had struck a chord. The murmurs in the streets and choruses in the taverns had all alluded to a rising fear among the people.

King Ionius rapped his jeweled scepter on the arm of his throne. "Your mask has outworn its purpose. You are no longer performing in an arena to the entertainment of gawking fools. You now make claim to a kingdom with a history as rich as mine own. Reveal yourself and show me this proof of your claim."

"I will not!" Dark Tidings bellowed. "The proof of my right is for my people alone. Never will a king of Ashai depend on a foreign monarch to legitimize his rule, nor will he allow one to denigrate him."

"But you are not a king," Ionius snapped. "Caydean, Bordran's eldest son and heir sits upon the throne."

"You, of all people, should know that a throne is more than a gaudy chair. It is an ideal, one constructed by the people. They carry the king's weight upon their shoulders because they have faith that he will shelter them from the rain and guide its torrent to grow prosperity beneath their feet. Caydean feels only a chair beneath his rear while raining madness down on his own people, a madness that you can be sure will not stop at the borders."

Ionius sat back in his throne with a look of calculation.

Dark Tidings continued. "When his people grow too weak to carry him, he will look for new slaves to bear his throne." He looked around to see a number of heads bobbing in agreement and noted Councilor Onelle's, in particular. After a dramatic pause, he added, "I do not need or desire your approval, Ionius, for your opinion in the matter is inconsequential."

Ionius lurched forward with his scepter raised, ready to expel an angry tirade. It seemed that kings did not care for being told they were inconsequential.

Before the man could unleash his fury, Dark Tidings said, "You should, however, consider the difference between Caydean and I." He gazed about the room theatrically. "Which would you prefer as your neighbor?"

Ionius's gaze flashed over the faces of his babbling audience. He leaned back again and said, "What is it that you want? Why have you come to my shores?"

"As you know, on the night of Caydean's attack on the tournament, all foreigners in Skutton were taken into custody to be sold into slavery or ransomed to anyone willing to pay. Any Ashaiians deemed important enough were also detained. Those unwilling to accept the king's tyranny have been sentenced to death, and some of these executions have already been carried out. Any who resisted or attempted to escape were killed. I led a group of escapees from the island, and we are now in search of sanctuary. On behalf of my people, I request asylum."

"How many of refugees do you have?" the king asked noncommittally.

"Many of the people on my vessel are foreigners who desire to return to their homes. The majority, however, are Ashaiians who no longer have homes to which they may return or are foreigners who choose to stay in my company. Some of them wish to fight for my cause."

"What cause is that?" Ionius asked. "It does not seem that you have the numbers or resources to engage in any cause."

"My army is greater than you think, and it grows with each day of Caydean's tyranny. I do not intend to stay abroad indefinitely. I will return to Ashai and take what was rightfully entrusted to me. Before that can happen, though, more refugees will continue to flee, crossing the border into your kingdom and others. I am seeking refuge for all of my people whom Caydean has failed."

In truth, Rezkin had no idea how many refugees were attempting to flee Ashai, nor did he know how many were successful. His intent was to shock the king and council to prevent them from accepting his proposal of asylum. He did not want them to approve the absorption and integration of his people into their own kingdom. He needed Ionius to propose an alternative. He needed Cael. Rezkin had to take the katerghen at his word that the sanctuary he sought would be available on the island, despite all reports to the contrary. If the katerghen failed to deliver on his promise, then Rezkin would still need to find refuge for his people. His hard work would not be wasted if he failed, since by the rules of engagement with the fae that had been documented for centuries, he would gain mastery over a powerful fae woodland nymph. He would benefit either way.

Ionius scoffed. "I will not permit thousands of destitute Ashaiians to invade my cities, filling the trenches that are already bursting with *deplorables*."

"A new place, then, separate from your people. Ashaiians are strong. We are survivors. We will make our own way," Dark Tidings said.

"And I suppose you want land, rich and fertile. Do you desire timber and ore, as well? You ask that I give to the Ashaiians resources that belong to *my* people—at no cost?" Ionius paused in his own dramatic gesture. He sat back and his heated voice cooled as he said, "I am not an ungracious man, and Ashai has been an ally for many generations. My people know that I am both merciful and honorable. The Maker smiles upon me." Ionius nodded toward the high priest at his side. "The Council will convene. You shall have your answer on the morrow. I expect you to return to your ship until you are summoned."

It was a slight for which Rezkin was appreciative. One could only expect such from a man who believed that murdering his own daughter so that he could blackmail a neighboring kingdom was somehow honorable. With Dark Tidings relegated to the ship, however, it left the Raven open to conduct business without suspicion of a connection.

As Dark Tidings and Roark were led from the chamber, Rezkin studied the faces of the onlookers. They were dressed in their own extravagant displays of wealth and status, but to him they were merely playing a game. He had looked upon this very hall from the rafters above and seen just how small these people truly were, the same rafters from which two sets of eyes spied upon him. He wondered if the two assassins were aware of each other. It was not as if they could lose themselves in a crowd. He gave no indication that he had seen them as he left the hall.

The party had arrived on a market street under escort when a commotion erupted involving a crowd of angry people, several stalls—two of which were overturned—a flock of chickens, a donkey, and a cartload of cabbages. No other guards or patrols were present, and the commander looked back to Dark Tidings with an unspoken question. Dark Tidings nodded a silent promise to stay put, and then the commander ordered his men into the fray. Rezkin ducked into an alley where Shezar waited already half undressed. The man assisted him in removing the braids while Rezkin shucked his own wardrobe. Roark leaned against the plastered building as he kept watch.

"How did it go?" Shezar asked.

The strikers were formal with him on the ship but knew better than to use names and titles while on a mission.

"All is going to plan," Rezkin said as he divested himself of his tunic.

Roark glanced back over his shoulder and said, "How so? For a man begging a boon of the king, you were disrespectful, antagonistic, and overbearing; your message was naught but terror; and your exaggerations all but guaranteed a rejection."

Rezkin raised a brow at the man's candid words, but Roark just shrugged. He thought the striker might have made a good trainer with his direct personality.

"Ionius may hate me, but he respects me. He would not have given a weaker man as much consideration. He needed to see a man with the strength to stand up to the challenges ahead. Furthermore, I needed both the king and council to reject my request and propose an alternative—one of my design."

Roark glanced at him sideways. "You mean you *planned* to fail?"

Rezkin tugged on his trousers and said, "If an opponent unknowingly hands you victory, do you call it failure?"

Shezar grinned as he slipped the mask over his face. Roark signed that their time was up, and Dark Tidings stepped into the street beside him.

Commander Cosp returned with his patrol having settled the ruckus. "For a moment, I did not see you," he said to Dark Tidings. With a chuckle he added, "I almost thought that you had slipped away."

As Dark Tidings and Roark were being led to the ship, Rezkin ambled toward the lower district as the unremarkable traveler called Roy. He had been in Serret for only a few days, but it felt as though the energy of the city had shifted since his arrival. People appeared agitated, fights were breaking out, and like the ITA office, more of the buildings bore the mark of the Fishers. He could not tell if this was the norm in Serret, though. He did not have the time nor desire to investigate since he did not foresee it affecting his mission.

About half way back to the brothel, he elected to take a detour to visit a magitorium. He had an idea that would make circumstances much easier in the future, *if* he could get it to work. It would require several mage materials and the expertise of mages with a specific *talent* set. He did not think that any of the mages in his company possessed such skills, but he decided it would be best to have the materials on hand if he ever came into such a resource. He placed the items on order to be delivered to the ship. The mage who sold him the items was suspicious, but Rezkin assuaged his concerns by telling the man that he was a servant to a master mage whose name he made up on the spot. The mage accepted his story after voicing his expert conclusion that the untalented *Roy* could not have devised the list on his own, nor would he have a use for the items.

Rezkin finally made it back to the brothel late in the afternoon and realized that he had little to do. All his plans were set in motion, and it was now time to let others do work *for* him. When he entered the kitchen, he found Grebella and Ilanet having a cup of tea. By Grebella's cackle and Ilanet's flushed face, he decided the older, more experienced woman was probably filling the princess in on some details that she was unlikely to hear anywhere else. He briefly wondered if he should sit in on the lesson but decided Ilanet would not appreciate his presence for that conversation. He slouched and squinted and ducked his head as he greeted them and then turned to leave.

Ilanet called, "Wait. I am glad you came back. I worried that you might not."

Rezkin glanced up and then dropped his eyes to the floor. "Said I would."

"People often say one thing and do another," she said.

Grebella came over and pulled him into the kitchen. "Aw, Roy's not like that, are ya?"

Rezkin glanced around and then shrugged. "I do what needs doin'. Keep what needs keepin'."

The madam raised a brow and said, "How long we plannin' on keepin' her?"

"We're leavin' in two days," he said with a glance toward Ilanet. Her eyes widened, and she bit her lip. "If she's a problem, I can take her somewheres else."

Grebella eyed Ilanet for a moment and then sighed heavily. "No, she ain't no problem long as Brendish don't see her. She's a pretty thing. If he sees her, he'll be wantin' his own kinda payment."

He fidgeted and rubbed at his mouth, snatched the floppy hat from his head, and twisted it anxiously. Finally, he stuttered, "H-he touches her, and we gonna have problems. I told you don't want no problems."

Grebella came over and straightened his tunic as she said, "Now, Roy, don't you be silly, and don't you even be thinkin' 'bout challengin' Brendish. He won't think twice 'bout turnin' ya into cat food. You hear me? Besides, Brendish only ever comes at night. I'll send her out to the stables if he stops by." The woman rounded the counter and took the tea cup from Ilanet. She shooed the princess away with a waving hand and said, "Now you two go on. Sounds like ya got things to talk about."

Rezkin shuffled through the yard with Ilanet at his side until they reached the stables. He surveyed the rooftops and shadowed recesses but did not detect any lurking spies. Once they entered, he straightened and threw off the Roy persona. He searched the stalls and the loft and jabbed at the hay to ensure that no one else was present. Ilanet appeared more anxious now that they were alone. He casually leaned back against a stall and attempted to exude a sense of peace and calm. The princess had already drawn the conclusion that he was an assassin, so he was not surprised that the attempted manifestation of his *will* was not working.

"Do you still wish to stay with me?" he asked.

He avoided using her title in case anyone was listening.

Ilanet chewed at her lip and then said, "First, you saved me from the poisoning. Then, you helped me escape"—she paused—"um … my home. Now, you go to great lengths to shelter me. You still have not told me why. What is it you want in return for your efforts?"

"I did not say that I wanted anything," Rezkin replied.

Ilanet said, "My father taught me that people do nothing unless they stand to profit."

Rezkin tilted his head and said, "It is a topic that has been debated for centuries by uncounted philosophers. Does altruism exist?" He shrugged. "Perhaps not. I cannot say."

She said, "I brought the gold and jewels that I promised. I know that you could easily take them and rid yourself of my inconvenience."

"I do not need your personal treasures. I do stand to profit from having you in my custody, politically if not financially. The cost of caring for a single small-woman is negligible in the scope of my responsibilities. I require nothing further from you, personally, except for your loyalty. I will not abide a traitor in my company."

Ilanet stared at him, her expression a mixture of relief and suspicion. "I am trying to be brave, but I am afraid. I have never been so alone, and I am at your mercy. As a woman of my station, my value, my *only* value, is defined by the political and economic deals made when selling me into marriage. What do you intend to do with me?"

"That is your father speaking. An individual's value cannot be determined by another. You are as valuable as you perceive yourself to be. Whether anyone else recognizes it is another matter." Ilanet's confused expression encouraged him to continue. "You see me as I am now. You have seen some of my *Skills*, and you have seen others with similar *Skills* defer to me. Therefore, you probably perceive that I have some value. Madam Grebella knows me as Roy. Roy appears to have few *Skills*, and is socially awkward, uneducated, and clumsy. Do *I* have less value when I am playing the role of Roy?"

"But you are not Roy. You are only play acting."

"Grebella does not know that. If your father were to meet me as Roy, he would determine that I hold no value. That does not mean that I suddenly am worthless. Incidentally, I believe that Grebella holds Roy in high regard. I think she would not care much for the me that you see."

Ilanet said hesitantly, "You are not so bad."

Rezkin scanned the rafters and then returned her gaze. "You have not yet seen me kill."

Ilanet shuddered and wrapped her arms around herself. He did not wish to frighten the small-woman, but the image of Frisha's distant and cold regard swam before his mind's eye. It was a vision that haunted him every time Frisha looked at him now. He had tried to warn her, but knowing a terrible truth and seeing it were very different. He did not know why he should care, but he had a desire for the return of the joyful and sometimes longing gaze with which Frisha had once looked upon him. Rezkin realized that he did not wish to see that same disenchantment in Ilanet's eyes when she finally saw him for truth.

"You do not know all that I am or could be. Many people, especially women, find me disturbing. Never fool yourself into thinking that I am anything like you. You will end up disappointed."

Ilanet could look at him no longer. She stared at the ground as she gathered her thoughts. The stranger's face was as impassive as usual, but his words resonated with soulful regret. She had little desire to pry into the assassin's personal life, but she wondered who he had lost. Deciding that he likely would not divulge his secrets either way, she sighed and looked up at him.

"You said we are leaving in two days. Where are we going?"

"It is best we do not speak of it for now," he answered. "You never know who may be listening."

Ilanet nodded, accepting the truth of his words. She had made a concerted effort to act less like a princess and more like one of the maids while she was in the company of the women of the house. The problem was, she only knew how the maids had acted when they were around *her*. She had never seen them when they were with their own people.

"So I am to stay here? What of this Brendish?"

The stranger said, "Do not concern yourself over him. If he causes any problems, I will take care of it."

She was terrified that the infamous man would pay the house a visit. She briefly considered asking to stay in the stables with the stranger but could not force herself to voice the request. Perhaps Brendish would not come at all. She would be better off in the house with the women, even if those women were entertaining a steady flow of men all night. She could not believe the stranger would bring her to a brothel, but she admitted that her father would never think to look for her in that place. If anyone did find her, her reputation would be ruined. No one would ever believe that she retained her virtue. She would not believe such a story either.

"What are we to do now?" she asked.

The man studied her for a moment and then said, "You are afraid. You do not wish to be left alone."

She shook her head vigorously.

He nodded. "Then you will not be inclined to attack me in my sleep. I will rest while you keep watch. I have slept very little for several days and cannot enter a deeper state while I am so exposed." He waved to the open doorways at either end of the stable, and she could see his point. "If I sleep now, then I will be more alert tonight while you are sleeping. I will not permit any harm to befall you."

Uratel listened from atop the window eave to the two men in the room below. He had set out from the Black Hall immediately upon receipt of the Raven's orders, which had been passed to him from the Grandmaster. The Black Hall had its own mage relay, but from what Uratel had heard, the orders had been received through the official relay in Kaibain. The Raven had developed a system to code messages that even the Black Hall would have thought legitimate had they not known better. The Raven had spies in nearly every criminal network, and they had been assigned to follow Hespion Mulnak, Duke Atressian's youngest son and heir, since he had left the tournament. When Uratel received his orders, he knew exactly where to find the man.

Hespion had left the tournament in Skutton early and therefore had escaped the chaotic tide of Caydean's forces. The king had declared war on all four dukes, making to replace them with men of his choosing who had no blood claim to the throne. Atressian's heir would have been taken hostage had he been captured. Hespion was now pressed to make it back to the Atressian estate before he was found by hostile forces—the same forces that, until a few weeks ago, would have been charged with keeping him safe. Hespion made good his escape before the travel ban was enacted, sweeping up the Tremadel and the River Straei by mage-powered ship. Unfortunately for him, the king's patrols were now on full alert looking for rebels and *traitors*, so Hespion was lying low in Drennil and hoping to make his way west to Atressian unnoticed. He would fail without assistance.

"You should have warned me sooner!" Hespion howled.

Uratel could not see the two men, but his unusual talent allowed for subtle eavesdropping with little chance of detection. It was one of the reasons he had succeeded in the rigorous training at the Black Hall where so many failed.

"I sent word as soon as I found out," said the second man, whom Uratel had recognized during his surveillance as Hespion's older brother Fierdon. Fierdon was not difficult to recognize even though Uratel had never before set eyes on him. "I am not to blame for your delay. And for what? Bragging rights? You actually thought you had a chance to become tier champion? I heard the Jebai trounced you, and not the good one either. Almost took your head, they say."

"Oh shut up, Fierdon. Malcius Jebai is a cheat. I could have bested him easily. He should have been snoring in his own vomit," Hespion muttered. "There is no way he could have recovered so quickly. It was that old healer woman."

"What are you talking about?" Fierdon asked. "You poisoned him. I knew it! It is so like you to try to take what does not belong to you. You are just like Father."

"You watch your tongue. Our father is a great man who should be king, not that paranoid, madman Caydean. You have never understood the true meaning of family. That is why *I* am the Atressian heir."

For weeks, a flood of information had been pouring into the Black Hall from the Raven's spy network that now covered every district in Ashai and several beyond. At first, the guild had been frustrated with the inundation of seemingly useless drivel, and it had been necessary to create a new division of librarians just to handle the mess. Uratel, however, was developing a new appreciation of the Raven's extremism. He now knew the Mulnak brothers' life histories, dark secrets and all. He knew Hespion's claim about his father's reasons for naming him heir to be untrue and that Hespion had been the cause of the elder brother's disfigurement that had led to his being passed over as the next head of house.

"Father has ordered you to take my advice. He knows I should be heir," Fierdon said.

"So he tells me every chance he gets," Hespion muttered. "But that is not an option, is it? *I* am the heir, and you will do as *I* say. And we shall see what becomes of the Jebais. I heard Simeon and Lady Jebai were imprisoned."

"Sentenced to death, I hear," said Fierdon.

Hespion grumbled, "Serves them right."

"For what? Defying Caydean? Like us?"

"We have every right!" Hespion spat. "The royal bloodline has obviously become tainted. The throne should be ours."

"Wellinven has a greater claim," said Fierdon.

"What? Give the throne to Tieran Nirius? The arrogant sot already thinks he owns the kingdom. His claim is through what—his *mother*? The wench will be drawing my bath when I am king. We need strong blood on the throne. Bordran and his predecessors sought peace. Peace! Ha! Peace is an excuse for the weak to sit on their hands stroking a feeble throne. Ashai has been bound by the same borders for hundreds of years. Why? We are the greatest kingdom on the Souelian. Ashai can be made even greater."

"Father has no desire to go to war with our neighbors," Fierdon argued. "To claim the throne is enough. We need no more land. We were great under Bordran, and we can be great again, so long as Caydean is removed from the throne."

"Which is why I need to get back to Atressian," Hespion said.

"Where are your guards?" Fierdon asked.

"Here and there. I told them to scatter so as not to draw attention."

Uratel had seen Hespion's guards, and they were certainly scattered. A few were playing bones in the alley, one was dozing on the front stoop of the rundown inn, and the rest were at the tavern drinking away what was probably the last of their pay until they made it back to Atressian.

"We should go by land," Fierdon said. "The rivers are being watched closely."

"*We*? What is this *we*? I cannot travel with *you*. You draw attention like a traveling freak show. How much money do you have?"

"Enough," Fierdon said hesitantly.

"Give it to me. I may need to bribe the patrols. My trunks are over there. I'll take what I can, and you bring the rest when you find a way back."

"I would have been back already if I had not waited for you. I cannot walk into a bank and request more funds!" Fierdon said. "I would be recognized and captured immediately."

"Which is exactly why *I* cannot visit the bank. Caydean would find no value in *your* capture. Everyone knows Father would never capitulate to any demands to get *you* back."

"Maybe not, but they will not stop at torture to find out what I know," Fierdon said.

"Then I suggest you do not get caught. If you do, you might consider using that sword to save yourself the pain of torture."

"You can get your own funds, Hespion, and find your own way back. When you are killed or captured, Father will be forced to choose a new heir."

"It would not be *you*. They say you are a monster, you know. They say you were using dark magic to summon demons, and that is why the healers could not fix you."

"If they do, it is only because *you* claimed it to be so."

"It no longer matters *why* they say it, only that they do," Hespion said. "Besides, if I fail to reach Atressian, Father will blame *you*. No matter how you look at it, you will never be duke."

"Then I will beget an heir."

Hespion burst into hardy laughter. "*You*? What of your noble ideals against forcing women? Have you changed your mind just to see me fall? Or do you think to take a whore? All the gold in Ashai could not buy you a minute in a woman's bed. Besides, any demon-born bastard of yours is more likely to be impaled on a stake and burned than be named … well, *anything* … much less heir to the duchy. Our impotent father is more likely to succeed."

"You had best hope he does not."

"I have no worries about that," Hespion said.

"What did you do?" Fierdon hissed, but the question was unnecessary. Even Uratel, sitting atop the roof, could catch the implication.

"You need not worry about that. Go to Justain and meet with our contacts there."

Fierdon scoffed. "You think I can just stroll into the marquis's estate? Besides, Ruald is now Head of House, and I believe his loyalty is with Wellinven."

"I am not an idiot, Fierdon. I did not intend for you to go to the estate. Urek is guildmaster of the Serpents. Explain to him that it is in his best interest to assist."

"You have not been paying attention to recent events. There has been a dramatic shift in power, and nearly all the criminal guilds are under the rule of the Raven now, including the Serpents. Urek has been replaced."

"Yes, I have heard of this Raven. Who is guildmaster now?"

"I believe it is Adsden, Urek's second."

"Adsden. Pah! He seeks to live above his station—thinks he is smarter than everyone else. Something is not right with him."

"I have not had the pleasure," Fierdon said. "I was busy with our family's *legitimate* dealings."

"Your hands are not so clean. You were just as eager to further our efforts against Caydean."

"I never claimed otherwise."

"Meet with Adsden," Hespion said. "If there is one commonality among men, it is greed. Do not give me that look. Greed is not a bad thing. It is what drives us toward greatness."

"I think you are confusing greed with ambition."

"You fool yourself if you think there is a difference. I am sure this Raven will jump at the chance for mutual profit. If he is cunning enough to take over the underworld, he will recognize the benefits of making friends with the duke and future king."

Fierdon stormed out of the room, and Uratel watched as the elder brother wrapped himself in rags and lugged his pack down the street with a distinctive loping gait. The limp was convincing, although Uratel knew it to be an act. While Fierdon was terribly disfigured by the fire that had consumed him as a boy, he was just as strong and capable as any man—perhaps more so for his determination. The Raven's spies had somehow managed to gain insight into the *accident* that had affected the man two decades prior, and the story goes that it was Hespion who set the fire to Fierdon's bed—with Fierdon in it. The young Hespion claimed a candle fell from the bedside table during the night, but that would not explain why the healers could not repair the damage. Whatever Hespion had done, the effects had been extensive and permanent. Presumably, the attack had been fueled by Hespion's jealousy of his father's adoration for the older brother and by Fierdon's success in pretty much everything he attempted.

Uratel shook his legs out and then shuffled across the rickety roof. He needed to find someone to deliver a message to Justain. Although he did not know Adsden, he had heard that the Raven himself had placed the man in charge of the guild. If the Serpent guildmaster was to meet with Fierdon, he would need to know the Raven's orders regarding Atressian. Uratel needed his assignment to succeed. He had been the first of the Black Hall to fall to the Raven, and somehow he felt that failure more so than did the others. The grandmaster had told him otherwise, but Uratel still felt a need to prove himself. He had never been dispatched to *protect* anyone before. The grandmaster had informed the guild that the Raven had officially endorsed Dark Tidings as king, so Uratel could not fathom why the Riel'gesh wanted Hespion Mulnak to reach his home safely.

Rezkin woke after a few hours of actual sleep to find Ilanet sitting only a few feet away from him. The sun was nearly set, and business at the house was picking up. He did not have to guess what the princess had been up to while he was asleep. She was seated in the hay as primly as one could sit in hay, and several tiny baskets woven from the straw were arrayed around her feet. She was busy weaving a much larger one that took up most of her lap. Her nimble fingers moved with expertise as she created the intricate structure. He watched her work for several minutes before she noticed he was awake.

She smiled and said, "Father did not care what I learned, or if I learned at all. One of the maids worked at her father's shop making baskets when she had the time. She offered to teach me when I was very young. Mostly, I think she felt sorry for me since I had nothing to do all day."

Rezkin had no respect for the outworlder king. The man had not trained his small-one to have any skills. She had not learned to fight or defend herself, and then he had tried to have her killed over a trivial matter. There were plenty of other ways to obtain what King Ionius wanted, and he had to know it. To him, Ilanet held no value, and his chances of marrying her to his ally and neighbor, King Caydean, had dissipated. Rezkin could not recall receiving any lessons that related to this type of situation, but he had come to the conclusion that killing a small-one who had committed no crime and could not defend herself was somehow intrinsically wrong. But why was it wrong, he wondered.

A gale of laughter burst from the house. Several men and women began singing, and someone committed to playing the pipes poorly. Ilanet glanced toward the aged structure with its awkwardly hanging shutters and chipped plaster.

"I would prefer to stay out here for a while, if you do not mind," she said as she continued twisting more straw into her creation.

No horses had stayed in this stall since he had mucked it, so at least it was clean.

Rezkin stood and stretched and then informed Ilanet that he would return shortly with a meal. He left her with instructions not to leave the stall and then slipped into the dusky streets. As he traversed across the district toward the vendors with fare more palatable than what was available at the brothel, he pondered over his earlier conclusion. Finally, he arrived at a decision. A small-one was potential. To end the life before its potential could manifest was a waste of valuable resources. Even if the small-one never became a mage, scholar, or warrior, he or she could always till a field or bear offspring. Potential *was* something the masters had emphasized, particularly during his lessons on potential ward manipulation. Potential could be shaped into anything. According to the masters, it was the greatest resource one could possess.

· · ·

Ilanet was alone outside for the first time in her life. There were no guards, no maids, not even a priestess or one of the women from the brothel. She might have been excited if she were somewhere more enjoyable, or at least *safer*. Sitting in a horse stall behind a brothel in the depths of a slum filled with deplorables was not her idea of fun and adventure. Of course, she had never had an adventure, but she had read about many in the castle library.

She wished she had brought a book with her. Eyeing his pack, she wondered if the stranger had a book she could read to distract her from how immensely vulnerable she felt at that moment. This time he had wedged the bag between the rafters overhead. She had no idea how he had gotten it up there, and she did not think she could reach it even with the pitchfork. She decided it was probably not a good idea to riffle through an assassin's belongings, anyway.

Again, she wondered what the stranger planned to do with her. He had said that he desired nothing from her and that he did not intend to sell her at the slave market. That was wonderful news, but could she trust an assassin to tell the truth? What else would he do with her? It was not as if he would set her up in a cozy chamber in a castle somewhere and provide her with everything she needed at no cost to her. He had to want something. He was probably keeping it from her so that she would not feel inclined to run from him. Perhaps she should flee now while he was gone and no one was watching. She had money. She could pay someone to take her somewhere safe. But then she would be in the same predicament as she was already. How could she trust anyone? At least she *knew* this man was an assassin. Thus far he had treated her well, with courtesy even, but she worried that what he had in store for her was worse than she could imagine.

Ilanet wanted to run home and listen to Mables chide her for being a silly girl worrying over trivialities. Mables would tell her that she was a princess, and everyone in the castle would protect her. Mables had betrayed her, though, and now the woman was dead. Ironically, it was the assassin who had saved her, and she prayed to the Maker that he would keep to his word.

7

Dark Tidings stood before King Ionius in the great hall. Dust motes danced in the rays of golden light that streamed in through the narrow windows high above their heads. Far below the vaulted ceiling, the rest of the room was dark by contrast, lit only by the wall torches that emitted scents of burning fat and sage. The councilors stood in lines beside the dais, and courtiers filled nearly every other space available beyond the aisle, Prince Nyan among them. Roark stood at Rezkin's back, and two hidden observers peered down from the rafters. Collectiare Tiblot stood behind the king to his left with his hand resting upon the back of the throne. Rezkin had never seen the collectiare in person, only a poor rendition on canvas, but the man's identity was betrayed by the black attire and golden pendant that hung from a torque about his neck. The collectiare's exact age had not been in the northern fortress's records, but estimates placed him near to eighty years old.

Rezkin had gone to the designated location near the docks after the sun rose to await the king's call. Luckily, Brendish had not shown the previous night, so Rezkin had spent his time in contemplation and exercise while he kept watch over the house. The messenger from the castle arrived with the summons less than an hour before his audience was supposed to begin. Apparently, the council spent the entirety of the previous afternoon and late into the evening in discussions and then met again for a few hours that morning before they finally came to an agreement. Rezkin thought it was probably the quickest decision in the history of the council. Serious matters like this usually took weeks or months, if they would consider them at all.

"The council and I have come to a decision," Ionius announced. His stately voice reverberated throughout the otherwise silent hall. With a sharp glare toward the councilors, he said, "We have agreed that the legitimacy of your right to the throne of Ashai is not of our concern. We neither endorse nor recognize your claim but respect your efforts to seek and provide refuge for the Ashaiian people who have placed themselves in your care." Ionius paused expectantly, as though some amount of gratitude was due to him for the weak praise. When none was forthcoming, he continued with irritation. "However, we unanimously agree that it is in the best interests of our kingdom not to accept *any* Ashaiian refugees onto Channerían soil."

The courtiers tittered and grumbled, and it was obvious they were not all happy with the decision. The councilors looked toward the king, eager for him to continue, but Ionius was in no hurry. He seemed to still desire a response from Dark Tidings, one that Rezkin was unwilling to deliver. Anything he said at this point, whether incensed, placating, or pleading, could be turned against him. Instead, he stood in ominous silence, a bastion of restrained power. He knew his visage alone was enough to wilt the courage of many.

Ionius inhaled sharply and then straightened with smug pride. "I submitted a proposal to the council for an alternative solution, one that pleases us and will rid us of a metaphorical thorn in our side. My proposal has won the council's approval. There is a place that has long been in contention between Channería and Gendishen, an island called Cael."

Ionius paused once again for a response.

Dark Tidings's disturbing voice boomed through the chamber. "I am familiar with the island of Cael, an uninhabitable rock on which nothing of significance grows and is almost completely inaccessible due to the high cliffs and sharp rocks that surround it."

Ionius grinned. "Yes, I can see that you know of it. We have agreed to withdraw our claim to the island and conditionally recognize your own." The courtiers muttered and shook their heads, and some of the councilors shifted anxiously, perhaps expecting retaliation for the poorly disguised offense.

Rezkin did not disappoint. "You mock our plight, Ionius? A brave people who have only just escaped death and persecution, many of whom are descendants of noble lines, a people bereft of home and succor. We, the neighbors to your west, who have held your borders with determination for generations and came to your aid when others threatened your own well-being, are deserving of naught but a barren rock that we must somehow wrest from another kingdom altogether?"

A number of courtiers were frowning and shaking their heads as if silently imploring a favorable response from the king. Although Rezkin doubted any of them would voice an objection, the sentiment was turned in his favor. The collectiare stared at Dark Tidings with black, clever eyes set deeply in an aged face. The seasoned veteran of political and spiritual intrigue revealed nothing of his thoughts.

Ionius scowled and said, "A begging cat accepts the scraps given him and does not plead for roast. We are not beholden to you or Ashai, and you have not yet heard our terms."

Dark Tidings raised an imploring hand, his first movement since arriving. The guards tensed, and the courtiers swayed. "Speak, Good King Ionius. Tell us of your gracious terms."

Ionius smiled greedily. "The first is a boon. I trust you are not yet wed, for I have heard no tell of a queen at your side. My daughter, Princess Ilanet, is to be yours. Her beauty is beyond compare, and she is of impeccable breeding." Rezkin was irritated with the way Ionius spoke of his daughter like a brood mare. "This is my gift to you to seal our pact and serve as a reminder of the alliance that has long stood between our peoples."

A voice sounded from the crowd as a stocky man nearing middle age stepped forward. "King Ionius, I protest! You speak of my betrothed. Ilanet has already been promised to me!" Prince Nyan was an unimpressive man. While he wore his princely attire with practiced comfort, he would have looked as suitable driving a farm cart to market.

Ionius spoke to the prince as a father scolding a willful son. "Prince Nyan, you failed to gain my daughter's favor so much so that she refused to attend her own betrothal celebration. As a father, I cannot in good conscience give my daughter over to such a union."

For once, the collectiare's stoic visage broke, and he smiled placidly, and nodding his head in approval. The councilors and courtiers smiled and nodded appreciatively in return.

Nyan was not satisfied, though. "You will not honor our agreement, but you will hand her over to this ... this ... masked *fraud*?"

"Prince Nyan, why would I choose a prince when I can marry her to a king?"

"But you have not even recognized his claim to the throne!" the prince protested.

Ionius was finished with the prince. "His claim to the throne is likely greater than yours will ever be!" After a calming breath he said, "These proceedings do not concern you. You will leave. Now. And since you no longer have business here, I am sure you will be desiring to leave my castle as soon as possible."

Nyan turned with a heated glare at Dark Tidings and then immediately lost his nerve when Rezkin graced him with the blackened gaze of the wraith. A guard stepped forward, making it clear that Nyan had been summarily dismissed before the entire court and council.

"My father will hear of this," the prince shouted as he stormed out of the hall.

"See that he does," Ionius rumbled. "I have it on good authority that he warned you against coming here in the first place."

Once the prince had departed, Dark Tidings redirected his gaze to the king and said, "Which one of these ladies is the princess?"

Tilting his head so that his perusal would be obvious, he surveyed the women closest to the dais. Most of them cringed away from his gaze, but a few looked more than willing to offer themselves to the mysterious, self-proclaimed king.

Ionius fisted his hand and then relaxed. "My daughter has been beside herself with grief over the pending nuptials with Prince Nyan. She refuses to leave her chambers. I am certain, though, that this news will please her, and she will anxiously await her departure in your care."

The collectiare's surprise was only evidenced by his decision to speak. "You will not require her to wed before departing?"

"You know as well as I that she is not yet of age," Ionius said with frustration.

"Exceptions can be made," the collectiare replied.

Dark Tidings interjected, "I am not interested in a betrothal, Ionius. I do not seek your daughter's hand."

"Then you will keep her as your ward until you are ready," Ionius snapped, making it obvious he would brook no further discussion of the subject.

The man's concern for his daughter's happiness and well-being was overwhelming. He also seemed to be putting quite a bit of trust in the Raven to keep his promise to deliver the princess.

Dark Tidings tilted his head and said, "I will accept this condition with the understanding that there is no expectation of betrothal between myself and the princess. I will care for her as my ward until she is wed."

"And she will remain *unharmed*?" the collectiare asked.

"No harm will befall her by my hand, and I will place her under my protection. I am sure you all recognize that my path is hazardous and harsh. She will be subject to the same fate that befalls the rest of my party, island *refuge* included."

Ionius waved a dismissive hand. "You have proven yourself a formidable warrior at tournament. I place her in your capable hands."

"And what of your other condition?" Dark Tidings asked. Rezkin wanted these proceedings finished. He had other things to do besides standing here jabbering and making deals with the king of Channería.

Ionius threw his hand up and motioned to the collectiare who stepped forward.

"The second is of *my* concern," the collectiare said. "The Temple wishes to ensure that you are worthy of the Maker's grace."

"Most of the people of Ashai, by far, are followers of the Maker," Dark Tidings replied. "The Temple does not hold power there, however,"

The collectiare nodded and said, "I am aware of that. It has never been our desire or policy to *force* our beliefs upon others, but the Temple of the Maker is the official guide for the soul in Channería, and you ask for Channerían soil. If we are to allow you to claim to Cael, we must certify that your actions and beliefs are consistent with the will of the Maker. We will send a small delegation with you to assess your suitability."

Rezkin did not care for that. He gave little thought to the subject and had no beliefs for or against the Maker. He had studied the religious and spiritual beliefs of a great many cultures, both existing and dead. Few of them sounded any more plausible than the others, and most possessed similar underlying guiding principles. The Temple's spies would surely find fault in his methods and unwillingness to impress them, and any support for his claim would be withdrawn. At least it would give him time to secure his claim by other means.

"How long do you intend for your priests to *evaluate* me?" Dark Tidings asked.

"You will be given a minimum of six months to prove yourself, but the priests may continue to observe for up to one year before submitting their final conclusions."

Rezkin would not agree to the collectiare's terms. He could play along with their demands, but they would see his cooperation as a weakness to be exploited.

"You may send *two* of your priests, no more. They may provide some consolation to the refugees in need. The priests may observe the daily concerns of the people, but they will *not* be accepted into my confidence, nor will they be privy to any official actions or plans. I will not abide spies in my midst, even for the Temple. The Temple will gain no foothold in the governance of Ashai *or* Cael through me."

The collectiare frowned. "We are already firmly planted in Cael as it is a part of Channería."

"It has been given to me by these proceedings. You would challenge the king and council's ruling? Do you claim such power in this hall?"

The councilors muttered to each other furtively, and Ionius straightened in his chair. "The collectiare is the voice of the Maker and the guide for our souls. He does not rule this kingdom," Ionius stated emphatically.

The collectiare donned a blank expression, and he bowed ever so slightly toward the king. "Of course, I could not claim such power as to overrule you, King Ionius, especially when you are backed by the council."

"Or *ever!*" Ionius snapped.

The collectiare smiled indulgently, "Yes, Your Majesty. I am only attempting to ensure that the conditions we discussed are met ..."

Ionius slammed his fist down on the arm of the throne. "The conditions are met. He has agreed to take your priests with him. The limitations he proposes are reasonable for a *king* to impose, especially one waging a war. Perhaps I should consider adjusting my own restrictions," he added with a sideways glance at the collectiare.

The collectiare bowed and stepped back, returning to his place behind the throne. The angry glare he directed toward the king's back and then Dark Tidings could not be misinterpreted. Dark Tidings ignored the collectiare and moved on to his final concern.

"Since we are to go to an island lacking in resources, it is pertinent that we consider a trade agreement."

"Yes, I assumed you would want that," Ionius said. "Ashai has suspended most interkingdom trade for reasons only a madman could conceive. Since you claim to speak for the people of Ashai, we will be gracious and recognize the same Channerían export agreements with you."

Rezkin knew the notion to be absurd, but it was not unexpected.

Dark Tidings said, "Those trade deals were negotiated by a wealthy kingdom with a prosperous economy, not a group of destitute refugees. During past negotiations, Bordran and Caydean have both agreed to higher prices in exchange for political and economic support for which *we* will not be reaping the benefits."

"And with that," Ionius said, "an agreement for Channerían cooperation in mining operations in the Zigharans with access to the Tremadel, which is something you cannot provide. You have yet to offer anything of value, and I do not foresee you finding it on that island."

"No, it is unlikely," Dark Tidings agreed. "Which is why we need assurance that, should we manage to acquire resources, valuable or otherwise, you will adhere to our agreement. If my people suffer through the challenges of colonization on an uninhabitable island, we will not give it up if something of value is discovered."

"You question my honor?" Ionius asked with indignation.

"You write your own story of honor, Ionius. I merely read the pages. The fate of kingdoms cannot depend on honor alone. I trust in yours no more than you trust in mine. If I am to stake my people's future on the gamble you have so graciously offered, then we need assurance it will not be taken from us should it pay off. We require a treaty with diplomatic recognition."

"You cannot have it," Ionius snapped. "I already told you that we do not recognize or endorse your claim to Ashai."

"I do not ask for Ashai. The recognition is for the Kingdom of Cael."

Ionius scoffed. "Here I thought you desired to be the king of Ashai, but it seems you will settle for a barren rock if someone will only call you king."

A few of Ionius's loyal supporters snickered, but most appeared anxious and unsettled.

The king waved his hand and said, "Very well, since the council has already voted to hand over the island, we will give you diplomatic recognition —with stipulations, of course. The first is satisfaction of the afore mentioned conditions for retaining the island. Second, if you should happen to find these mysterious resources that have somehow eluded both Channería and Gendishen for a thousand years, we will have the right of first refusal on any trade deals."

"So that you can bypass the free trade agreements of the ITA and lock us into unfair prices? We will give you first refusal but retain the right to reject your offer and seek fair compensation elsewhere."

"A paltry kingdom with no resources, hardly any people, no army, and no navy. Do you really think anyone will trade fairly? We shall see how that goes for you. I think you will find it more difficult considering your third and final stipulation. Our recognition of the Kingdom of Cael will be contingent upon the acquisition of diplomatic recognition from Gendishen."

Collectiare Tiblot stepped forward in protest. "King Ionius, these people are already destitute and seek only to find a place in this world. You place an impossible task before them. For hundreds of years, Gendishen has rejected every attempt to reconcile."

"This is a secular matter, Collectiare. I do not require your input," Ionius said.

"I disagree," said the collectiare. "I know you have heard the fable of the old woman who only ever offered her starving cat the fish bones and kept the meat for herself. Every child who has attended Temple services has heard the tale."

"What of it?" Ionius asked.

"If you recall, the cat ultimately ate the woman."

"That hardly applies here," Ionius argued. "That woman was old and feeble. Channería is a great and powerful kingdom, and this man in the absurd mask has no teeth or claws with which to scratch."

The collectiare shook his head in exasperation. "You miss the point, Ionius. The moral of the story was not what the cat did. It was about …"

"I do not care. That ridiculous children's story has no bearing here. My ruling stands."

Dark Tidings bowed slightly and said, "The Kingdoms of Cael and Ashai will not forget the *generosity* of its neighbor and long-standing ally Channería." He motioned to Roark and began backing toward the exit.

"*Dark Tidings*," Ionius called, "Do you bear the blood of the royal family? Prince Thresson, perhaps? If we are to call you *king* then we shall need a name."

Dark Tidings retorted, "You may have a name when you call me king."

Ionius smirked. "You are overbearing and offensive but intelligent and competent. This will no doubt be a test of your fortitude. If you can make a kingdom of *Cael*, then perhaps you have what it takes to seize Ashai. I admit you seem well suited for your station."

Dark Tidings tilted his head in acknowledgement and said, "That is something that *you* had best remember, Ionius."

Arrangements were made with the king's seneschal for the treaty to be drawn and delivered by noon on the following day. It seemed Ionius wanted them out of his kingdom as quickly as possible. Rezkin wanted the ship ready to depart upon arrival of the documents. Once they reached *Stargazer*, Rezkin called a meeting with his strikers.

"I do not understand what just happened," Roark said. "Yesterday you went in asking for asylum for less than a hundred refugees, and today the king and council offer up an uninhabitable island and call you king."

Surprised, Shezar said, "Ionius recognized him as King of Ashai?"

"No, he made him King of Cael," said Roark.

Kai furrowed his brow. "Cael? You mean that rock in the northern Yeltin Isles? Why would he do that?"

Roark shook his head. "It was approved by the council in less than a day. Not only that, but the king essentially forced his daughter on him."

"You are to marry the princess?" Kai asked with a pleased grin. "Last I saw her, she was only a child, but I hear she has grown to be quite the beauty."

"And befitting a royal union," Shezar added.

Rezkin was pretending to ignore their conversation as he pored over the list of supplies that had already been obtained and those which still needed to be acquired. He glanced up to see all three men staring at him.

"I am not marrying Princess Ilanet. Besides, she is still only a small one—a *child*."

"She was already betrothed to Prince Nyan of Jerea," Roark said. "I do not understand why Ionius would suddenly try to force a union with *you*, a rebel in a mask without a name or official station."

"Ionius does not care for his daughter, only her fiscal and political value. Ilanet has no desire to marry Nyan, and Ionius is eager to see her gone," Rezkin said.

"Why is that?" Kai asked.

"Two nights ago, Ionius tried to have Ilanet killed in an attempt to blackmail King Vargos. He failed, and now he needs her to disappear."

Kai released a long whistle. "What prevents him from trying again?"

Rezkin said, "Ionius no longer has possession of his daughter. I do."

Roark huffed in frustration. "You are saying that you already have the princess? You acted like you had never seen her before. Does Ionius know?"

"No, Ionius does not know that I have her, and it must stay that way. He expects her to be delivered before the ship departs. He may or may not send her belongings with the treaty. It would be best if we do not announce her presence aboard the ship right away. Princess Ilanet is now a refugee like the rest of us."

Following the meeting, Rezkin slipped off the ship and joined the shuffle of people delivering cargo to the dock. Since everyone had orders to stay below decks during the daylight, he did not chance running into anyone else that knew him. A large crowd had gathered in the market that he generally would pass through on his way back to the brothel. Most of the people appeared angry as they jeered at the guards, and some even began throwing produce and dung. Having no desire to get involved, he slipped down an alley to an adjacent street and completed his trek without further complications. Even on this street, though, most of the people were moving *toward* the growing mob, except for the priests, who were gathering anxiously in groups heading into the closest temple. It was all the more reason for Rezkin to hurry on his way. If serious problems erupted in the city, he would need to be close to Ilanet.

The princess was pacing anxiously in the stables when Rezkin arrived. As soon as her eyes fell on him, she rushed forward and grasped his tunic. Rezkin frowned down at her.

"You have to do something," she blurted.

He pulled her dainty hands from his shirt and said, "What is it that I am expected to do?" Her distress was plainly written on her face.

"He is here," she said. "Brendish. He is in the house. Grebella sent me out here so he would not see me."

"Obviously, he has not found you, so I do not understand the source of your concern," Rezkin said.

"He is angry, *livid*, even. Just before you arrived I could hear him yelling at Grebella about money. He hit her, I am sure of it. Now it is quiet, and I am worried."

"Brendish will not seriously harm Grebella. He has an investment in her well-being. They have a working relationship. It is not my place to intercede, and I have no desire to become involved."

Ilanet grabbed at his tunic again and tried to shake him. "But you must! Grebella is … well … *uncouth*, but she has been kind to both of us. This

Brendish smells of spirits, and he is covered in *ink*. I do not believe he is thinking about his *investment* right now. He is *hurting* her!"

Rezkin inwardly sighed. He had learned from his masters that outworlders would take any opportunity to weaken and subjugate other outworlders. Since he left the fortress, he had seen this in truth. Roughly half of the outworlders had managed to keep the other half weak by doing nothing more than convincing them that it was not socially acceptable to defend themselves. Grebella was responsible for a household of vulnerable women, yet she had few means of protecting them, forcing her to depend on men like Brendish. Neither Grebella nor Ilanet were Rezkin's responsibility. They were not his friends. They were not even Ashaiian.

He shook his head. "Grebella is a resourceful woman. She does not require my assistance."

"You are horrible!" she said. "You protected me, but you will not lift a finger to help *her*? Why? It is because she is a ... a ... oh, you know."

"That has nothing to do with it," Rezkin said as he grabbed his pack and took a seat in the hay. The little tortie came prancing into the stable as if it had been summoned. He frowned as the cat climbed into his lap uninvited and bumped her head against his chin. He looked back to Ilanet and said, "Grebella depends on Brendish to protect her and her house. If I stop him from hurting her now, he will only take it out on her later. I could kill him, but then she would have no protection from the other predators. Once I leave, someone else will just step into his place. I could not sufficiently protect her without further insinuating myself into the Channerían underworld."

"Why so much? Why not just this one?" Ilanet said pleadingly.

"People would be suspicious and fear the rising of an unknown power. They would seek to smother it before it grew. Grebella and her household would be the unfortunate collateral damage, which would completely defeat the original intent. I would have to gain sufficient power and instill enough fear to deter others from challenging me, and I would have to do it in one night since we are leaving on the morrow."

Ilanet's hopeful expression fell. "I see. That would be impossible."

Rezkin continued searching his pack as he said, "Not impossible, just tedious and tiring. I have more important things to do. Besides, I made an agreement with your father that I would limit my meddling in this kingdom if he gave me what I wanted." He looked up and narrowed his eyes as he stared at nothing in particular. "Then again, he did not exactly follow my instructions.

There will have to be a reprisal. He has to learn not to push the bounds where I am concerned."

"What do you mean? What deal?" Ilanet asked. "Does it have something to do with me?"

"Yes," Rezkin said as he pulled the writing kit from his pack. "In addition to my own considerations, we came to an agreement concerning you. I have arranged for your independence from your father."

"That is great news!" she said as she hurried over to sit beside him. Her eyes were filled with anticipation as she eagerly asked, "How so? What is to happen to me?"

Rezkin set the kit aside and kept his eyes on the princess, cognizant of the fact that she might not like what he had to say. "According to your father, you are to be married."

"Yes, I *know* that," Ilanet huffed. "You took me away from the celebratory ball, remember?"

"No, not to Nyan," Rezkin said. "Are you familiar with the one known as Dark Tidings?"

With furrowed brow, she said, "You mean the King's Tournament Champion?"

"Yes. Are you also aware that he has made claim to the throne of Ashai?"

"So I had heard. Only rumors, surely."

"Indeed not. His claim is legitimate. He is in Serret right now. While his crew has been resupplying, he has made a few arrangements with your father. I may have *encouraged* your father to send you with Dark Tidings. The betrothal was your father's idea."

Ilanet's eyes widened. "You mean I am to marry this Dark Tidings?"

"So your father would have it. Dark Tidings made no such agreement. He has only conceded to taking you as his ward until you do marry."

"So I am his ward until I am of age, and then I must marry him?" Ilanet's voice rose in pitch as she spoke.

"That is not what I said."

A piercing shriek erupted from the house, assailing their ears and causing the cat to skitter out of the stables. A few moments later, two men could be heard squabbling with several women. Loud cracks, crashes, and squeals escaped the building's confines, and then the back door burst open releasing a furious bruiser. The barrel-chested man gripped a club spiked with rusted nails as he pounded across the yard. A second man followed close behind, tromping through the dust in untied boots. He was a head shorter than the first, and he was still struggling to tie his pants as he stumbled toward the stables. Both men's arms were adorned in purple-black tattoos, and the glazed fury on their heated faces made it obvious they were out for blood.

Rezkin pushed Ilanet toward the rear stall with orders to remain silent. He positioned himself so that the women peering between the curtains could not see what was happening. The two men entered the stables and came at him without pause. The bigger man roared as he swung his spiked club at Rezkin's head. He ducked under the swing and slipped around the man to bring a swift upper cut to the second man's chin. The second man fell back from the unexpected attack, and Rezkin dodged another swipe of the club. He turned and punched the man in the kidney, eliciting another roar as the man grabbed at the back of Rezkin's loose tunic. Rezkin bent forward and then lurched back, slithering out of the tunic. He grabbed the ends of the long sleeves as he disrobed, wrapping one around the arm that gripped him and using the other to block the next swing of the club. He twisted the sleeve and yanked, causing the assailant to lose his hold on the weapon, and then he slipped around the man's side, pulling his other arm across his body and toppling him off balance.

Rezkin kicked backward, striking the second man in the chest just as he regained his feet. As the second man stumbled back again, Rezkin hooked the bigger man's head and then threw his body weight to the side while bounding off one of the horse stalls. The tangled, off-balance assailant could not recover, his head was wrenched around, and his eyes stared sightlessly behind him as he slumped to the ground. The second man jumped at him, but Rezkin turned to the side and then used the man's own momentum to smash his face into the stall with such force that he was rendered an unrecognizable corpse.

Ilanet watched the encounter through the space between the wooden slats of the stall. Her heart pounded against her chest, and she held her hand over her mouth to prevent her unbidden shouts from escaping. The exchange was vicious and abrupt, not like the duels between knights that she had spied upon during training sessions in the yard. No one here was laughing or congratulating the winner. The losers were rendered dead in a matter of seconds. One had a face smashed to a bloody pulp, and the other stared at her with empty eyes, his head twisted unnaturally. The stranger was half naked but far from bared since he had multiple knives and other odd sharp things strapped about his arms and torso. The instruments of death flowed with every motion of his body, as though they were part of him. He called to her as he bent over one of the bodies.

"You may come out now," he said.

Ilanet exited the stall and approached with caution. She had seen many men become angry during and after sparring sessions, even those who had won. This had been far worse than sparring, and she had no desire to draw the stranger's ire. She turned so that she could see into the yard without looking past the dead bodies or at the half naked assassin.

"What happened?" she asked. "Why did they suddenly attack?"

The stranger stood after collecting the men's purses and retrieved another tunic from his pack. Ilanet was glad when he covered himself and the armory he carried with him. No matter her father's expectations, Ilanet was not ready to be alone with a man, much less an unclothed one.

"We will go to the house to find out," he said as he strapped on the armor he had been wearing the night they met.

Ilanet glanced down at the dead men and then quickly averted her eyes. "Are all assassins as good as you?"

The stranger looked at her quizzically. "If by *good* you mean *Skilled*, then no. If you are referring to morality, then I am sure most of them are far better than I." Ilanet thought she might have seen uncertainty behind his cold gaze before he continued. "I have come to realize that the principles under which I operate are inconsistent with the standards by which outworlders judge themselves and others."

Ilanet did not know what an *outworlder* was but figured she must be one of them. With another glance at the bodies, she decided that she would save that question for another time. It was strange the way he referred to himself, almost as if he were only a soldier following orders with no choice in the matter. Perhaps he was. She wondered whom he served and how anyone could hope to leash such a deadly creature. The stranger had said that he had never loved anyone, so she doubted his master was holding the safety of a family over him. Perhaps he served out of loyalty or honor.

She had heard her father warn her brothers on many occasions never to trust in a man's loyalty or honor. *Loyalty and honor are enough for knights who may win you battles*, he would say, *but eventually knights become tired and jaded. If that does not kill them, then fear and greed win their hearts. Fear and greed lead to wealth and power, and* they *will win you a kingdom.*

Whatever the stranger's motives, she knew one thing. She had no desire to get involved in anything that was about to happen in that house.

"Maybe I should just wait here," she said.

"You will come with me," he said, dashing that hope. "Neither of these men is Brendish, and we cannot know for sure that these are the only two he had with him. By now they may be aware of your presence. You are safer with me."

At least that made sense, she thought. Ilanet supposed she should be glad he had offered an explanation at all. Although at times the stranger seemed high-handed, his explanations for his actions always provided good reasons for being so. The man strapped his swords across his back but left his hood hanging. After situating his belongings in his pack, he picked it up and motioned for her to follow. The curtains swayed in the window as they approached the house, and the stranger did not wait for permission to enter. Urmel and Rella were in the kitchen. Both stepped back with fearful expressions, and Ilanet could understand their distress. The ragged traveler they knew as Roy was no longer the bumbling, self-conscious boy. This man dominated the room with a stern bearing and sharp gaze.

"Gather everyone in the parlor," he said.

Rella seemed eager to leave his presence as she pushed Urmel toward the doorway. Ilanet stepped quietly as she followed the stranger through the house. Somehow, he did not make a sound, an oddity that she now remembered from their castle escape but had forgotten. When they arrived in the parlor, Urmel and Rella were standing pensively behind the settee, a woman Ilanet had not met stood by the hearth gripping the fire poker with attempted subtlety, and a second unknown woman sat on the bench by the front window holding an empty candelabra. Tiani was on the settee embracing a shaken Grebella. The madam's hands trembled as she dabbed at the mixture of tears and blood trailing down her face. Grebella glanced up when they entered, and Ilanet slipped into the room to one side at the stranger's direction.

Fresh tears bathed the madam's cheeks upon seeing them. "Oh, Roy, I'm so sorry. I shouldn't've ..."

Her voice broke off, and she blinked up at the stranger several times. For a moment, he was still as a gravestone, and then he began stalking back and forth in front of the doorway. Ilanet thought he looked like one of the giant cats sizing up his prey, searching for the ideal position from which to pounce. He stopped in front of Grebella, his icy blue eyes seeming to swallow the woman's soul.

"What happened?" he asked, his voice deep and harsh.

Grebella was silent as she stared, and then she abruptly sucked in a breath as though just remembering to breathe. "I, um, Brendish was angry," she said with a glance toward the floor.

For the first time, Ilanet noticed the bloodied body of a man that was mostly hidden from her view by the coffee table.

"More than that. He was furious. He was yellin' at me to get him more money, but I already done paid him *twice* this month. I didn't 'ave the money he wanted. He started hittin' me, and I jus' ... I don't know what happened ... I jus' *stabbed* him with the knife! I don't even know how it got in my hand." She shook her head and wiped at her bloodied mouth and nose. "Then, Tiani came in and screamed."

Tiani looked up with tearful eyes. "It was my fault. I shouldn'ta screamed. Just, I saw all the blood."

Grebella squeezed Tiani's knee and shook her head. "Those two idiots came poundin' down the stairs, and when they saw, they started comin' at me. I thought they'd kill me an' the girls. I don't know why I did it. You gotta believe me, Roy. It jus' slipped out. I-I told 'em you did it. I told 'em *you* killed Brendish and ran out the back."

The stranger was silent for several moments as he stared at the woman. Finally, he said, "Perhaps some of the fault is mine. I wanted you to feel comfortable and safe in my presence. When you felt threatened, your thoughts were instinctually drawn to me."

The women's concerned glances toward each other spoke to their confusion. While it was obvious that *Roy* was not who he had led them to believe, no one yet dared the question.

Grebella looked to the floor shamefully. "No, it ain't none of yer fault. Truth is, I didn't expect ya to live." Doubt and remorse filled her gaze when she sought the stranger once again. "Where they gone? How'd ya escape?"

The stranger's voice was soft, almost consoling. "You and I both know that would not have been possible—not for *Roy*. The result of your actions is that Royance is dead, and now you are left with *me*."

Grebella swallowed, and still her voice was but a whisper. "W-who are you?"

"You do not wish to know me, Madam Grebella. Those men you sent after Roy and this young lady"—he tipped his head toward Ilanet, and Grebella glanced at her guiltily—"are dead. You have three corpses on your property, and no one left to protect you. The investigators may be slow to pick up on the disappearance of a few *deplorables*, but they are tenacious and will not disregard any murder. The other businessmen in the area will become aware of Brendish's absence much more quickly, and you will be at their mercy. You may find your own protection, or you may serve me. The choice is yours."

"Serve you? You're not goin' to kill us?" Tiani asked.

The stranger tilted his head and fingered the hilt of the dagger at his waist. "Until recent events, you were kind to me, and you have been kind to the girl."

Tiani huffed an anxious laugh. "Recent events? You mean sendin' people to kill you."

"Yes, a minor infraction," he replied with a shrug. Ilanet was just as dumb-founded as the others judging by their expressions.

Tiani asked, "How's tryin' to kill you a *minor* infraction?"

"You sent men to kill *Roy*. I expect you will not make the same mistake with me. Previous events are no longer relevant. You survived. I survived. Brendish and two of his men are dead. Shall we move on?"

Grebella stood to face the stranger. Her face was swollen, but most of the bleeding had stopped. Ilanet remembered how it felt to bear such injuries. Although she was angry that the woman's actions might have meant her death under different circumstances, she could not completely fault the women. There were times when the beatings her father had given her had been so painful that she would likely have thrown someone else to the wolf had it been an option. She also knew the shame of even thinking of committing that horrible deed. No, she did not blame Grebella. Oddly, she thought that neither did the assassin.

"What would ya 'ave us do, and how are ya gonna protect us?" the madam asked.

Instead of answering, the stranger said, "How many entities did Brendish oversee?"

Grebella glanced around at the other women, "Oh, um, I think there was three brothels includin' this one, two gamblin' houses …"

"Don't forget the fights," interjected the woman by the hearth.

Grebella nodded. "Right, they call it the Burrow. It's where they fight for sport, if ya can call it that."

"Very well," the stranger said. "I will secure Brendish's holdings. It will be up to you to maintain them."

Grebella balked. "*Me?*"

The stranger spread his hands and glanced around the room. "Who else?"

"No, I couldn't ..."

"Then I suggest you find someone who can," he said, "and hope he does not stab you in the back. Really, Madam Grebella, you are better off attempting the management on your own. You will have all of Brendish's resources at your disposal."

"How's that? What makes ya think they'll listen to *me*?" Grebella asked.

"Because they will fear *me*," the stranger said.

"But you won't be here, will ya?"

He smiled fiendishly and said, "No, but I have a certain reputation."

With a nod toward the dead man, she said, "What about him an' the other two?"

"I will take credit for their deaths. When the investigators come around, you tell them that I killed these men and forced you to submit. With my mark upon the bodies and those that are to come, the investigators will not doubt your story."

Tiani rose from her seat. "You're gonna kill more people?"

The stranger shrugged and said, "Not so many. These people are like wild animals. I must show my teeth to assert dominance."

Ilanet's voice erupted of its own volition. "But the investigators will come after you!"

The stranger turned to regard her with his eerie blue eyes. "Perhaps, but I doubt it. The investigators' job is to discover the culprit. In this, they will have no doubt. Ionius knows he would need a much greater force to take me. I was going to have to do something to punish his insolence anyway."

The way he spoke of her father was disconcerting, and yet she found herself mentally applauding him. Ilanet had never heard anyone mention her father without a hint of fear. Still, this man was an assassin, and these were her people.

She said, "You told me you had no desire to make a claim here."

"I do not. I am perfectly willing to walk away and leave these women to their fate. However, it was only minutes ago that you implored me to help this woman, did you not?"

Ilanet glanced at Grebella. "Well, yes."

"Then let this serve both our purposes. I will take only the smallest piece" —he tilted his head toward the women—"as a warning to Ionius." He must have read the horror on her face, for he smiled most disturbingly and said, "Of course, I will only do so if they agree."

Grebella glanced between them and then said, "You speak of the king as if ya know him, and it don't sound like yer on his good side. Mayhap I don't wanna know who ya are, but I think I'm needin' to—'specially if we're gonna be dependin' on this reputation of yers."

The stranger tilted his head and then bowed a most courtly bow. "Madam Grebella, allow me to introduce myself. I am called the Raven."

~

"It's not so bad, you know," said Reaylin.

Frisha huffed but refused to rise to the bait.

"No, really. How many people can say they know the *king*? And he's never said so, but I think he considers me a friend."

Frisha looked over at the woman who was thumbing through a book that one of the healers had assigned her to read. "Friends? You've finally given up on trying to claim him?"

Reaylin shrugged. "I thought he was just a warrior like me. Two warriors are a good match. We'd understand each other, you know? But a king needs a queen, and we both know I ain't no queen."

Frisha could not help but notice the small smile that crept across Jimson's face as he peered through the porthole at the gulls swooping down to catch their dinner from the bay. She was surprised by the other woman's sensible response. It all seemed so clear and uncomplicated the way Reaylin said it. She wondered why it was such a mess in her own mind.

"You're not a queen either."

Frisha abruptly pulled herself back to the conversation. "What?"

Reaylin rolled her eyes and closed the book. "Don't be daft, Frisha. There's nothing about you that says *queen*. You don't walk like a queen, you don't talk like a queen, you don't *dress* like a queen."

Frisha scowled as her face heated. "What do *you* know of being queen?"

"That's the point. *I* don't know what they do. Do you?"

"I could learn ..."

"Oh, please. Kings marry duchesses or princesses. A king's bed is big, though, and there's always room for a mistress," Reaylin said with wicked grin.

Frisha felt the fury radiating from her face, and Reaylin's smirk fell.

The woman shrugged and said, "Where there's room for one mistress, there's bound to be room for two."

Jimson turned and, for once, his feelings were plain on his face. He shouted, "You would settle for being a king's mistress when you could be an officer's *wife*?" He snapped his mouth shut and glanced away. He then bowed to no one in particular and said, "Pardon my outburst. Please excuse me."

Reaylin watched in apparent shock as Jimson stormed out of the cramped quarters and down the narrow corridor, and then she skittered out in the opposite direction. Frisha hated Reaylin at that moment more than ever. It was not that Reaylin was wrong—just the opposite. Reaylin was voicing the doubts that had been plaguing Frisha ever since she discovered that Rezkin was the True King.

Before she met Rezkin, she had been tormented every night by nightmares of her future husband. She would travel to Kaibain and there be auctioned off like a prized sow—or perhaps not so prized by noble standards. Every nightmare was different. In one, her husband was a slovenly old man, grown fat by the toils of his servants, who raged at the least offense. In another, he was stern and sanctimonious, prized piousness and propriety in equal measure, and believed laughter and joy to be sin. Other times, he was wonderfully handsome and yet a terrible philanderer, locking her away while he laughed and lounged amongst the frills of other women's petticoats.

Rezkin had been different. He had been a gentleman and a savior. Even when she thought he was merely a young traveler of little consequence she had felt insecure and a bit inferior. She had lived a sheltered life. She had never traveled, and she had no special talents. She had always known that one day she would marry and raise children. What else was there for her?

Rezkin did not talk much, though. It had been difficult to get to know him, to find out what he liked and disliked. She had tried to find common ground, even going so far as to attempt to learn the sword. She figured that if he carried two of them then they must be important to him, and she did want to be able to protect herself. The metal monstrosity had been terribly heavy, and she had been afraid that she would cut off her own leg. Anxious about disappointing him, she had given the excuse that she could not carry a sword because she was a woman. The disapproval in his eyes had her worried that she had made a mistake. When he showed up with the set of knives, she had been elated. He was at least trying to meet her half way. Truthfully, she hated the knives almost as much as the sword. She kept at it, though, because she wanted to prove to him, and to herself, that she was capable. He seemed to put value in that quality. Plus, the gift had been costly, and she did not want to appear ungrateful.

Frisha knew she had shortcomings as far as many of the others were concerned. She had not been trained as a warrior, she had no *talent*, and she was not of high standing among the nobles. Frisha had always been a romantic, though, and she knew that her greatest gift to her future husband was her love and devotion. She had thought to give those to Rezkin, but that was before she had seen his emptiness. She was no longer certain she could offer those to him. Her mother had once told her that if you pour water into a well with no bottom, the well will never fill, and you will keep pouring until you too are empty.

"Pay no attention to Reaylin, Frisha," Malcius said.

Frisha had almost forgotten his presence. Malcius was sitting on a short stool leaning back in the corner behind her. He, too, was reading a book, but his appeared to have something to do with military tactics. She briefly wondered if he chose it intentionally or if nothing else was available.

"She is crass and simple minded," he continued. "Rezkin chose you, and she has not yet accepted it—not that she was ever truly an option. I know not what the good captain sees in her, but I suppose he is used to dealing with commoners."

"Perhaps he was struck in the head too many times during training," Brandt proposed as he ducked into the room and settled himself in the chair that Reaylin had vacated.

Frisha fought back the tears and said, "I don't know, Malcius. I think she may be right."

Malcius and Brandt shared a look that was too close to pity.

Malcius said, "Look, if this is about your speech and style, we can teach you what you need to know."

"Shiela is the expert on modern fashion," Brandt added, "or so she claims."

Malcius nodded and said, "The strikers have spent much time in the palace, and Tieran is as close as you can get to royalty. They will be able to tell you about queen's business."

Frisha nodded and said, "I'll think about it."

She was both appreciative and irritated by her cousin's show of support.

When first they set out on their voyage he would barely look at her. Had they grown so much closer through their trials, or was the prospect of her becoming queen encouragement enough? She glanced out the porthole just as a gull swept past with a fish clutched in its beak. At least Reaylin was honest in her opinions and intentions, she thought. Then, she felt guilty for doubting Malcius. She buried her face in her hands and wondered, *How did life get so complicated?*

Bilior padded through the human settlement. It was larger than those he had visited on the few unfortunate occasions in the past. When first he had arrived, he donned the aura of a human female. People had spoken to him, though, and he did not care for that. He wished to interact with the humans no more than he desired to be in their settlement. The humans were strange, rejecting the balanced variety of animals in the wild but permitting the small felines to enter their domain unhindered and unmonitored. If only they knew the felines' thoughts, they would not be so careless. Still, it was a boon to Bilior, for he much preferred the aura of nature's beast. It mattered little that these had been tainted by the meddlesome humans' standards of selective breeding. The little felines were still wild in spirit.

He followed the scent of the young king. It was difficult to pick out at first, amongst all the noxious smells of the settlement. The sensitive nose of the cat, enhanced by his own powers, was both a blessing and a curse. By the scent trails, he could tell that the king had been all over the settlement, but they were focused strongly in one area. The structures in this section were built of old wood that had long lost its soothing energy, and Bilior mourned the sacrifice. Like the Ahn'tep peoples before them, the life energy of the humans lacked the balance of the other animals. He supposed that was the intent of the gods, but he did not care for it all that much.

The strongest scent of the king was in a deadwood structure that was partially open to the elements, and the ground was covered in piles of dried, dead plants. Bilior would never understand why the humans chose to surround themselves with death, but he supposed it had something to do with their connection to Nihko, Goddess of Death and the Afterlife.

The Ahn'an were created only of the essences of Rheina, the Goddess of the Firmament and the Realm of Life, and Mikayal, God of the Soul. Thus,

Bilior did not possess a connection to Nihko. The humans and the other Ahn'tep bore the essences of all three of the Ahn, who the humans called gods. Ahn'tep souls were hosted in Rheina's realm for a time, and then they passed into Nihko. Sometimes, the Ahn'tep returned, only to leave again. It was an intriguing cycle, and Bilior occasionally wondered about where they went when they left Rheina, but he would never know. His kind had no Afterlife, no realm to keep his soul separate. Once removed from its body, the Ahn'an returned to Mikayal, becoming part of the whole, an individual no more. Bilior liked being *one*, and he would fight to keep his *self*.

That *self* was threatened so long as he remained in the Realm of Life. The Ahn had reserved the Realm of Life for the Ahn'tep, and any Ahn'an who did not accede to the will of the Ahn were removed, sent to Ahgre'an. While the Ahn'an were blessed with Ahgre'an, the Daem'Ahn were contained within H'khajnak. The Ahn'an were permitted to stay in the Realm of Life only so long as they did not interfere too much with the lives of the Ahn'tep. It was for this reason that the Daem'Ahn were not permitted in the Realm of Life. The humans called the the Daem'Ahn *evil*, but truly they were *chaos*. The Daem'Ahn were composed only of Rheina and Nihko, lacking the soul of Mikayal that would render them *alive*. Thus, they felt not even the most primitive connection with other beings, and they could not comprehend the need for balance or order or growth. Bilior wondered if the Daem'Ahn saw the soul as an infestation that needed to be destroyed.

Just as it was possible for the Ahn'an to reside within the Realm of Life, so too could the Daem'Ahn—under the right conditions and against the will of the Ahn. It was to the misfortunes of both the Ahn'An and Ahn'tep that those conditions had been met.

Bilior decided that he would wait in the structure where the king's scent was strongest. He eyed the dead plant material but had no desire to touch it. The dry dirt was filled with potential, though. After selecting a few seeds from the soil at his feet, he encouraged lush greenery to grow into a thick patch and then curled his feline body into a ball atop it. His feline aura was happy in this position, although he would have preferred to be higher. He turned his gaze to the dead wood above and found a pair of similar eyes staring back at him from atop a dead branch that had been straightened and smoothed. The furry creature looked back at him and hissed. Bilior sloughed the feline aura, returning to his comfortable self. He released a tendril of power to encourage the feline to come to him and licked his lips in anticipation.

~

Rezkin sat in the chair beside the king's bed. It was dark, and Ionius was asleep, as was the young mistress beside him. He briefly wondered how she could possibly sleep through the cacophony emanating from the old king, but the strong scent of spirits was explanation enough. Rezkin took a moment to rest before the imminent confrontation. Earlier in the evening, he had gone to each of the brothels and the gambling houses and the Burrow and made it clear to Brendish's men that he was now in charge. Some of them had taken more convincing than others, but after the first several deaths that had been bloodier than necessary, they began to fall in line. His hold would be tenuous and probably would not last long, but at least Grebella was off the hook for the deaths of Brendish and his lackeys. Additionally, since all Brendish's holdings had been hit by the Raven, no one would focus on the single brothel in which he and the princess had been staying. It was now time for Rezkin to use the evening of unplanned bloodshed to his own advantage.

"Ionius," he said.

The older man did not stir. Rezkin shook the king and then shook him harder. It was reaffirmation of the need to stay vigilant and clearheaded, even in one's sleep. He slapped the man hard and then barely gained his feet in time as the chair in which he had been sitting was ripped from beneath him and shattered against the wall in a burst of wind. Ionius sat up with a shout and lashed out with another violent gale. The bed curtains billowed, a lamp crashed to the floor, and a tapestry was ripped from its hooks. Rezkin made a mental note to establish a larger focus shield the next time he antagonized a wind mage.

"Guards! Who dares enter my bedchamber? Guards!" Ionius shouted.

"You may stop yelling, Ionius. No one is coming. They have all been ... incapacitated."

"Who is there? Show yourself!"

"A task made difficult by the fact that you destroyed the lamp," Rezkin mused. "Again, we find ourselves enjoying the peace of darkness together, Ionius."

"You! What are you doing here, Demon, and what have you done to my guards?"

"I am inclined to believe that your inquiry is made less out of concern for your guards' well-being than it is for the fact that they are unable to save you from *me*. I am curious about your companion, though. Are you sure she is alive?"

"What? Of course, she is alive," Ionius muttered. He nudged the woman with a firm jab to the ribs, and she snorted but did not awaken. "See? Now what do you want, Raven?"

"Very well. Let us move past the pleasantries and on to business. You failed to comply with our agreement."

Ionius gained his feet and snatched a night robe from the floor. He donned the garment and stepped toward the Raven, shaking his fist in the air. "I gave him that worthless island *and* my daughter. It is what you wanted. *I* am king of this land, not you, and I shall not bow to a demon in the dark."

"You could have been rid of me, Ionius, but you failed in the simplest task. Everything was arranged, the difficult part done, but you had to add your own stipulations."

"Bah! Minor things to get the collectiare and the council off my back."

"Lies," the Raven hissed. "The council was already in line, and you could have rejected the collectiare's *advice*. You placed those stipulations to satisfy your own ego, and now you will feel the sting of consequence."

"What are you going to do? You agreed to stay out of my kingdom!"

"It is not what I am going to do but what I have already done. I took a *minor thing* and have graced you with a mere taste of my abilities. In a matter of hours, I have claimed a slice of your capital city. You leave it be, or I shall claim more."

"You expect me to turn a blind eye as you invade my city?" Ionius spat with disgust.

"It is no worse than what was already there. Only, now you know that it is *mine*, and you will remember in the future that your *deplorables* keep the remainder at my behest."

"You may keep the filth if it suits you. You are nothing but a gutter-born criminal, a rat. Where there is one rat, there are hundreds, and still they are just rats. Do you know what hungry rats do when they sense weakness? They turn cannibal. I need not spend the time and effort to exterminate you. The other vermin will eventually do it for me."

The Raven paced toward the open window where the first lightening of the sky turned black to indigo. "You conveniently hide behind an ill-conceived metaphor when the task becomes too daunting. Much the better for me, but you should remind yourself that I am not, in fact, a rat. I am an intelligent and powerful man like you."

"You are nothing like me!" Ionius snapped. "I am a king of rich, royal blood, born of a line of kings that have held this kingdom for centuries. The Maker smiles upon my house."

"Oh? And what of your daughter? You have not asked to her well-being," the Raven said.

"I have washed my hands of the useless whelp. No doubt you have sullied her virtue and any price she might have brought. She will wed this Dark Tidings, and if he should win the Ashaiian throne in truth, perhaps then she may carry the honor of my royal house again."

"I see. That rich, royal blood flows only through the veins of male line then. Tell me, Ionius. How many sons do you really need?"

Ionius stormed toward the Raven shouting, "You stay away from my sons!"

The Raven smiled and said, "All in good time, *King* Ionius."

Then, he was out the window, vanishing into the dark as Ionius shouted obscenities that could make the moon blush.

8

The clouds were awash in gold and magenta, and the first rays of dawn were spreading across the eastern sky as Rezkin slipped into the stables. He could have claimed a place in the house, but he preferred to be alone. The thought crossed his mind that he might have liked the company of Tam or Malcius, or possibly even Tieran. Then, he considered that, if any of them knew what he had been up to that night, they would not want to be near *him*. The realization troubled him because he could not find fault in his actions. Ilanet, Grebella, and the other women of the brothel were in trouble. His plan was the most efficient and effective method of ensuring their survival in the allotted time, while also furthering his own agenda to save the refugees and take the first steps in creating the kingdom and army demanded by the katerghen so that he could face an impending demon invasion. A few dozen criminal casualties seemed a small price to pay.

Releasing a heavy breath, Rezkin decided that his concerns were ill conceived. It was potentially a violation of *Rule 37—separate from one's emotions* and was inconsistent with the intent of *Rule 42—reconsider actions that end in failure*. Thus far, his actions appeared to be successful, so it was unnecessary and unwise to second-guess himself. He entered the dark stables cautiously. Now that the women knew he was the Raven, there was the chance that one of them had told someone else. He searched the recess overhead and the first few stalls, poking at the hay with the tip of his sword. When he reached the opposite end where he slept most often, he found a most incongruous sight. There, amongst the golden hay and drab dirt, barely lit by the rising sun, was a black-and-grey striped cat curled upon a bed of thick, green grass. The cat opened one yellow eye and peered up at him. It yawned and stretched, completely unconcerned by the potential predator that had just entered its den. It then turned and sat facing Rezkin expectantly with its tail wrapped around its legs.

Rezkin did not care for the creature's behavior or the odd greenery beneath it. "Shoo, go!" he said with a wave of his free hand.

The cat blinked lazily but remained comfortably perched upon its bed. It meowed a pretty little trill, and then jumped as though startled by its own sound. It smiled. He had spent little time around cats, but even so, Rezkin had never seen one smile. He thought it disturbing. He wondered if sleep deprivation was having a detrimental effect on his mind, and this seemed to be confirmed when a moment later the cat began to change. Its fur appeared to retract into its skin, and its body and limbs elongated to hardened, thin twigs. The yellow-orange eyes of the katerghen stared back at him from beneath fronds of feather-leaves that rattled with the sound of rain. The creature grinned, and Rezkin spied between its tiny razor teeth little tufts of fur.

Unexpected anger surged through him, and Rezkin snatched the katerghen by throat. The creature's feet did not leave the ground, but rather his neck and torso elongated to reach Rezkin's height. An icy fire splashed against Rezkin's insides as battle energy swept through his veins, and a distant voice warned Rezkin that he had somehow lost control. His thoughts, however, were for one thing only.

"Where is it? Where is the little cat—the one with black and brown splotched fur?"

The katerghen grinned again, and then a thunderous boom rocked the stables as Rezkin was thrown into the far wall. He blinked several times, and the ceiling swam into view. He frowned as he pondered in the darkness. His first thought was that the fur between the katerghen's teeth had been white and orange. Then, his reaction to the katerghen began to dawn on him, and he was confused. It had been as if he were visiting a dream, aware that he was dreaming and yet unable to control the events. Except this had not been a dream. His lungs finally filled with air, and he gasped. When he had finally caught hold of his breath, he realized he was no longer staring at the ceiling. Yellow-orange eyes set in the face of a demonic tree stared back at him from only inches away. The katerghen was sitting on his chest and appeared to be studying him like one would a foreign insect.

Rezkin coughed once and said, "What do you want, Bilior?"

He felt as though he were being pulled into the katerghen's gaze as it said, "Light behind darkness—the curse of thy soul. Fracture thine heart, and broke becomes whole."

Rezkin did not move. It was obvious the katerghen could defeat him with a thought. Still, he had no idea what the thing was talking about.

"We had a deal," Rezkin said. "A haven, a kingdom, for an army. It will take more than a couple of days to create an army."

With the creaking of boughs in a breeze, Bilior said, "Yes."

Rezkin sighed under the weight of the katerghen, which seemed to be increasing by the minute. "Then, what is it you want?"

Bilior jumped from his perch and clung to a rafter for no apparent reason. He swung several times before tumbling to the floor and ending in a crouch just as Rekzin regained his feet.

"The *you* needs care—you and yours. Safety was promised. A kingdom, I said. Far away an isle—long left to the dead."

"I know the deal—"

"And so must be reached."

"You are here to fulfill your part of the bargain?" Rezkin asked with surprise.

He had thought that Bilior's responsibility was already met with the gift of information. Bilior crouched lower to the ground, and his twiggy hair seemed to droop.

"Safety reached, a kingdom made—the price be paid."

"You are saying that if my people and I fail to establish this kingdom of safety, then you will be in breach of contract? You must serve me?"

Thunder rumbled and the katerghen hissed. "I, I, I—not *I*. Of the Ancients am I. For the council, I speak."

Rezkin could hardly believe his ears. This playful, irritating little creature was one of the rulers of the fae, an Ancient of the Ahn'an.

"You speak on behalf of the Ancients? I did not make this deal with only you?"

"For all the we, you did agree."

Until that moment, Rezkin had not seriously considered the existence of demons. The katerghen had requested an army to invade Ashai, or at least defend against it. At the time, it had seemed a reasonable price since Rezkin already intended to create one. If Bilior had been sent to strike a deal on behalf of *all* the Ahn'an, presumably the most powerful, albeit aloof, creatures on the planet, then the demon threat had to be serious. If the Ahn'an were threatened, then so was everyone else. It was the kind of threat that could end the world, and it seemed that the fae had thrown all their eggs into one basket. That basket belonged to Rezkin.

Rezkin felt a heavy weight settle onto his shoulders. He had left the northern fortress with no more purpose or direction than to find Farson and protect and honor his mysterious friends. In a few short months, he had taken on the burden of usurping a throne, rescuing hundreds, possibly thousands, of refugees, creating an entirely new kingdom, and becoming the savior of the Ahn'an and human races.

A shriek from the doorway drew him out of his shock.

Ilanet cried, "What is *that*?"

Bilior bounced up like an uncoiling spring and bounded over to the frightened young woman. Ilanet backed away but not fast enough. The creature boxed her into a corner and peered at her as it clung to the top of the doorframe. He licked his lips and looked back to Rezkin.

"I may eat this?"

Rezkin sighed and said, "No, you may not eat her. She is one of mine."

Bilior's twigs trembled in what Rezkin thought was disappointment. "A *human* yours," he muttered.

Ilanet placed her hands on her hips and looked at Rezkin with a stern countenance that, for some reason, nearly brought a smile to his face.

"Do not call me yours, *Raven*. I do not belong to you." She looked away and said, "Apparently, you and my father have conspired to give me to *Dark Tidings*."

Rezkin furrowed his brow. The princess had not seemed angry with him when he had left the previous night, although she had been quiet after he revealed that he was the Raven. He wondered what had happened to incite her ire. Perhaps the women of the house had said something.

Bilior watched the princess with rapt attention as she fussed. He tilted his head and looked back to Rezkin. "Raven they call you? This be your name?"

"No," Rezkin said.

"Yes," Ilanet followed with a huff. "He is the infamous Raven, the criminal overlord of Ashai, possibly the most powerful *deplorable* ever! He has killed hundreds of people in his bid to build an empire of the most despicable human beings alive."

Bilior muttered, "Kills humans, saves keurg?"

Ilanet looked back at the creature. "What is a keurg, and what are *you*?"

Bilior skittered to the ground, thrust his arms out to the sides, and said, "I be a tree."

With a dubious look, Ilanet said, "I do not believe you."

The katerghen twisted its torso, and an instant later there stood a tree—a small one—in the middle of the stables. The princess gawked and then turned a questioning gaze on Rezkin.

"Ignore the tree for now," he said. "I think there will be plenty of time for explanation later."

"I doubt that," she snapped, "since you will be handing me off in a few hours."

"Is that what has you so angry?" he asked.

Ilanet dropped her arms as the wind left her sails. "I am not angry. I am afraid."

"I see. You need not fret," Rezkin said. "Dark Tidings travels with a large entourage and many refugees. There will be nobles from several kingdoms, mages, healers, and plenty of other women. It may set your mind at ease to know that he has agreed to take on a couple of priests of the Maker. You will not be alone."

"But I am not just *traveling* with him. I am to be his ward, and, if my father has his way, his wife. No one knows anything about him—not even what he looks like."

Rezkin wished he could tell her the truth and set her mind at ease, but he could not for the same reason he had avoided using her name or title. He could not risk someone overhearing or chance that she might let it slip.

Instead, he said, "Your father does not always get his way."

"Oh, yes, he does," she argued.

"Perhaps in Channería, but you will not be in Channería."

"Where will I be?"

"It is best not to speak of it now. So long as you are awake, you might as well get ready."

"I am ready. I had only the one pack, remember?" she said, pointing to the tightly packed sack on the ground by the door.

A tingle of mage energy swept over Rezkin's chest, and he dodged out of the way just in time to avoid a glowing green javelin that smashed into the ground where he had been standing and then disappeared. His back collided with the princess who yelped as she was shoved farther into the corner. He pressed her into the wall restricting her movement, and, hopefully, preventing her from accessing any of his weapons. Peering through the open doorway and across the yard, he saw a shadowy figure perched on the rickety roof of the adjacent building. The man was too far away to reach with his daggers or the miniature crossbow latched to his belt.

"Stay here," he said to the princess before he dove across the opening. Two more javelins of green mage power struck the ground behind him as he scrambled for his pack that lay buried in the hay. Meanwhile, the tree that was Bilior stretched its boughs to wrap the flailing princess in a tangle of branches.

Rezkin strung his bow and grabbed four arrows before taking a position beside the doorframe. Peering around its edge, he saw that the figure remained where he had been, as though presenting himself as a target. Rezkin stuck one of the arrows into the ground beside him in the shadow of the doorframe. With two of the arrows held between his knuckles, he knocked the fourth and spied his target. Rezkin knew the man could see him, and yet he still did not hide or advance. The first three arrows shot through the air in quick succession, and the assailant used a tendril of power to smash them to pieces before they struck. The man had not seen the release of the fourth arrow, though, and did not have time to compensate. He dodged to one side and tumbled from the roof. Rezkin could not see what happened to the man beyond the wall of the yard.

"Did you get him?" Ilanet asked, peeking through the creature's branches. She was hesitant to touch the creepy creature-tree, and she did not care for being surrounded by it. The Raven did not appear concerned, but she was not optimistic that the notorious criminal overlord would have such feelings for anyone, much less a useless, displaced princess.

"No," Rezkin said as he searched the yard and beyond with a sharp gaze.

"Will you go after him?" Ilanet asked.

"It may be a ploy to draw me out, to lure me away from you," he said as he rested the bow against the frame. "But I think I need not go to him. He will come to me."

"And this ... *tree*—it is protecting me?" she asked hesitantly.

Rezkin spied the creature from the corner of his eye. "Perhaps ... or it is preparing to eat you. It is difficult to say."

"What?" Ilanet shrieked as she struck the branches and kicked at what she thought to be the trunk.

Rezkin drew Bladesunder while tracking a shadow that swept over the yard. "Calm yourself. I believe you have little reason for concern."

Ilanet did not find his words encouraging. After all, *little* reason was not *no* reason, and she was trapped. She was startled when a face appeared in the bark of the trunk within her cocoon. It studied her curiously with yellow-orange eyes and grinned. Her gaze was riveted on its dozens of needlelike teeth.

In a strange, sing-song voice, it said, "Raven's sparrow entwined. A deal kept. Safety in mind."

Ilanet's heart pounded furiously, but she tried to grasp the meaning of the creature's words. "Raven's sparrow? That is *me*? I am safe? You are saying that I am safe?"

The creature did not answer, and the face dissolved back into the trunk. She tried to contain her fear-filled whimpers as she tugged at the branches with shaking fingers, hoping for a better view of her surroundings. She caught sight of a shadowy figure just as it sailed past the Raven.

Rezkin dodged out of the way as the assailant swung down from the roof. The man kicked out at his head, but Rezkin ducked and grabbed the offending foot. The skillful assailant used the leverage in conjunction with his own momentum to wrap around Rezkin's body. Rezkin dropped to the ground, landing on the man with his full bodyweight. He jammed the pointed, teardrop shaped pommel of Bladesunder into the man's ribs, eliciting a heavy grunt, and then rolled out of the assailant's reach before regaining his feet. The assailant lurched to his feet and bowed to stave off Rezkin's attack.

Maintaining his guard, Rezkin said, "Xa Jeng'ri, must I be prepared for this kind of greeting each time we meet?"

Xa grinned and said, "One must always be prepared."

"Of course," Rezkin said, "but why have you come?"

Xa's smile fell. "I have been cast out—at least until the Ong'ri passes judgment. In essence, I am on suspension." An expression of remorseful acceptance slipped across his face. "It is better than I expected."

"That does not explain why you are *here*," Rezkin said.

"I thought to convince you to present yourself to the Order so that they, too, may recognize you as the Riel'gesh."

"I do not have time for frivolities," Rezkin said as he sheathed Bladesunder.

Xa winced. "I may not return to the Order without you. If you will not go to them, then I shall accompany you."

"I am ever cognizant of the dangers that surround me, but I cannot travel with those who seek to test me at every turn. You are an unnecessary risk."

"You are the Raven Riel'gesh. You wage war from the shadows on more than one monarch. You need all the resources you can get. I will serve you with honor."

Rezkin pondered the opportunity. The Jeng'ri would be a major asset, but could he afford the risk? He said, "You are quick. I do not miss my target often."

Xa tugged the torn fabric at his shoulder, and his finger came away bloodied. "Still, you do not," he said.

Rezkin knew as little about Xa as he did the strikers with whom he traveled. Xa was perhaps the lesser threat so long as he believed Rezkin to be the Riel'gesh. Still, he could not afford continuous *testing* by his presumed allies while also remaining vigilant against his enemies. After a moment of contemplation, he said, "Beware, Xa Jeng'ri, the next time you attack me, I will kill you."

Xa bowed. "I will not test you again."

Rezkin did not believe the man. It was the way of the Order to gain rank through exploiting weakness in one's superiors. With the consequences of failure known, though, Xa would not attack unless he believed he could win. For the moment, at least, Xa believed Rezkin indomitable and perhaps even immortal.

Rezkin asked, "How did you find me?"

"I followed the bodies."

Rezkin nodded. Xa was more skilled than most, but if he could find Rezkin, then others would soon follow. It was time to leave. "Bilior, release the girl," he said.

The creature's face grew out of the trunk, peering at Rezkin and Xa. Bilior said, "Sparrow squawks and flitters. Not harmed."

The branches retracted as the tree-like body untwisted and shrank into

Bilior's previous form. Ilanet was left shaking as she hugged herself and stared at Rezkin and Xa with wide eyes.

"*Assassins,*" she hissed. "Always trying to kill one another and then congratulating each other on their failed efforts." She glanced at Bilior. "And trees with eyes and teeth that try to eat you! What have you gotten me into?"

Xa's expression held disapproval as he looked to Rezkin. "She seems ungrateful that you granted her life."

Rezkin raised a brow. "Says the man who just tried to kill me *again.*"

The easy smile returned to the Jeng'ri's face. "It was a good battle." He pointed at Bilior and asked, "Did you create this golem?"

Rezkin shook his head. Although he had never seen one, he had learned that golems were structures, usually constructed of inanimate objects, that were given only the semblance of life by their mage creators. "Bilior is not a golem. He is Ahn'an."

"What is Ahn'an?" Ilanet asked as she shuffled out of the corner while still clinging to the wall as far from Bilior as she could manage.

"If I am not mistaken, Ahn'an is the ancient name for the fae, the name still used by his people," Rezkin said with a gesture toward Bilior. "Specifically, he is a katerghen."

"You have one of the fae at your command?" Xa asked, again looking at Rezkin with a reverence that made him uncomfortable.

"I am not his master," Rezkin said. "We have entered into a deal, a treaty, if you will."

Xa's disapproval was evident. "I will refrain from questioning your intelligence and say that you are brave. What is this deal?"

"That is none of your concern," Rezkin replied as he shot a meaningful look at Bilior. The creature snapped his mouth shut, and the seam of his lips disappeared into smooth, wood-like flesh. Rezkin doubted the fae wanted to advertise the weakness that was their deal with him.

"He protected the girl but not you," Xa observed.

Bilior chittered as his twigs and leaves shook. Rezkin thought it might have been a laugh. "Sparrow breaks when Raven flies, but Raven falls to no human foe."

Xa stepped forward. "Then it is true? He is not human?"

"That is not what he meant," Rezkin said as he unstrung his bow and secured it to his sack.

Bilior tilted his head all the way over to rest on his shoulder and peered at the two warriors out of the corners of his yellow-orange eyes. It was an odd gesture that Rezkin had not yet seen and could not interpret. Bilior's head suddenly snapped upright, and he skittered out of the stables.

"What did he mean?" Ilanet asked.

"Only that he has confidence in my *Skills*," Rezkin answered. "Collect your belongings. You are leaving now."

Ilanet looked at him in alarm. "What? You are not going with me?"

Rezkin turned to Xa. "Your belongings are near?"

Xa nodded and glanced at the princess.

"Good," Rezkin said. "Since you are here, I have a task for you. Escort her to Dark Tidings's ship, *Stargazer*."

"You trust me to escort her?"

Rezkin shrugged and feigned disinterest. "Once you leave here, it is no longer my concern. If you fail to deliver, then you must contend with Dark Tidings."

"Is he such a threat?" Xa asked skeptically.

"You will see soon enough," Rezkin answered. "You are not to disclose who she is, only that you are passengers boarding at Dark Tidings's behest. He does not wish for others to know her identity until you near your destination. You will conduct yourself as her escort and guard until further notice." Turning to the princess, he said, "You will act as though he is your most trusted ally and friend. You have known him most of your life. After it becomes known who you are, you may identify him as a longtime member of the king's guard."

Ilanet glanced at the assassin. "No one will believe *he* is a member of the king's guard."

Rezkin turned to study Xa. In his unrelieved black and grey, studded with weapons, ropes, and hooks, he certainly did not look the part of a Channerían king's guardsman. "She is correct. Acquire a uniform on the way and stow it for later use. Remove the insignia of rank. Try to refrain from needlessly killing anyone."

Ilanet huffed. "That is not what I meant. He does not *act* like a king's guardsman."

Rezkin said to Xa. "Act like a king's guardsman."

Xa snapped to attention and saluted smartly. "By your command, sir." He followed the performance with a wink for the princess.

Ilanet left with Xa, making sure that Rezkin knew in no uncertain terms that she was angry with him for abruptly dumping her on the assassin. Although she knew he was the dreaded Raven, she had not treated him any differently. She was still a small-woman, though, and innocent. He doubted she truly understood the extent of the terror he had rained down on Ashai and, more recently, on a small portion of Serret. Had she seen the bodies, she might have felt differently. As it was, he had protected her, and she was intelligent enough to take advantage. He knew, both from the teachings of his masters and from his observations of outworlders, that the weak often attached themselves to the strong. Ilanet was physically weak and lacked endurance and skill, but she had shown true strength of spirit. It was a kind of strength that he would have undervalued before meeting Frisha.

With that thought, he turned and collected his pack. Just as he was approaching the open doorway, Bilior made an abrupt reappearance. The creature stretched himself upward to reach Rezkin's height, standing nearly chest to chest. Rezkin was uncomfortable with the proximity, but remained steadfast. The katerghen grinned and then thrust a fury beast between them. The little tortoiseshell cat hung limp as a kitten between the Bilior's twiggy fingers. It peered into Rezkin's eyes and mewled pitifully.

"What am I supposed to do with that?" he asked.

Bilior examined the cat and then looked back at Rezkin. By the odd tilt of his head, he appeared confused, but Rezkin could not be sure. "Black and brown, brown and black, small feline be your cat?"

"It does not belong to me. It is a wild animal," Rezkin said.

Bilior's leafy-feathers fluttered, and he grinned. "I may eat?"

Rezkin scowled. "No, you may not eat it." He snatched a burlap sack from a pile in the corner and emptied the rotting alfalfa and oats. Holding it open, he said, "Put it in here."

Bilior looked as though he was about to strangle the little beast.

"*Alive*," Rezkin added.

The katerghen's twigs drooped, and he slowly lowered the cat into the bag. He glanced at Rezkin several times, as if searching for approval. Or, Rezkin thought, maybe Bilior was hoping to gobble up the little furball without his noticing. He cinched the sack tightly with a short length of rope and then thought better of it. He did not want the cat to suffocate. Removing the rope, he elected to hold the bag closed until he reached his destination. He considered that at least the cat would be able to escape if something happened to him.

The streets were oddly desolate as he made his way toward the port district. He could hear shouting in the distance, but it was coming from the opposite direction, near the city center. Once he was in an area where the structures were more stable, he climbed atop the tallest spire, the bell tower of a temple, and peered across the sea of mismatched rooftops. Although he could see little detail from his vantage, it was apparent that masses of people were converging on an area that held several official residences. The city guards were overwhelmed, and it looked as though reinforcements were slow to respond. He briefly wondered if any of the guards had escaped to report the uprising, and then he decided that he did not care so long as his treaty and the princess both arrived at the ship.

9

The ship's crew was scurrying about hollering, hoisting, and hitching as they prepared *Stargazer* for departure. A group of passengers, mostly the wealthier foreigners, were gathered on the deck waiting for permission to disembark. Rezkin had ordered everyone to remain on board until the ship was ready to cast off, and the strikers were skillfully enforcing his will. In his drab traveler's clothes, he was able to slip into the stream of workers loading last-minute acquisitions with little more than a nod from Shezar as he boarded the ship. Tam's enthusiastic reaction upon seeing him was far more animated, and, for some reason, Rezkin felt pleased.

"Hey, Rez! I'm glad to see you're back, and it looks like you're in one piece. Kai said you made it to Serret, but I admit I was a bit worried." With a cheeky grin, he added, "More for us than you, I think." He leaned in and lowered his voice. "I never know if I can believe anything Kai says."

"It is good to see you, Tam," Rezkin said with a friendly smile as he mentally applauded his friend's assessment of the striker.

He stepped around Tam, continuing to his quarters, and Tam fell in beside him. Tam's eyes were drawn to the bag that seemed to be moving of its own accord at Rezkin's side.

"What's in the bag?" Tam asked.

"A cat," Rezkin said.

Tam looked at him quizzically. "Why do you have a cat in a bag?"

Rezkin looked at Tam sideways. "It was easier to carry this way."

The cat screeched and jerked against its confines before settling down again. Rezkin glanced at the bag and wondered why the little beast had suddenly become agitated when they boarded the ship.

Tam chuckled and said. "Yeah, but ... uh ... it doesn't seem very happy. Don't you think we should let it out?"

Rezkin looked around at the chaos of the ship's crew and passengers. "You want to let the cat out of the bag *here*?"

"Let the cat out of the bag about what?" Tieran asked as he sauntered up to them.

Rezkin frowned. "What are you talking about?"

"That is what I want to know," Tieran said, narrowing his eyes suspiciously.

Tam's gaze bounced between the two as they stared at each other in mutual confusion. Finally, he said, "Uh ... Rez has a cat in a bag. I was trying to find out why."

The cat chose that moment to protest its predicament again. Rezkin kept a firm grip as the bag lurched, a violent motion that was accompanied by an angry yowl.

Tieran's brows rose. "You have an *actual* cat in a bag."

"What other kind of cat would I have?" Rezkin asked as he passed the two and headed toward his quarters.

Tieran and Tam shared a look and then followed.

"Why do you have a cat?" Tieran asked.

"You have a cat?" Malcius asked, nearly colliding with them on the stairs.

Rezkin sighed. "Yes, I have a cat, and I am taking it to my quarters."

"*But why?*" Tam and Teiran blurted simultaneously.

"So it will not get injured on the deck," he said as though it was obvious.

He held on to the bag as he searched the room for hidden dangers.

"Rezkin, what is the purpose of the cat?" Malcius asked.

Rezkin scowled at his friend. "It is a cat, Malcius. Its purpose is to be a cat."

"Fine, but what is *your* purpose in having the cat?" Tieran asked with bemused frustration.

"Do I need a purpose?" Rezkin asked. "Everyone in Channería has a cat. Why is it odd that I possess one?"

Rezkin was irritated that they were interrogating him about his decision to bring the cat. He had no idea why he had claimed the little beast. It had been an impulse. Rezkin paused when he noticed the mood between his friends had suddenly lifted. They were smiling. Why were they smiling?

Malcius remarked, "I did not know you were a cat person, Rez."

"A what?" he asked.

Malcius and Tieran snickered as Tam said, "Someone who, you know, likes cats."

"There is a name for such a person?" Rezkin would never understand outworlders' obsessions with frivolous details. He shook his head. "I did not say I liked it. It is a practical animal."

"A dog is practical," Tieran argued. "Cats are just annoying. One of my aunts had a cat that she adored. Then, my cousin got one of those fancy, colorful birds. The cat ate the bird, and my cousin was so angry that she kicked it out of the third-floor window. The cat lived, but it did have a limp ever after. It hated my cousin." He paused upon noticing Rezkin's expression. "What?"

Tieran's story had ignited within Rezkin feelings of anger, although he did not know why he should care. It was just an animal, and it was not even his. Still, he felt it was wrong to punish an animal for doing what it was naturally inclined to do. The cat had not been malicious, just hungry. He was reluctant to express the undesired emotions, so he struck upon Tieran's other remark.

"Dogs can be useful, true, but they require maintenance. They must be bathed and fed, and you must ensure they get enough physical activity. They are impractical for keeping indoors since you must continually take them outside to relieve themselves. Cats are self-sufficient, and their hunting activities reduce the rodent population."

He released the cat from the bag, and it immediately hid under the desk, its yellow eyes glinting in the candle light. Rezkin glanced around the small space. The creature would need somewhere to relieve itself. He headed for the door and ascended the steps. Malcius, Tieran, and Tam followed.

"I cannot believe we are having this conversation," Malcius said. "It never goes anywhere."

"You have had such a conversation before?" Rezkin asked as Shezar and Kai approached.

Tam laughed, "I think everyone has this conversation."

"I have never had this conversation," Rezkin said.

"Welcome to the club," Malcius remarked with a chuckle.

"There is a club for this?"

They paused in their conversation to greet the strikers.

"You all look a bit tense," Kai observed. "What is happening?"

Rezkin said, "Apparently, I joined a club of individuals who argue over their preferences for certain domestic animals."

The strikers exchanged a quizzical look.

"Cats or dogs?" Tieran muttered with a smirk.

"Dogs," Kai answered immediately.

"Cats," Shezar said. Kai frowned at Shezar with disapproval, and Shezar shrugged unashamedly.

Rezkin looked at them in wonder. "You too?"

Tam grinned, "See, I told you. *Everyone.*"

Rezkin wondered why anyone would care to have the conversation at all, much less a large percentage of the outworlder population. It was a tradition that had even managed to span the gap between common carpenters and high-standing nobles, and it had been denied to him. Although he doubted the actual importance of the conversation, it reminded him once again how poorly he fit into outworlder society. For such a menial custom, the apparent lack on his part left him feeling even more distanced from his companions.

"Tieran, what did your aunt do to contend with the cat's need to relieve itself?"

Tieran sniffed as though he could smell the offensive odor at that moment. "I cannot say that I ever cared to know. I am sure the servants dealt with such issues."

Rezkin could feel a sense of irritation creeping up on him, another unde-sired emotion. He smothered it and said, "Find out what we need and make sure we have the appropriate supplies."

Tieran's expression was a mixture of bewilderment, disgust, and annoy-ance. "You do realize you are ordering the future Duke of Wellinven to procure supplies to collect cat excrement."

"You would prefer that *I* do it?" Rezkin asked.

"No, but ..."

Tam said, "I could ..."

"Just do it, Tieran," Rezkin snapped.

Tieran clenched his jaw and glared at Tam before storming away. Malcius glanced around uncomfortably and then hurried after Tieran. Rezkin turned to Kai and Shezar, who were both watching him with calculating eyes, and demanded an update. After learning that neither the treaty nor the priests had yet arrived, Rezkin sent Kai into the city to determine the source of the delay. He then dressed in the guise of Dark Tidings in preparation to receive the king's envoy and the princess. Shezar informed him of the ship's affairs and security concerns, and Tam went over the cargo manifest. Rezkin conferred with the captain and then did a quick inspection of the ship and passengers. One issue concerned him more than any other—he was growing impatient. He told himself the emotional upwelling was due to sleep loss, but never had he felt such a slip in control. He needed deep sleep and time to meditate—and food. He was hungry again.

As he was crossing the deck, he came upon a deckhand lugging a crate filled with soil and a small tree. "You!" he called. "Where did you get that?"

The deckhand paused, startled. "Ah, it were brought aboard with the cargo, Yer Majesty."

Rezkin sighed, but the disturbing sound that emanated from the mask caused the deckhand to step back. "Take it to my quarters," he said. Then it occurred to him that if he was not careful, that tree would eat his cat. Abruptly, he said, "No!" The deckhand jumped with a start and nearly dropped the crate. "Take it to the women's quarters, those in which Lady Frisha is staying. Place it in front of the porthole. Also, prepare another bunk."

He had no idea if a katerghen tree required light, but he had no need of an irritable fae creature aboard his ship. Fleetingly, he considered that Bilior might eat the women. The creature had assumed a protective role over the princess, and Rezkin hoped that he would continue to do so.

Turning to Shezar, he said, "You should prepare for another occupant in your berth as well."

"A striker?" Shezar asked.

"No, he is the guard for the young lady that will be joining us—the one that I told you about before."

They paused upon Captain Estadd's approach. "Your Majesty, a large group of people is demanding to be allowed to board."

Rezkin began to step away and then thought better of his decision not to inform the strikers that a master assassin would be bunking with them. He turned back and said, "He is of maximum threat level and should be watched carefully."

Rezkin caught the disgruntled expression on Shezar's face as they followed the captain to the railing. None of the strikers would appreciate being left in the dark about the Jeng'ri. Below on the pier, over thirty bedraggled people were huddled before a unit of the king's guards. Most of them appeared to possess no more than they could carry, but a few stood beside small carts or pack animals loaded with belongings. Some of these even had cages and crates filled with smaller livestock. To one side stood a few people of higher station, wealthier merchants or nobles, as evidenced by their apparel and the servants who were tending to their belongings.

One of the guardsmen and two of lesser rank pushed through the crowd to ascend the gangplank. These were followed by three additional men dressed in the garb of priests.

"Permission to board, Captain?" said the senior officer.

With a glance at Dark Tidings, Captain Estadd said, "Permission granted. What is this about?"

"I am Dronnicus, captain of the Channerían royal guard." He held up a rolled parchment tied and secured with the king's seal. "I seek an audience with the King of Cael. I come to deliver the treaty."

Shezar stepped forward and took the proffered parchment. After a quick examination, he handed it to Rezkin. Of course, they would need to name him in the document, and Dark Tidings was hardly an appropriate name for a King. As usual, Rezkin did not care what people called him so long as his claim to the island was legitimate. The treaty was succinct, the terms exactly as agreed, without the flowery embellishments typical of interkingdom bureaucracy. It was very much like Ionius. So was the unexpected mass of people on the pier.

"Who are they?" Dark Tidings said with a nod toward the crowd.

"By order of King Ionius, all Ashaiians, regardless of station or immigration status, are to vacate the kingdom, by force if necessary. Our merciful collectiare suggested you might have a desire to provide aid or refuge to those we have collected from the city thus far. He has generously directed us to deliver them here under his authority."

Rezkin turned his fathomless dark gaze on the guard. "If I do not?"

"Your Majesty?"

"If I do not desire to take on the responsibility of additional refugees? If I choose not to take them on a ship with a questionable fate to an uninhabitable and inhospitable island? What then? What becomes of the Ashaiians who came to this kingdom under the banner of friendship and trade within a centuries-long alliance?"

Dronnicus's gaze flicked away and then returned so quickly it might have been missed by a less observant man. It was a subtle, involuntary gesture that spoke volumes. Then, his hazel eyes hardened and glazed over with professional detachment as he repeated his orders. "All Ashaiians are to be detained and removed from the kingdom."

"A costly endeavor. I doubt Ionius intends to absorb such a deficit."

"Indeed, he does not," Dronnicus said. "Deportees are required to pay for their own travel expenses. If they are unable to pay, they will be delivered to a willing patron."

"And the identities of these so-called patrons?" Rezkin asked.

"We are not required to keep record of identities or destinations. Those without a patron will be hosted in guarded camps and made to work."

"Tell me, Dronnicus, captain of the Royal Guard, how do you feel about slavery?" Rezkin asked.

Dronnicus's gaze sharpened, and he met Dark Tidings's black stare. "It is a despicable practice in direct opposition of the tenets of the Temple and has long been illegal in Channería."

"Is it?" Rezkin asked.

Dronnicus glanced away, and any response he might have made was lost when the eldest priest stepped forward.

"The collectiare has issued a proclamation of temporary sanctuary within the temples to be granted any Ashaiians who wishes to seek refuge in Cael. He apologizes that he was unable to discuss this matter with you in advance, but the king's decree was issued only hours ago. You will, of course, need to arrange for transportation of future deportees."

"The collectiare did not seem particularly supportive of me or my efforts," Dark Tidings said.

"I cannot speak to the collectiare's personal opinions, but the Temple is of an open mind. As Captain Dronnicus has said, the Temple does not suffer slavery. You are an unknown, unstudied and untested. A man cannot be judged by his origins nor by his actions alone."

"How do *you* judge a man, Minder?" Rezkin asked.

"By his intents, his purpose, his desires. We shall see what flourishes in your heart, Dark Tidings."

"I do not claim to have one beyond that which pumps blood though my veins," Rezkin said. "I did not get your name, Minder."

"Ah, forgive me, Your Majesty. I am Elder Minder Barkal." He motioned to the middle-aged man behind him and said, "This is Minder Thoran, and the younger one there is my assistant, Minder Finwy."

"Which of you will be travelling with us?" Rezkin asked.

Barkal smiled graciously and said, "We all intend to accompany you. With so many people, you can use the assistance."

What the Elder Minder said was true. This many frightened and angry refugees would be a delicate burden, but the assistance of the priests came with a price that he was not willing to pay.

"The agreement was for two priests, no more. Two of you may stay, but the third must depart."

Barkal protested, "But Minder Finwy is an assistant."

"Then Minder Thoran may leave," Rezkin said.

"I see," Barkal said with resignation. "Travel of this sort will be rough. Perhaps it is best to leave it to younger men." He met Dark Tidings's gaze and said, "You should know that the results of your decision are not likely to be in your favor. Minder Thoran is not as understanding as I."

"So be it," Rezkin said. "I will not cater to the desires of the Temple."

Barkal pursed his lips and bowed, the gesture imitated by the other two priests, and then they stepped to one side to engage in heated conversation.

Rezkin turned back to Dronnicus. "We will take these refugees," he said, gesturing toward those gathered on the pier, "so long as they swear allegiance to the Kingdom of Cael. We sail to the unknown, though, and our resources are restricted to what we carry with us. There is no guarantee that we will even be able to land on the island. I require time to consider the retrieval of additional Ashaiians."

Dronnicus nodded and spied the bickering priests out of the corner of his eye. "I believe the collectiare acknowledges this, but even his patience is limited. I would not expect it to extend beyond the spring." Rezkin nodded once, and Dronnicus took pensive breath. "There is another, more sensitive, issue," he said with a glance toward the ship's captain and the gawkers that had gathered around the deck.

Rezkin tilted his head and then strode toward the railing on the starboard side. Deck hands and passengers scattered like sheep from a wolf, and he was left alone with the royal guardsman. He lifted his gaze and spied Wesson standing afar on the quarterdeck. With a nod toward the ever-observant mage, Rezkin felt the tingle of a mage ward surround them. Dronnicus tensed at the sensation.

"What is this?" Dronnicus asked with barely contained alarm.

"A sound ward. I am sure you are familiar with them," Rezkin said.

"Composed of nocent power," the captain mused. "I have never seen one so finely woven—and subtle. I doubt I would have noticed the destructive power if it were not my specialty."

Rezkin tilted his head. As usual, his knowledge of magical things was lacking, but he found it particularly odd that he had not been informed that the captain of the Channerían Royal Guard had an affinity for destructive magic. Although he could not be expected to know everything about everyone in every kingdom, this was one man about whom he knew many details. He knew, for example, that Dronnicus was partial to the Ubellian martial style, preferred ale to wine, and spent much of his free time reading in the north castle tower. Yet, he had not known the man was a *battle mage*. This revelation led Rezkin to wonder why Ionius had not depended on the man for defense against the Raven. Perhaps all was not well between the king and his captain, or maybe Ionius feared the loss of Dronnicus's loyalty should he discover the plot against the princess.

Dronnicus's gaze was fixed on Wesson, but the younger mage met his stare without wavering. "So young to have such skill," the captain absently muttered.

"What is this about, Captain?" Rezkin asked.

Dronnicus returned his attention to Dark Tidings. "It is the matter of the princess. She is ... not quite ready to depart."

Although the man was steady, Rezkin had seen the flash of uncertainty—or distress—in Dronnicus's eyes. In the guilt of a lie, Rezkin saw an opportunity. He could not blame Ionius for his stubborn refusal to bow to the demands of a notorious criminal. In fact, he would have lost respect for the king had he been so malleable. As it was, though, Ionius had proven himself unworthy purely through his own actions. With a glance toward Wesson, he considered his previous assertion that destruction was not always a bad thing. Rezkin decided to stir the pot.

"You mean to say that you have not yet found her."

The royal guardsman failed to conceal his surprise. With more caution, he said, "What do you mean?"

"Exactly as I said. The princess is missing, and you do not know where to find her. It must be quite embarrassing since it was Ionius who insisted that I take her."

With a dash of hostility, Dronnicus asked, "What do you know of it?"

"I know *why* she was taken, *when* she was taken, and by *whom*."

"Tell me what you know," Dronnicus said. "On behalf of the king, I demand you tell me."

Rezkin shook his head and said, "Be careful for whom you speak, Dronnicus. Ionius already knows all but her location."

"You lie. King Ionius has been beside himself since she was discovered missing this morning. He has charged me with the task of finding her and bringing the abductors to justice."

"Then your king has set you up for failure, Captain. Her location is simple enough. In fact, she is below on the pier, hidden in the crowd." Dronnicus gave a start but restrained himself from rushing to the other side of the deck. "Her location is no longer of consequence to you, however. Do not forget that your king has *given* his daughter to me." Rezkin saw the tightening of muscles as Dronnicus clenched his jaw. "She is now a ward of Cael. *You* should be more concerned with the *why*, *when*, and *whom* of her disappearance. Be warned, though. Your king does not wish for you to know the truth."

"Yet he has tasked me with the endeavor. Speak your lies, and I shall learn the truth of it."

"Very well," Rezkin said, "but I suggest we keep the fact that you know between us. We do not wish for you to have an *accident*. Ilanet has been missing since the night of the ball."

"Impossible," said Dronnicus.

"Is it?" Rezkin watched as the past few days' events danced in the guardsman's gaze. When Dronnicus appeared sufficiently uncertain, he continued. "Ionius plotted with the archmage to murder Ilanet that night and blame the death on Prince Nyan. The king intended to take the prince prisoner and blackmail Vargos. His plan failed when the princess was rescued and secreted away."

Dronnicus's face reddened with fury. "That is absurd. My king would never harm his own daughter."

"Do you truly believe that?" Rezkin asked. "Rumor has it that Ionius bears a heavy hand." Again, Dronnicus seemed at a loss. "You do not have to take my word for it, though. The Order knows." After a brief pause for effect, he said, "You may even ask the princess,"—he tilted his head toward the pier—"but do not make a scene. I do not wish for others to know her identity, and *your* chances of survival are higher if no one knows you have spoken with her."

Dronnicus glanced toward the pier again and asked, "You have spoken to her?"

"How would I do that? She arrived at the same time as you and has not yet boarded the ship."

"Then how do you know what has occurred?" the guardsman asked.

"Ionius underestimates my strength and resources. You should not."

"Why would you tell me this? I am the captain of the Royal Guard. What I know, Ionius knows."

Rezkin shook his head. "You would tell him what? That I know of the plot? That *you* do? A war is brewing unlike any our kingdoms have endured. Ashai is only the beginning. Kingdom borders are invisible to this foe, and old allegiances will carry little value. You will remember this when the time comes to choose your side."

Dronnicus's fury radiated from him in his every word and expression. "I serve my king and kingdom by oath and allegiance. If you think I would so easily betray that, then you do not understand the meaning of honor, *Your Majesty.*"

Rezkin shrugged and said, "Honor is a relative term. For now, we have a group of passengers wishing to disembark so that they may return to their homes, and the new arrivals must be accommodated lest your kingdom sell them into slavery. We shall soon set sail."

Ilanet pensively stared up at the ship's railing from beneath her hood. She could no longer see the masked man who appeared as a demon incarnate. She wondered why anyone would desire to look like such a fiend but reminded herself that this was a warrior, or more aptly, a warlord. Of course, he would want to frighten his foes, even incite such terror as to seize submission without a fight. Ilanet had no intention of submitting to him, mask or no. A man skulked behind that mask—just a man. She nearly laughed aloud at herself for the sentiment. Men were dangerous, perhaps more so than demons. Men were real, and from her experience, were easy to anger, and they hit *hard*. For the Maker's sake, she was standing beside an assassin who, for all the world, looked to be nothing more than a weary traveler. She was disheartened at how easily these beasts disguised themselves. At least the one on the deck was honest in his concealment.

"Stop staring," the assassin called Xa whispered in her ear.

"Everyone else is staring," she whispered in return.

"No longer. They have lost interest. Pay attention," he hissed.

Ilanet glanced around and saw that it was true. The deportees were huddled in groups of three or four, some with children. Those who were not crying or simmering in anger were grumbling their frustrations about being plucked from the streets or yanked from their beds. Most had been given only moments to gather their most prized possessions, at least those they could carry, and then were shoved out the door under escort of the city guard. Some of the Ashaiians had apparently immigrated to Channería years, even decades, ago and had families who were either left behind or forced from their homes. Ilanet was disgusted with her father once again. These people had nothing to do with the crimes of that distant King Caydean.

After what seemed an endless wait, Dronnicus, the captain of the Royal Guard, came tromping down the gangplank followed by his men and the elder of the priests. Behind them flowed a group of people who looked to have been aboard the ship for a while. They were worn and carried little. Ilanet noticed that most appeared to be foreigners not of Ashai. Her gaze returned to the guardsmen. When first she had seen Dronnicus ushering the crowd toward the pier, she had worried that he or his men would recognize her. None of them had paid much attention to the sea of unfortunates being forced from the kingdom at sword point, though, and Xa had maintained position between her and the guardsmen. Much like her experience with the Raven, she was both relieved and petrified by the presence of the assassin. She had confidence that he could protect her from most threats and equal confidence that he would kill her if he so desired.

As he descended the gangplank, Dronnicus's gaze roved over the crowd. When they landed on her, she quickly ducked her head. At first, she worried that he had seen her, but when she looked up again his attention had passed. A sudden chatter surged through the crowd followed by a round of hisses demanding silence. The dark wraith was standing at the top of the gangplank. A chill ran down her spine as he began to speak in Ashaiian.

"King Ionius has decreed that all Ashaiians in Channería are to be deported, sold, or detained in work camps," he said. A rumble of disgust rolled through the crowd. "Some of you may know that I lay claim to the throne of Ashai by *Right of Ascension*, as King Bordran's true heir. You may or may not believe I bear this right. It matters not. A new kingdom has been born, the

Kingdom of Cael, negotiated lawfully and recognized by the Kingdom of Channería."

"Cael is worthless!" hollered a voice from afar.

It was Lord Braxen, a lesser Ashaiian noble who had attempted to gain favor with her father to receive an exemption from an import tax. Ilanet had little interest in taxes, but for her own edification, she had tried to listen to most of the court proceedings from the hidden balcony. Lord Braxen was repugnant, though, and Ilanet would have been pleased to never see him again.

"You can hardly call it a kingdom when ownership of the land is disputed by Gendishen," Braxen added.

"I will deal with Gendishen," Dark Tidings said. "That is neither here nor now. You all must leave Serret immediately if you do not wish to be sold or imprisoned. I have a ship, and I am offering you refuge in my kingdom. You may accept or find your own way. If you accept, you must swear allegiance to the Kingdom of Cael."

A strongly built man with dark hair and eyes leaned in to whisper something to Dark Tidings. The man wore armor and bore a sword, so Ilanet thought him a guard, but he held himself with more self-assurance than a typical soldier.

Dark Tidings added, "You, Lord Braxen, are not invited. The rest of you may begin boarding. You will be questioned and your identities recorded."

The crowd began to surge around her as people pushed and shoved toward the gangplank. Ilanet felt a tug on her arm from Xa, and then she suddenly tripped, toppling to the ground. Xa abruptly crouched over her, but when she looked up, a second set of eyes had found her. Dronnicus was also crouched, giving the appearance that he was gathering her spilled belongings. In a rush, he said, "My lady, did you leave the castle of your own accord?"

"What?" she asked in alarm.

"Quickly please, there is little time," he hissed. "Did you run?"

Ilanet paused as she considered whether to confide in the captain. He had always seemed a good man, but she was not confident in her ability to identify such an anomaly. Finally, she said, "Yes."

The captain's gaze flicked to Xa, and for the first time Ilanet noticed the dagger the assassin held over her in warning to the guardsman. Dronnicus dropped his gaze back to her and hesitated. His voice was choked when he asked, "Did your father try to kill you?"

With conviction and without pause, she said, "Yes, I believe he did."

Dronnicus inhaled sharply and looked away. "Be well, my lady. By the Maker, may you find your way."

Before she could respond, the captain was moving through the crowd. Xa pulled her to her feet, and they shuffled with the others toward the gangplank. Ilanet could not understand why people were pushing to get ahead when they knew the ship would not be leaving until everyone was aboard. Maybe they worried that the ship would run out of room, or perhaps they hoped to find the best spots to call their own. She wondered what kind of accommodations she might expect. As the king's ward, she should be afforded the best available, but she was supposed to be incognito.

She hoped she did not have to share a berth with Xa or be relegated to a common room in the hull. If there was a chance she would marry Dark Tidings, he surely would not expect her to sleep and dress among other men. No, the Raven had said women were aboard, and at least some of them were nobles. Some measure of propriety had to be observed. She chided herself for overthinking things again. Mables had always said she worried too much, and truthfully, most of the things she had worried over were inconsequential. Ilanet figured she had plenty of valid reasons for her anxiety at that moment.

When she arrived at the front of the line, Dark Tidings was no longer at the railing, but the dark-haired warrior who had been speaking to him was still present. He was standing beside a younger man with shaggy brown hair that was pulled back with a ribbon. The warrior looked upon the crowd with the sharp gaze of a viper, but the younger one had an easy smile. Both wore swords with comfort, though. The younger man did most of the talking and recorded information onto a scroll. His attention was on his writing as he began speaking to her.

"Greetings. My name is Tam. You may see me if you have any questions. What's your ..."—he looked up and met her gaze where she peeked out from beneath her cowl—"ah ... your um ..."

The warrior's stern expression gave way to a smirk, and he jabbed an elbow into Tam's ribs.

"Your name, I mean, what's your name?" Tam finally finished.

Ilanet opened her mouth and realized that, in the midst of her rambling, anxious thoughts, she had forgotten to come up with a story. Now, she was on the spot. "I am ... um ..."

Xa stepped partially in front of her and said, "Her name is Netty. I'm Lus."

Seemingly out of nowhere, Dark Tidings appeared behind Tam, as if manifested from invisible smoke. Ilanet ducked behind Xa, but the assassin provided a poor shield since she was nearly as tall as he was. She could not be sure, but she thought the black voids of Dark Tidings's eyes had met hers over Xa's shoulder.

He turned to Tam and spoke in a most disturbing voice. "Lady Netty will bunk with Frisha, Shiela, Yserria, and Reaylin."

Ilanet thought that Tam appeared abashed and perhaps disappointed when he looked at her again. "Pardon me, Lady Netty. I meant no offense." Oddly, though, he lowered his voice and spoke to Dark Tidings with comfort and familiarity. "Are you sure you want to subject her to *that*?"

Ilanet wondered how anyone could ever be less than disturbed in this man's presence.

Dark Tidings said, "It will be cramped, but they will make due. Lus will join the strikers."

Beside her, Xa met the dark-haired warrior's calculating gaze with a grin. She realized the man must be one of the legendary Ashaiian strikers. While she had been in the presence of a few over the years who had come to visit her father for diplomatic reasons, most of what she knew of them was from rumors. The loyalty of the strikers to their king, though, was renowned. She considered Dark Tidings anew. If he had somehow acquired the loyalty of the strikers, then his claim to the Ashaiian throne had to be genuine. Either that or he had stolen the title and begun calling his own men strikers for effect. The dark-haired warrior's confidence had her doubting the latter.

Dark Tidings stepped closer to the striker and whispered something in his ear. He then said, "Striker Shezar will show you to your quarters."

With that, he stalked away, presumably to survey the other new arrivals. Ilanet watched with curiosity as people shied away from him even though he had done nothing overtly threatening since he first appeared. Ilanet was jarred from her thoughts when the striker named Shezar spoke.

"Please follow me."

Ilanet looked back to Tam, but he would not meet her gaze. She had found his manner of Ashaiian speech slightly difficult to follow, but not as difficult as some of the others. She had the sense that it was common speak. As she followed the striker, she wondered who the young man was and how he had gained his position of trust with the rebel king. She was so wrapped in her thoughts that she nearly collided with the striker when he stopped. From her position behind Shezar, her quick survey of the room had her both relieved and agitated. Two sets of stacked bunks lined the walls, and a fifth had been placed adjacent to the door. There was barely room to maneuver without stepping on people's bunks or belongings. Five women were present, two of them were obviously a lady and her servant. She was uncertain about the other three.

The lady, a brown-haired beauty dressed in a frilly yellow frock stood beside one of the bunks as she tugged at a lacy gown laid out on the bed. "Tami, this will not do. How am I supposed to present myself in something so dreadful? These wrinkles! Fix it. Get one of the mages to do it if you must."

The waif-like servant girl was practically buried in fabric as she gathered the dress and scurried out of the room, bumping into Shezar, Ilanet, and Xa as she passed. The lady huffed and sat on the bunk, furiously fanning herself.

Another woman reclined on the bunk above reading a book. She was attractive but plainly dressed in pants and a tunic, quite unlike the lady below. Oddly, she was not afraid to speak her mind despite her appearance of lower status. "Shiela, nobody cares if your dress is wrinkled. Where exactly do you intend to present yourself? We are on a cramped ship, and everyone is miserable. Who are you trying to impress?"

"The *world*, Frisha. Of course, I would not expect *you* to understand." Lady Shiela raised a hand mirror and ran her fingers through her flawless curls. "A lady must appear as perfection at *all* times."

Ilanet had heard those same words enough in her lifetime, though they were in a different language. She wondered if she had looked so ridiculous. Then, she realized it was not the behavior that was absurd but the setting. If she had appeared as anything less than the perfect princess at the castle, it would have been court gossip for weeks, and her father would have punished her for the embarrassment. She had found a kind of freedom in her plain clothes and boyish disguise.

Shezar interrupted the exchange. "Ladies, you have a new bunk mate."

He turned, and Ilanet was forced to show herself. Lady Shiela took one glance at her and rolled her eyes. "Another commoner? Why must she stay in *here*? Put her with all the others below."

Ilanet was now faced with the disadvantage to her newfound freedom. She no longer had the respect of her peers, and she could not blame them. While she would never have been as brash as Lady Shiela, she would have expected the same courtesy the young woman was demanding.

Striker Shezar met Lady Shiela's glare and said, "The *king* assigned her to this berth. This is Lady Netty. You may disregard her present state. She is a

Channerían refugee who has been in hiding. I expect you will treat her with due respect."

Ilanet glanced at the striker upon realizing that he knew more about her than he should. But how much did he know?

The woman who had been sitting on the bunk by the door bounded to her feet. She had bright red hair and freckled skin. She was beautiful and feminine, but, oddly, she wore leather armor over pants and a fitted tunic. Her smile was open and friendly, but grief swallowed the light of her bright green eyes. She clasped hands with Ilanet and said, "I'm Yserria Rey of the king's royal guard. It's nice to meet you. Please come in and join us."

The woman Lady Shiela had called Frisha climbed down from her bunk and said, "Yes, please ignore Shiela. She doesn't mean to be rude. She just doesn't know any better. I'm Frisha Souvain-Marcum, and that's Reaylin de Voss."

Ilanet glanced around the room as her brain attempted to translate the strange style of speech. For some reason, as with Tam, Yserria and Frisha's words were a little difficult to make out. It was as if they slurred some of them together, and she had to concentrate harder to understand. She was startled by the snap of Shiela's fan as she slapped it closed in her hand, and then the young woman sidled over to join the conversation—or, rather, to take it over.

Shiela looked at Frisha and said, "I was *not* being rude. We must maintain our boundaries, *Cousin*, or before you know it, the room will be filled with refugees. Already we can barely move in here." With a condescending glance at the striker, she said, "The *men* do not consider the needs of a proper lady. We must voice them loudly and often if they are to be met." She looked back to Ilanet and said, "I am Shiela of House Jebai. It is a pleasure to meet you, Lady Netty."

It was easier for Ilanet to follow Shiela's speech, but she was surprised by the sudden turnabout.

Frisha gasped. "Oh, I'm sorry. We just assumed. Do you speak Ashaiian?"

Since she had rarely been permitted to speak to visitors at the castle, Ilanet had never had the opportunity to speak Ashaiian outside of her lessons, but her tutor had said her grasp of the language was adequate. "Yes, thank you for asking, Lady Frisha."

Shiela rolled her eyes and looked at Frisha disdainfully. "Of course she speaks Ashaiian, Frisha. Everybody with a decent education speaks Ashaiian. I apologize for my cousin. She was raised by *commoners*."

"Thank you, Lady Shiela. This is no concern," Ilanet said. "Do you speak Channerían?"

Shiela tittered. "Of course not. Why would I?"

Ilanet forced herself to maintain a courteous smile, but Frisha was not so obliging.

"Shiela, you should apologize for the offense you just threw at our new friend."

"What are you talking about, Frisha?" Shiela appeared genuinely oblivious. "Everyone knows that Ashaiian is the common trade tongue. Those doing business outside of their respective kingdoms must speak Ashaiian. It is only proper for a noble-born lady to learn. Nobody needs to know Channerían except the Channeríans," she said with a wave toward Ilanet. She then turned to Ilanet and said, "I apologize, again, for Frisha's discourtesy. She has no understanding of the workings of high society."

Ilanet glance between the two uneasily and then looked back to the tall warrior woman. "You are a member of the king's royal guard?"

Yserria smiled broadly and said, "Yes, our king does not discriminate. He values my skill with the blade." She nodded toward Striker Shezar and said, "The strikers are training me in their ways. I believe I am the first woman to hold the honor."

Shezar nodded, but his response was swallowed by squeals and shouts that accompanied the sudden rocking of the ship. Ilanet stumbled, but Xa steadied her before she became entangled in the piles of packs, trunks, and bedding. The armor-clad blonde, whom Frisha had identified as Reaylin, groaned and rolled over, burying her head in her blankets. The striker turned to Ilanet and said, "Lady Netty, I am to escort you and your guard to the king's quarters for a proper introduction. You may leave your belongings here."

"Striker Shezar, are we still to remain here? Can we not go above for some fresh air?" Shiela asked with a flutter of her lashes.

"The order to remain in your quarters stands. As you were informed, we have taken on additional passengers, and we must see to your security. The newcomers must be questioned and briefed on protocols. You will be informed as soon as Lord Rezkin lifts the order."

Shiela huffed again and began fanning herself. "This room is too hot, and that tree is blocking the window. Why is it in our room anyway?"

Ilanet eyed the little tree suspiciously. It appeared to be an average sapling of the kind she had seen in many of the gardens in Serret, but she was sure she had seen this particular tree before. She shivered. Was the creature following her? Had the Raven sent it to spy on her? To spy on the king?

"Is he well?"

Ilanet's attention returned to the conversation, and she realized Frisha was speaking to the striker.

"Is Rezkin well?" Frisha clarified. "I haven't seen him."

Striker Shezar said, "He did not inform me otherwise, Lady Frisha. Would you like me to deliver your regards?"

"No, that's okay. There's no need to bother him at such a busy time. I'm sure I'll see him soon enough."

"Who is Lord Rezkin?" Ilanet asked.

Shezar turned to her and said, "He is the King's Voice when Dark Tidings is unavailable. Please follow me now. We have delayed long enough."

The striker led Ilanet and Xa down a short passage to a berth that looked to be an office more than a bedroom. A small bunk sat in one corner, and the walls were lined with cabinets and drawers that were all latched shut. A large desk occupied the center, upon which rested a stack of maps, neatly bundled scrolls, and tools she could not begin to name. Ilanet jumped when she noticed the pair of reflective yellow eyes peering up at her from beneath the desk. A cat was curled around itself and appeared terrified. Like the tree, the cat looked familiar, but it was dark beneath the desk, and she could not be certain.

"Lady Netty, is it?"

The deep, unnatural voice caused her to startle once again, and she realized the masked king was seated behind the desk watching her. She knew he had not been there a moment ago. She was nearly certain of it. Surely she would have noticed.

"And Lus?" he said.

She stepped back. Behind her, Xa said nothing. Dark Tidings had spoken several times now, yet in each instance, it was as though she was hearing his eerie voice anew. Dark Tidings flicked a hand, and Ilanet turned to see the striker shutting the door as he exited. She was left alone in the small room facing the infamous rebel king with an assassin at her back. Belatedly, she remembered her manners and curtsied as elegantly as she could in her baggy trousers.

"Your Majesty, thank you for receiving me. I apologize for my present state of dress. I assure you that I am capable of looking the part of a lady."

The thought had occurred to her that, if this king found her lacking, he might throw her off the ship. Then where would she be? The Raven was gone, and she had nowhere to run. Worse, her father might find her and finish what he had started the night of the ball.

"I do not doubt that, Princess Ilanet," he said.

The Raven had told her that Dark Tidings would know who she was, but it was still unnerving to hear it confirmed. He stood and rounded the desk.

"You have no need of the weapon in here, Lus," Dark Tidings said. "Unless you intend to take her hostage or kill me."

Out of the corner of her eye, Ilanet saw the flash of steel.

"I am to protect the princess," Xa said.

"Yes, but not from me." As he reached up to remove the mask, he said, "I did warn you what will happen if you attack me again."

"You!" Ilanet exclaimed upon seeing the brilliant blue of the Raven's eyes. Incensed, she tromped forward and stuck a finger in his face. "Why did you keep this from me? *You* are Dark Tidings!"

The Raven nodded and said, "Yes, *and* I am the Raven—a fact that is known only to the two of you."

"The strikers?" Xa asked.

Ilanet noticed that the assassin had moved to stand in the corner. His expression was inscrutable, but his stance was tense, and still he bore the knife.

The Raven shrugged and said, "If they suspect, they have not yet broached the subject with me. They have had much to contend with, and the activities of the Raven are the least of their worries."

"Why have you revealed this to us?" Xa asked.

He was far from the self-assured assassin he had been earlier, even in the Raven's presence, and Ilanet wondered why he seemed so disturbed by the revelation.

The Raven frowned and said, "Because I am also Rezkin, whom you will be seeing about the ship. A few aboard know that Rezkin is Dark Tidings, a fact that will be revealed to the others in time; but none, besides the two of you, know that Rezkin or Dark Tidings are the Raven. I wish it to stay that way."

Rezkin watched the princess carefully. Her posture was hostile, and a streak of fear showed in her eyes, but she accused him with courage—or maybe she was too inexperienced to recognize the danger. He was more concerned that she had realized he posed her little threat. He had no desire to harm the princess. In fact, he felt the need to extend his protection to her as he had with his friends. Perhaps he would make her one of them, but for now, he needed to make sure she understood the severity of the situation.

"Consider this. Right now, only two people stand between the notorious killer known as the Raven and complete anonymity."

Ilanet stepped back—and then stepped back again. She wrapped her arms around herself and said, "I understand."

Rezkin turned his attention to the Jeng'ri, who looked like a wild animal caught in a trap.

"My people have seen you here on the ship when I know you to have been elsewhere," Xa said.

Rezkin turned Dark Tiding's visage over in his hands and held it up for the assassin to see. "Anyone can wear a mask. The strikers don the guise in my absence."

"Even so, you seem to be everywhere at once and you bear so many personas of great importance—the unscathed tournament champion, the leader of the Ashaiian underworld, the Riel'gesh, the True King of Ashai, the new King of Cael, this Lord Rezkin. Yet you are also no one. The Order does not know who you are, nor the Black Hall and the Adana'Ro. Ionius and Caydean would pay dearly for such information, and so would all the other leaders by now. You are bold yet hidden. It is impossible."

"Not so impossible when I am the only one keeping the secret," Rezkin mused. "The two of you are an unnecessary risk."

"Why are you doing this?" Ilanet asked. "Why did you take me away from the castle and arrange for me to come here—with *you*?"

Rezkin returned his gaze to the frightened small-woman and said, "Because you asked me to."

Rezkin believed Ilanet would do her best to keep his secret, but he wondered at her ability to succeed. While Xa was physically the greater threat, he was more likely to keep Rezkin's secrets, so long as he *wanted* to. Rezkin needed formidable resources, though, and he could not afford to reject them merely because of the potential for them to turn foul.

After sending Ilanet and Xa to their quarters, Rezkin changed into his doublet and breeches, plaited his hair, and affixed his swords to his belt. Part of him wanted to simply return to Ashai, kill Caydean, and be done with this mess. At this point, though, killing Caydean would solve only the most obvious problem. The mad king had already caused too much turmoil. While he was destroying his own kingdom from within, he was equally abolishing long-held friendships with Ashai's neighbors and inciting the wrath of every nation's leader. By the time he was through with Caydean, Ashai would be swamped in foreign armies. Rezkin's refugees needed immediate help, as did all the Ashaiians in foreign kingdoms who were no doubt becoming the targets of hatred and vengeance.

While many of the foreigners in his company chose to disembark in Serret, almost everyone had left their belongings behind in Skutton during their flight. Many did not have the funds to travel home. While he had been generous in providing for those who chose to leave, others preferred to stay and earn their passage. Foreign nobles and diplomats saw it as their opportunity to gather information or possibly ingratiate themselves to the True King of Ashai. Of the suffering slaves, few were well enough to identify themselves, and most who could claimed to no longer have families to which they could return. As for the Ashaiians, they were all considered traitors. By now, most of their families would have been gathered and killed or sold into slavery. Some of the more ambitious refugees thought to go straight to the slave markets to seek their loved ones.

Rezkin promised to do all in his power to help the refugees, but he reminded them that it would take much time and effort. Although he was not able to save those that had been killed and could not ensure rescue for the others, he did promise justice, which many interpreted to mean vengeance. The passengers were filled with fear and loss, but for many, these feelings were overshadowed by anger and betrayal. The refugees' rage and resentment was only balanced by their intense devotion to their new liege. All aboard knew the warrior Dark Tidings had saved them and that he was the most wanted enemy of the Crown of Ashai. The strikers and many of the nobles already recognized him as the True King. Thus, the people had faith that the one man who spoke openly and adamantly against the usurper Caydean could bring them the satisfaction and justice they demanded.

After concluding his urgent matters, Rezkin's first order of business was to check on Pride. The battle charger was in good health, and the strikers and life mages had managed keep him as content as a horse could be on a ship. Upon seeing him, Pride stomped his hooves, tossed his mane, and released a whine that was not difficult to interpret. Rezkin took a few moments to brush the stallion's coat even though it did not appear to need it. All the while, Pride watched him with a suspicious gaze. Rezkin did not know if a horse could pout, but Pride seemed to be mimicking the behavior to perfection. He stepped around the horse, and his attention was captured by a small brown mouse slipping beneath the hay. He eyed the spot for a moment and then decided that the creature was indeed just a mouse. The thought occurred to him that he would need to have a talk with Bilior about not eating his horse.

Rezkin then met with Kai who confirmed that the newest passengers had been vetted and assigned stations, so he rescinded the order for the others to remain in their berths. There was little room to move about the ship without interfering with the duties of the crew, so although they were free to roam the decks, people were asked to remain at their stations as much as possible. Most chose to do so anyway for fear that their few belongings would be claimed by desperate neighbors. Tam was assigned to the distribution of blankets, clothing, and soap that they had acquired in Serret. Rezkin felt it was good for his friend to learn the complexities of equipping large groups and the difficulties that arose with unexpected events—like the unplanned arrival of more than two dozen additional bodies. To his advantage, most of the passengers seemed comfortable with Tam. The commoners knew he was one of them, and the nobles recognized him as the apprentice to the King's Voice.

With the updates passed and the passengers settled, Rezkin was finally able to take a breath of fresh sea air. The respite did not last long as he was descended upon from both sides.

"So, are you going to tell us what you were up to?" Malcius asked as his group came to a halt. Tieran, Brandt, Tam, and, oddly, Xa were gathered around him.

"When?" Rezkin asked as he leaned back against the deck railing.

"*When*, he asks! Since you left the ship, of course! The rest of us have been stuck here bored out of our minds while you go gallivanting through western Channería."

Rezkin's gaze swept across the others, paused on Xa, and then landed on the women. Frisha and Shiela stood at the fore with Reaylin and Ilanet in the rear. She tried to hide behind the others, but Ilanet's wide eyes and rapt attention exposed her interest.

He smiled broadly and bowed. "Ladies, it is a pleasure to see you all again. Shiela, I trust you are as comfortable as possible."

Shiela harrumphed and fanned herself as she said, "I know you think me selfish, but I am not inconsiderate of our present conditions. You have provided me with the best that can be had, and for that I am appreciative."

Rezkin was surprised by the woman's turnabout, but he acknowledged her effort. He glanced to Malcius expecting him to be pleased, but his friend's expression was one of sad acceptance. Resolving to question Malcius later, he turned to Reaylin and said, "How go your studies with Healer Jespia?"

Reaylin balled her fists. "I hate that woman. She thinks she knows everything, and she won't let me carry my weapons during lessons. She can't accept that I'm to be a healer *and* a warrior."

"Can *you*?" Rezkin asked.

Reaylin lifted her chin and said, "If you can do it, then I can. Besides, I'll not give her the satisfaction of seeing me fail."

"I do not think Healer Jespia wishes you to fail," he replied.

"Who knows what she wants—besides to hear herself speak," Reaylin muttered.

Rezkin shook his head and turned to Frisha. He took her hand and brushed his lips across her knuckles. "Frisha, you are well?"

She pulled her hand back and frowned at him. "Stop that. You left us alone on the ship."

"You were hardly *alone*," he said. "More than a hundred people are on this ship, many of them talented fighters and mages, in addition to *three* strikers. Besides, it was only for a few days, Frisha. It was not to be forever."

Frisha huffed. "You know what I mean. You went off on your own while we were stuck here wondering what might have happened to you."

Rezkin smiled. "You were worried about me."

"Of course," she said lightly, and with a shrug added, "but only because you didn't tell us the rest of the plan. We wouldn't know where to go if you didn't come back."

"Frisha, you wound me," he said, testing a teasing tone he had picked up from Brandt.

Frisha rolled her eyes and muttered, "As if you could be wounded."

"Yeah, not likely, Rez," Tam said with a grin. "You look well enough."

Tieran said, "Yes, did you enjoy your *vacation*?"

"I think you and I have different definitions of a vacation," Rezkin said.

"Yes, mine is laying back relaxing with plenty of food and drink. You were probably off taking on armies, battling magical creatures, and rescuing fair maidens."

Behind Tieran, Xa grinned. Rezkin hummed under his breath and said, "Well, Tieran, I did have a long run to Serret and then tasks to perform. I am pleased to see that you were able to keep things in order here—between your periods of relaxation, that is."

Tieran scowled. "Thank you for that, by the way. I divest myself of the responsibility only to be saddled with it at inopportune times."

"For you, *every* time is inopportune," Kai remarked as he strode up behind the group. The striker nodded meaningfully, and Rezkin knew that it would soon be time for another meeting.

Rezkin turned to Frisha with a smile. "At least you are speaking to me again."

Frisha crossed her arms and pursed her lips. "I haven't decided about that yet, but it would have been rude not to greet you."

Tam leaned over and said in a stage whisper, "Don't ruin her good mood. Your girlfriend has been a bear since you left."

Rezkin raised a brow and said, "Only since then?"

"You two!" Frisha huffed. She spun to storm away and ran into Ilanet. "Oh! I'm so sorry. Right, um …"—she turned back to Rezkin—"We forgot to introduce Lady Netty. Have you met?"

Rezkin knew that Frisha was aware of Ilanet's meeting with Dark Tidings, but she was not practiced at deception, and her uncertainty was obvious. In fact, all his friends appeared to be waiting for some indication that the young lady knew he was Dark Tidings. Keeping this kind of secret was difficult for them, which was one of the reasons he knew he would have to reveal the truth to the rest of the passengers before long.

"Yes, I met Netty and Lus"—he nodded toward the assassin lurking behind Tieran—"in Serret. I invited them aboard. They are aware of my relationship with the king."

Everyone appeared to relax as they nodded toward the newcomers. Frisha took the initiative to introduce *Netty* to the other men, and once it became clear that Tieran was not interested in making introductions, Malcius did the same for *Lus*. Rezkin briefly wondered what the Jeng'ri had said to gain entry to their inner circle, but he was not surprised that the assassin had managed it.

Rezkin nodded toward Ilanet and said, "I see that you were able to acquire your belongings." She was wearing a green dress with draped sleeves embroidered with gold thread. It was too elegant for travel, but because it lacked the characteristic voluminous bustle of Channerían court dress, it was more practical than anything Shiela donned.

"Yes, Lord Rezkin. Two trunks were delivered."

She smiled, but her pain was obvious. Under normal circumstances, the princess would be wed in a lavish public ceremony and then sent off in grand spectacle complete with a parade, celebratory feast, and substantial dowry. Rezkin doubted that either of her trunks contained any wealth beyond the value of her apparel.

Tieran narrowed his eyes and asked, "Do I know you? Have we met?"

Ilanet smiled sweetly and curtsied. "I doubt that, Lord Tieran. I have never been to Ashai."

"No?" He looked up thoughtfully and said, "I visited the castle in Serret with my father once. I think it was about seven years ago. Yes, we celebrated my twentieth birthday. Perhaps I saw you then?"

Ilanet flushed and said, "I am sorry, Lord Tieran, but I had only nine years at then."

Upon seeing Tieran's perplexed expression, Ilanet whispered to Frisha, "I am saying this correct, yes? I had nine years?"

Frisha smiled and patted the girl's back. "It's fine. We understand."

Tieran shook his head and said, "No, your Ashaiian is quite good. It is just —you seem so familiar—and you are younger than I realized."

"Or you are *older* than you thought," Brandt muttered with a snicker.

Rezkin stood and said, "I have duties to which I must attend. I will join you all again for the evening meal." He turned to Tam and asked, "Did you complete your training this morning?"

"Yes, of course, with Waylen, Malcius, and Brandt," Tam said.

Rezkin looked to Tieran questioningly.

"*What?*" Tieran threw a hand out toward the main deck and said, "I was busy fielding problems with these insufferable passengers. The Torreli are the worst! You should all be glad I am not king or we would be at war with them already."

"You have issue with Captain LuDou?" Rezkin asked. He was surprised since the captain seemed even tempered and courteous whenever they spoke.

Tieran pursed his lips and said, "No, and thank the Maker for that. *He*, at least, seems to have some sense."

"What, exactly, is your problem with the Torreli?" Rezkin asked. From his studies and limited experience, Torreli culture was not so different from Ashaiian.

Tieran scoffed. "They strut about with nothing but complaints, that Lord Gerresy especially. They come to *me—Me!*—with demands, as though I am somehow responsible for their comfort. Can they not acknowledge that they were *rescued* and be grateful? They think they are entitled to the best, and they cannot accept that, so long as we are on this ship, there is no *best* to be had!"

Rezkin's lips turned up at the corners of their own volition, and everyone else wore similar expressions—everyone but Shiela. The young woman appeared wrapped in loss and longing as she stared over the water.

Rezkin turned his attention back to Tieran and said, "Since, as far as I know, no blood was spilled, and I have heard of no declarations of war from either side, I think it is safe to assume your performance in my absence was acceptable. Now that I have returned, you will train double to make up for lost time."

"*What*? I was planning for a break!"

"The exercise will help relieve your stress, Tieran. You and Tam will be joining the strikers and me on the quarterdeck this evening after the meal." He looked to Tam for confirmation.

"Yes, I know. I guess I was already expecting it, knowing you," Tam said with a cheeky grin. "Can't say I'm looking forward to it, though. You're always worse when you think we've been slacking."

"Have you been?" Rezkin asked.

"Like I would tell you if I were!" Tam said.

Tam laughed as Rezkin shook his head and walked away with Kai. He then turned, intending to speak with Frisha about how she was feeling since Rezkin's return, but she was focused on her cousin. Shiela had been acting weird for the past few days. After Palis's death, she had screamed and moped and cried mostly. Now, she seemed like her ordinary, irritating self one moment, and the next she would become somber and almost *mature*. He thought it disturbing in a way.

He looked around and found that Reaylin had disappeared, and Malcius and Brandt were tromping away, deep in discussion. They had also been different since Palis's death, and Rezkin's absence seemed to have made it worse. Tam thought they had both become more aggressive toward Rezkin, but in a passive kind of way. Many of their remarks were delivered in jest, but it seemed to Tam that they were meant to injure. He felt guilty for even thinking it of the nobles that had deigned to befriend him, but he had begun to wonder if Kai was right. The striker had said that Malcius, especially, felt a strong resentment toward Rezkin. He had said that if allowed to fester, that resentment could turn to contempt. Kai had instructed Tam to keep an eye on them for signs of betrayal.

Tam suddenly had the feeling he was being watched. He turned to discover that he had been left alone with Tieran, and the lord was staring at him. Until now, he had been successful at avoiding Tieran much of the time. It had been simpler when he knew his place with respect to the high lord and the potential consequences of stepping outside of it. Now things were muddled, and Tam did not know how to act. Glancing around anxiously, he said, "I-Is there something you need of me, Lord Tieran?"

Tieran narrowed his eyes, and then his gaze briefly flicked to something over Tam's shoulder. His countenance abruptly changed, and he smiled. "No, my friend. Nothing at all. I was just wondering if you are well. You looked lost for a moment. Now that your mentor is back, I am sure you will have much to keep you busy."

"Yes, I suppose so," Tam said cautiously.

"You will be dining with us tonight?" Tieran asked. "I do so love to share a meal with my friends."

"Well, I expect to sit at my usual place …"

Tieran laughed, and his tone was jovial, but a fire burned in his eyes. For just a moment, Tam thought he had seen the previously elusive family resemblance to Rezkin. "Nonsense, Tam. We have not dined together in some time."

Tam knew that they had, in fact, *never* dined together—not at the same table, anyway. The Maker forbid that the great Tieran Nirius share a meal with a commoner. Except, it seemed, that was exactly what he was proposing.

"You wish for *me* to dine with *you* tonight?"

"Of course," Tieran said as he stepped forward. "One should keep his friends close." He grinned as he leaned in and whispered, "You owe me." Tieran abruptly straightened and passed Tam with his usual swaggering gait and nose to the air. Tam then heard him say, "Hello, Lady Netty, pardon me."

Tam spun to see Netty peeking around a stack of crates that had not been moved to the hold yet. He had thought she had gone with the women, but now he wondered if she had been spying on them the whole time. The revelation made Tieran's behavior seem even more inexplicable. It seemed Tieran had been trying to make him look good in front of the lady, but Tam could not conceive of a world in which Tieran Nirius thought it appropriate for *any* commoner to approach a noble lady. And, why would Tieran do anything for *him*?

Netty's gaze followed Tieran until he was gone. She turned to Tam and smiled. "Hello. You are Tam, yes? You said I should speak with you if I have questions."

"Oh, right," Tam said as the wind abandoned his sails. "Yes, Lady Netty. I'll be happy to assist you with anything you need."

Netty smiled, and it was as though she had been painted by the Maker's own hand. She strolled closer and motioned to one of the crates. "May we sit?"

"Yes, of course, but ... um ... is it appropriate? I mean ... you and me alone—not that I'm thinking of anything like that. I mean. I wouldn't, of course not. I just mean—are you comfortable?"

Oh, smooth, Tam, he thought to himself. *She's going to think you're an idiot.* The crystal bells of Winterfest were not as soothing as Netty's laughter.

"I appreciate your concern for my comfort," she said. "We are in the open,"—she nodded toward a dark figure looming in the shadow of the upper deck—"and we are not so alone. Lus is my guard."

"Ah," he said as he glanced anxiously toward the shadow.

"What is it?" Netty asked.

"Um, he kind of gives me the creeps," Tam said. "It's like he's ready to put a dagger through my eye at any moment."

Netty tilted her head and studied Tam curiously. "I do not understand your ... I am sorry ... I do not know the word. Your *place*—what you are to the others here."

"Well, I don't have a specific role. Not really. I kind of got caught in Rezkin's wake. We all did, I think."

Netty only looked more confused.

He said, "I'm Rezkin's best friend. He keeps me along for the ride, and he's taken me on as an apprentice."

"So you are like him?" Netty asked, and he thought her expression betrayed disappointment or, more likely, skepticism.

Tam laughed. "I don't think anyone is like him. He's teaching me to fight —to wield a sword and a few other weapons. I'm also learning strategy and things like that. I don't know what good it'll do me though." Realizing he would never have a chance with Lady Netty, Tam decided it was best to be honest. "Before I met him, I was just a carpenter's apprentice about to join the army."

"But you are friends with Lord Tieran as well? He is the heir to Wellinven and next in line for the crown of Ashai, yes?"

Tam rubbed the back of his neck. "No, I can't say that we're friends, truthfully. I don't know why he said all that. He's trying to prove a point or something. Since I'm friends with Rezkin, he thinks he needs to be friends with me too."

"Is Lord Tieran a hostage, then?"

"What? No! Why would you think that?" Tam asked.

"He is heir to the throne, but Dark Tidings has made claim. Since Lord Tieran is here, I thought he had been captured."

Tam sighed. He could understand how it would be confusing to an outsider —or anyone, really. He glanced around to make sure no one was within hearing distance and then whispered, "Rezkin is Tieran's cousin, and we believe King Bordran intended for Rezkin to be named his heir."

Netty appeared skeptical. "Intended?"

Tam nodded. "Regardless of the intent, though, Bordran gave Rezkin the power to rightfully claim the throne—it's signed and certified—and Tieran, whom you pointed out was the heir after Thresson, has already willingly sworn fealty to Rezkin."

Netty followed his lead and lowered her voice. "So Rezkin is the king, and you are his apprentice?"

Tam laughed boisterously. Lowering his voice again, he said, "Well, yes, but I'm not apprenticing to be king. You know it doesn't work that way."

"So, you apprentice to his ... *other* ... skills?" Netty asked.

"Not *everything*. Honestly, I think it's impossible for a single man to be all that Rez is. He's teaching me to be a warrior, I guess, but not just the fighting. He wants me to be smart, too. He makes me read a lot, and we talk about different cultures and history." Tam furrowed his brow. "Honestly, I don't know *what* I'm supposed to be."

"It sounds like you are very important," Netty said, and Tam's heart skipped a beat.

He swallowed and met her eyes. "Maybe to him, in a way, but I'm still only a commoner."

Netty nodded and then asked, "You said that Lady Frisha is Lord Rezkin's girlfriend? This means they are courting?"

"Yeah, well, that's complicated too. There was talk of a betrothal, but I'm not sure they're anything now. It's kind of awkward for me, since Frisha and I have been friends all our lives."

"You have known Lord Rezkin long?" Netty asked.

"No, only a few months." When the questions were asked so simply, he began to recognize how strange the truth sounded. "I guess it's just one of those things. Some people you meet and never care to meet again. Others you feel like you've always known. You know what I mean?"

Netty's smile fell. "Outside of formal occasions, I have not met so many people. It was not permitted." After a pause, she asked, "You know Lord Rezkin well?"

Tam had a growing suspicion that he was being interrogated. Lady Netty wanted to know a lot about Rezkin, and he was unsure how much he was permitted to say. "No, I guess not. He keeps lots of secrets."

She tilted her head. "You accept that he keeps secrets from you?"

Tam shook his head. "I don't think I *want* to know everything about him. What do *you* think?" he asked.

She smiled playfully and said, "I think it is strange that you are afraid of Lus but are very comfortable with Lord Rezkin."

Tam laughed again. "There's no need to be afraid of Rez. He's harmless. Well, not really, but he is. I mean …" Tam abruptly ceased his rambling and wondered what in the bloody hells he was trying to say. "What I mean is, Rezkin is a good man. I don't worry that he would harm me or Frisha or anyone who wasn't a threat—unless he needed to, I guess."

He ran a hand through his hair and became frustrated when it tangled in the queue. He had forgotten how long it had grown. "I guess I don't really under-stand it either. I just know that if I ever needed anyone for any reason, Rezkin would come through for me." He looked up and met her eyes. "*Me*, a simple carpenter's apprentice. And, I would do the same for him. That's why I gave him my fealty. I didn't have to. He didn't ask for it, and sometimes I think he would have preferred I didn't. But I did, and I don't regret it."

Ilanet was having difficulty with the juxtaposition of Lord Rezkin and the Raven. What Tam said made sense. Rezkin had been there for her when she needed him, and he had not even known her. There were plenty of reasons someone would want to save a princess, though, and he had admitted it was to his political advantage. However, her father seemed to have washed his hands of her, and she could not see any advantage to her presence any longer. She knew that she was not practiced in intrigue and politics, though Tam seemed to know much about these things.

She looked to the young man sitting next to her. She thought he was perhaps only a few years older than she, and he was handsome but not arrogant. He smiled and laughed often, and he was friendly with everyone, regardless of station. His manner seemed genuine, so unlike the contrived pleasantries of the people she had known. Prior to absconding with the Raven, the only commoners she had met were the castle staff, and she had not been permitted to converse with any of them. Her father had always made commoners seem like crude half-wits, but it did not seem to be the case with the few she had recently met. She wondered if maybe these Ashaiian nobles had found something special in Tam. For these few moments, while sitting with him, her perpetual anxiety had eased, and she felt calm.

"L-Lady Netty, was there anything else you needed?" Tam asked.

Realizing she had also been silent for too long, she said, "No, not now. Thank you, Tam. I am understanding more."

Tam smiled and stood, somehow able to maintain his feet as the ship began to roll in earnest. He held out a hand to help steady her as she rose. The ship dipped on the waves, and although she could feel the deck beneath her feet, it felt as though she was suspended in the air. Then, the ship rose, and she thought her knees would likewise rise to meet her chest.

Tam smiled and said, "It takes some getting used to."

Ilanet held her stomach as it began to quiver. "I think I should lie down. I fear I am to become ill."

"Right. I'll help you to your quarters," he said. He nodded toward Lus who suddenly appeared, much closer than before.

"I am just escorting her to her quarters ..." Tam began.

"I know. You two should be more careful when you speak," Lus said. "There are many mages aboard who could listen in even if you do not see them. I took the liberty of placing a sound ward around you this time."

"So you could hear us?" Tam asked, slightly abashed. He had not thought of the mages. He should have known to be more careful. If he found out,

Rezkin would make sure he learned his lesson—probably with more grueling hours of practice.

Lus grinned menacingly, and Tam cringed. He turned away quickly and took Ilanet by the arm as he escorted her down to the berth she was sharing with the other women. When they arrived, he led her to the bunk that Reaylin had previously occupied. The pretty blonde was now sitting on the upper bunk reading a book while muttering unhappily to herself.

"Reaylin," Tam said. "Lady Netty isn't feeling well. Will you help her?"

A heavy thud sounded on the bed above her. "Anything to distract me from reading that book," Reaylin grumbled. She dropped to the ground and said, "Did you know there are twenty-six bones in your foot?"

"I didn't know that," Tam said as he poured a cup of water from a skin hanging from the bunk and handed it to Ilanet.

"No, and you probably didn't care to either. Just like I don't care. But now I have to know, and Healer Jespia expects me to be able to name them all."

"Well, I guess if you're going to heal someone's foot, then you'd best know what you're healing."

"You're no help. Go away, Tam. I'll take care of her," Reaylin said in a huff.

Ilanet was disappointed when Tam left, but she was also thankful that he would not be around to see her lose her stomach. She lay back against the wall and looked up at Reaylin. Ilanet did not think Reaylin to be much older than she.

"You are a healer?" Ilanet asked.

Reaylin rolled her eyes and said, "I guess. An apprentice anyway. It won't help, you know—lying down. You were probably better off on deck where you could see the horizon and breathe the fresh air. Took me a while to learn that. Don't worry, though. I can already help with the sea sickness. I've been doing it *a lot*."

Tam wandered the short distance toward his own berth, one he shared with Wesson, Jimson, Drascon, and Millins. A few of the foreign former tournament competitors had also been sharing the space, but they had disembarked in Serret. His new bunkmates would be settling in, and he intended to see if they needed anything. Before he made it to the room, however, he was set upon by a band of unscrupulous nobles. They yanked him into their own berth and tossed him to a bed. Malcius, Brandt, and Tieran surrounded him. Waylen watched from across the small room, but the baron was not to be seen. It was too bad, Tam thought. The baron might have talked them out of whatever troublesome antics they intended.

"Well," Tieran said as he crossed his arms imperiously. "How did it go?"

Tam glanced between their fervent gazes. "How did what go?"

Brandt popped him upside the head and said, "With Lady Netty, you twit. You two were up there for a while—*alone*."

Tam scowled at the insinuation. "We weren't alone. Lus was guarding her the whole time." He straightened his tunic and said, "We just talked."

"Yes, but what did you talk about?" Malcius asked with a grin. "Is she besotted already?"

"Probably. She asked a lot of questions—about *Rezkin*." Tam knew they could hear his disappointment.

Tieran rolled his eyes. "Of course she did. They *all* want to know about Rezkin. She came to *you*, though. Soon enough she will realize she cannot have him, and she will look elsewhere."

"Who knows?" Tam asked. "She might have him. She's gorgeous … and refined. She seems really nice, too. I don't think things are too good with him and Frisha. He might choose someone else."

Shaking his head, Tieran said, "Even if he and Frisha do not wed, he would not marry Lady Netty. Frisha was never an appropriate choice for a king. We have only been forced to accept her because he wanted her. Now, he is to be king of Cael, at the least, and eventually Ashai. If he chooses someone else, she must be of appropriate standing, someone of good breeding—a princess or duchess most likely."

"Or a master mage," Waylen added.

"Right," said Tieran. "Lady Netty obviously lacks importance. She has no wealth that I have seen, and I have asked around. Nobody recognizes her."

Brandt said, "And, come on. Nobody names their child *Netty*. Terrible! Obviously a false name. She does not wish us to know who she is."

"She is probably a runaway," said Tieran, "a stray that he picked up along the way. You know how he is. He thinks he needs to save everyone."

"Until he gets them killed," Malcius muttered. "But seriously, Tam. Lady Netty has been traveling *alone* with Lus and Rezkin. If nothing else, her virtue is in question. If the healers cannot be satisfied, then she holds little or no value to any noble who cares for his reputation."

"You shouldn't say such things," Tam snapped. "You don't know anything about her."

"That is the point," Tieran said. "And it is to *your* advantage."

"How is it to my advantage? I'm a commoner. She's a noblewoman. Even disgraced nobles don't marry commoners."

"Aunt Terissa did," Malcius said. "You know her—*Frisha's mother*—and she certainly was not in disgrace."

"That was different," Tam argued. "She was in love, and Frisha's father is as wealthy and successful as a commoner can be. What am *I*? I have nothing to offer."

"*You* are the king's apprentice and his friend besides," Malcius said. "He has made it clear to us more than once that you are to be treated with respect. I think he would give you anything if you only ask, including permission to marry a noble lady."

"So you think I actually have a chance with her?" Tam asked, still utterly confused about the turn of events. It had not been that long ago that these same people were berating Palis for pursuing a commoner. Although he was buoyed by their support, he was hesitant to get his hopes up for something too fantastical to consider.

"Unless you screw it up," Brandt said as he popped Tam in the head again.

"It is best you move quickly," Malcius added.

"Why is that?" Tam asked as he rubbed his crown. "She is only sixteen, not even of age."

"That hardly matters. She will be of age next year. It is common for these details to be arranged ahead of time. Besides, if she *is* pregnant, you will want people to assume it is yours."

"*What?*" Tam asked in horror. "Why would I want people to think I knocked up a young girl?"

"Because then you can marry her, and the babe will be thought legitimate," Brandt said as he moved to strike Tam in the head again.

This time Tam ducked. Brandt fell forward with the failed attack, and Tam's palm came down on Brandt's shoulder. With a shout, the young lord fell, his face smashing into the planks. Tam jumped to help upon realizing what he had just done.

"I'm so sorry, Lord Gerrand. It just happened, I swear! I didn't mean to ..."

He was cut off when Brandt broke into boisterous laughter. "Stop your blubbering, Tam. You got me by rights." He rolled over and pushed to his feet.

"Nobody messes with the king's apprentice. You can tell Lady Netty that you laid me out."

Tam blinked at the grinning faces and asked, "Why are you doing this? Why would you help me?"

"Protect and honor your friends," Tieran said. "It is the first rule, Tam. King's orders."

10

Adsden watched the door shut behind the latest messenger and then sat back in his chair contemplating the turn of events. He surveyed his office in the Serpents' guildhall as he tried to piece together the intent behind the orders he had received the previous day. For the life of him, though, he could not figure out the Raven's plans. Adsden rather liked puzzles—anything to keep his overactive mind intrigued, and the Raven had become something of an obsession. The first messenger had been a runner from Drennil, a life mage with the ability to drive his horse faster than was naturally possible. The cost of procuring such a messenger was not insignificant, so the directive had to be important.

"Were the orders from the Raven?" Benni asked.

"I do not believe so, though I cannot say for sure. Reports place the Raven all over Ashai. One even claims he has begun an assault on the Channerían King's Seat in Serret. I think that overreaching. It is more likely the Raven was responsible for the recent annexation of the guilds in Vogn."

"That's in the southern peninsula, right?"

"Yes, and it would make more sense with these orders. By all accounts, Duke Ytrevius, who presided over the southern peninsula, fell under Caydean's assault. There have been reports of refugees, or traitors as the king is calling them, fleeing east to Channería. The Raven could take advantage of the unrest and go west to Vogn. He could then travel up the western coast to Atressian lands in the north, hence the interest in the Mulnak brothers."

"What if he did go east?" Benni asked.

"I admit, I have not yet determined the Raven's motives, but I can think of nothing that would draw him east when so much is to be had here. Now, move to your position. The messenger said that Lord Fierdon Mulnak will be here shortly."

He did not have long to wait. Duke Atressian's eldest son did not ask for permission to enter, nor had Adsden expected it. Fierdon might be considered the black sheep of the family, but he was still an Atressian. He swept into the room wrapped in the rags of a beggar.

"Guildmaster Adsden, your men may go."

Fierdon's shoulders appeared tense, and he had the countenance of a man prepared to defend himself—perhaps more from verbal onslaught than a physical one, Adsden thought. He motioned for the man at the door to leave but did not acknowledge his protégé hiding in the rafters. Benni was to prove that he could remain undetected *and* remember most of the conversation. The Raven had seen promise in the boy, and he had not been wrong. Benni was quickly becoming one of the Serpent Guild's best sneaks.

The door shut softy, and Adsden motioned to the settee. "Lord Fierdon, would you care for a drink? I recently acquired a Leréshi red-gold that is rare in these parts. It is both sweet and bold."

Fierdon paused and eyed the crystal decanter that sat amongst the goblets on a silver tray. "I ... yes, that would be fine."

Adsden poured the proffered spirits as he spoke. "Please, let us sit. I trust you are not in a hurry? May I take your coat?"

Fierdon glanced down at the rags he wore over his tunic. "Yes ... I ... it is a disguise."

"Of course," Adsden said as he handed the goblet to Fierdon with a practiced smile. The man was truly hideous, but he could not be blamed for his appearance. Adsden had been informed of the circumstances surrounding the man's deformities. "You wear it well," he said. Fierdon looked at him questioningly. "I hope you take these words as the compliment they are intended to be. As guildmaster of a prominent thieves' guild, I am practiced at recognizing talent. You would have made an excellent thief or assassin had you not been born to privilege. Obviously, it is far below your station, but ..."

"No, I appreciate your candor, Guildmaster, and your recognition of my efforts. My … appearance has been both a boon and a hindrance. Obviously, I draw attention, but most people would rather not see."

Adsden watched as Fierdon's eyes were drawn to a sculpture that had been conspicuously positioned on a side table for this meeting. It was a dreadful rendition of a bestial man ravaging an ancient goddess.

"It is unfortunate," Adsden said.

Fierdon blinked, and his attention snapped away from the sculpture. "What is?"

"That we should live today in this place. Long ago existed a people called the Svellites. Have you heard of them?"

"No, I cannot say that I have," said Fierdon as he took the goblet and tested its contents.

"The Svellites were a unique culture," Adsden said. He paced toward the side table and paused, as if admiring the sculpture. "They were first and foremost artists, but their culture was strongly immersed in an unusual perception of beauty. They believed that aesthetically pleasing things, those that we today consider beautiful, were incomplete. They felt that true beauty could only be achieved in balance—a juxtaposition of light and dark, good and evil,"—he waved a hand over the sculpture—"desirable and appalling. They were fascinated by extremes. The more attractive, the more adored. The more grotesque, the more respected. To be included in a union of the two was their greatest privilege and honor. After all, a lady was not considered to be truly beautiful if she was not accompanied by horror."

Fierdon had been captivated by the sculpture, but he now looked to Adsden uncertainly. "It seems unfair," he said, "to curse someone so lovely with something so hideous."

"Some*one*, some*thing*?" Adsden mused as he took a seat in the high-back chair across from Fierdon. He held his goblet with the refinement Adsden had observed of the aristocracy. "Their contemporaries felt as you say. They called the Svellites heathens and even accused them of demon worship. Eventually, the Svellites were slaughtered by their enlightened neighbors, and most of their abundant artwork was destroyed. But, consider this—not everything that is beautiful on the outside is beautiful on the inside, and not everything that is ugly is a demon. I, personally, think the Svellites sought to see the truth in things. In the balance, they were acknowledging the beauty and ugliness that exists in all things and sought to bring them to the fore."

Fierdon's gaze swept back to the statue, and Adsden knew he had the man's attention. A knock sounded at the door.

"Enter," he said.

Attica strolled into the room with a swaggering gait and a smirk on her lips. Her confidence faltered briefly when her gaze landed on Fierdon, but she recovered so quickly one might have thought to have imagined it. Fierdon probably had not noticed because as soon as the woman stepped into the room, he became preoccupied with raising his hood, which, in present lighting, could not possibly conceal his face. One of Attica's enforcers, Kendt, surveyed the area before closing the door with his departure.

Adsden rose to greet the woman properly and make the introduction. "Lord Fierdon, this is Attica, guildmaster of the Diamond Claws. Attica, this is Lord Fierdon Mulnak of Atressian."

Attica crossed her arms beneath her breasts and cocked a hip to one side. "Pleasure."

The woman appeared different every time Adsden saw her. One day she would be dressed as a seamstress or scullery maid and the next, a mercenary. Today, she was wearing a fitted shirt, indecently unlaced to a point below her bosom, tucked into pants that hugged her curves. Knee-high boots graced her calves over raised heels that made her already long legs seem endless, and her raven-black hair was pulled back tight, emphasizing large green-brown eyes. Her strong nose and sharp chin rendered her striking, if not exactly beautiful.

"You are a guildmaster?" Fierdon said. "It cannot be."

Attica grinned and said, "That's what *I* keep saying." She strolled forward and plopped into a chair in a very unladylike fashion. She crossed her legs, looked up at the men, and said, "Well?"

"Do not be fooled by her appearance, Lord Fierdon," Adsden said. "Attica was hand-picked by the Raven to run her guild, and she is ruthless."

He poured the woman a drink, and then both men took their seats. Fierdon seemed to be looking for a shadow in which to hide.

He kept his face averted as he said, "Forgive me, Madam Attica … Guild-master. I did not intend insult."

"No forgiveness necessary, and it's mistress, not madam. I don't run a brothel, and I'm not married," she said with a wink.

Fierdon finally met her gaze and ventured, "You are not disgusted by my appearance?"

Attica shrugged. "So your face is a bit melted. You seem like a nice enough guy."

"Attica, you are talking to a lord of Atressian," Adsden said.

Attica raised a brow and smirked. "Right. Sorry, Lord Fierdon. I'm not used to talking to important people."

"I—do not claim to be important, exactly. It is true that I am a Mulnak, but any significance I held burned away with my flesh." He gritted his teeth and said, "Hespion is heir."

Attica laughed. "And we are heirs to nothing. Are we not important? We've survived, made our own ways, impressed the right people. Besides, Hespion's a fraud. From what I hear, you're the brains of the family. Oh, sorry. I guess I shouldn't have said that. Don't mean to disrespect the future duke and all."

Fierdon appeared mesmerized, and Adsden thought the woman was delivering a magnificent performance.

After an uncomfortable silence, Attica said, "*What?*"

Fierdon blinked several times and glanced away. "I apologize. I did not mean to stare. It is just that ... well, I have never spoken to a woman for so long. They usually run away, screaming in terror."

This last he said with a lift of his lips that Adsden thought to be a smile, but it tugged the skin around his eyes and twisted his face into an almost menacing expression. Still, Adsden admired the man for his ability to find humor in the darkness.

"A terror?" Attica said with a chuckle. "No, *you* are not a terror." Her smirk fell, and her eyes lit with intensity. "I have seen terror. I have met the Raven, and *nothing* is so terrifying as he."

This, Adsden knew to be a truth and found no fault in her words. He stared into the red-gold liquid in his glass, swirling it as he once had another goblet in the demon's very presence.

"And yet he is so beautiful," he mused.

Attica raised a brow and said, "I can't seem to remember."

Adsden looked up. "Nor can I ... and neither can any of my men, for that matter. But I remember how I felt. He is enticing, yet horrifying," he said as his gaze wandered to the statue on the table. He looked back to his guest and said, "What may we do for you, Lord Fierdon."

Fierdon glanced between the two. "I was under the impression the guilds were at odds."

Attica grinned. "We are."

Adsden added, "But we are united under the Raven."

Fierdon paused, and Adsden saw the realization dawn. "You knew I was coming."

Smiling, Adsden said, "The Raven knew."

"But how? I found out only a few days ago, and I was very careful not to be noticed on the way here."

"The Raven's network is extensive," Adsden said. "I think greater than any of us realize."

"What does he want with me?" Fierdon asked.

Attica said, "The question is, what is it *you* want?"

Fierdon's gaze grazed the woman's form, and he quickly glanced away. "I need funds—and protection. I need to return home."

"Do you?" Adsden asked as he refilled Fierdon's glass.

"What do you mean? Of course I do. I will not be safe until I am back on Atressian lands. Caydean's forces are everywhere."

"Yes, that is true," Adsden said. "Though, not everyone is loyal to Caydean."

"That hardly matters in my case." He motioned to his face. "Anyone would be glad to see me captured, and the promise of a reward is more than enough incentive."

"You are probably right," Adsden said. "I imagine the son of a duke might find it difficult to make genuine friends, friends on whom you may depend in difficult times. As you say, it is likely more difficult in your case. *Fear* drives Caydean's forces, though. Their hearts are not in it. Caydean's greatest adversary is not your father or any of the dukes. It is not even his own madness. It is hope. So long as his people have hope of redemption, his power will never be consolidated."

"Hope?" Fierdon growled. "What hope is there? He is destroying this kingdom. Even if the dukes combined their might—which will never happen—and managed to prevail, too much damage has been done. He has angered our allies and prodded our enemies. I fear that before a Mulnak sits the throne, foreign armies will be overrunning the palace.

Adsden said, "If not for the knowledge I bear, I would concur. The battles between opposing powers will rage across this once great kingdom, and they will not end until there is nothing left to desire."

Fierdon fisted a gloved hand and nodded once.

Adsden added, "But there are rebels."

Fierdon scoffed. "The rebels have been around for years—a bunch of common thugs, brigands and bandits, using rebellion as an excuse to take what they want."

"For some," Adsden conceded. "For others, they are potential. Have you heard of the True King?"

Fierdon's face screwed up in disgust. "Everyone has. It is a sham. Bordran never mentioned choosing an heir besides his own son. I doubt he could see the savage inhumanity behind Caydean's icy eyes that were otherwise so like his own. Fathers are like that. So long as the son looks the part, they will excuse anything to preserve the family name."

Adsden tipped his goblet up, which prompted Fierdon to do the same. He said, "I hear Tieran Nirius was last seen in the True King's company, and he was very much alive. Rumor has it the True King is protecting the Wellinven heir. It seems odd to protect the person most likely to succeed Caydean upon his death if this *Dark Tidings* truly hopes to claim the throne. The strikers seem convinced—at least some of them. More importantly for *us*, the Raven has declared his support for the True King." Adsden set his goblet on the table beside him. "I cannot say *why*—perhaps only to vex Caydean. His machinations are a mystery to me. The Raven gets what the Raven wants, though, and the Raven wants *you*."

"*Me*? What does this Raven want with me?"

"Again, I cannot say. He has extended to you his protection. You need not risk the return to Atressian. You are welcomed here, with us," he said with a nod toward Attica.

"I would stay here? Hiding in an abandoned warehouse?"

"Well, it is hardly abandoned, but I agree that it is not one of our nicer establishments. We move the guild house every so often to throw off Caydean's spies. Oddly, they have had little interest in us. It would seem strange for a king to allow thieves and deliverers of death and destruction to run rampant in his kingdom, except that Caydean seems to thrive on such chaos. What I do not think the king realizes, though, is how organized we truly are. We are no longer lawless mongrels fighting each other for bones. We serve the Raven, and the Raven has an agenda. You can help further that agenda."

"What agenda is that?" Fierdon asked with skepticism.

"We each receive orders related only to our particular functions. Perhaps the Raven has confidants who are privy to his designs, but I suspect only he knows what he is doing. Regarding *you*, our orders are to extend an offer of friendship and mutual advancement. If you reject the opportunity to participate, then we are to provide you with whatever you require for your journey. Of course, we expect that you will remember our generosity in the future."

Fierdon's expressions were difficult to interpret with the way his waxy skin twisted around his orifices. His eyes held a healthy suspicion, however, which Adsden thought reasonable. Such an offer never would have been extended to the son of a duke before the Raven—not without a fantastically profitable deal, anyway. The younger brother, Hespion, had been involved in unscrupulous dealings with former Guildmaster Urek, but those had been arranged by the previous Marquis Addercroft.

"You said 'participate.' What am I expected to do?" Fierdon asked.

"You may be as involved as you wish, in whatever way you consider useful; *or*, you may sit here drinking and relaxing until the war is over. The choice is yours, but I cannot tell you the details of our mission until you have agreed."

Fierdon glanced at Attica, who smiled and winked at him. He said, "My father has always depended on me to be the voice of reason in Hespion's ear. My brother no longer listens to me, though, and I do not see a place for myself in his household once Father passes. At home, I am ridiculed. I am not permitted to participate in important occasions and events. I wish to feel useful, to be welcome. Despite my appearance, I am an intelligent man. I know that you and the Raven have an agenda, and that your attitude toward me is defined by that agenda. If I am to be regularly treated with this kind of respect, then perhaps the Raven's agenda should be my own."

He paused and stared at the statue for another moment. Then, he said, "I accept your proposal."

"Welcome to our family," Adsden said. His smile slipped away, and his eyes spoke promises as he caught Fierdon's gaze. "No one leaves the family— not alive."

Attica leaned forward and stroked Fierdon's arm. He jerked with surprise but did not pull away. "Will your skin take ink?"

"I do not *ink*," he said with disgust.

Attica chuckled and pulled up her sleeve to reveal the black Diamond Claw tattoo. "I meant regular ink."

Adsden exposed his own tattoo. Both had been modified recently. The symbols of their respective guilds were now clutched in the talons of a black raven.

"I am to receive one of those?" Fierdon asked.

"Of course," Attica said. "You are family."

A fire lit in Fierdon's eyes, and he looked to Adsden. "What is our mission?"

Adsden smiled and said, "We are thieves. We are going to steal something."

"What are we to steal?" Fierdon asked.

"People," Adsden said with a grin.

～

"I was betrothed."

"Betrothed?" Tam asked.

Ilanet nodded and hurriedly added, "Yes, but no longer."

In her mind, she told herself she knew not why she had said it but, in truth, she did. She wanted Tam to know that she was not a child. While she was not ready to consider marriage, she felt comfortable with Tam. Over the course of the week that they had been on the ship, he had always treated her with deference, and she knew he would never act presumptively. The Raven—or Rezkin—had said that he would not marry her and neither would he sell her. She knew it would be impossible for her to marry a commoner, but Tam was not just any commoner, and she was not much of a princess. If he was truly Lord Rezkin's best friend, then maybe?

After a moment of uncomfortable silence, Tam said, "But you're too young."

"I will be of age next year," she said. "It is not uncommon to make these arrangements early."

"So I have heard," Tam muttered. "Is that why you are here? Did you run away?"

"Well, yes—and no. I am not so eager to wed, and my betrothed was"— she tapped her lip as she searched for the word—"*insufferable*."

"You two didn't get along?"

"I did never speak with him," she said, "but I did hear him speak to other people. He is terrible, and I wished for a younger man."

"Why would your parents want you to marry someone you don't like?"

Ilanet gathered her hair again, drawing it over one shoulder. She had never worn her hair loose before, but some of the other women on the ship did so often. Somehow, it made her feel free. She was free to choose how to wear her hair, and no one would scold her for her unkempt tangles.

"My mother died. I was very young. My father did not marry again. He had ... how do you call them? Other women?"

"Mistresses?" Tam said uncomfortably.

"Yes, *mistresses*, but he sees them for only servants. All women are servants to him. He does not care for me."

She glanced at Xa, who was standing several paces away pretending he was not listening to their conversation. He flicked his fingers in the way that meant he had erected a sound ward. She was fascinated with the silent method of communication she had witnessed between Rezkin and Xa or the strikers. Xa was not a striker, though. He was not even Ashaiian. She wondered if they were using different signals in the same way that they spoke different languages.

"He's your father," Tam said. "I'm sure he cares—"

"He tried to kill me."

His head snapped up, and he looked at her in alarm. "What?"

Ilanet kept her gaze on the rolling sea. It was soothing and mesmerizing—when it was not making her ill. She blinked several times to clear the moisture from her eyes. She told herself it was only the salty breeze that drew the tears because she would not cry for that horrible man.

She took a deep breath and said, "He thought it would give him a political advantage. He wished to blame my death on my betrothed so he could blackmail the man's family. A stranger saved me, and he arranged for Lus and me to escape with all of you."

"That's terrible!" said Tam. "I can't imagine ... I mean, I don't even want to think about how horrible it would feel to have my own father betray me like that. I'm so sorry, Lady Netty."

Ilanet turned to Tam. "I should like to wait a while before marriage, maybe five or six years."

Tam smiled and said, "I think that sounds like a good idea—for you, I mean. Not that it's any of my business."

"What about you, Tam?" Ilanet asked.

"I haven't thought about it, really. I don't have much to offer right now. Mostly, though, I kind of feel like I'm just starting this big adventure. It's frightening, and I feel horrible about all the terrible things that are happening. I don't even know what has become of my family. I guess I feel like I shouldn't even be considering starting a family in a time like this."

Ilanet frowned and then smoothed her face out of habit. A lady should always remain composed and never don unattractive expressions. "I read a book about a war that lasted over a hundred years. Well, the book was not about the war, really. It was about horses. But, the war, lasted over a hundred years. It lasted such a long time, that these horse breeders created a new breed. The new horses had greater endurance, and they were bigger, stronger, and more aggressive than the others. The book claimed that it was because of this new type of horse that the war finally ended."

"That's really interesting. I'm kind of surprised that you are interested in wars and horses, though."

Ilanet laughed. "I cannot say that I was interested in the book. I read anything that was available. I like learning. I like horses, too, even though I have never ridden one. They are majestic animals."

Tam ventured, "Yes, but ... I'm not exactly sure what this has to do with the previous conversation."

"Oh, I apologize. Sometimes my mind makes ... um ...connections, and I forget others cannot follow. I am thinking that if a war can last over one hundred years, you cannot afford to wait until it is over to find happiness. People must keep living and find love where they can. They must enjoy what happiness is to be had."

Tam was silent for a time. Finally, he said, "I think your father made a big mistake in undervaluing you. You're an intelligent lady, and I imagine you will do great things as you get older—that is assuming you don't end up with someone who treats you like he did. Ah, sorry. I shouldn't have said that."

"No, I appreciate you saying it, Tam," Ilanet said with a smile. She laid her hand on his where it rested on the crate that served as their seat. "It means much coming from you."

Tam was not sure why it meant so much coming from *him*, but he was glad to see Lady Netty smile. Now that he knew the source of her melancholy, he completely understood. Over the past week, she had been friendly and smiled often, but the cheer never reached her eyes. They always held sadness, a look that was shared by most on the ship. Loss and betrayal were a commonality among the passengers, and Lady Netty's had been most personal.

Tam looked up as Frisha approached. She had also been making friends with Lady Netty, taking the younger girl under her wing in hopes of making her feel more comfortable on a ship full of strangers.

"Hi, Netty," Frisha said as she sat down to Tam's other side.

"Greetings, Frisha."

"Oh, right. *Greetings*," Frisha said.

Lady Netty had been helping Frisha to become more *ladylike*, and since she never acted condescending or judgmental, Frisha had been open to her assistance.

"We were just discussing the value of pursuing relationships during a time of war," Tam said. "Relationships in general—not one between us, I mean, of course not." Tam could feel his face heating, so he quickly moved on. "Lady Netty is wise beyond her years." To Lady Netty, he said, "You kind of remind me of Rezkin, you know."

Her eyes widened. "*Me*? No, I am nothing like *him*."

"You say that as if you don't like him," Frisha said, leaning around Tam to see the other girl.

Lady Netty shook her head and said, "No, I do not dislike him exactly. I am afraid of him. I am sorry. I do not wish to say more for fear of offense. I know you are close with Lord Rezkin."

"No, it's okay," Frisha said. She looked at Lady Netty thoughtfully, and Tam wondered what silent communication was happening between the two women. Whatever it was, it had somehow passed through him without pause. "You've seen it, haven't you? The emptiness."

Lady Netty gazed at the dark blue water as she nodded. "My father is not a good man," she said, "but always his eyes were *filled*—filled with anger, mistrust, ambition, and sometimes … what is it? … *glee*. I suppose I was always in fear of him. His moods changed without warning. Lord Rezkin is steady. I have not seen him lash out in anger, even when it was warranted."

"How is that a problem?" Tam asked.

Lady Netty looked as though she wanted to say more. "We should not discuss such matters. I-I should go." She stood to leave, and Tam jumped to his feet.

"Wait. We can talk about something else. I'd like to show you something."

She looked at him with skepticism and glanced at Frisha, who also appeared to be at a loss.

"Great!" he said with a grin. Without thinking, he grabbed her hand and pulled her along behind him. After a few steps, he realized what he had done and dropped it quickly. "S-sorry, Lady Netty. I didn't mean—"

Netty smiled and said, "It is fine, Tam."

Tam happily led the two women to the stall where Pride was kept. The life mages had been doing an admirable job of keeping the horse calm. Even so, Pride protested with snorts and stomps whenever anyone got too close. Tam grinned and held out a hand showing off the horse.

Lady Netty and Frisha both stared at the beast and then looked to Tam.

"Lord Rezkin's horse?" Lady Netty asked. "I have seen him already—from a distance. He looks much larger up close."

Tam grinned. "What did they call that new breed of horse in your book?"

"*Cuorstuvor*," she said. At their questioning look, she added, "This translates as, maybe, *horse of war*."

Tam nodded toward the horse and said, "We call them battle chargers."

Lady Netty's face brightened. "This is a *cuorstuvor*? I have not seen one. I read that they are sometimes gifted to royalty outside of Ashai but are made unable to breed."

"This one's sire was King Bordran's own," Tam said.

Lady Netty drew her gaze from the horse to look at Tam with surprise. "How did Lord Rezkin get the king's horse?"

Tam and Frisha shared a look. "Well, that's still not clear," he said. Pausing as a burst of short whistles announced the midday meal, he shook his head and smiled. "Time to eat!"

Tam turned to escort the ladies to the mess and nearly ran into Lus. He had forgotten about the guard and was unnerved that the man had been hovering behind him without his noticing. Rezkin would be disappointed if he knew how oblivious he had been. Lus grinned and flipped a knife end over end in his hand. He caught the blade by the tip and offered it to Tam, hilt first. Tam stared at the knife in wonder and then realized it was his own belt knife.

"Your master will hear of this," Lus said.

"Oh, come on!" Tam protested.

"I am to hear of what?" a deep voice said from the doorway.

Tam groaned. "As if having the strikers watch my every move wasn't enough. Now you have Lus doing it too?"

Rezkin raised a brow. "If Lus is harassing you, he is doing it of his own accord. I suggest you learn to defend against it."

"*What*? But he's an experienced guardsman," Tam argued.

"How else do you expect to gain experience?" Rezkin asked. "If you wait until you meet a foe in truth, you will be dead before you realize your mistake. It is better to do so here, where he knows I will cause him great pain before his death should he kill you."

Tam scowled at Lus. "Are you so sure he won't anyway?"

Lus glanced at Rezkin and said, "I have no desire to die a meaningless death."

"Then I hope my death never has meaning for you," Tam muttered.

The man met Rezkin's gaze and said, "We shall see."

A dark shadow appeared to pass through Rezkin's icy blue eyes. A chill descended in the stall, as if frost had been carried on an absent wind from the great Void itself. Tam shivered and could have sworn he saw his breath in the still air. Wood cracked loudly in the stillness when Pride suddenly kicked at his stall. Lus was the first to break eye contact, lowering his gaze as he bowed toward the silent warrior. Tam sucked in the breath he had lost and glanced back to the ladies. They had moved closer together and were gripping each other's hands.

Rezkin blinked lazily and turned his clear gaze on them. His facial expression had not changed, and yet he seemed a different person than he had seconds before, a friendly person, a *decent* person.

"Lus will escort the ladies to the mess," he said, as if death had not just been hovering in the air. "Tam, you will accompany me."

Frisha and Lady Netty scurried out of the stall ahead of Lus, both women appearing as if they wanted to be nowhere near the strange guard. Tam thought it odd considering that Lus was supposed to be Lady Netty's escort. He wondered if she was upset with her guard for antagonizing Rezkin. Then he questioned why anyone who knew the reputation of *Dark Tidings* would do such a thing.

Rezkin led Tam far from the mess, spying Wesson on the way and insisting the mage attend him as well. When they finally reached a satisfactory position, Rezkin turned to face them. Tam noticed that Rezkin kept a close eye on the entrance to the mess as he directed Wesson to erect a sound ward. Tam could not feel or see anything, but Rezkin seemed to approve.

"What were you doing in Pride's stall with Lus?" Rezkin asked.

"I wasn't doing anything with Lus," Tam said. He rubbed the back of his neck and said, "Actually, I forgot he was there. I was showing Pride to Lady Netty. She has an interest in battle chargers."

Rezkin tilted his head. "Lady Netty is interested in battle chargers?"

"So she says," Tam said. "She read a book about them."

Rezkin stared contemplatively at the mess entrance and then said, "Tam, this is important. Do not underestimate Lus. He is dangerous."

"Yeah, I figured that. You can't tell me he's a normal guard, Rez. Something's not right about him."

Rezkin held Tam's gaze for an uncomfortable moment. Finally, he said, "You are correct, and I am glad that you have become so discerning. He is not a guard. He is an assassin."

"An assassin," Tam shouted and then, upon realizing his error, was glad no one could hear his outburst through the ward.

"A highly skilled assassin," Rezkin clarified. "Be vigilant." He looked to Wesson and said, "He is also a mage, trained to use his *talent* in battle and subterfuge."

"I sensed his power," Wesson said, "although he conceals it well. I believe he may employ a misdirection spell so that mages will think the power is emanating from someone or something else nearby."

Tam was furious that Rezkin was *just now* bringing this to his attention. "Did you know he was an assassin when he came aboard?"

"Of course," Rezkin said.

Even more dissatisfied, Tam asked, "Does he know that you know he's an assassin?" Without giving Rezkin a chance to respond, he yanked at his hair in frustration and said, "Why would you bring an assassin onto our ship, anyway?"

Rezkin waited for Tam to stop huffing before he answered. "Yes, he knows that I know, and I brought him because he may be useful. We are at war, Tam."

"And Lady Netty?" Tam asked. "Is she an assassin, too? Tell me she isn't. She can't be."

"No, she is not an assassin. She is innocent."

Gritting his teeth, Tam said, "Then why does she have an assassin as her guard? Does she know?"

"He is guarding her because I assigned him to the position. She knows he is an assassin, and I do not believe she cares for the circumstances."

"Why would you assign an assassin to guard her? Make it stop, Rezkin. I want her safe."

Rezkin sighed. "Assassins do not go about randomly killing people, Tam, and he is not a savage animal. He will do as I command. As I said, he is highly skilled and, besides the strikers, is the most capable warrior on this ship."

"If he respects you so much, then why did he threaten me? I know he was doing it to goad you. I just don't know *why*."

Rezkin said, "I would prefer not to involve you in this, but it seems he has singled you out. I will not have you going about unaware of the danger. He is not just any assassin. He is a very high-ranking member of the Order, the premier assassin's guild in Channería. The Order is to Channería as the Black Hall is to Ashai."

Tam's heart pounded harder with every word Rezkin spoke. "When you say *very high*—"

"He is the Jeng'ri, second to the Ong'ri, the grandmaster of the guild. His name is Xa. The Order has a strict set of principles. For now, he is beholden to me for reasons I will not discuss. So long as he sees me as the superior warrior, he will do as I say. He continually searches for weakness, though, and he was hoping to find one in you. He knows already that I will kill him if he attacks *me* again."

"Again?"

Ignoring Tam's interruption, Rezkin said, "He was testing to see what I would do if he threatened you, my *best friend*. If I had been more protective of you, warning him off, he would have thought you one of my weaknesses. If I failed to stand up to his challenge altogether, he might have believed I lack conviction. The assassins fight amongst themselves, but the guild stands together against their enemies. He knows you are my apprentice. By ordering you to fend against him yourself, I have placed you in the tiers. It is dishonorable for a superior assassin to challenge a trainee to the death. Henceforth, any moves he makes against you will be within the relational constraints of master to student. This does not mean you cannot get seriously injured or killed. Again, I emphasize vigilance."

"Wait, you're saying that I am to train to be an *assassin*?"

"I am not saying that you must become one, Tam, only that you will acquire the *Skills*. Aside from outright killing Xa, which would be a terrible waste of a valuable resource, it is the best protection I can provide for you. Besides, such *Skills* will aid you in any battle."

Tam was overwhelmed. He looked to Wesson as if the mage could magically fix things. Wesson shrugged at Tam, clearly at a loss, and then crossed his arms as he looked accusingly at Rezkin.

"Why do *you* know so much about assassins?" the mage asked.

Tam looked at Rezkin as well. He had been too astounded to think of the obvious question. He knew a little more about Rezkin's training than most, but Rezkin had never mentioned assassins.

"For the same reason I know about mages, healers, nobles, and blacksmiths," Rezkin said. "It is my responsibility to know about *all* of the people I may encounter, *especially* potential enemies. Now that you know of the potential danger, you will both be better prepared to deal with it. If you become overwhelmed, you know to come to me or one of the strikers. I believe Xa has been *testing* them a bit as well. At least it should keep them sharp."

"Is this how you want to live?" Tam asked. "Always on edge?"

"Who said anything about *want*?" Rezkin replied. "This is life."

Tam said, "No, this is *your* life. My family never had to deal with anything like this."

"Let us hope they never have to, but you are not like them. *You* are an adventurer," Rezkin finished with a grin.

With another groan, Tam said, "I'm starting to wish I had been born boring."

Rezkin turned to Wesson and said, "What say you, Journeyman?"

"I suppose not much has changed," Wesson said. "It seems as if death has been following us since the moment I met you."

"Not true," Rezkin said. "Your donkey lived."

11

The trio joined the others in the mess, and Tieran beckoned Tam to sit between him and Wesson. Rezkin looked at them both curiously and then sat at the same table beside Frisha. This conveniently placed him across from Xa, who was seated between Ilanet and Shiela. Malcius, Brandt, and Waylen were dining with the baron at a smaller table. Kai sat in a chair with his back to the wall by the door that was kept locked while they dined. It was Wesson's job to make sure their conversations were not overheard.

Ilanet glanced up from her meal. "*Lord Rezkin,*" she said in Channerían, "*the 'tree' in our room has not moved since we left Serret. Should we be worried?*"

Rezkin shrugged and said, "*Probably not. The thing is ancient. I am sure it can take care of itself.*"

Frisha turned to him and remarked, "I didn't know you speak Channerían."

Leaving Rezkin no chance to respond, Tieran interjected, "Not only that, but they must be speaking in code."

"How so?" Rezkin asked, thoroughly confused by Tieran's assertion.

"Why would she expect a tree to *move*, and how is it supposed to take care of itself? Have you been watering it? Plants need water, you know."

"I trust in your expert judgment," Rezkin replied as he shoved a bite of fish into his mouth.

Ilanet glanced at Tieran and then back to Rezkin. Switching to Ashaiian, she said, "Lord Tieran is an expert in ... *trees*?"

Rezkin shook his head, which earned a frown from Tieran. "He is a life mage with a strong bond to plants."

Ilanet relaxed her shoulders. "Just plants."

"Now wait a minute," Tieran said. "What are you two talking about?"

Ilanet smiled and changed the subject. "I do not yet know if I possess the *talent*. My father is a wind mage, and my mother was an illusionist."

Rezkin looked at her sharply, but the damage had already been done. He mentally commended her, though, for keeping her secret so long. He had not expected it since she was only a small-one, untrained in subterfuge.

"Illusionism is an unusual *talent*," Tieran said as he scrutinized the young lady.

"What is illusionism?" Tam asked from beside him.

"Perhaps Journeyman Wesson can explain it better," Tieran muttered.

He furrowed his brow and sank into deep contemplation. Rezkin could see that his cousin was working toward the solution, and it was only a matter of moments before the secret was revealed.

Wesson swallowed the bite he had just stuffed into his mouth and took a drink while bobbing his head. Finally, he said, "It is an unusual ratio dominated by the elemental powers of pyris, or fire, and tropestrian, which is wind, with a miniscule concentration of amber, the power to bond and interact with plants and animals, in the tertiary envelope—or so it is defined by the readers. Weak illusionists can manifest images or sounds that do not really exist, but strong ones can make the illusions physical, seeming so real that you cannot tell them from reality. An illusionist's power produces the illusion and then invades the mind to convince someone that it is real. It has been suggested that the talent is rare because it is possible for an illusionist to be seized by his own power, during which time it drives *itself* until the wielder dies from overexertion—that and the fact that illusionists are often murdered because people fear any power that can manipulate the mind."

"Like Rezkin's spell," Frisha said with a generous scowl in his direction.

"What?" Wesson looked at Rezkin with wide eyes. He sat back in his chair and then groaned as he ran his hands through caramel locks. "Why did I not think of it *before*?"

Tieran suddenly slammed a hand down on the table and lurched to his feet.

"You went to Serret to file some paperwork, and you came back with a new kingdom, a treaty, and a *princess*?"

Rezkin sat back in his own chair and calmly looked at Tieran.

"What princess?" Tam asked, and Rezkin could see the anxiety growing behind his friend's eyes.

"*Netty*," Tieran said mockingly with a derisive laugh. "Sixteen, her father a wind mage, her mother an illusionist—Ilanet! *Princess* Ilanet!"

Ilanet's cheeks flushed, and she looked back to Rezkin. "Oops."

"When were you going to tell us?" Tieran exclaimed.

"Probably never," Malcius muttered from the adjacent table. "At least, not until he is standing over all our graves."

"Malcius, that is uncalled for," Frisha said.

While Tieran and Malcius were absorbed with berating Rezkin, Tam was focused on Ilanet. She looked as if she wanted to disappear under the table. She must have felt him staring because she turned to meet his gaze. Her eyes held pain and sorrow, and her gaze was pleading.

Tam said, "Your father—the man who tried to kill you—was the *king*? King Ionius?"

She blinked a few times, her lips quivering with words unspoken.

Tieran caught Tam's remark, which drew his attention to Ilanet. "Is this true?"

Ilanet closed her mouth and nodded.

Tieran looked back to Rezkin. "Did you steal her? Did your incessant desire to save people drive you to *kidnap* a princess? What about the treaty? Ionius will go to war over this!"

Rezkin said, "Do you think me so irresponsible? The princess was part of the treaty. In fact, Ionius insisted."

"Kings do not simply give away their daughters," Tieran said with a glare.

Frisha's anxiety had also spiked with the revelation. Like Tam, she stared not at Rezkin but at Ilanet. "Why are you here? What was the deal?" she asked.

Frisha tried to remain calm and congenial, but by the look on Ilanet's face, she thought she might have failed. She did not want to scare the poor girl, whom she had come to think of as the younger sister she never had, but as her own dark thoughts welled within, her tone had acquired an unbidden edge.

Ilanet looked at Frisha and thought that this was how the mouse must feel when cornered by the cat. "Well, I was not present," she started, but by the hard glare directed her way, she knew Frisha would not be satisfied with that answer. She glanced at Rezkin and then swallowed. "But I am told that my father believes I am to marry Dark Tidings."

Tam said, "You told me you were no longer betrothed!"

"I am not," Ilanet said, quickly turning back to him. "My father broke my betrothal to Prince Nyan when he gave me to Dark Tidings."

Tam turned his glare on Rezkin, who was by that point receiving the same from almost everyone in the room.

Rezkin held up a hand. "I will tell you the same as I told Ionius. I do not intend to marry Princess Ilanet. By the treaty, she is here solely as my ward." He met Tieran's angry gaze and said, "I did not aim to deceive you indefinitely. It is true that Ionius planned for Ilanet to die. It was for her safety, and everyone else's, that I wanted to get as far from Channería as possible before her identity was revealed. This was to diminish the possibility that someone aboard might be capable of sending word back to the mainland."

Brandt broke his silence to say, "But if Ionius agreed to the treaty, then he knows already that she is aboard."

Rezkin nodded. "True, but where royalty is concerned, we must recognize the potential for more than one enemy. She was disguised upon boarding, and it may be that others did not recognize her. Without the fanfare, as would be typical for the departure of a royal, some may question whether she made it aboard at all. So long as people are speculating, they will be unlikely to implement any plans, at least until their suspicions are confirmed. You must remember that we are only one ship sailing to a questionable destination. Most aboard are already wanted in Ashai for treason and sedition. We are a prime target for pretty much anyone who wants to make a lot of money and is in possession of a few ships."

Tieran narrowed his eyes. "Which raises the question, why did Ionius not send at least a couple of war ships as escort? And why only one guard?"

"Remember, Ionius wants her dead, if for no other reason than to cover up his failed attempt," Rezkin said.

Brandt added, "He would be more likely to blow us out of the water than to help."

Tieran dragged his chair back over the floorboards and retook his seat. "So how did she end up *here*?"

Rezkin looked at Ilanet, whom he noticed glanced more often at Tam than anyone. Tam now sat brooding with his elbows on the table and head buried in his hands. "As I said, King Ionius insisted. It seems her rescuer made a deal with the king to see her to safety."

Tieran said, "And you, Lus, are you this rescuer?"

Xa tilted his head and grinned. "No, I do not possess—how did you say? —an *incessant desire to save people*. I was also unaware of the plot against the princess. I had only a small part in the events."

"So who saved you, then?" Tieran asked the princess.

"I think I am not supposed to say," she said without meeting his eyes.

Kai took the opportunity to interject his thoughts. "I will tell you who it was. It was the *Fishers*."

Tam's head jerked up, and he looked at the striker incredulously. "*Fishermen* saved the *princess*?"

"Bah! Not fishermen," Kai said. "The Fishers. They are an underground group of activists dedicated to exposing corruption within all facets of Channerían society—the nobility, guilds, merchants, military, and even the Temple."

"A bunch of commoners?" Malcius asked.

"Not at all," Kai replied. "Anyone can become a fisher, and their members span all classes. In Ashai, people vie for power, and corruption exists, but in the end, the king commands all. It works well when a good king sits the throne, but when the king harbors a dark soul—well, such is the nature of our own predicament. In Channería, the king still bears the ultimate authority, but the power to make policies and carry them out is divided between the various offices of the council, the Temple, and the military. If the king wants to change anything, he must seek approval from those entities. More people are in positions of greater power, which means a greater chance of corruption. Such an environment inevitably leads to the formation of groups like the Fishers."

Malcius glanced at Rezkin with narrowed eyes and then returned his attention to the striker. "What makes you think these Fishers have anything to do with Princess Ilanet's rescue?"

"You might recall there was a delay in the arrival of the treaty on the day we departed. I was sent to investigate. It turns out there was an uprising. The Fishers had somehow uncovered a plot by one of the council offices to usurp funds from the military, or something to that effect. I did not have time to get the whole story. This was brought to the attention of another council office, which took the issue before the council. The general of the army, who also holds a seat on the council, went to Ionius for support. Ionius hates having to answer to the council for anything, so when they cause trouble, he comes down hard on them.

"Meanwhile, Ionius was also in negotiations with our own Dark Tidings. The council, already in hot water, voted in favor of Ionius's proposal. The general, however, was incensed that he was not included in negotiations, and the Temple was angered that, for the most part, its stipulations were rejected. The council blames the Fishers for the whole debacle. The military has historically been opposed to the Fishers but has sided with them anyway, since it was they who revealed the plot to steal military funds. The general and the council both have concerns about the repercussions of Ionius's treatment of Prince Nyan of Jerea. In addition, the general has been ordered to carry out the internment and sale of any Ashaiians found in Channería, which does not sit well with him, from what I hear."

"What does this have to do with Princess Ilanet?" Tieran asked.

"I was getting to that," Kai said with a huff. "Now, you have to understand that this information was not easy to get in such a short time, although some of it was discovered during other outings. I did not have the luxury of validation, and it is difficult to put together with such limitations. I only share it with you now because Rezkin gave us permission to do so once Princess Ilanet's identity was revealed." He paused with a look at Rezkin for confirmation and then continued. "There are rumors within the council that the Fishers are involved with someone called the Raven."

Frisha exclaimed, "You mean the one that took over the thieves and assassins in Ashai?"

Kai paused. "You know of him?"

"Yes, he was in Justain when we were there. Uncle Marcum was concerned that he might also have been in Kaibain."

"Was he now? Interesting," Kai said with an almost imperceptible glance at Rezkin.

Tam said, "We were told not to talk about it, Frisha."

Frisha rolled her eyes and waved at the striker. "It's not like it's a secret. They all know now."

Kai glanced between the two and then said, "I admit I was a bit behind on those events, but Shezar and Roark filled me in on what they know. Anyway, it is said that the Fishers have been emboldened by apparent support from the Raven. I think, under normal circumstances, they would never align themselves with someone who so obviously lives contrary to their creed; but with the council cracking down on their activities, it seems the Fishers have decided to rally behind him."

Rezkin had noticed Ilanet becoming more troubled by the moment, so it was no surprise when she finally spoke. "You are saying that the *Fishers*, the men and women who have fought against corruption for decades, now serve the *Raven*?"

Kai stroked his beard thoughtfully. "I did not get much information about that, but I doubt they actually *serve* him—more like they are using his reputation and influence to advance their cause."

"That is a dangerous game," said Xa. "If a man hides behind the shield of a demon, he had best be willing to serve when the demon calls."

Kai grunted. "They are probably hoping he will not notice."

Malcius glanced at Rezkin out of the corner of his eye and then turned back to Kai. "Then he was not in Serret?"

With a shrug, Kai said, "It seems doubtful. The other strikers told me that all the reports received prior to boarding in Skutton indicated he was moving west. We intercepted intelligence in Serret that appears to confirm this. In the past month, the Raven's influence has spread from Vogn in the Southern Peninsula nearly to Zigharan's End in the north. Of course, he cannot be everywhere that the reports claim, but he has been impossible to pin down. We believe members of his network, probably those from the Black Hall, are posing in his stead."

"So he could have been in Serret," Malcius said.

"I suppose," Kai said with another glance at Rezkin, "but I see no reason for him to go there when he has been running a highly effective campaign in Ashai."

"Why has it been so effective?" Ilanet asked.

Rezkin thought she was intentionally avoiding his gaze, but he could not tell if she did so to preserve his secret or because she was afraid—perhaps both.

"He is a mass murderer," Tam interjected, and Ilanet looked at him with surprise.

Xa also considered the young man. He glanced at Rezkin with a blank expression. Rezkin noted the assassin's interest but put the concern aside for the time being. Instead, he observed the anger and disgust on his *friend's* face. It was the second time Tam had referred to him as such, and he did not care for it. He

was conducting a war. People died in war. None of his victims had been innocent, and his standing orders protected the lives and property of those who were.
Of course, no one on the ship knew of the changes he had made to the way the
Ashaiian underworld conducted business. He hoped Tam would understand if he
learned the truth. He turned his attention back to Kai who was explaining.

"He or his surrogates kill the opposition and spare anyone willing to serve.
Criminals are, by nature, a selfish lot. It is rare that any are willing to put their
own necks on the chopping block for loyalty's sake. It seems most have realized it is in their best interest to serve the Raven. It was his acquisition of the
Black Hall that solidified his dominion; though, I have no idea how he
managed that."

"You knew about this?" Malcius asked with a hard stare at Rezkin.

"Knew about what?" he asked.

"About the Fishers' involvement in saving the princess and their possible
connection to a notorious criminal overlord."

Rezkin tilted his head. "The strikers informed me of their findings and
subsequent conclusions. It is best for everyone that I not divulge how the
princess came into my company. What does it matter anyway?"

"It matters because *she* might be somehow involved in a plot by the
Raven! How do we know we can trust her? Or *him*, for that matter," Malcius
said, pointing at the man he knew as Lus. "Who knows what evil is behind the
plot."

"You think saving a princess's life is an evil plot?" Rezkin asked.

Malcius said, "No, but he could be using it to his advantage."

"Malcius makes sense, Rezkin," Frisha said. "Saving someone without any
strings attached does not sound like something the Raven would do."

Xa grinned and looked at Rezkin as he said, "No, but it does sound like
something the Fishers would do."

"If it's true, and the Raven is involved, then maybe he isn't really evil,"
Frisha said.

Everyone turned to her with questioning stares.

Startled by the sudden attention, she said, "What? From everything I've
heard, the Raven has only attacked criminals. Maybe he's like a rebel for
justice—or something."

Tam said, "He's killed a lot of people, Frisha, and he didn't just attack the
criminal guilds. He claimed them as his own. Why are you always so eager to

excuse killers?" Tam shut his mouth and glanced at Rezkin, who raised a brow in response.

Frisha flushed and scowled at Tam. "I'm just saying that we don't know the whole story."

Having allowed the striker to seed their minds with his erroneous deduction, Rezkin finally said, "Frisha is right. Not enough information has been recovered to reach a conclusion, and this kind of speculation leads only to inaccuracies that may continue to propagate until we forget they are not facts. Malcius's concern about the motives behind the princess's rescue is understandable given the extent of your conjecture, but considering that there is no conclusive evidence to prove that the Fishers or the Raven were involved, treating her or any of the passengers who boarded in Serret differently would be unjust and divisive. Based on my own knowledge of her rescue, I am reasonably confident that she currently poses little threat. Remember that Dark Tidings has accepted her as his ward, so she must be treated as a member of his family."

"For how much longer must we keep up this charade?" Tieran asked. "It is confusing and makes things uncomfortable every time I speak with the other passengers."

"I intend to make the revelation soon. I must do so in order to carry out the next stages of my plan."

Tieran looked at Rezkin for a long moment, and no one else seemed willing to breach the wall of silence that stood between them. Finally, he said, "If it were not for your plan, you would never reveal yourself, would you?"

"Why would I?" Rezkin asked.

Tieran scoffed. "Perhaps because you are *king*! It is a position of power and honor coveted by all."

"All except by you and Thresson," Rezkin said.

"I cannot imagine why anyone who knows what the position entails would want it," Tieran said, "but if you are going to have the responsibility anyway, you might as well reap the benefits."

Rezkin rose from his seat and stared down at Tieran. "You do not want the position because you already have power and wealth. Caydean is trying to take that away from you. Without me, the only way to preserve your family is for you to take the throne. Given the choice, would you rather bear the weight of the crown or die an exiled pauper whose entire family was executed?"

Tieran snapped his mouth shut and swallowed hard. "I am reminded that I am lucky you are here."

Rezkin walked toward the door and paused beside his cousin. He leaned over and said, "Remember, Tieran, if anything happens to *me*, the task of liberating Ashai from a mad king is *yours*."

Rezkin had not yet reached the door when it shook with a series of heavy thuds. Kai opened the portal to reveal Captain Estadd standing on the other side. Jimson followed the ship's captain into the mess.

Estadd saluted and said, "Lord Rezkin, we have sighted land. We should be at Uthrel by dusk."

"We are not going to Uthrel," Rezkin stated.

Everyone looked at him in surprise.

Estadd cleared his throat and inquired, "My lord, did you not order us to sail to the Yeltin Isles?"

Rezkin nodded and replied, "I did, Captain, but we will not be disembarking in Uthrel. We go to Cael."

Estadd said, "I knew that Dark Tidings had been granted dominion over the island, but Cael is deserted. Nothing is there! No people, no shelter! And, it is nearly impossible to make land since the entire island is surrounded by jagged rocks and cliffs."

Rezkin stared at the captain as the man shifted uncomfortably.

"Ah, pardon me, my lord. I did not mean to question you, but—"

"I think you will find there is more to Cael than you believe," Rezkin said. "We will make land in a cove on the northern side of the island. I will assist you in finding the place."

"You have been there?" the captain asked skeptically.

"No, but I trust in the knowledge imparted to me," Rezkin stated. "See to it, Captain."

"Aye, my lord," Captain Estadd replied with a formal salute.

After the captain left, Tieran asked, "What is so special about Cael?"

Rezkin tilted his head and contemplated his companions before answering. "On the island of Cael stands an ancient stronghold that predates modern civilization. The people who existed there were long departed when our forefathers crossed the mountains. At least, that is what the legends claim."

"Legends?" Tieran asked, his gaze shifting over the other faces to observe an equal level of confusion.

"No one has actually *seen* the stronghold in recent history," Rezkin replied. "Our knowledge of the place exists solely in the legends of these eastern regions, although I am sure Gendishen has spent no small amount of resources looking for the place."

"What do you mean by 'looking for the place'?" Tieran asked in alarm. "I thought you and the captain knew where it was!"

Rezkin nodded and said, "Like I said, it is supposed to be on Cael, the northernmost island of the Yeltin Isles, but no one has actually found the stronghold. The island is uninhabited as it is quite rocky, has no fresh water source, and is without decent land for farming and grazing. As the captain said, it also lacks a place to make landfall."

"Except for this cove," Jimson observed.

"Yes."

Tieran shook his head and said, "I admit that my knowledge of geography is not great, but I happen to remember that the northern islands of the Yeltin Isles are very small. If such a fortress exists, surely the Gendishen found it long ago."

"Yet, they have not. Some claim it never existed at all. I believe that not only does it exist, it can only be accessed from the cove," Rezkin explained.

Malcius said, "If there is such a cove, someone must have found it already. As Tieran said, the island is not that big. You could probably sail around it in a few hours."

"True," Rezkin conceded. "I believe the reason no one has found it is because it is warded."

Tieran scoffed. "I am sure the Gendishen have thought of that. Most naval ships have at least one mage on board."

"Yes, but I do not believe they had sufficient *Skills* to detect the ward," Rezkin replied.

Wesson said, "Rezkin, any mage can sense a ward."

Rezkin shook his head. "I believe this ward is different. These were ancient people. We should not assume they used the same kind of magic or wards that are used today."

"Okay, then how do you propose we find this cove?" Wesson asked. "If you are expecting *me* to be able to find it when all the other mages could not, I doubt we will be successful."

"I think you underestimate yourself, Journeyman; but no, I was not expecting you to find the ward. I believe I may be able to find it. I have mastered the *Skills* of *Mage Ward Detection and Circumvention* and *Potential Ward Manipulation*."

Kai said, "What are you talking about? There are no such *Skills* in the training."

Rezkin shrugged. "There were in mine."

Tieran said, "Rezkin, mundanes cannot detect wards. Only those with mage power can do so."

"That is true," Wesson added, "which is why I have always found it fascinating that you are not only able to detect and walk through wards, but you are also capable of sensing when people are *using* mage power. As a mundane, you should not be able to feel anything."

"Are you sure you are not a mage?" Tieran asked with suspicion.

Rezkin shrugged and said, "I have been tested. Surely you or Wesson would be able to sense it if I were."

Tieran looked to Wesson who shook his head and said, "No, I have never detected any mage power coming from him or anywhere around him, for that matter—except of course, from his enchanted items."

"But, if he is my cousin, then he *must* be a mage," Tieran argued.

"You are assuming he is your cousin on your mother's side. It may be that the two of you are related on your father's side," Wesson replied.

"That is absurd," Kai said. "He looks just like the royal family."

The mage shook his head. "It is a conundrum, but we will not know for certain unless we have a blood sample willingly provided by someone of that line, and I doubt Caydean will be so accommodating."

Rezkin said, "It does not matter at this point. Right now, I need to see if I can find this warded cove."

Tam, Tieran, and Wesson followed on Rezkin's heels as they emerged into the sunlight. The sky was clear and the breeze balmy. More than a month had passed since the fateful tournament, and summer's stifling heat had waned. Rezkin returned to his quarters and donned the guise of Dark Tidings. As soon as he set foot on deck, he was greeted by Tam, who followed him to find Estadd at the helm discussing their plans with his first mate.

"Captain, how long until we reach the island?" Dark Tidings asked.

The captain turned and genuflected before answering, "The northern island is much closer than Uthrel. We should arrive within the hour."

"Very good. Sail past the island and turn back to approach from the east. We will trail the northern coastline."

"Aye, Your Majesty. What will we be looking for?" the captain asked.

"I will tell you when I see it," was Dark Tidings's curt reply. The captain saluted, but his dark eyes held only doubt.

Rezkin turned to the mage at his side. "Journeyman, gather all of the mages and any others with *talent* on the deck."

"Yes, Your Majesty," Wesson said as he scurried away.

Ever since leaving Skutton, his friends had taken to calling him *Your Majesty* or *King* when he was dressed as Dark Tidings. They claimed his title only held weight so long as people respected it, and that respect had to start with those who were closest to him. Rezkin could not argue the point, but he still inwardly cringed every time.

Tam asked, "Your Majesty, would you like an update while we wait?"

Rezkin inwardly winced. He especially did not care for it when Tam or Frisha used the honorific. "Yes, Tam, please go ahead," he replied.

Feeling somewhat useless, Tam had taken it upon himself to deliver regular reports and updates on the passengers and supplies. As such, people had begun going to the former carpenter's apprentice whenever they had requests or sought an audience with Rezkin or Dark Tidings. Some had begun referring to Tam as the king's seneschal in jest, but the humor seemed to have faded while the title remained. Rezkin figured that if he needed a seneschal, it might as well be Tam. The young man was decently educated, thanks to Frisha's successful merchant father, and Rezkin trusted him as much as he could trust anyone.

"Okay," Tam said as he rattled off lists from memory, since paper was a luxury in short supply. "The medical supplies are still sufficient, although Healer Jespia says we will need to resupply sometime in the next two weeks. Fresh water is still not a problem due to the desalination efforts of the water mages, which also provides us with an abundant supply of salt. Food is an issue, though. People tire of fish and seaweed," Tam said with disgust, "but the beans and potatoes are running low. Lord Tieran's little garden project doesn't provide enough for everyone."

Rezkin nodded as he maintained focus on the passing island. Bilior had not been as helpful as he had hoped in deciphering the puzzle of the island. It turned out the ancient fae had never actually been there. The creature was confident, though, that Rezkin possessed the *Skills* he needed to breach the wards. Since the katerghen was so powerful, Rezkin wondered why the creature did not use his own *talent* to get them through.

Eventually, all the passengers with *talent* gathered on the deck, and Rezkin arrayed them around its perimeter with orders to focus on sensing any ward or other use of *talent* emanating from beyond the ship. Because they had fled Skutton from the King's Tournament, most of the escapees were men and women of note. Of the refugees, about two-thirds were accomplished swordsmen or weapon masters, and a quarter had the *talent* to some extent. Two healers and three apprentice healers were aboard, including the unwilling Reaylin. He also had one life mage and two life mage apprentices, including Tieran, three elemental mages, one journeyman elemental mage, and four apprentice elemental mages. His battle mages included the unwilling but extremely powerful, naturally *talented* Journeyman Wesson and the battle-trained assassin of unspecified constructive *talent* Xa.

The remainder of the *talented* individuals did not have sufficient power or their ratios were not efficient enough to be considered for an apprenticeship. In fact, most of the apprentices had only entered into the positions since boarding the ship and did so at Rezkin's behest. Nobles usually did not formally apprentice because it meant stepping from the noble class to the mage class. While mages were highly respected, it was a respect that each mage had to earn by his own merit. Many nobles did not care for the idea of starting at the bottom of the hierarchy and having to earn their way to power.

The ship had been far from shore on the first pass of the island, but on the return, they hugged the coastline as close as the captain dared. Other passengers gathered on deck out of curiosity and an eagerness borne of enduring weeks at sea. None of the mages detected anything from the island, and many passengers were becoming concerned and restless. The northern side of the island was nothing but steep cliffs without even a hint of recess.

Rezkin tilted his head as he focused nearly all his attention on the barren cliff face. For the past several minutes, he had felt ... *something*. He was not certain at first, but the sensation grew as the ship crashed through choppy waters. A chill had seeped into his flesh, and it had gradually increased. He asked the mages around him if they sensed anything, to which they all responded in the negative. The chill clawed at his skin and then drove deeper into his muscles causing them to tighten. The bitter cold reached a sharp peak, and he could stand it no more. He knew something was different about this section of steep, rocky cliff standing before them in defiance of the sea.

Dark Tidings strode to the helm and said, "Captain, bring the ship to port."

"But, Sire, it is a solid wall," Estadd said, "and, as you can see, there are jagged rocks all around. We cannot get any closer without smashing the hull."

Dark Tidings said, "I gave you an order, Captain."

"You are the king, and I would follow your orders any other time, but I have no intention of smashing the ship to pieces and killing all these people." Estadd spoke with unconcealed anger and disgust that Rezkin would not have expected from the generally steady man.

He held the captain in stasis with his empty, black gaze and said, "Do you think I wish to die, Captain? Do you think I wish for these people to die? I said, *bring the ship to port*."

Frisha's soft voice interrupted him. "Y-Your Majesty, maybe we should …"

"Silence!" he shouted.

Frisha snapped her mouth shut, and Wesson pulled her away.

"Captain, bring the ship to port, or I will have your men do so without you."

The captain stared for only a moment before he had to look away. The older man began barking orders to his crew to turn the ship. A wave of unease and fear washed through those on deck, and the passengers' confusion was clear. The inhuman being they trusted, believed in, and some nearly worshipped, would take them all to a watery grave.

Standing at the bow, Rezkin felt the cold seep deeper into his bones and tried to *will* his body to warm. It was a struggle to keep from shivering. Others did not seem to feel the cold, but all around, their eyes were filling with an unnatural panic. It was not the fear of sailing toward a vertical cliff through rocky waters that had them so riled. The frantic, wild eyes were the unnatural result of an intrinsic *need* to move *away* from the area. The ship's steady motion faltered as panicked sailors began discordantly pulling at the rigging, and passengers and crew alike started screaming. They stumbled over each other as they attempted to run toward the stern.

"Halt!" the king's voice boomed over the chaos. Rezkin focused his *will* and pressed back against the cold that threatened to invade his core as he intoned, "Dismiss your fears and lend me your *will*. I will deliver you to safety!"

All turned their attention to the king, the dark and powerful warrior with black eyes. The words had been overly dramatic, but the katerghen had been clear on this point. The people had to *believe* that Rezkin could save them to break the spell. Frozen tendrils lashed at him as he focused on the minds of the people aboard the ship, even those below in the hold. Motions steadied and gazes cleared as the passengers' panic fled. Those closest to him would later swear the man had radiated light and power. The crewmen returned to their stations and righted the ship as they confidently sailed the rocky waters toward the cliff.

Without warning, Wesson abruptly tried to dart away. Rezkin reached out and seized the journeyman's robes. "To where do you run, Journeyman?" he asked, his voice deep and grating.

The mage's fear-filled blue-green gaze was caught in the black depths of his own enchantment. "I-I have to get away," he exclaimed with absolute certainty.

Rezkin pulled the mask from his face and held the mage's attention. "No, Wesson. All will be well."

The young mage swallowed hard as his terrified eyes blinked back at Rezkin.

A wash of cold flowed over Rezkin's skin and through his entire being, as though he had just stepped through a doorway into winter. The cold quickly travelled down Rezkin's arm, and when it reached the mage's fisted robes, Wesson was torn from Rezkin's grasp. The young mage screamed and flailed as an invisible force shoved him across the deck. Rezkin ran after him, grabbled the tousled mage from the wet planks, and dragged him away from the encroaching force to the stern. He stood Wesson on his feet and shook the distraught mage violently to break through the young man's panic.

"Wesson! Look at me!" Rezkin said. The mage's eyes once again seemed to focus on Rezkin's steely gaze, and Rezkin commanded him. "Give me your *will*, Wesson! Trust in *me*. I will carry you through."

Wesson blinked several times and gulped. Sweat beaded on his lip and brow as his frantic gaze bounced about. He noticed several people were staring at the two of them, but more people were exclaiming excitedly and smiling. Several were even running toward the bow, rather than away from it. Wesson glanced back at his employer and saw the concern and sincerity in Rezkin's gaze. He inhaled deeply and then made the conscious decision to abandon his fears and accept Rezkin's *will* as his own. For as long as he had known the warrior, Rezkin had never failed at anything he claimed he would accomplish. If Rezkin said he would get him through, then he would.

Rezkin felt the cold wash over them both, but Wesson did not seem to notice, nor was he thrown from the ship. He smiled down at the mage and announced, "It is over, Wesson. We are through the ward."

12

The cliff, it turned out, was not one massive wall, but two overlapping walls of rock that were several hundred feet high. Between the two walls was a deep channel just wide enough for two large ships to pass. After a few hundred yards, the channel turned back on itself and continued to where it ended in a cove surrounded by towering cliffs. A stone slab ran the length of the landward curve, and it was obvious this was not a natural feature. The flawlessly smooth platform possessed ornate stone pillars spaced at regular intervals along its length and was perfectly designed to secure several ships at a time. The *Stargazer* was a large merchant ship, and this dock could easily fit four or five such vessels. The entire cove might have held two dozen more ships with room to maneuver.

At the far end of the platform was a long, shallow ramp leading from the water into a massive cave that appeared to be a dry dock. Beyond the platform, set into the stone cliff that seemed to rise forever into the sky, were four sets of evenly spaced, massive stone doors at least thirty feet in height. They were hewn from the same stone as the cliff, and only their cathedral shape and the elegant carvings upon their faces betrayed their existence.

Above the doors and across the full length of the landward wall, was a banner of life-sized, beautifully detailed bas-reliefs depicting strange people, plants, and animals. Many of the people appeared elegant with flowing robes and long, formfitting dresses, while others were unmistakably warriors with massive physiques, magnificent armor, and wicked weapons. All of them were unusually tall, if they were carved to scale, and had smooth hair, well-defined muscles, and upswept, pointed ears. Rezkin felt possessed of reverence in this place, and he thought the other passengers might have sensed it as well. Voices were subdued as people gawked and pointed to the beautiful depictions and impressive architecture.

The ship drew alongside the dock, and crewmen threw ropes around the stone pillars, cinching them until the ship was held fast. Passengers and crew stood in tense silence as they waited for anyone to appear from the towering citadel. When no one appeared, most turned to Rezkin. Their sense of awe upon entering the channel and cove had distracted them from the fact that he was unmasked, but now they were looking at him expectantly.

Rezkin turned to Captain Estadd, who appeared hesitant to speak. "Yes, Captain. I am Dark Tidings."

"But, Lord Rezkin ... uh, Your Majesty, I have seen you ... and him ... together, at the same time, and ..."

"The strikers took turns filling in for me to maintain the ruse."

"I see ..."

"Implement the security measures we discussed. The landing party will go ashore now."

"Aye, Your Majesty," the captain said.

The two strikers were first down the gangplank, darting forward as they inspected the doors and dry dock. Rezkin already wore the guise of Dark Tidings with the tabard of green lightning bolts on a black field. The Sheyalins were at his hips, and the black blade and great axe were strapped across his back. He would have preferred to forgo the great axe, but the Eastern Mountains men had opted to stay with him until he reached his destination. The axe was a source of pride for the men and the symbol of Rezkin's position as their chieftain. He donned the ominous black mask just in case someone was observing their arrival.

Rezkin was not the only one who had dressed for the occasion. While in Serret, Kai had taken it upon himself to purchase several skeins of thread and bolts of fabric in black and green. A wife of one of the tournament competitors who had fallen in their flight from the arena was a seamstress. Although she was from Jerea, she swore fealty to Rezkin solely because of his promise to bring justice to her husband's murderers. Due to her efforts, and those of her assistants, all sworn to Rezkin now wore black and green tabards, tunics, or robes bearing his emblem. The hastily made garb was not a full uniform, but Kai stated that they would complete the ensemble when they had more time and supplies.

Kai and Shezar flanked the end of the gangplank. Swords were drawn, and they stood ready to strike down any encroaching foes. The king tromped down the wooden plank with his new guard in his wake. Yserria Rey, Malcius, Tieran, Jimson, Drascon, and Millins followed in two columns, and each wore a tabard of black and green over whatever armor and gear they could find. When they reached the dock, Rezkin stood tall and waited as his guards fanned out to the sides.

Wesson led Tam and Frisha down the ramp. The young journeyman was in the same grey robes he had worn when they met, but he now wore black panels with red trim to indicate his affinity for nocent and pyris power. Tam wore the same black and green tabard as the guards with the sword Rezkin had gifted him at his hip, while Frisha donned a long black skirt and fitted black tunic with green trim and a green lightning bolt embroidered over her heart. She also wore the corset-like knife belt filled with throwing daggers.

The second wave of guards followed, which consisted of soldiers who had joined the company during their escape and the tournament fighters who had opted to remain with Rezkin's cadre for the time being. The group of ten Eastern Mountains men was among them. While the massive men did not don the tabards worn by the others, they did each tie a black and green strip of cloth about the left bicep in honor of their chieftain.

A number of fighters remained on the ship. Several were arrayed around its perimeter, along with the ship's crew, not so much because they expected attack, but to make it obvious to any observers that the ship had not been left unguarded. The last to disembark were four of the elemental mages and the life mage, each wearing their grey robes with colored panels indicating their affinities. Rezkin knew it was no mere coincidence that Nanessy Threll, the elemental mage mysteriously associated with his former trainer, Striker Farson, was among them. The woman had attempted to hide her identity throughout the month-long voyage, and Rezkin had yet to expose her. He was interested to see what the woman would do if she believed she had succeeded in her deception. He had alerted the strikers to her presence, though, and given orders to keep an eye on her.

Once the entire landing party was ashore, the military personnel split into units and headed toward each of the four grand doors. The strikers informed

Rezkin that a fifth door, like the others, could be found within the dry dock, but they had not been able to open the monstrosity. The soldiers pushed at each of the doors and searched for handholds or levers to no avail. Wesson stepped up to the second set of doors in the line and thrust a powerful burst of energy at the sealed portal. The energy struck the doors with enough force to blast through five feet of solid rock, but they did not rupture as expected. The surge of energy left no mark upon the intricate carvings but rather rebounded on the young journeyman. Wesson was pitched across the dock with such force that his momentum ceased only when his body collided with one of the carved pillars.

Healer Aelis, who had been watching from the ship's deck, came bounding down the gangplank to check on the injured battle mage. Aelis was a gangly man. With his long legs and arms and overly large eyes, set in an almost skeletal face, he reminded Rezkin of a praying mantis. The healer must have found something to repair, because it was several minutes before Wesson unsteadily regained his feet. Concerned faces followed the journeyman as he gingerly approached his king.

He said, "I would not suggest doing that."

Rezkin shook his head and then approached the door that Wesson had nearly killed himself attempting to open. After seeing the battle mage fail so painfully, the other mages had ceased their own attempts. Rezkin examined the carvings and then reached out to feel along them in hopes of finding some hidden mechanism. As soon as he pressed his hand to the stone, a chill colder than anything Rezkin had ever experienced shot up his arm. His survival instincts nearly overwhelmed his focus when the ice approached his heart. He feared that if it succeeded in reaching the vital organ, its life-sustaining cadence would cease. Due to a lifetime of training and sheer instinct, the battle energy surged through him, and Rezkin pushed back at the cold with a tidal wave of *will*-induced heat.

The fire and ice clashed within his core, and Rezkin felt as though his chest might burst before the victor prevailed. He pushed against the icy assault with every vestige of his strength. He was no longer aware of the world around him. His entire being was consumed in an internal struggle for survival, and it had been very long while since he had truly feared failure. While the battle raged in earnest, all that remained of his conscious mind began to fail.

Rezkin felt his heart falter, and he knew he could not maintain his *will* for much longer. He thought of all those who depended on his survival and the promises he had made to them. The only power Rezkin knew he had at his disposal was the spell that lay over him—a spell designed to respond to his *will*, to aid in concealing himself and influencing the minds of others. Although he doubted the spell was intended for such a purpose, he felt he had little to lose from the attempt. Rezkin formed in his mind an understanding of himself—he, the elite warrior, the Raven, Riel'gesh, Dark Tidings, King of Cael, True King of Ashai. He focused on all that he was, his confidence, and his power to dominate. He commanded the ice to disperse.

The ice angrily surged against him in response. Just as Rezkin felt something burst inside him, the frozen flame was abruptly snuffed. His lungs flooded with air as they were inundated with a new kind of fire. His heart skittered and fluttered as it attempted to find its rhythm, and he realized he could feel the tingle of vimara flooding his system—someone else's vimara. The stars dancing in the darkness before his eyes were replaced with red, throbbing veins before faces came into view. He felt a cool hand on his cheek, but when he turned his head, he saw not the soft brown eyes he had anticipated. Instead, overly large bug eyes stared back at him.

"My king, can you hear me? King Rezkin. Are you awake?" the voice asked, but the words did not match the lips. The bug-eyed man turned and said to someone behind him, "He is burning up. I cannot say what happened, but he is breathing again … and his heart is beating regularly, if a bit fast."

Rezkin sat up and immediately regretted the action. The world swam before him, and he nearly toppled back to the hard ground. He listed to one side, but his short plummet was halted by a hard tug on his arm. His wandering gaze followed the length of the offending appendage to see that his hand was still resting upon the door. No, resting was not the right word. It was *stuck*. He tugged at his arm, but the door would not release its grip. He pulled and then pushed, and the door came free, swinging inward on soundless hinges until it came to rest against the inside wall. Staring into the black chasm, Rezkin blinked several times.

Firm hands jerked at his shoulders. "Rezkin …"

He lurched to his feet and drew Kingslayer in one fluid motion, its point coming to rest at the throat of his assailant. Wide, fear-filled brown eyes stared back at him. A drop of crimson trailed down Frisha's exposed neck. Rezkin blinked several more times, lowered his sword—but only slightly—and then back-pedaled. He needed something solid at his back. With the swift realization that he had no knowledge of his surroundings, Rezkin immediately went on the defensive. His heart was racing, but the battle energy refused to heed his call. He could see dozens of eyes peering at him, but the images were disjointed, and he could not find even the simplest focus.

Kai stepped forward and pushed the terrified young woman behind him. "My king," he said with raised, empty hands as he took a step forward.

Rezkin saw the striker's advance and immediately raised his sword in preparation to defend himself.

The striker glanced around and then lowered his voice. "Rezkin, please. No one intends you harm. Please, put the sword away."

Blinking a few times, Rezkin attempted to clear his vision. He ran a hand over his face and then looked down at the hand. Reaching up again, he touched his cheek. His mask. His mask was gone. Where was his mask? His frantic gaze darted over the spectators and finally found the stolen object in the hands of the battle mage. Wesson watched the king pensively while chewing on his lip.

The dark warrior narrowed his crystal blue eyes at the mage and tightened the grip on his sword. Wesson's eyes widened when it suddenly appeared that Rezkin might attack. Kai took a step forward, and Rezkin's attention shifted to the advancing striker.

In his king's clear, blue eyes, Kai saw what he could only interpret as panic —at least, the closest thing to *panic* that Rezkin had ever shown. The striker decided it was best to give him space.

"Everyone back. Regroup," Kai ordered. "The king desires a private conference to discuss how we will proceed."

Striker Shezar stood facing the crowd to block their sight of the disturbed king. With the striker's back to him, Rezkin immediately zeroed in on the elite warrior's vulnerability. If he needed to fight, Shezar would be the first to die.

"Rezkin," came Kai's deep voice.

His attention darted to the older man, forgetting all about Shezar.

Kai said, "Do you know who I am?"

Rezkin narrowed his eyes at the patronizing striker. "Of course I know who you are. I have not lost my mind."

The striker raised a questioning brow, his expression still seeking an answer.

Rezkin grumbled, "You are Kai, my most uncooperative vassal."

Kai grinned unapologetically. "Good. Do you know *where* you are?"

"Caellurum," Rezkin stated with confidence.

"Yes," Kai drawled, his tone patient as though speaking to a small-one. "So what is the problem, my king? You seem to be a bit ... defensive."

Rezkin knew it to be true. He blinked several more times as Kai's face swam before him. In a sudden rush, he realized he had forgotten his surroundings again. He had no idea where anyone was or who might be listening. A horde of enemies could be bearing down on him at this very moment, and he was completely exposed. Rezkin raised his sword and backed up again, hoping to feel the second door behind him. His back pressed against the solid rock, and he was momentarily relieved—until the goliath began to swing open as silently as the first.

Rezkin darted to the frame and pressed his back to the stone. He could not leave the vast, unknown space at his rear, and a multitude of potential attackers occupied the dock. The two strikers glanced at each other with looks of concern and then spied the sea of curious faces.

Wesson, who had stayed to help, said, "I placed a sound and light shield around this entire opening. They cannot see or hear anything. For all they know, we are exploring the interior."

"The mages," Shezar asked, "can they see through it?"

"No, and I will sense it if they try," Wesson said.

Shezar released a breath and turned to observe his liege as Kai closed the distance to the king.

"Rezkin," Kai tried again. "What concerns you?"

Rezkin's attention was fully on Kai. After a long stare, he said, "I cannot focus ... or rather ... I cannot split my focus." He shook his head, and then his eyes abruptly sought Kai again. "I can focus on you, but then everything else disappears. When I focus elsewhere, you disappear."

Kai thought that, in that moment, Rezkin sounded like the scared trainee he should have been at his age.

"How can I see my attackers?" Rezkin asked. "How will I anticipate the danger?"

The strikers' gazes met, and they nodded in understanding. They turned back to their king. Focus was one of the fundamental principles of their training. For the young man who had probably learned to focus before he could walk, having little or none of it would undermine everything he knew.

"Did you not train to fight while intoxicated?" Shezar asked.

Rezkin's eyes grew wide, his gaze flashed to the speaker. He gripped his sword before him in ready battle stance. "Yes, of course, but this is different.

Kai was only a few feet from you, yet I had somehow forgotten that you were present. I could not even see you when I was focused on him."

At Rezkin's own mention of the other striker, he abruptly sought Kai. He became panicked when he realized the striker was not where he thought the man should have been. His gaze shot around, but he once again found Shezar, who was also not where Rezkin thought the man had previously been standing. Drawing his second blade, Rezkin held a sword in each hand ready to defend himself from their hostile maneuvers.

"I see what you mean," Kai said from beside the mage, a good ten feet from where Rezkin thought the man had been. With Rezkin's back to the wall, both men should have been within his field of view at all times, and their movements would have been obvious. Wesson's presence had not even registered until Kai had spoken from beside him.

"Look, Rezkin, we are your servants, your guards," Kai said in a calming tone. "We are on your side. Let us focus *for* you. We will allow no harm to befall our king."

"I cannot," Rezkin replied. *"Rule 8 – Know your surroundings, Rule 84 – Do not allow your attention linger, Rule 164 – Do not depend on others, Rule 165 – Trust no one ..."*

"Truly?" Kai interrupted with a deep frown. "Is there no one you trust enough to guard your back? Even as strikers, we trust in our brethren. We all fight for the same cause."

"Do you?" Rezkin asked, and Kai winced. "I have no brethren," Rezkin said. "I am alone—a weapon—an *intent*."

"He is vulnerable," Shezar observed. "It is instinct to fall back on his training."

"I always follow the *Rules*," Rezkin argued, his attention drawn back to the second striker.

"Perhaps," the striker conceded, "but you are usually more reasonable about it. You understand that some of us are less likely to attack you than others."

"I know little of you, Shezar," Rezkin said with unusual candor. "I have no reason to trust you any more than the others."

Shezar's face dropped. He replied, "I concede the point, but surely there is someone. The woman perhaps? Frisha."

"Yes," Wesson said from out of nowhere. Rezkin had once again forgotten the mage. "You have said on several occasions that you trusted her to some extent."

"She is angry with me. She no longer speaks to me … and … and I have injured her," he said as the vague memory of crimson blood resurfaced. "She may seek reprisal."

"Rezkin! I cannot believe you would say that!" Frisha shouted.

Rezkin nearly jumped out of his skin. Where had she come from? These people appeared from the void like specters. Rezkin was beginning to wonder if he was truly conscious. This felt more like a twisted dream than reality.

"Lady Frisha, you should not be here within the ward. He is not well," Kai said to the angry woman.

Rezkin swung his sword in the direction of the deep voice. His gaze landed on the striker, and he blurted, "Where is she? What have you done with her?"

"Who?" Kai asked in surprise.

Rezkin heatedly said, "Frisha. You were just speaking to her."

"Rezkin, I'm right here," the young woman answered.

Rezkin's gaze followed the voice across the distorted expanse, and the woman could not have been more than a few feet from the striker. Frisha's brow was furrowed in concern. She took a step forward, but Rezkin raised his sword in warning.

"Okaaaay," she drawled as her anger appeared to deepen. "What about Tam? Would you trust Tam to help you?"

"I …" he paused as he remembered Tam calling him a mass murderer. "No," he said, "Tam is conflicted. He may yet retract his support."

Cold sweat began dripping into his eyes, and he wiped at his brow with his sleeve.

Frisha's mouth parted in surprise. "Uh, what about Malcius?"

"He blames me for his brother's death, and possibly those of his parents."

With more than a hint of frustration, she suggested, "Tieran?"

"May still change his mind about wanting the crown."

"Brandt?"

"His house declared support for Caydean."

Frisha shifted uncomfortably. "Jimson?"

"Is an officer of the Ashaiian army, which currently seeks my head."

Frisha could not believe her ears. "Is there no one you trust, Rezkin?"

"Everyone I know has cause to want me dead, Frisha. Any who know of my … condition … could seek to take advantage."

Frisha could not decide which she felt more keenly, pity or anger. Her voice was filled with scorn as she said, "I had no idea you were so fearful of our betrayal."

"Not fear, Frisha," Rezkin said. "Acknowledgement and acceptance. In recognizing the potential for attack, I will not be surprised when it occurs."

Frisha's attention darted to the side, and she spoke to someone Rezkin did not see. "What happened to him? Whatever it was has made him paranoid. He speaks nonsense."

Frisha hated seeing her stoic warrior so frightened and vulnerable, but, even more so, she hated to hear his opinions of his friends.

Rezkin tore his attention from the woman to see to whom she spoke and was surprised to see that Wesson was present.

The mage replied, "I cannot say what happened. I have not been able to get close enough to determine if he is under a spell."

Rezkin's gaze darted to the side. He did not know to whom the mage was speaking, but he worried that the unseen individual could be an attacker. His gaze landed on Frisha. He had forgotten about her.

From somewhere to the left, a man's voice said, "I think perhaps we are getting an unusual glimpse into the mind of our king."

Had Shezar been there the whole time, or had he just arrived?

"You mean he thinks like this all the time?" Frisha said with abhorrence.

"Perhaps to some extent," Shezar said.

Frisha was aghast. "You're saying he's paranoid?"

"Not paranoid—*prepared*," the striker said. "We are all trained to think in such a way to a degree. From what I have gathered, our king's training was more brutal and intense than the rest of ours. The strikers do not begin training until we reach adulthood. We have years of developing personal relationships and trust with others before we are instructed otherwise. King Rezkin *finished* his training at that age, having never experienced anything else. I would say he is usually better able to prioritize his concerns, and his masterful skills of observation enable him to develop a reasonable threat level analysis. At this moment, however, he is incapable of observing more than one point of focus at a time. Therefore, everything is, in essence, at the same threat level. Because of his training, he is on highest alert."

Rezkin said, "You speak of me as though I am not present."

The striker met Rezkin's fitful gaze. "Do you reject my assessment?"

Rezkin narrowed his eyes. "To whom were you speaking?"

Shezar shook his head. "This is getting us nowhere. We must do something quickly. The others are becoming anxious." To Rezkin he said, "Can you at least *pretend* you are confident in our loyalty and dedication?"

"Who is *we*?" Rezkin asked.

The striker sighed in exasperation and glanced at someone to the side.

"Do not look at me," Wesson said. "He would likely view anything I do as an attack."

"Journeyman," Rezkin said upon noticing the mage's presence for the first time. "Place a ward around me."

It had suddenly dawned on Rezkin that his behavior seemed erratic to his companions, and he could not afford to show such vulnerability.

"Are you certain?" Wesson asked with uncertainty. "You usually view wards with contempt."

Rezkin could not believe he was going to have to put faith in a mage ward to keep him alive. "Yes, do it. As far as I know, none of our traveling companions are able to breach your wards, at least not without your knowing about it, yes?"

"Yes ..."

"The others. They are here, are they not?" Rezkin asked.

He looked beyond the immediate vicinity and saw a multitude of people ... and a ship. Yes, they had been traveling on a ship, and now he was in Caellurum. But, what had he just been doing? He shook his head. *Talking to the mage. Where is the mage? Ah, there he is.* Rezkin felt the faint tingle of mage power envelop him, and he stiffened.

"What are you doing?" he asked in alarm.

"You told me to put a ward around you," Wesson responded with wide eyes.

Rezkin stared at the mage. After a moment, he relaxed his stance.

"Yes, so I did." His thoughts were slowly piecing themselves together. "Kai and Shezar ... and Frisha ... they are here as well?" He maintained eye contact with the mage as he spoke so as not to lose him.

Wesson nodded. "Yes," he said slowly. "They are right here, only a few feet from me."

"I cannot see them while I am looking at you, but I remember they are here, at least. I can feel your ward, though, and can see you at the same time. Your ward will keep *me* safe, and I will keep *you* safe. It is the best I can do for now."

Wesson nodded and replied, "Yes, that seems reasonable ... unless you decide I am a threat, and you attack *me*."

"Mage," Kai scolded from ... *somewhere*.

Rezkin sheathed one of his swords and took a step away from the wall. He gripped the other sword casually, rather than in preparation to strike.

"Attacking you would be counterproductive ... unless you become hostile, and I cannot think of a reason you would seek to harm me right now."

"And me? You think I could hurt you?" Frisha asked.

Keeping his eyes on the mage, Rezkin replied to the disembodied voice. "No, Frisha. I find the prospect doubtful."

"Doubtful but not impossible," she observed.

"Everyone is capable of violence," he said. "It is best to always expect the possibility."

Kai muttered, "Well, at least he is making more sense now."

Rezkin had forgotten about the striker again, but at least now he could focus on the voice and Wesson at the same time.

"What happened?" Wesson asked. "When you touched the door?"

"A minor setback," Rezkin replied. "I am recovering."

Wesson said, "That was no minor setback, Rezkin. You *died*."

"What?" Rezkin said in astonishment.

Wesson shifted uncomfortably and added, "Well, a little bit, anyway."

Rezkin frowned. "How can one die *a little bit*? A person is either dead or alive."

"You weren't breathing," Frisha said, "and your heart stopped."

Wesson held up the mask and said, "I had to break the enchantment securing your mask to remove it. Healer Aelis said you were getting hotter and that something was causing your blood to rush even though your heart no longer beat. He said he has never heard of the like, and neither have I."

Rezkin tried to focus long enough to recall the memory but was concerned he would lose track of his surroundings again. With his peripheral vision returning, he could now see that Frisha was standing beside the mage. He could also remember that Kai and Shezar were present, but he could not yet determine their locations.

"I cannot speak on it, yet. Shezar said the others are becoming restless, did he not? I need more time to collect myself before we explore the interior, but you may drop the shield blocking us from view of the others." With a smirk, he added, "I will behave myself."

As soon as the shield dropped, Tieran, Malcius, Brandt, and Tam rushed forward.

"Rez, are you okay?" Tam asked with obvious concern.

Rezkin continued to hold Wesson in his gaze as he raised a hand and said, "I will be fine." He was not sure of the statement's veracity, but optimism was better than exposure.

"What happened?" Tieran asked. "We saw you collapse, and the healer said you *died*."

Out of the corner of his eye, Rezkin could see Tieran standing next to Wesson, so he felt relatively confident he would still be able to see the mage if he looked at Tieran.

He met Tieran's gaze and said, "Well, obviously, I am not dead." Without looking behind him, Rezkin motioned to the gaping chasm beyond the massive threshold and said, "I managed to open the door."

"Yes, I can see that," Tieran said facetiously. He may have matured along the voyage, but he was still Tieran. "*How* did you do it?"

"I am uncertain," Rezkin admitted.

"Is that a Sheyalin?" Malcius asked.

Rezkin gripped the hilt and risked meeting Malcius's gaze, hoping he would still be able to see Wesson.

"Yes," he said.

"You are a swordbearer," Malcius said. He threw his hands in the air and said, "Of course, you are a swordbearer. Why would you *not* be a sword-bearer? You are everything else. Why not a swordbearer?"

"I told you that Bordran had given me unlimited authority," Rezkin said. "This is how he did it."

Tam leaned over to Frisha and said in a forced whisper, "I'm friends with a *swordbearer*!"

Frisha rolled her eyes. "You're friends with a *king*."

Ignoring them, Malcius said, "That is why you never drew it in our presence. You did not want us to know." With a suspicious perusal of the weapon, he added, "You said before that you do not draw it unless you intend to kill someone."

Rezkin motioned over his shoulder. "We do not know what lies within the darkness. We should all be prepared."

The others took this as a command and drew their own weapons. Rezkin almost regretted his words now that so many unseen blades were bared, but the mysteries that lay in the darkness were potentially more dangerous than those who had sworn to him their support or fealty.

"Check the other doors," Rezkin ordered. "See if they are still sealed."

"Are you sure, Sire? That did not go so well for *you*," Kai said.

"Of course it did. The door is open, is it not?" Rezkin said. At the striker's huff of dissatisfaction, Rezkin added, "Whatever spell assaulted me did not seem to affect anyone else who examined them. We have no reason to believe it will begin doing so now."

The striker motioned to Jimson to have the men check the other doors. Rezkin gained a respite while the soldiers did his bidding. No one questioned him further, and he wondered how bad he had looked. Even those who had not seen the worst of his reaction were eyeing him speculatively. He was glad he had ordered Xa to stay aboard the ship with Ilanet.

Several minutes later, Jimson reported that the doors were indeed unlocked.

"Very well," Rezkin said. "Split into five units with at least one mage in each. Gather torches as well. I do not wish to depend on *talent* in this place. We will enter each doorway in unison to ensure that no one flanks us. I will take this one."

Shezar suggested, "Your Majesty, perhaps you should allow us to perform the forward reconnaissance while you maintain the command center here."

Rezkin knew what the striker really meant was for him to stay behind because they did not trust him to keep his wits. Shezar might have had a point, but *Rule 239* said to *protect yourself before others to the exclusion of Rule 1*, and *Rule 1* was to *protect and honor your friends.* Rezkin would not allow his friends to go into potential danger without him. He was not yet fully recovered, but he could now recognize the presence of multiple people around him.

"An unknown power resides in this place, and I am apparently the only one trained to sense it. I will not allow you all to enter at a disadvantage," he said.

"We do not sense it because there is nothing to sense," Wesson replied. "Whatever power resides here seems to affect only *you;* therefore, you are in the greatest danger."

"I disagree," Rezkin said. "The spell on the door did not affect you when you touched it because you were not a threat. When we sailed through the island's ward on the ship, you were violently shoved across the deck as the ward prevented you from passing. That proves this power *can* affect you, even when you cannot sense it."

"Yes, we must discuss what happened on the ship as well as with the door," Wesson said. "Still, the unknown power only prevented me from passing through the ward. It did not *attack* me, as it did you."

"I do not believe it was attacking me," Rezkin mused thoughtfully.

"Then what?" Tieran asked. "Rezkin, you almost died!"

"I believe it was testing me, and I prevailed. As you can see, the doors are now open. Let us get on with this."

13

Rezkin ordered Tam and Frisha to remain behind on the dock, to their disappointment. Kai insisted on accompanying his king, but Rezkin sent Striker Shezar to lead another unit. Reaylin was fuming when she learned she also had to stay behind. With the high percentage of skilled swordsmen and warriors in their company, the young woman's skills as a healer were more important.

With the strikers in the lead, Rezkin donned his mask and entered the dark chasm beyond the monstrous stone doors. The torchlight carried a few dozen feet in every direction, but still they could not see the walls or ceiling. To the party's right and left, torches appeared as the other units passed the thresholds. Far on the other side of the cavern, a fifth torch appeared from a gap in the side wall where the dry dock was located. Every door opened to the same massive chamber.

Kai waved his torch to signal the advance. Each of the five units methodically made its way into the depths of the hall. It was nearly a hundred yards in length and at least fifty in width. Evenly spaced columns rose from the smooth, polished floor into the eerie darkness above. Upon each column were carved fantastical scenes in intricate detail. Some were of terrible, bloody battles, others bore images of festivals with lavish feasts and joyous dancers, and still others held depictions of great, mythical beasts or tiny fae creatures.

A fresh breeze blew in from the open doors, sweeping around the columns to elicit a haunting call that echoed into the darkness that embraced them. The peaceful serenity induced by the stillness was suddenly broken by a shout from the team that had entered through the first door to the right. The cry clattered off the walls and floor and reverberated throughout the immense chamber before fading into the gloom. The others turned to join those who had sounded the call.

Rising from a recess in the far right-hand corner of the chamber was a grand staircase wide enough for at least fifteen people to stand abreast. The steps were carved of the same stone that made up the rest of the chamber and were slightly taller than was customary in Ashai. While Rezkin would have no problem scaling the blocks, the petite Reaylin and some of the small-men might find the ascent awkward.

"What do you think?" Shezar asked in a gruff voice that was quickly swallowed by the still air. "A warehouse?"

"Or a staging ground for troops," Kai suggested as he stroked his beard, his eyes glinting in the firelight with visions of an army standing ready for battle in the darkness.

Keeping Wesson in his peripheral view so he would not lose him, Rezkin studied a shoulder-high pedestal that stood to one side of the stairs. The smooth stone twisted like the roots of a massive marglow tree that abruptly ended at a flat top, into which was embedded a metallic claw molded like the talons of a great raptor. The talons faced upward and were gripping a long, prismatic crystal about the length of Rezkin's forearm.

"What is it?" he asked the mages.

Wesson, who was closest, leaned in to examine the beautiful structure. "It looks like a mage stone, but I do not see or sense any spells. Based on what you told us about the place, it has been a very long time since this was in use. Most likely, the spells or enchantments have long since dissipated."

"Like the one on the door?" Rezkin mused.

Wesson shrugged and looked to the other mages. No one offered additional answers.

Rezkin reached out to touch the stone, but Kai halted his arm with a firm grip. Rezkin's muscles clenched in alarm. He had not realized the striker was so close.

"My king, perhaps you should avoid touching anything. We would not want a repeat of what happened earlier."

Rezkin raised a brow and remarked, "We would not be standing here if not for the earlier incident."

The striker begrudgingly released his hold, and they all held their breaths as Rezkin's fingers slid across the smooth surface. The crystal was flawless and perfectly translucent and ... *cold.* When the chill began, Rezkin's first instinct was to snatch his hand away, but this power did not attempt to seize him like the other. It was cool and inviting—like a shaded pond on a hot summer day. He had the sense that the power wanted something from him, but he could not say what it was. He peered deeper into the crystal, but the torch-light was insufficient to expose the mystical object's hidden secrets.

He opened his mouth to ask one of the mages to produce more light, but as soon as the thought formed, the crystal blazed to life. Pale blue tendrils of light snaked and twisted like lightning within the lattice. Everyone jumped back. As Rezkin blinked away the stars in his eyes, he saw that the crystal before him was no longer the only source of blue light in the room. The entire ceiling, which he could now see was at least forty feet high, was ignited with a soft topaz glow. Rings of glowing blue crystals wrapped around every pillar, and the walls were adorned with beautiful carvings and swirling mosaics of illuminated crystals.

"How did you do that?" Wesson exclaimed in wonder.

"I only thought to ask you to produce more light, and then *this,*" Rezkin said with a wave of his hand around the bright chamber.

"Then, it works on intent," said another mage named Baelin Gale.

Baelin was an elemental mage whose affinities were wind and water. Waves of dark brown hair framed his face where they hung at the sides nearly merging with an equally wavy, silky beard.

Baelin suggested, "Perhaps it is enchanted so that anyone can activate it."

"I do not sense even the slightest use of power," observed Mage Ondrus, the only Master life mage in Rezkin's company.

"Nor do I," Wesson agreed.

The mages began chattering about various aspects of magery that sounded like intelligent gibberish to untrained ears.

Although he was much recovered, Rezkin was still attempting to regain his focus. He needed time to process what had happened earlier, especially if it was true that he had actually *died.* With his focus shattered, he had entirely too much to consider while standing in a foreign room illuminated by an unknown power in a mythical fortress that had been nearly forgotten by time. He did not like leaving the rest of his friends on the dock and ship, and he had no idea what lay at the top of the stairs.

"Enough," he said, interrupting the increasingly heated debate regarding the nature of the power illuminating the chamber. "Drascon!"

"Yes, Sire," the second lieutenant responded with a salute as he made his way to the front of the group.

People often underestimated Drascon's intelligence due to his charming good looks, large stature, and quiet demeanor, but he had proven himself to be both observant and intuitive. Rezkin still did not know how far he could trust the man, but he would use him nonetheless.

"Your unit will maintain position here. Send a runner to inform the others of our progress." Rezkin looked over the others and said, "Jimson, Shezar, and Leyton's units will advance with my own to the next landing where Jimson's will hold position. Shezar's unit will cover the left, Leyton's the right, and mine will go forward. Make no more than two turns before reporting back to Captain Jimson. Designate a runner. If you encounter any resistance, the runner will not engage. He will report back to the captain immediately. Any questions?"

Everyone shook their heads and then shuffled around to take up their respective positions. Rezkin could now observe most of the people at the same time, but recognizing any details about the individuals was still beyond him.

The troop ascended the stairs with weapons at the ready. The light from the chamber below struggled to reach beyond the lower half of the stairs, so the remainder of the climb was made by insufficient torchlight. Rezkin decided that he was a bit more comfortable with the poorer lighting conditions. Those around him could not see him any better than he could focus on *them*; and now that he did not have to concentrate on as many visual cues, he could focus on his other senses to greater effect. He only hoped that any inhabitants of the ancient citadel were at similar disadvantage.

At the top of the staircase was a wide corridor running to the left and right, and to one side was another crystal-topped pedestal. Wesson placed his hand on the crystal but nothing happened. He focused his vimara into the foreign object and even searched for the trigger for the spell, but he found nothing that indicated the crystal held any power. The mage considered Rezkin's explanation for how he had managed to light the crystal on the lower level and then concentrated his *will* on creating more light. When that failed, the four other mages surrounded the pillar, and their attempts were met with the same results.

"By the Maker," Kai grumbled. "How many mages does it take to light a mage lamp?"

Deciding the mages could play with the crystals later, when there was less chance of being set upon or surrounded by unknown, hostile enemies, Rezkin slipped his hand over the crystal and *willed* it to light. In an instant, the entire corridor was flooded with glimmering blue luminescence. Swirling mosaics of topaz-blue crystals reflected off the smooth, polished stone walls in both directions. Some of the crystals glowed softly while others shimmered or sparkled, and these seemed to be organized in a purely aesthetic arrangement.

"Apparently, the answer is *none*," Shezar said wryly.

The mages began muttering amongst themselves when Rezkin not so subtly reminded them that they were on a mission. If these people were to be his army, much training was in their futures. They would be lucky to survive invading an empty fortress. With a quick flick of his hand, Shezar's unit moved down the corridor to their left. Rezkin's unit accompanied Leyton's in the opposite direction.

LeukCaptain Leyton Wuald was retired from the king's army and had been employed as a guard for House Nirius for the past ten years. Although he originally had misgivings about the pompous *Lord Rezkin* he first met in Skutton, he could not deny the might of the infamous Dark Tidings. Ever since the dark warrior's identity had been revealed, Lord Rezkin had been a completely different man. Leyton had to have faith that his wife and children were safe at Wellinven under the protection of the duke who, according to the last reports, still held his position against the king's forces. The leukcaptain felt that his best bet at seeing his family again was to stay near Tieran Nirius, and the young lord was dedicated to *King* Rezkin.

The corridor was clean and free of dust, despite the countless ages that had presumably passed since anyone had last set foot in the citadel. Although the passage branched to the left several times, the two units continued forward. The corridor ended at an intersection that diverged to the left and right, and the passage was clean and illuminated just as the previous one had been. The king directed Leyton's unit to the right while his own surveyed the left.

The former guardsman led his people down the passage with more than a little caution. Leyton was a decent swordsman and had held a position of authority while serving in the army, but he felt more confident with the quality of fighters currently at his back. Swordmaster Yserria Rey had been impressive during the King's Tournament, surprising everyone who claimed she would fail due to her being both a woman and a commoner. Viscount Abertine of Sandea had competed in the fourth tier and the melee and had finished well. The man claimed to remain in the company of the refugees to show his support for the True King of Ashai, but Leyton suspected the lord was more interested in gathering intelligence.

Also on his team were Yerlin and Marlis Tomwell, brothers from a noble line so distanced from the great houses that they might as well have been commoners. The brothers had found other ways to set themselves apart, however. Sir Marlis had competed with the spear in the melee event and was an accomplished swordsman of the fifth tier, although he had not claimed a prize. Four years prior, he had been named a knight of the realm by King Bordran for several acts of bravery and accomplishment. Marlis's older brother, Yerlin, was a life mage employed as a horse trainer for the knights of the realm and had set his hopes on becoming a master at the Mage Academy.

Additionally, Leyton had three of the Eastern Mountains men who claimed King Rezkin as their chieftain due to his mountain-man-style defeat of their leader during the tournament. The final members of the unit were two king's army soldiers, Sergeant Millins and Corporal Namm. Millins had apparently been in King Rezkin's company for close to a month prior to the tournament, and Namm had spontaneously elected to assist the refugees in escaping the arena rather than fight against them.

The unit passed two small rooms to the right on their way down the corridor. Neither had a door, although piles of dust lay at the thresholds. Within the dust were perfectly preserved nails and hinges that looked as pristine as the day they had been forged. Along the walls stood metal racks of weapons and armor, some of them strange and completely foreign. Despite the thousands of years that had passed since these items had been stored, each metal article was polished and sharp, without a hint of rust. Many of them were missing handles and straps, however. Smaller piles of dust were strewn about beneath the armaments. It seemed that while the stone and metal were preserved, anything made of wood, leather, or fabric had long ago turned to dust.

Just past the storage rooms, the corridor narrowed, and the patterns of crystals on the walls abruptly changed to a geometric design that repeated at regular intervals every few paces. Each arrangement looked as if it would frame some item that had once hung from the wall but was now missing.

"Perhaps it is a decorative feature," suggested Viscount Abertine.

Yserria looked at them curiously and mused, "They almost look like arrow slits."

"Except that they are being solid rock," said Grath Jaeg, one of the mountain men.

Mage Yerlin ran his fingers over the polished stone wall. In an instant, the stone within the frame vanished, and the mage was struck with a cool burst of sea breeze. The deep cobalt blue of the ocean and the sky's lighter cornflower hue replaced the drab grey of the stone. The crystals that framed the opening no longer glowed blue but now radiated green.

"It *is* an arrow slit!" Yserria exclaimed. "Look there. It opens out of the cliff over the ocean."

Grath ran his hand over the stone on the opposite wall, and it, too, disappeared. "This is being the channel up we sailed to be getting in the cove."

"We're inside the cliff that hid the cove," Yserria said with excitement. "It's perfect! We could rain arrows down on anyone approaching from either side."

"Interesting," Yerlin muttered, "but how do we close them?"

The mage ran his fingers over the green crystals, but nothing happened. He noticed a horseshoe-shaped string of red-glowing crystals to the upper right of the frame. The other frames held the same design, but the horseshoes adjacent to the closed slits glowed blue. The mage pressed his hand to the symbol to no effect. Thinking perhaps it was a kind of rune, he traced the symbol with his fingers.

"Gah!" shouted mountain man Prask Berly as a sword materialized from the air and sliced deeply into his arm.

The insubstantial sword was held in the grip of a tall, wraithlike being. The phantom sword glowed red, while the smoky wraith that wielded it was blue like the crystals. The being was tall and built like a warrior, but its features were indistinct. While the entire form, sword and all, appeared as wisps of glowing vapor, its strikes were as solid as any steel.

"Defensive positions!" shouted LeukCaptain Leyton. "Corporal, report to Jimson as soon as you can get around the thing! Abertine, Marlis, watch our flank. The rest of you surround the creature!"

The corridor was too narrow to wield the bulky battle axes, so the mountain men drew the smaller axes and knives at their belts. Small was a relative term, though, since the curved, single-edged knives were nearly the length of a short sword.

Grath slashed at the phantom, but his knife and, in fact, his entire arm, passed straight through the vapor. The phantom jabbed at the injured mountain man, and Prask instinctually parried with the knife in his good hand. The blades met with the *clash* of metal. Grath stabbed at the wraith again, and Prask attempted the same, but their knives cleaved only air. The vaporous form twisted and slashed at Grath, and the burly warrior dodged to the side. He returned the attempt with a strike of his own, catching the phantom's blade as it tried for another attack. Again, the blades met solidly and powerfully. The reverberation trailed up the thickly corded muscles of the mountain man's arm, rattling his teeth.

"We are not for hitting it. We can only be defending!" Grath shouted.

"See if you can drive it to the side. Get the corporal through!" ordered Leyton.

Hult Moraug, the third mountain man, took Prask's position as the injured man stumbled back while attempting to stem the flow of blood from the deep laceration on his arm.

"Mage! Can you not do something?" Leyton shouted.

"I am *trying*," Yerlin snapped as he continued waving his hands in the air to no effect. "Nothing is working. I do not believe it is actually *alive*."

The mage came to a sudden realization. He darted back to the red-lit horseshoe-shaped crystal arrangement. The symbol was no longer alone amongst the surrounding blue crystals. Five more runes were now lit in a ring around the central red horseshoe. The other symbols were glowing green, and each was unique. Yerlin ran his finger around the horseshoe again. When that did not work, he tried tracing it backward. Finally, he started tracing the other symbols.

Around him people shouted, and metal clashed with vaporous metal, but the mage methodically traced the symbols over and over again in different sequences. He had no idea if what he was doing would have any effect, but it seemed no less useful than trying to fight the misty phantom directly. A pain-filled cry sounded just as the green crystals suddenly flashed and returned to the normal topaz-blue color. Yerlin spun around and saw that the phantom warrior was gone. Three of the members of his unit were injured, but none seriously. As a life mage, Yerlin had some healing ability, but he was by no means a true healer.

"What happened?" Leyton barked.

"It was a spell," Yerlin responded as he began tending to the wounded. "The phantom was not real. I inadvertently activated it when I traced the red rune beside the arrow slit. It must be some kind of emergency defensive spell, but I have never heard of anything so marvelous."

"Marvelous?" Grath exclaimed. "This spell did almost take the arm of Prask."

"Yes, of course. I am sorry that happened," Yerlin acquiesced. "You have to admit, though, that it was a very effective spell. I cannot imagine the complexity involved. I have never seen a spell emulate a person like that, and the way it fought was amazingly realistic."

"Too real," Yserria remarked through clenched teeth as she gripped the slash to her forearm.

"What of the injured," Leyton commanded.

"I have stopped the bleeding and begun the repairs," Yerlin said as he stepped away from Prask. "He should have full functionality after he sees the healer, but he can continue now if he is up to it."

The Eastern Mountains man growled and pounded on his chest with a meaty fist. Everyone took that to mean he was willing to continue. Yerlin saw to Yserria's arm and healed the shallow cut completely. The young woman thanked the mage with a brilliant smile that made her bright-green eyes sparkle.

"We may continue, now. Marlis and Swordmaster Yserria are completely healed," Yerlin said. His brother had received only a cut to the cheek when he failed to dodge an errant slash that had been deflected by Grath.

"Very well. Let us continue," Leyton said.

Rezkin strode down the corridor with Kai to his right and Wesson at his left. Chieftain Gurrell Yuold of the Viergnacht Tribe of the Eastern Mountains, and his second in command, Myerin Ilgoth, followed close behind. Tieran and one of his guards, Dennick Manding, were also present. Both Tieran and Dennick had entered into mage apprenticeships since becoming refugees. While Tieran had a small amount of formal education as a life mage, Dennick's aquian, or water *talent*, had been deemed too insignificant to be worthy of training. Rezkin insisted on making full use of his resources, though, so anyone with the slightest amount of *talent* was required to train so long as he or she remained in the king's company.

The corridor was brightly lit with glowing crystals in brilliant hues, the mosaics they formed capturing scenes from the lives of a long-dead race. In some, an alien people joyously danced within a colorful, swirling breeze or splashed about in clear, blue waters. In others, the people were playing happily with small-ones or strange animals. The most foreboding images showed brutal warriors battling fierce beasts or fearsome foes that were shrouded in darkness. These were not the glamorous tapestries of glorified heroes surrounded in the golden light of valor that could be seen in so many of the affluent estates in Ashai. These were images of true battle with blood, anguish, and death presented in brilliant color for all to see.

The continuous crystal mosaics were broken only by empty doorframes leading to uninteresting rooms. Most of the rooms appeared to have been used for storage or as workrooms. Some had stone tables and benches upon which sat mundane objects such as pots, pitchers, and tools. Piles of dust lay where pieces of wooden furniture might have once stood. Some items, many of them broken, were scattered in the dust. Only those items created from earth seemed to have survived. Anything that might have been made from plant or animal had degraded.

At the end of the corridor, the people disappeared from the mosaics, and the crystals were arranged to show images of the elements. In one mosaic, brilliant yellow, orange, and red crystals flashed and flickered to look like flames climbing up the wall. In another, blue, green, and white appeared to flow across the surface like water, with hints of gold dazzling atop the crests of stylized ripples. A third had a variety of colors swirling in draughts and eddies that depicted the wind; and in another, browns, pinks, and greys seemed to tumble for eternity from the top of the wall to the bottom, like falling rock. Plants and animals interwoven within the elemental scenes stretched from one to the next interconnecting each of them. All the plants and animals were running or reaching toward the final doorway where the corridor terminated. This doorway was not empty like the others, but rather, held a solid stone door similar to, but smaller than, those through which they had entered the fortress.

Rezkin's companions were mesmerized by the fantastical crystal images. Never had anyone seen *moving* scenes, and it was all accomplished with light since the crystals were stationary. The warrior might have been more enraptured if he was not working so hard to maintain his focus. He could not afford to become distracted in such a threatening place. The mysterious fortress had power running through it that nobody understood. Despite Rezkin's apprehensions regarding the security of the citadel, he felt an unrelenting and disturbing sense of peace and serenity in the place. He was concerned that the soothing chill constantly infusing his body would lull him into complacency.

"What are you doing?" Wesson asked with alarm.

Rezkin turned to look at the journeyman, and the young mage drew back from the ominous visage of Dark Tidings. "I am going to open the door," he replied.

Wesson suggested, "Perhaps you should wait until we are certain you are recovered from the last time you opened a door."

Ignoring the comment, Rezkin turned back to the stone slab and placed his hand upon the cool surface. The entire portal glowed a brilliant white and then disappeared.

Rezkin made to step across the threshold when Kai called out, "Sire, please allow me to go ahead to ensure that it is safe."

Rezkin was frustrated with everyone wanting to keep him safe. His safety was his own responsibility. He was a warrior, trained to be dependent on no one. If he desired to survive, then he would follow the *Rules*. The strikers should understand that, but he knew that they *were* following the *Rules*—at least, *their* version of the *Rules*. Kai had informed Rezkin that *Rule 1* was to *protect and honor your king*. Rezkin wondered why the *Rule* had been changed for him, but he thought perhaps it was because he was supposed to *be* the king. It would not have made sense to tell him to protect and honor *himself*.

Pushing those errant thoughts aside, he forced himself to focus on the present. Something felt strange about the room before him. He did not want the striker to enter the room. In fact, he did not want *anyone* to enter the room but him. He realized the thought was peculiar and seemed almost foreign to him. The chill washed over him again, and his resolve was reaffirmed. He did not want the striker to enter the room. He wanted to enter alone.

"I will go. You will all remain here," Rezkin said. As Kai opened his mouth to protest, Dark Tidings barked, "Do not question your king!"

The striker snapped his mouth shut, but his eyes spoke of disapproval. Rezkin stepped across the threshold alone. The room was mostly dark with only a few glowing crystals scattered across the ceiling. Other crystals covered the ceiling and walls, but they were clear and devoid of light or power. The lit crystals were pulsing and appeared to be fading. As he stood surveying the dark space, another crystal winked out, joining the other empty vessels.

The floor was smoothly polished but held a grid of thirty carved bowl-like structures, each about the size and shape of a buckler. The bowls were smooth, less than a foot deep, and each contained a few crushed stones that might have been the ore from which the glowing crystals were derived. The warrior wondered if this was where they processed the stones, using the basins for grinding or crushing. He could even see grooves along the sides of chamber where water might have been flushed out of the room.

Rezkin wove his way around the basins, glancing into each to make sure he had not missed anything. He bent to retrieve some of the crushed stone and was instantly inundated with sensation. It was as though a stream of ice flooded up his arm until it reached his chest, and then it was gone. Gasping for breath, he dropped the crushed stone and clutched his hand to his chest. With disbelief, he realized that his hand was neither injured nor cold. Carefully examining the discarded material, he noticed that it no longer resembled the crystals. The stone had turned to dust, but he felt revitalized, and his focus seemed to have improved a bit.

Rezkin skirted along one wall as he made his way back toward the door where he could see the others anxiously watching with curiosity. A small stone skidded across the floor after colliding with his foot. Somehow, he had not seen the tiny object in his path, and Rezkin admonished himself for the misstep. It was unacceptable for him to make such an egregious mistake. He had just broken *Rules 8 – Know your surroundings, 10 – Do not leave evidence, 12 – Do not make sound,* and *149 – Map your body,* all in a single step.

Rezkin cautiously collected the object of his failure and found that it was a perfectly smooth cobble about the size of his thumb. The clast was rounded like a river stone and appeared to be uncut crystal. Faint, colorful swirls played across its translucent surface, but the interior was opaque. Rezkin did not receive the cold jolt from the stone that he had experienced from almost every-thing else he touched in this alien stronghold. Instead, the cobble seemed to warm to his touch, siphoning away some of the chill from his body. The peaceful sensation that had invaded his senses since entering the fortress subsided to a more acceptable level, and Rezkin could feel his warrior's edge returning. He placed the stone in a pouch at his waist, but the protection it provided abruptly ceased when the stone left his hand. Rezkin was once again inundated with the calm, cool chill of the citadel's strange power.

He pulled a length of leather lacing that he would typically use for restraining prisoners from one of the pouches at his belt. He wrapped the lace around the stone until it was secure and then tied the lace in a loop to hang around his neck. The stone rested against his skin under his tunic, and Rezkin felt relieved that his mind was clear and his senses alert. After looking around the dark room again, he decided, to his disappointment, that no more of the stones were present.

When he finally emerged from the room, Wesson asked with excitement, "What was in there? It is so much darker in there that we could barely see anything."

"It was nothing—just an empty room with a few crushed stones. It may have been where they processed the ore for these crystals," Rezkin said, motioning to the brightly glittering crystals around them.

The mage furrowed his brow and looked around at the crystals again. "Yes," he said slowly. "I suppose they may have placed great importance on such a place, but it seems odd that they would put so much work into decorating the corridor leading to this very impressive door for it to hold only a processing room. Still, these crystals are unlike anything I have ever seen. They would be very valuable, and these people may have even placed some religious significance on them."

Just then, pounding footsteps could be heard charging down the hall. A runner from Captain Jimson's unit came into view, and Rezkin strode forward to meet the young man. It was Fedrin Malto of Torrel. Fedrin's brother had been a fifth-tier competitor in the King's Tournament, but the Swordmaster had been killed during their escape from Skutton. Fedrin wanted to return to Torrel and demand justice from his king on his brother's behalf, but his desires had been dashed when Brendam LuDou, the Torreli captain of the Royal Guard for King Desbian, had instructed him to stay near Ashai's so-called True King until further notice. LuDou had escaped Skutton with them but had disembarked in Serret with intentions of returning to Torrel to report to his king.

Fedrin abruptly stopped and saluted smartly while attempting to catch his breath. "Sire, Leyton's unit has been attacked," he said in a smooth Torreli accent. "Corporal Namm reported that it was some kind of wraith or specter."

"How fare the men?" Rezkin asked.

"I cannot say, Your Majesty. I was sent as soon as we heard from the corporal, and his unit was still in battle when he departed to deliver his report."

Rezkin took off down the corridor with his unit trailing behind him. Kai quickened his pace to overtake the king, and Rezkin begrudgingly allowed it. The man was, after all, attempting to do his job. They turned at the intersection of the two hallways and had not gone far when they spied Leyton's unit coming toward them. The unit did not appear to be in a hurry, so Rezkin slowed his pace while Kai jogged ahead. The striker conferred with the unit commander and then, satisfied they were in no immediate danger, escorted the disheveled unit toward them.

Leyton saluted and bowed upon approaching his king and then reported what had happened during their encounter with the phantom warrior. Mage Yerlin provided additional information regarding the magical entity, which Wesson and the other mages found to be fascinating.

"Do you recall the sequence you used to terminate the spell?" Rezkin asked.

"My apologies, Sire, but no," Yerlin confessed. "I was tracing the runes as quickly as possible, hoping for the best outcome. I was using a pattern while attempting to break the code, so I could *eventually* come to the same sequence again."

"Very well. We will investigate the runes another time. For now, we must return to Jimson and see if Shezar's unit encountered any trouble."

Shezar's unit had, in fact, not gotten very far. The corridor ran straight for a time, and the unit passed several doors made of stone, but the mages had not been able to open any of them. The hallway ended at a staircase leading to an upper level, but at the top of the landing stood three stone doors that likewise could not be opened. Although the mages attempted spells and everyone searched for hidden mechanisms, they had made no better progress than they had with those on the lower level.

After listening to the update, Rezkin made the decision to push forward. While, most of the stronghold was yet unexplored, he knew it was getting late and the sun would be setting in a few hours. He did not want his people out in the open where they were vulnerable. While they could spend the night on the ship, he decided to make use of his newest resources.

"Move everyone into the warehouse," he said. "Place guards on the ship and dock, and create a station in the corridor that overlooks the sea. We will call that corridor the seawall." To Yerlin he said, "Show them how to open and close the arrow slits, but make it clear what they are *not* to touch. We cannot have the guards slaughtered by phantom warriors." Rezkin turned to Striker Shezar and said, "Post a rotating guard here at the top of the stairs. No one is to go beyond this point, except for the lookouts in the seawall. I will take my unit to see if we can open some of the doors on this level."

After a round of tiresome genuflecting and *Your Majesties*, Rezkin could finally get back to the business of exploring the fortress for threats. The corridor to the left was lit by the same blue crystals as the other hallways, but most of the decorative touches were mundane carvings. Still, the carvings were beautiful and appeared to depict what life had been like among these ancient, alien people. Rezkin desired to study the images when he had more time.

He stopped at the first sealed door with his entourage arrayed around him. He pressed his palm to the stone, but it did not assault him or immediately open or dissolve as the others had. Instead, a series of crystal runes lit beside the frame. Wesson, who stood at his side, stroked his fingers along the rune as Mage Yerlin indicated he had done at the other end of the corridor. The door dissolved into nothing right before their eyes.

"This magecraft is phenomenal," Wesson remarked without realizing he had spoken aloud.

Kai entered the room beyond the threshold and was disappointed when it appeared to be nothing more than living quarters for servants or dockworkers. The other rooms on the lower level were equally unimpressive, but the mages were fascinated.

"The door runes remain lit now that they have been activated," Wesson observed, "and it seems that they can now be operated by anyone."

"But, what is powering them?" Tieran asked.

"I have yet to determine the source of their power," the journeyman said as he considered the possibilities.

The *talented* members of Rezkin's unit were studying the runes while the mountain men guarded the corridor. Rezkin removed his mask, clipping it to his belt, and turned to Kai. "Move the guard station to the end of this corridor. No one is to go up the stairs, but we will make use of these rooms. Assign one to the healers for their patients, and divvy up the rest between those most in need, such as the women and those with small-ones."

"The nobles will not approve," Kai said, although he did not disagree with the order. "They will desire the private rooms for themselves."

"I care not what the nobles think," Rezkin replied. "They can suffer community living for another night or two. They should be relieved that they are no longer forced to endure the hardships of the ship."

"And you? Which will you take, *Your Majesty?*" Kai said, emphasizing the honorific to remind Rezkin that he was a king and needed to be treated as such.

"I will rest in one of the armories in the seawall," he replied.

"Sire, those rooms do not even have doors," Kai said, "and some kind of phantom warrior resides within the walls."

"From what Mage Yerlin deduced, the phantom warrior will not appear unless it is activated," Rezkin said. "I believe it is a failsafe mechanism in case the citadel is overrun, and I doubt the seawall is the only place in which such a security measure exists. Likely, a number of places exist in this fortress from which the phantom warrior may be called forth. For all we know, an army of such warriors is secreted within the runes. I will study the phenomenon later."

"You want to *activate* the thing?" Kai exclaimed. "What if we cannot rid ourselves of it afterward?"

"Mage Yerlin said he could figure out the code again. We need only hold it off until he does so."

"We?" Kai asked.

"You are not confident in your *Skills*, Striker?" Rezkin said.

"I was not speaking of *me*," the striker replied with irritation.

"You doubt *my Skills?*" Rezkin said, feigning surprised indignation.

Kai sighed in exasperation. "Of course not! You are the *king*. You need not take such risks for the sake of curiosity. If you insist on doing this, then Shezar and I will fight the phantom, and you can observe from afar."

Rezkin said, "I am not one of these weak outworlders in need of coddling, Kai. I am a warrior first, and these people need to see me as such. They depend on me for security, both physically and mentally. As a striker, it is your responsibility to protect me, but only if or when I am incapable of protecting myself. You are to provide backup. If I am overrun or incapacitated, then you may intervene; but I cannot have you attempting to fight my battles for me."

Kai stared at the young man he called king and knew the words to be true. Upon noticing the attention of the others who had witnessed the king's admonition, Kai bowed and said, "Forgive me, Sire. I must adjust to serving a king as capable as you. The kings of past were not warriors."

"No forgiveness is necessary, Striker Kai," Rezkin said. "You are performing your duties admirably. You are correct that my needs are not the needs of past kings who had grown soft in the years of peace and protection. Cael is a warrior kingdom," he declared.

14

"Cael?" Kai said.

"Come," Rezkin said as he motioned to the others. "We will return to the staging grounds to further discuss matters."

As they retraced their path back to the lower level, Rezkin issued orders to be disseminated. When they reached the warehouse, he surveyed the activities of the refugees who were disembarking and setting up a temporary mobile camp. Rezkin wanted to be able to retreat to the ship in the event they were attacked from within the unexplored citadel. He also wanted to be able to take refuge in the fortress should they come under attack via the waterway. He thought the latter scenario far less likely, considering the nature of the enchantments on the island, but the Ashaiian Navy was still seeking the notorious Dark Tidings and escaped refugees. Kai, Shezar, and Wesson flanked Rezkin as he watched the outworlders fumble through setting up what he thought to be a ridiculously disorganized camp.

Rezkin eventually voiced his thoughts. "We are no longer in Ashai. I am claiming this island and declaring it the Kingdom of Cael, as was agreed to by King Ionius. The capital city is named Caellurum, as the histories have indicated this place was once called."

"I think Gendishen may have something to say about that," Kai muttered.

"King Privoth may reject the claim, but he will not be able to reclaim the island," Rezkin said. "Although Gendishen officially holds all the Yeltin Isles, never has anyone inhabited this one—not since its original inhabitants. We are the first; therefore, the island is ours."

"Perhaps, but we will not be able to get supplies if Privoth's navy enforces a blockade," Kai said. "Aside from that, if we cannot trade with Gendishen, it will take weeks to receive shipments from Channería; and that is dependent on whether Ionius keeps his word and does not impose sanctions against us to maintain the peace with Gendishen."

"I have considered that, which is why I intend to meet with King Privoth to inform him of my decision."

Kai scoffed. "You expect to just walk into a king's court and say, *I am claiming your land; and, by the way, we would like a good trade deal.*"

"Of course not. I am not an idiot, Kai. Gendishen has no use for an island it cannot access, and, as far as they know, has little or no value. Privoth does have other needs and desires, though. We must discover what he wants in exchange for this useless rock."

"You propose a trade?" Shezar asked.

"Indeed," Rezkin said. "I do not intend to *fight* for everything. I *do* have other *Skills*."

Shezar said, "If you do not mind me asking, Sire, just what *are* your *Skills*?"

"All of them," Rezkin replied as he watched the heated exchange between a couple of foreign lords engaged in an inconsequential disagreement.

"What do you mean by *all of them*?" Shezar asked.

"And then some," Kai added. When Shezar gave Kai a questioning look, the older striker expounded. "King Rezkin claims to have mastered twenty-seven major *Skills* and sixty-three minor ones."

"Impossible," Shezar said. "No one can master all the *Skills*. Besides, there are only twenty-five major and forty-seven minor."

Kai laughed. "That is what *I* said."

Rezkin said, "We will discuss the *Skills* another time. Right now, I want you two to enforce some order in this chaos."

The two strikers looked over the refugees who had gathered in groups around small piles of supplies. While the arrangement did not possess the structure of a trained army, it could hardly be considered chaotic. Both strikers said, "Yes, Sire," before slipping away to carry out their orders.

Still feeling out of sorts, Rezkin backed up until his body was pressed against the wall. Glancing around, he realized Wesson was standing quietly several paces away studying him. While he knew this behavior was typical for the mage, in his current state of vulnerability, Rezkin did not care for the close scrutiny.

"What is it, Journeyman?"

After a moment, the mage looked away and said, "We can discuss it later."

Rezkin nodded and then pushed away from the wall, retreating up the steps into the corridor. Wesson maintained the ward that surrounded the king as he followed Rezkin down the passage leading to the seawall. The guards stood at attention and saluted as he passed, and Rezkin pretended to ignore them. By tradition, the king was not supposed to acknowledge his retainers while they were performing their duties unless he needed them.

Upon entering the section of the corridor with the arrow slits, Rezkin slowed his pace. He surveyed the crystal-lit walls as he addressed Wesson. "Journeyman, do you sense any mage power in this corridor?"

Wesson stretched his senses, struggling to detect even the faintest seep of power. Finally, he answered, "No. I sense nothing."

Several paces down the corridor, Mage Yerlin was speaking with one of the officers. Both turned as Rezkin approached. "Mage Yerlin, show me these rune crystals that control the enchantments."

"Yes, Sire," Yerlin replied with a bow. "These crystals, here, activate the enchantments and spells. Right now, they are lit blue like the others. Once the defensive spell is activated, they glow green and are arranged in patterns, which I have interpreted to be runes, although I have never seen the like. I do not believe they control the enchantments, however. They seem to be a trigger. The actual source of power is unknown to me. I believe the colors of the trigger runes may be indicative of their nature. The red one, there," he said pointing to the largest rune, "triggered the phantom warrior. When the crystals turn green, they are ready to perform some function but require the operator to trace them in a specific sequence. In this case, they cease the defensive spell."

"By defensive spell, you are referring to the phantom warrior?" Rezkin asked.

"Yes, Sire. I do not believe it is an actual entity or wraith. I believe it is simply a manifestation of the spell."

"You could detect this with your mage senses?" Rezkin asked.

"Ah, no, Your Majesty. I sense no use of vimara whatsoever. The other mages have all agreed on this point," Yerlin said, nodding toward Wesson. "I assume it is somehow shielded from our senses."

"Have you encountered other instances where mage power was shielded from your senses?" Rezkin asked.

Yerlin stared at Rezkin for a moment and then glanced to the journeyman before answering. "Not before joining your party, Sire."

"Thank you, Mage Yerlin. Please activate the phantom warrior now," Rezkin said.

"Sire? You wish me to activate it *now*?" he asked as he looked around the relatively empty corridor. The life mage glanced again at Wesson for guidance. Rezkin thought it curious that the mage would question the king and look to a journeyman for approval.

"You would not be doing what I think you are doing, would you?" asked a gruff voice that grew progressively louder as its owner approached.

"We are activating the phantom warrior spell," Rezkin replied.

"And you were planning on doing this without your guard?" Kai said.

"You are here, are you not?" Rezkin responded as he noted several other people following in the striker's wake with Tieran in the lead.

Tieran strode imperiously down the corridor with all his usual decorum. Whatever humbling effects Rezkin had impressed on the young man had not travelled far beyond his circle of friends. Tieran was a high lord by all accounts. The men who followed carried satchels and trunks and practically plastered themselves to the wall as they passed their king. Tieran stopped before Rezkin with a slight bow that was befitting a young man of his station.

He smiled broadly. "A delivery of comforts for the king." He sniffed disdainfully and remarked, "What few I could find, anyway." Then continuing with his winning smile, he said, "I was hoping my gracious cousin would be so kind as to share his quarters with me, seeing as how decent accommodations are difficult to acquire."

"I doubt there are any to be considered decent by your account," Rezkin muttered.

The sarcasm was lost on Tieran as he tilted his head replied, "I am sure you are correct," with complete sincerity. He looked around and the others. Finally, he asked, "What goes on here?"

Rezkin waited until the servants had either retreated into what he assumed was to be his quarters or passed by on their return trip before answering. "Mage Yerlin was about to activate the phantom warrior spell. I wish to ensure that no murderous vapors will be seeping from the walls while we sleep."

"Excellent! I would very much like to see this. I have heard it is quite impressive," Tieran said.

"Word travels fast," Yerlin muttered.

Tieran shrugged and remarked, "After a month at sea, everything that is not wood, water, and salt is interesting. Shall we see it, then?"

"It would probably be best for you to depart," Rezkin said. "This phantom warrior is reportedly quite dangerous, and we have no idea how long it will take Mage Yerlin to find the deactivation sequence again."

"Nonsense. I am sure you can handle whatever we encounter," Tieran replied with confidence.

Rezkin said, "I am not infallible, Tieran."

"Perhaps not, but you have mentioned on many occasions that you would not undertake an activity if you did not have confidence in your success. Besides, I may be of some assistance if we need fight the thing."

Rezkin just wanted to get on with his investigation, so he turned and said, "Very well. Go on, Mage Yerlin."

"Yes, Your Majesty. Lord Tieran may wish to move, though, since last time the specter appeared just about where he is standing."

Tieran skittered to the other side of the corridor, and then he, Rezkin, and Kai drew their swords in preparation for the fight. The apparition did not appear where Tieran had previously been standing. Rather, it appeared directly behind Rezkin. He immediately felt the cold slither up his spine, and he quickly spun to intercept the expected attack. Rezkin's sword sailed through the vapor without effect, but the entity did not respond in kind. In fact, it did not move at all as it stood expectantly with a confused expression on its insubstantial face. After a moment of study, the phantom warrior spun its sword into a reverse grip and then pressed the pommel into its free hand, holding its arms at shoulder height. Lowering its gaze to the floor, the specter bowed deeply and intoned, "*Pereliou evé Spirétua Syek-lyé. Rienau adue feyel mes. Ah'Casue oleri rienau.*"

As the phantom warrior held its stance, presumably waiting for a reply, Tieran asked in a loud whisper, "What did he say?"

Rezkin cocked his head and responded, "I have no idea. I have never heard the language." He glanced to the others, but none knew the foreign language. He said, "Based on the images of the original inhabitants recorded on the walls and the appearance of this entity, I would say it is most likely Fersheya."

"What is *that*?" Tieran asked.

"The language of the elves!" Wesson blurted with wide eyes. "Some of the terms used in magery are derived from Fersheya, or so we are taught. It is said that mage power originated with the elves and was somehow passed to humans. We use too few of the words to constitute any semblance of a language, though."

"I can think of maybe a dozen," Mage Yerlin commented, "though I doubt our pronunciation would be appreciated by the elves."

"I thought all the elves died off," Tieran said.

"Perhaps," Rezkin replied. "We cannot say for sure, but they have not been seen in these lands for more than a thousand years—since the founding of Ashai, at least. Based on my studies, I had considered that it was likely the elves were the original inhabitants of Caellurum, but I could not confirm my suspicions until we arrived. I believe we now have sufficient evidence to prove that it is so."

"What do we do about *him*," Kai asked as he motioned toward the vaporous entity. The specter still had not moved and did not seem to tire of his stance.

"It does not appear that it intends to attack," Rezkin observed. "Mage Yerlin, perhaps you should start trying to figure out the sequence to arrest the spell."

"Yes, Sire, but might I make a suggestion?" the mage asked tentatively.

"Of course, Mage Yerlin. Please do."

Yerlin motioned to the entity. "Well, the specter is a spell. So far, the other spells in the citadel, like the doors and lights, have responded to your *will*. Perhaps this phantom warrior will respond to you as well."

Rezkin considered the mage's suggestion and figured it could not hurt to try. He gathered his *will* and tried to impress upon the entity what he wanted of it. "Speak Ashaiian," he commanded.

The phantom warrior straightened and dropped its hands as it stood at attention with its sword resting in a reverse grip behind its arm. From his perspective, Rezkin could barely see the glowing sword through the vaporous form. Rezkin maintained a ready battle stance.

The specter looked into Rezkin's eyes with gaseous orbs and replied, "*Ah'Treyia aduleue*."

"Perhaps if you skip the language altogether," Wesson suggested. "Just *will* it to do what you want."

"How will it know what I want if I do not tell it?" Rezkin asked.

As far as he knew, people were influenced by the spell that lay over him only if he outwardly encouraged them in some way. If he wore a convincing disguise, they would be more inclined to believe it. If he told them to do something, they would be more likely to comply if they were already inclined to perform the action or had neutral feelings about the activity. He did not think he could make people do things simply by thinking the commands in his mind, but he had never actually tried.

"It is not a real person," Wesson reminded Rezkin. "It is just a spell. The spell recognizes your *will* whether you speak it aloud or not. I do not have to say '*create ward*' every time I wish to create a ward. In this case, you are not even creating a spell. You are influencing one that already exists."

While Rezkin's knowledge of spellcraft was better than that of most mundanes, it was nearly insignificant when compared with the mages' knowledge. He wondered why that subject had been so sparsely covered in his training. He thought perhaps it was because he was not a mage, so his masters felt it unnecessary for him to learn.

Rezkin formed a simple understanding in his mind of what he wished the specter to do. He wanted the phantom to understand and speak his language. Once he felt his desire was clearly communicated, he pressed his *will* against the phantom. To his surprise, he did not feel the sensation of pressing back that usually came with exerting his *will* on another. He realized this was because the phantom warrior was not an actual living being; therefore, it had no *will* of its own.

The specter cocked its head curiously, eerily mimicking Rezkin's mannerism. "*Thresia Spirétua Groyt* King. *Elyiliis* alert *mirahk*. Danger *yuolg fresté'imal* me *queld*," it said.

"I do not believe it worked," Tieran observed. "What was that? I thought I recognized a bit of Old Channerían."

"I believe some of it was Pruari," remarked an astounded Kai. "And Jerese?" he muttered as he scratched at his beard.

"I apologize," Rezkin said. "It was my error. I *willed* it to speak my language, but I neglected to specify which one. I will correct the oversight now."

"You speak Adianaik?" Wesson asked skeptically as he glanced between Rezkin and Mage Yerlin.

Rezkin did not care to emphasize once again how different he was from the outworlders, so he chose to say nothing in response. While at times he felt as though he was starting to make a place for himself in their society, it was increasingly clear that he was not one of them. He pressed his *will* upon the phantom again, this time with a clear understanding of Ashaiian in the forefront of his mind.

The warrior preformed its strange genuflection and said, "By the honor of the *Spirétua Syek-lyé*." Straightening, it continued, "We have been alerted to danger. With great respect, please identify the enemy."

"Well, that was better, but it is still not completely translating," Tieran observed.

"It must not be able to find a word in Rezkin's vocabulary to adequately translate *Spirétua Syek-lyé*." Wesson suggested, "Perhaps it is a title."

To the specter, Rezkin replied, "There is no danger. Stand down."

The phantom warrior dropped its arms and straightened to what was presumably an appropriate stance of attention among elven warriors. "Your weapons are drawn," the specter observed. "Do you wish to spar?"

"Fascinating!" exclaimed Mage Yerlin. "The enchantment is capable of observing its surroundings and making conjecture about the intentions of the people around it."

"I do not wish to spar," Rezkin replied. "I desire information. What is your purpose?"

"We are *shielreyah*," the specter said.

"Well, that clarifies things," Tieran remarked.

Ignoring his cousin, Rezkin asked, "What is the function of shielreyah?"

"Shielreyah are the protectors of the People, the Guardians of Caellurum," the phantom said.

"How many shielreyah are in Caellurum?" Rezkin inquired. He had no desire to be overrun with phantom warriors.

The phantom tilted its head curiously and replied, "We are seventeen, and we are one."

Rezkin considered the answer and then asked, "So there are seventeen entities like you, but you are all manifestations of the same spell?"

The specter paused, and it appeared as if some uncertainty crossed his vaporous features. "We are *Eihelvanan*."

"You mean you are elven," Rezkin clarified.

The phantom warrior frowned. "This *human* word is crass and means nothing to us. We are *Eihelvanan*, and this means much."

Rezkin lifted a brow at the mages in inquiry. "A spell with an opinion. I think it is offended."

Yerlin rubbed at his chin thoughtfully and said, "Curious. I have never heard of such a thing."

The specter grimaced and then bowed with reverence. "With great honor to the *Spirétua,* we are not a *spell,*" he said with disdain. "No *human* construct could capture the essence of *shielreyah.*"

"Wonderful," Kai barked. "An enchanted phantom warrior that hates humans."

The phantom turned his attention away from Rezkin for the first time and fixated on the burly striker. "We do not hate humans. It is simply a fact that human *spells* cannot create *shielreyah.*" The specter turned back to Rezkin and said, "*Spirétua,* we are one, but we can become many if you prefer."

"Explain," Rezkin commanded.

He had the sense the specter was attempting to be succinct in answering the questions, but the being seemed to be under the assumption that Rezkin, at least, understood more about elven matters than was so.

The specter studied Rezkin for a moment. Appearing to come to a decision, he said, "You are not of our age. Your knowledge of the *Spirétua* is lacking, even for one so young." Surveying the corridor with obvious concern, the phantom warrior asked, "Where are the other *Eihelvanan?*"

"There are none," Rezkin replied. "At least, none *here.* The original inhabitants of this citadel departed more than a thousand years ago and have not been seen in these lands since."

The phantom blinked in surprise, a variety of emotions passing across his vaporous visage. "We are alone," he observed sadly. "You have acquired a new people. You have brought to our land the humans."

"These people are my subjects and guests, and I have claimed this land," Rezkin said. "You have yet to explain how you can become many."

"*Pereliou evé Spirétua Syek-lyé,*" the phantom said with a bow. "We are now one, but we were once many. Our numbers were seventeen. Seventeen of the *LyréRheina* gifted to *Caellurum,* our essence to be preserved in the halls until we may be released to the Afterlife. Our *chiandre* are attached to this vessel as once they were to our living bodies. We now speak as one, but we may separate to serve as individuals again, by your *will, Spirétua.*"

"I see," Rezkin said.

"Then perhaps you can explain it to the rest of us," Tieran interjected. "I do not understand anything he is saying, even when he speaks Ashaiian."

Rezkin nodded and then asked the specter for clarification before continuing. "*LyréRheina* ... this means *Knights of Rheina*?"

The phantom cocked his head in contemplation and then grimaced as he answered, "This is an *adequate* translation, *Spirétua*."

Rezkin kept most of his attention on the specter but spoke to his companions. "The Knights of Rheina, or *LyréRheina*, were a warrior class of elves." The specter winced at his usage of the human term, but Rezkin continued, "They were servants and priests of Rheina, the patron goddess of elves and humans blessed with Her power."

"Rheina? I have never heard of her," Tieran remarked.

"Rheina is one of the three gods that were worshiped in places and times before the settling of this land and are still revered in the old kingdoms," Rezkin explained. "While none of the gods were technically male or female, Rheina is usually referred to in the feminine sense. She is the Goddess of the Firmament, of all things physical, and the Realm of Life exists within Her essence. All of the physical mage powers, including healing, are *Blessings of Rheina*."

"It does not sound as if much is left for the other gods," Kai interjected.

"Not so," Rezkin replied. "The other gods are just as important, but we may discuss religion another time. This warrior was a Knight of Rheina, and it seems that he and sixteen of his brethren essentially donated their souls to this citadel."

"Their *souls*?" Mage Yerlin exclaimed. "You are saying he is not a spell?"

"Yes and no. The phantom mentioned that the shielreyahs' *chiandre* were attached to Caellurum. To put it simplistically, the chiandre is the path of the soul. It is the tether that ties the soul to both the body and the Afterlife. When a person dies, his or her soul leaves the body and the Realm of the Living and travels the chiandre to the Realm of the Afterlife, which exists within the Goddess Nihko. It sounds like the chiandre of these seventeen warriors were disconnected from their bodies and reattached to this citadel."

"So the citadel is actually *alive*?" Wesson asked in alarm.

Rezkin tilted his head and considered the specter before him. At times it seemed to be very alive, while at others it was little more than a vaporous statue. "I do not believe so. I would venture to say that their souls reside in the

Afterlife but are still able to maintain some of their essence here in the Realm of the Living through the connection of their chiandre to the citadel."

The specter abruptly bowed his head slightly and said, "Your conclusion is accurate, *Spirétua*."

"So they truly *are* phantoms!" Tieran exclaimed. "I thought they were a spell. How did you influence them with your *will*?"

Spellcraft truly was not one of Rezkin's strengths, but he thought he understood enough about the old religion to venture a guess. "A soul cannot inhabit a non-living thing like this citadel. The soul must possess a body capable of sustaining life to exist in the Realm of the Living. It seems that a very powerful spell has been constructed to mimic life just enough to sustain the warriors' essences and maintain the connection with the chiandre, but it is not strong enough to carry the soul itself."

"The elves must have possessed power far beyond that of our mages to do such a thing," Mage Yerlin observed.

Rezkin shook his head and replied, "I cannot imagine they did it by themselves. The *Eihelvanan* may have had the power to construct the life-mimicking spell, but they had no power over the chiandre."

The phantom warrior bowed again and said, "You are correct, again, *Spirétua*, except that we are not a *spell*. *Spells* are human constructs. During the unprecedented visit by SenGoka Ga Ka Ahn-Den, the *Spirétua* and Sen worked together to create the *shielreyah*."

Rezkin's brows rose in surprise. "The Jahartan Emperor came *here*? With the *Eihelvanan*? I was under the impression that the *Eihelvanan* did not care for the Sen."

"It was so throughout most of our history," the phantom replied. "But SenGoka Ga Ka Ahn-Den was exceptional."

Tieran rubbed his jaw and said suspiciously, "Did you not say it was the Jahartan Empire that was trying to conquer this land before the founding of Ashai?"

The specter turned his attention to Tieran who swayed back in response. "It was more than just *this* land, but it was SenGoka Ga Ka Ahn-Den's predecessor who was responsible for that widespread death and destruction. SenGoka Ga Ka Ahn-Den brought an end to the Empire's reign of terror."

Tieran narrowed his eyes at the phantom and spoke to Rezkin without averting his gaze. "I remember you mentioned the Sen before. They were the necromancers, yes?"

"That is so," Rezkin affirmed. "The Sen were capable of seeing into the *Void*, the space between the Realm of the Living and that of the Afterlife. They could see the soul and the chiandre and draw the soul back to the body if it had not already passed beyond the Gates of the Afterlife. I had never heard that they were capable of actually manipulating the chiandre itself."

The phantom warrior inclined his head. "In general, they were not, but SenGoka Ga Ka Ahn-Den was exceptional."

"So you have said." Turning the discussion back to the original topic, Rezkin asked, "The *shielreyah* are presently of a single mind, but you can separate into your original personas?"

"Yes, *Spirétua*, but we are a mere essence of our former selves."

"And if I change my mind?" Rezkin asked. He was hesitant to make any permanent decisions regarding something so foreign and fantastical.

"We shall be as you *will*," the shielreyah replied with another graceful bow.

"Then so be it," Rezkin said as he exerted his *will*.

The phantom vapors began to swirl madly within the shape of the warrior, and then the entity separated into two identical, featureless forms. Slowly, the vapors morphed into identifiable features until the two beings were obviously Eihelvanan but individual and unique.

Both shielreyah abruptly took to one knee with their swords held in their strange pose. A broad-faced, full-lipped Eihelvanan said, "Thank you, *Spirétua Syek-lyé*. We were one for too long. *I* ... am thankful to be *myself* once again. I am Shielreyah Opohl, and I concede to your *will*."

The second's wide eyes looked past a sharp nose and high cheekbones as he said, "I thank you, as well, *Spirétua Syek-lyé*. I am Shielreyah Elry, and I concede to your *will*."

Rezkin nodded, and said, "Thank you. I am honored by the shielreyah."

Without knowledge of Eihelvanan customs, he was not sure how to respond. Most people liked being thanked and honored, though, so he went with that. Both specters smiled and stood. It seemed he had chosen well.

15

The ground was hard beneath the thin leather mat. Rezkin reclined against his pack as he closed his eyes and cleared his mind.

"Are you sure we can trust them?"

Tieran's words resonated through the void of Rezkin's subconscious. Rezkin's hollow voice echoed in his own ears as he replied.

"I have no reason to trust them any less than most of the citadel's current occupants."

"Gutterspit," Tieran snapped. "We all owe you our lives, some of us several times over. *They*, on the other hand, are foreign and … *creepy*."

Tieran did not take his gaze off the two silent wraiths standing guard outside the open portal, one that he thought should have held a sturdy door … with locks … many, many locks.

Rezkin did not open his eyes or stir to consciousness as he answered. "They are now an extension of my *will*, at least to some degree. For whatever reason, the citadel and its guardians have accepted my authority. I am fairly confident they will at least attempt to protect *me*, if not the rest of you."

Tieran scowled at his cousin. "And what of us? They could slaughter us in our sleep … or while we are perfectly awake and armed, for that matter. How do you know they do not seek to deceive us? Perhaps they are aware that we know how to dispel them and hope to lull us into complacency."

"I have considered the prospect, Tieran," Rezkin said as colors began to swirl behind his eyelids, "but in truth, there is little we could do if they choose to attack. The reports from the first encounter were consistent. The shielreyah can harm us, but we are incapable of mounting an effective counter attack. Therefore, we have little reason to concern ourselves. Either they speak truth and we live, or they are deceiving us and we die."

"Again with the comforting words of wisdom," Tieran grumbled.

"Do you propose an alternative?" Rezkin said with minimal interest.

Tieran said, "We could leave, abandon this haunted, albeit extravagant, graveyard."

In Rezkin's mind, twisting strands of colors separated and then came together into brilliant cords of white, only to split again in a moving tapestry of rainbows, a never-ending dance. At times, during deep meditation, the dance was accompanied by a soft, lulling melody that soothed his tense muscles and eased his aches. Not so this eve. Tieran's nattering and the multitude of potential threats prevented Rezkin from entering the deeper meditative state that he often sought in lieu of sleep.

"And go where, Tieran?" Rezkin asked, his voice a mere whisper as he slipped farther away.

"We could seek asylum in one of the other kingdoms," Tieran called across the chasm that separated them. "They are all in a riot over Caydean's treachery. Surely they would welcome his greatest contenders to the throne."

Rezkin responded from afar. "Hmm, likely they would capture us for use in a prisoner exchange. Some very important people are held in the dungeons of Kaibain. You should be grateful that we have found such a fortuitous refuge." His whisper was a shout in the darkness hidden beyond eddies of light.

"*Fortuitous?*" Tieran exclaimed, the intensity of his anxiety reflected in the green bolt that streaked through a field of orange before Rezkin's mental gaze. "We are in a haunted fortress infused with who knows what kind of power, guarded, or perhaps held captive, by the disembodied souls of elven wraiths who died over a thousand years ago. Not only that, but there is no game to hunt and no decent land for farming. What a stroke of luck!"

Tieran's words were punctuated with a dash of yellow in Rezkin's mind.

"You desire to become a farmer now?" Rezkin said.

"I desire to have a full belly and a bottle of wine," Tieran grumbled, "maybe two."

Pink and red washed over the orange.

"Fear not, Tieran," Rezkin droned. "I doubt the eihelvanan ate air."

"They could have eaten rocks for all we know ... or these disturbing crystals," Tieran muttered as he gazed at the pulsating blue gems on the ceiling.

The ebb and flow of light within the crystals seemed more synchronized around Rezkin. It almost reminded Tieran of a breath ... or a pulse ... and he could not help but wonder if somehow Rez was driving it. An icy chill ran through him as he thought of the alternatives. What if the citadel was *feeding* off Rezkin? What if an unseen spirit was trying to take over Rezkin's mind and body? It made sense for the spirit to target the strongest among them, and the rest of the refugees would be trapped on the haunted isle until they, too, were consumed. The dead were recruiting.

Light skittered away as a dark shadow plummeted through Rezkin's mind toward him. He ripped himself from his meditation and lurched to his feet as he deflected the projectile with a serrated knife and strength borne of a lifetime of training. His heart pumped furiously, but the battle energy was slow to respond. A quick perusal of his room reassured him that he had not somehow missed an encroaching assailant. Tieran was frozen in wide-eyed trepidation as two vaporous wraiths stood over him, their blazing-red blades bared at his throat.

"*Spirétua Syek-lyé*," Shielreyah Elry intoned, "this human assaulted you in *eskyeyela*. Shall we carry out his sentence now?"

Rezkin studied the floor, the *assault* evidenced by the torn sack and beans strewn across the grey stones. He looked to his cousin with a questioning lift of his brow.

"I-I was just seeing if you were awake ... I mean, if you were *you*." Tieran swallowed hard as he felt the sharp edge of the phantom blade press against his throat. "Y-you were speaking ... but it did not seem right. I cannot explain it, but I thought that ... um ... maybe something was trying to possess you."

Tieran's confidence seemed to wane with each word spoken. Rezkin cocked his head curiously at his cousin. Tieran closed his eyes and released as much breath as he dared.

Terrified, he muttered, "I know, it sounds stupid when I say it aloud."

Rezkin said, "Shielreyah, what is the sentence for attacking someone who is in ... *eskyeyela*?"

"Immediate death, *Spirétua Syek-lyé*," the phantom warrior answered tonelessly.

"And yet, you did not kill him," Rezkin observed.

A wisp of energy flitted between the two wraiths, and the second answered. "We sensed that you did not desire his death, *Spirétua Syek-lyé*."

Rezkin smiled at his cousin, but Tieran did not find the fiendish grin consoling in any way.

"There, see?" Rezkin said. "They were responding to my *will*."

His cousin frowned in sharp reply. "It is your *will* that they bare their blades to my throat?"

Rezkin sheathed his knife and said, "No. Release him and return to your posts."

The wraiths bowed their heads and then evaporated in a vaporous puff, only to reappear at attention outside the open portal. Tieran rubbed at his throat and was relieved to find no blood.

"What is this *eskyeyela*?" he asked as Rezkin retook his resting place on the floor.

"It would seem it has something to do with a state of meditation, although it must be more than that or the shielreyah would have translated it as such."

"So that is what you were doing? Meditating?" Tieran asked as he sucked in a calming breath.

"Yes," Rezkin answered. "At least, I *was* until you *assaulted* me," he said as he tossed a small packet to his cousin.

"What is this?" Tieran asked as he unwrapped the leather pouch.

"A needle and thread—to mend your pillow."

"*Mend my pillow?*" Tieran exclaimed in dismay. "What do *I* know of mending? Besides, the beans are all over the floor! Where is Colton when I need him?"

"Yes, it may take you awhile to collect them all," Rezkin said. "And, you do not need your manservant to mend a sack of beans."

The heir to the duchy of Wellinven stared at his king. Rezkin sighed and stood. He snatched the torn sack from the ground and then sat beside his cousin.

"It is like this," he said as he showed Tieran how to thread the needle and then demonstrated the highly complex task of stitching. "You have to loop the thread back like this or the seams will pull apart ..."

"What are you doing?" a deep, gruff voice asked from the doorway.

"What does it look like?" Tieran snapped.

Kai huffed and said, "I see the King of Cael, True King of Ashai, sitting on the floor teaching the Archduke and Crown Prince how to sew."

Tieran scowled and rebuffed, "I am not the duke … or *arch*duke. My father still lives. I know it. And what is this Crown Prince business?"

"While I realize all of this is new," the striker said as he twirled his finger in the air to indicate *everything*, "and we have yet to hold any official ceremonies or make announcements, the fact remains that *you* are Rezkin's only confirmed kin. Therefore, *you* are the closest thing he has to an heir, not to mention that you are already in the direct line of ascension to the throne of Ashai."

Tieran said, "I never wanted to rule Ashai and have even less desire to rule over this haunted abomination."

Rezkin interrupted before the striker could reply with one of his usual acerbic remarks. "What are you doing here, Kai?"

The striker grunted. "The *ghosts* came for me. One of those phantom elves popped right out of the wall and told me you were under attack. I am not ashamed to admit I nearly lost my skin when he suddenly appeared over my pallet. I have to say, though, Lord Tieran, that a sewing needle is a poor choice of weapon."

Rezkin said, "It was a pillow, actually."

"He tried to suffocate you?"

Rezkin shook his head and smirked. "No, he threw it at me."

"You mean I was pulled from my bed by phantom elven warriors because the two of you decided to have a pillow fight?"

"What is the problem?" Striker Shezar asked as he appeared behind Kai, his sword drawn in preparation for a fight.

Kai muttered, "Our valiant king is hosting a sewing circle."

"Consider it a test of sorts," Rezkin said as he stood. "We now know the shielreyah are highly intuitive and considerate of my desires …"

"Or so they would have us think," Tieran mumbled.

Rezkin tilted his head in recognition of Tieran's pessimism. It was, after all, a valid concern. "We also know that, although they have divided themselves into separate entities, they are still, in a way, of one mind and can communicate between multiple locations within the citadel. Additionally, it seems they are aware of your status as my guards and they will alert you if I am in danger. It was a very informative encounter."

Rezkin settled himself onto his makeshift pallet and said, "Now, if you all do not mind, I intend to get some rest."

. . .

Rezkin was up well before dawn, as usual. Somehow, he felt both refreshed and drained. He had not actually slept, but after Tieran fell asleep, he had finally entered a state of deep meditation. He could typically function on meditation alone for a few days, but for some reason, it had been less effective that night. He wondered if he could not reach the meditative depth he intended due to his perceived need for constant vigilance in the mysterious citadel. He would need to get some real sleep soon if he were to feel truly revitalized.

Most of the refugees were still abed, except for the few guards. Rezkin did not wish to disturb his slumbering subjects, and he felt even less inclined to deal with the guards—not that he expected any trouble. On that morning, he did not feel like dealing with people in general. After donning his night stealth armor and dark hood, Rezkin swept through the crystal-lit corridors on silent feet. With a few well-timed turns, some minor distractions, and the expert use of shadows that somehow always appeared where he needed them, the dark wraith slipped past the guards and through the warehouse to the dock. Hand over hand, he scurried up one of the ropes securing the ship to the dock and slinked over the rail without notice. He was both thankful and irritated that it had been so easy to infiltrate the ship without raising the alarm.

After a quick sweep of the decks, Rezkin stole into the captain's quarters. Captain Estadd was just beginning to rouse. The man grumbled and rubbed at his face as he shifted his feet to the floor. He used a firestick to light the candle on his bedside table and then lurched back with a shout.

Undesiring of frivolous chatter, Rezkin remained curt. "Captain, report."

The captain sputtered and clutched at his chest as he attempted to regain his senses. A moment later, two of the ship's crewmen charged into the room, weapons bared.

Captain Estadd snapped at the men. "Why did you not announce the king's presence?"

"S-sorry, Cap'n. We didn't know he was aboard," the first mate answered, his eyes shifting anxiously between king and captain.

Rezkin scowled at the late arrivals and then looked back to Estadd. "Captain?"

"Ah, Your Majesty ... nothing to report. All is hale," Estadd said as he hurriedly tucked his shirt into his trousers.

"You have heard of the phantom warriors in the citadel?" Rezkin asked.

Standing straighter, the captain replied, "Yes, Sire. Quite disturbing, I would say."

"Have they made an appearance on the ship?" Rezkin asked, his words clipped and brusque.

"No, Sire. We have seen no phantoms on the ship ... save for you, perhaps." Then catching himself, he said, "Pardon me, Your Majesty, I am not quite awake ..."

Before Estadd could finish his sentence, the king was out the door. The two crewmen and the captain quickly followed, but when they reached the deck, the king was gone.

Upon reentering the warehouse, Rezkin was momentarily pleased to see that Tam and Waylen were up and just beginning to work through their warm-up routine. He knew Malcius and Brandt would be joining them soon. Palis's death had been difficult for everyone, but it had lit a fire under the young lords. Waylen had been Palis's most avid training partner, and over the past several weeks, Tam, Malcius, and Brandt had begun to fill the void. Rezkin was not exactly sure what was driving Tam, but he knew Malcius and Brandt sought vengeance.

He did not think vengeance was an appropriate driving force. His masters had emphasized the need to distance himself from any emotions or personal desires. But Malcius and Brandt were not training to be like *him*. Rezkin now understood that outworlders had little knowledge of the *Rules* and even less motivation to follow them. He thought this odd since the *Rules* were intended to keep people alive. From everything he had observed, though, outworlders tended toward complacency and even apathy. It was deeply rooted in their society and perhaps even encouraged by those in power. Fewer aspiring minds meant easier targets to control.

Rezkin also realized that his upbringing was considered odd and harsh to the outworlders. He had trained with no clear understanding of his purpose and none had been necessary. He trained because it was expected; it was what he *did*. He had not known anything different, and frankly, it was painful when he failed. The threat of pain could be enough to drive any man, at least until he learned to resist the pain; but by then he was already conditioned for training. Rezkin decided the young lords probably needed a sense of purpose, so he accepted their thirst for blood—for the time being.

As he passed the two young men, Rezkin said, "You two are with me."

Tam and Waylen glanced at each other and then hurried to catch up to their king. The blue crystals were dim in the corridor at the top of the stairs, barely shedding enough light to illuminate the floor in front of them.

"Uh, Rez, where are we going?" Tam asked as he reached Rezkin's side.

Waylen strode to the king's other side with piqued interest. It was not often that Rezkin addressed him outside of training, and he was excited to be included in whatever excursion the king had planned.

"We go to explore the citadel," Rezkin quietly replied so as not to wake those sleeping in the side chambers.

"What?" exclaimed Tam. At Rezkin's scowl, he glanced around and lowered his voice. "All alone? Just us?"

Rezkin rounded on his friend and grumbled, "Would you rather stay behind?"

"No!" Tam blurted. "I mean, shouldn't we have a team or something? You know, like with guards and mages?"

"I agree with your apprentice," remarked a shadow as it separated itself from the other shadows along the corridor. Striker Shezar's eyes appeared tired but alert as he blocked their passage. "These boys are not warriors. You are not truly considering going to the next level without your forward units?"

Rezkin's reply was terse as he pushed passed the striker. "Since you are here, you may attend as well,"

"Sire, we should gather a team ..."

"We go now," Rezkin said. "The shielreyah have assured me that I am in no danger."

"And you believe them?" Shezar muttered. His generally smooth voice and steady tone did nothing to disguise his irritation. "Then Lord Tieran speaks sense."

"And I do not?" Rezkin snapped.

The striker stepped in front of his king when they reached the foot of the stairs leading to the next floor. He leveled his gaze at the imposing young warrior and said, "I fear you are still not recovered from yesterday's incident. You are not acting like yourself."

"I am fine, Shezar. I just do not feel like dealing with people today."

"You would dismiss the danger and threats simply because you are feeling asocial?" Waving his hand toward the stairs, Shezar said, "This, here, is an unnecessary risk, Sire. It is in violation of the *Rules*."

Rezkin paused. Was he in violation of the *Rules*? Was he taking an unnecessary risk? Perhaps he would have been if he were not certain that he had no need for concern. As it was, he *knew* the wraiths spoke truth, and he had no apprehension about the unknown that resided above.

"*Spirétua Syek-lyé*, you summoned?" a phantom said as his vaporous form took shape beside the striker.

Rezkin was momentarily thrown, as he did not remember calling for the phantom. He narrowed his eyes at the vaporous entity. Had he unconsciously summoned the being, or were the specters listening to them argue?

"Who are you?" Rezkin asked.

This phantom appeared younger than the others he had met, with fine features but a serious countenance. He stood about an inch shorter than Rezkin and wore his hair in an intricate braid that trailed down his back to his waist. Although it was impossible to tell the man's coloration since he was composed only of bluish vapors, Rezkin thought the young eihelvanan might have had much lighter hair and eyes than the others.

The phantom thrust the pommel of his glowing red sword into his vaporous palm and bowed deeply. "*Pereliou evé Spirétua Syek-lyé.* My name is Yeshri," he intoned in an accent unlike the others. "How may I serve?"

Rezkin studied the phantom for a moment and then said, "My companions believe you intend to lead me into a trap."

"*Sire* ..." Striker Shezar protested with a scowl for his liege.

Tam and Waylen glanced at each other but were otherwise frozen in place. Neither wanted to attract the attention of the wraith ... or the angry striker ... or the unpredictable warrior-king. Shielreyah Yeshri straightened to attention with his sword hidden behind his back at the ready. He looked curiously at Rezkin but said nothing.

Rezkin looked to the striker and remarked, "They can hear everything that occurs in the citadel." Looking back to the shielreyah, he asked, "Is this not true?"

The shielreyah tilted his head and answered, "This is true, *Spirétua Syek-lyé*, but one of us must be listening."

Shezar looked accusingly at his king. "They might not have heard, then."

Rezkin shook his head and asked the phantom, "You are always listening to *me*, are you not?"

Yeshri tilted his head again and replied, "Yes, *Spirétua Syek-lyé*. We are ever at your call."

It suddenly dawned on Shezar that the king might not have been behaving oddly after all. Perhaps Rezkin was allowing the wraiths to *believe* they had his trust for a reason. The striker was now faced with a conundrum. Either the young king had become mentally unstable and erratic, or he was fully cognizant of the dangers and had a plan. Shezar had not known Rezkin for long, and during that time, they had mostly been confined to the ship. He knew the young man to be an indomitable warrior with a sharp mind, but Rezkin's upbringing had been brutal. It was possible the young king was not altogether sane. Plus, the enchanted citadel had done *something* to the king upon their arrival. Shezar did not know Rezkin well enough to tell if he was under a spell.

Rezkin looked to the shielreyah and asked, "So, is it a trap?"

This time it was the shielreyah who looked at Rezkin as if he were crazy. "You would ask me if I am leading you into a trap?"

"Yes. Is it a trap?" Rezkin asked with irritation.

"No, *Spirétua*. We have no reason or desire to *trap* you." Yeshri glanced at the striker and then back to Rezkin. "The humans do not understand. We heed the *will* of the *Spirétua* and serve the *Syek-lyé*."

Rezkin gave Shezar a single nod. He said, "See. No trap. Let us go."

With that, the young king pushed past the striker and started up the stairs to the unexplored level.

Shezar said, "Please, at least bring the battle mage. We know not what surprises await."

Rezkin snapped, "Fine. Yeshri, summon Journeyman Mage Wesson."

Yeshri floated ahead of him as they ascended the steps, his vaporous form providing additional light to the dim stairwell. This passage was not as wide as the one that led from the warehouse to the first level, only allowing for two or three people to stand abreast. At the landing, Rezkin and his comrades stood before three closed stone doors. Several minutes later, Rezkin could hear the patter of feet in the corridor below, followed by heavy panting up the stairwell. Wesson stopped behind Tam and Waylen as he sucked in air like a man dying for breath.

"The ... the phantom said it was urgent," Wesson huffed as he leaned on his knees gasping for breath.

Rezkin raised a questioning brow at the shielreyah. The phantom appeared concerned that he had somehow offended the king.

"I sensed your frustration and thought it best for the mage to attend quickly," he said apologetically.

Rezkin was a little unnerved that the phantom warriors were so attuned to his moods. "That was very ... efficient ... of you, Shielreyah Yeshri."

The young elven wraith smiled with pride, obviously pleased to have been of service to the king. Yeshri did not appear to be much older than Rezkin, and he wondered why the young eihelvanan had sacrificed his life to the citadel. It was not the time to ask, though, and such an invasive question might be offensive to the phantom warrior.

The king looked over the three doors and asked Yeshri, "What lies beyond each of these doors?"

Yeshri stared at the three doors in much the same way Rezkin had. He tilted his head curiously in a parody of the king that was a bit disturbing to Rezkin's companions. Finally, the wraith replied, "I do not know, *Spirétua*."

Rezkin narrowed his eyes at the shielreyah. "You are a guardian of this citadel, and you do not know what lies beyond the doors?"

Yeshri appeared similarly confused. Wisps of vapor whipped into and out of the phantom, like tiny insects flitting away into oblivion and then returning to their nest just as quickly. His facial expression eventually morphed into one of understanding, and he said, "I do not know what lies beyond the doors because you have not yet unlocked them, *Spirétua*."

"You cannot access that part of the citadel?" Rezkin asked in surprise.

"I have access to all of the citadel, *Spirétua*, for we are one and we are many. I cannot carry the knowledge across the threshold," Yeshri explained.

Rezkin looked to Wesson for clarification. Wesson pondered for a moment and then suggested, "It sounds like the spells are compartmentalized. The phantom warrior spell cannot access knowledge of that part of the citadel once it passes through the ward spell. He will not be able to do so until the ward is deactivated."

For the first time, Yeshri's eager but determined visage turned to one of irritation. "We are not a *spell*, human. We are *shielreyah*."

"Ah, my apologies, *shielreyah*," Wesson mumbled at the phantom's hostile gaze.

Rezkin approached the door on the left and pressed his hand to its cool stone surface. An icy tendril wound its way up his arm, but he focused on pressing it back. The cold chill snapped away like a snake from a hot brand. With the slightest push, the door swung wide to reveal a short, empty corridor that ended in another door. Along the left side was a solid stone wall polished smooth with intermittent, beautifully sculpted images in bas-relief. The wall on the right was lined with massive floor to ceiling windows of frosted glass, the sun's early morning glow evident through the panes.

"That makes no sense," Waylen said. "That wall abuts the mountain. How is it the sun shines through?"

Rezkin pressed his hand to the door on the right and found a winding stairwell leading upward into darkness. Finally, Rezkin opened the central door. He was not prepared for what lay beyond. His companions gasped as their eyes lit with the sun's rays. Without further consideration, Rezkin stepped into a courtyard. It appeared to be a side yard, for he could see the wall of a large building to the left. In front of him and to the right was a stone wall, perhaps eight feet in height, that ran the remaining perimeter of the courtyard. The ground was paved with tightly fitted stones, and directly across from him was a tall gate. The most astounding aspect of the courtyard, though, was the brightening sky above, splashed with the vibrant pinks and oranges of sunrise.

Rezkin took a few steps into the courtyard and was quickly overtaken by Striker Shezar. The striker bounded past him, alert to the foreign surroundings. Rezkin and the striker both scanned the tops of the walls and checked for arrow slits and windows in the adjacent building. Far at the top was an open window, but neither saw any movement within the dark recess. Rezkin turned to observe the wall through which they had entered the courtyard, the wall that lined the corridors of the citadel. It was almost completely missing. A short perimeter wall stood in its place, alone with the doorway through which they had exited. With a few quick steps and expertly placed feet, Rezkin was atop the wall in seconds. From there, he could see the hidden cove and the sea beyond. It was fascinating. When they had been on the sea and later standing on the dock, they could see naught but a solid cliff face on a mountainside.

"What do you see, Rez?" Tam asked.

"The ocean," he replied, mesmerized by the mystical view.

Turning back to the courtyard, Rezkin unceremoniously dropped to the ground.

"Are you okay?" Tam exclaimed as he rushed forward.

Rezkin paused in confusion. "What?"

"Are you hurt?" his friend asked.

"No. Should I be?" Rezkin said, still not understanding the source of Tam's distress.

"That wall is like ten feet high!" Tam said.

Rezkin scowled and shook his head. "It is closer to eight, and I am fine."

Rezkin was uncomfortable with the way everyone was scrutinizing his every move. It was not the technical observation he was used to from his trainers. These people were not watching to ensure that he performed correctly and efficiently. *They are suspicious*, he thought. *Is Tam searching for a weakness?*

Rezkin met Tam's concerned gaze with a hard stare.

Tam shifted, glancing around anxiously. "W-what?"

Is he plotting with someone else? Rezkin wondered. His cold, blue gaze slid to the side. *Shezar. Shezar seems more suspicious than the others. And Tieran. Tieran attacked me last night.*

Rezkin frowned at the thought. No, Tieran had not attacked him. Tam was not plotting against him. Tam would never do that. His friend was loyal. Tam's oath of fealty had been genuine, Rezkin was sure of it. He shook his head and felt his thoughts clear.

"Let us get on with this," Rezkin said as he turned and stalked toward the gate.

"What was *that*?" Shezar muttered beneath his breath to Tam.

Tam shrugged and stopped himself from wringing his hands. It was a bad habit he had developed at some point in his travels.

"I don't know," he said. "For a moment, it looked like he wanted to take my head. I've seen that look before but never directed at *me*. I can honestly say I never want to see it again."

The iron gate was free of rust and swung open smoothly on silent hinges. Beyond the gate was another astounding sight. It was a city square—one so massive as to rival the main square in Kaibain. To their left, the square curved around a semicircle of steps leading to the grand entry of an elegant palace. A central tower rose above the square, the solid stone façade twisting around like a unicorn's horn. Behind it rose a second, larger tower, the walls bulging and curling like an enormous bonfire. Between the curves and licks of flames were windows, some with balconies, and a multitude of arrow slits disguised as part of the monumental sculpture. An array of crystals reflected the sun's rays off the tower's surface, but none glowed as they did below in the citadel.

Across from the palace was what looked to have been a market lined with empty structures that might have held shops. The stone buildings were pristine, as though recently constructed. The roofs were made of slate, and iron rods that likely once held signs protruded over many of the doors. Three equally grand streets radiated away from the central square. Rezkin proceeded down the central street with Wesson, Tam, and Waylen excitedly chattering behind him. Shezar bounded from one building to the next looking for hidden assailants. Smaller streets crossed the larger street, but none of the roads were straight as they mean-dered around what might have been small gardens or sitting areas. Eventually, former stores and workshops gave way to residences. The scene was surreal, though, since there was no evidence at all that anything had ever lived within the city. There were no plants, birds or insects; no rat droppings or pollen; no wood, fabric, or leather of any sort. Only metal and stone had survived the centuries.

After the last house on the last cross street, the city ended. The end was not denoted by a wall or sign but by lush and vibrant greenery. The boulevard quickly narrowed to naught but a small path that wound its way through what was obviously once a garden, now overgrown and wild. A dry, stone fountain lined with clear crystals dominated the center of the garden, three statues grasping toward the sky in its center. One statue was of a majestic horse rearing onto its hindquarters, a single, twisting horn jutting from its brow. The second was of a magnificent bird, a raptor as large as the unicorn with feathers that flowed and curled like tongues of flame. The third creature was an enor-mous serpent twisting around the trunk of a young tree. At the top of the tree, the serpent's jaw gaped as though to swallow the sun and stars. In its maw was a blue cabochon crystal larger than a man's head.

The stone path and fountain had been preserved like the rest of the city, but the plants had been left to grow wild and uncontrolled. The path was littered with leaves and roots, and vines curled over the fountain like living lace. A step beyond the dense greenery of the garden revealed, in the distance below the mountain upon which the city stood, distant fields of swaying grasses, green meadows dotted with colorful flowers, and scattered copses of trees through which birds and small animals flitted and skittered. The fields and meadows stretched nearly to the horizon and, in their center, was a massive lake fed by a myriad of sinuous streams. In the far distance was a vast forest undisturbed for over a thousand years. Far, far beyond, perhaps more than a week's ride from the palace, was a ring of purple mountains stretching from one end of the horizon to the other.

"It is a bowl," Waylen whispered in awe.

"What say you?" Shezar said as he finished checking the immediate area for danger.

Realizing he had been heard, Waylen muttered, "We are on the rim. See? The mountains stretch all the way around."

Shezar took in the distant scenery for the first time. "So it is." With mounting apprehension, he said, "It is strange, though. The amount of land here is far greater than the size of the island."

The explorers beheld the mysterious countryside, baffled by its very existence.

Finally, Shezar said, "There is plenty of space and terrain in which a sizeable force could hide. We should retreat to the citadel and organize units for reconnaissance. Already someone could have easily flanked us and cut off our escape route. We have no idea what has been living in this city. Do you not see? It is too clean."

"Exactly," Rezkin replied. "Nothing lives within the city."

"Perhaps there is a reason for that," Shezar countered.

Rezkin studied the striker for a moment. His voice was cold and unfamiliar as he said, "You would deny my claim to the city?"

"*What*?" Shezar exclaimed in confused exasperation. "No, nothing of the sort. I am just saying ... look there," he said pointing to the wild garden. "Nature takes its hold when it can. But, the life stops *there*. You can see the line. Nothing grows beyond it. *Something* is either keeping the life *out* or is killing everything *within*—without leaving a trace."

"Which makes it much easier for us to occupy," Rezkin agreed.

"That is not what I am saying, and you know it," Shezar said, now nearly certain the young king had lost his mind.

Rezkin turned back down the path that led into the city. "We will return to the warehouse. Shezar, you will oversee the reconnaissance and scouring of the city for signs of life."

Shezar released a breath. That, at least, was sensible. With a suspicious glance toward his liege's back, Shezar asked, "What will *you* be doing during that time?"

"I will be exploring the palace, of course," said Rezkin, as though it were obvious.

Ignoring the disapproving glare directed his way, Rezkin stepped across the demarcation between the untamed garden and the dead city. Shielreyah Yeshri reappeared in front of him, also wearing a disgruntled expression. The shielreyah examined Rezkin with a critical eye. His wispy facial features relaxed, as he was apparently satisfied with what he found.

"What is it, Shielreyah?" Rezkin asked as he passed the phantom warrior.

The specter bowed and said, "I seek only to ensure your well-being, *Spirétua Syek-lyé*."

"Did you have reason for concern?" Rezkin asked, his tension mounting.

"Not as such, *Spirétua.* Our power is tied to Caellurum. We cannot follow or see beyond the *corveua* ..." Yeshri paused, his face a mask of deliberation. "The *boundary*, perhaps. My apologies, *Spirétua.* This term does not translate properly."

"Sire," Striker Shezar interrupted. "Would you please join me in the garden for a moment?"

Yeshri narrowed ghostly white orbs at the striker and said, "*Spirétua Syeklyé,* the warrior seeks to lure you beyond the limits of my protection. His motives are not to be trusted."

Shezar's attention snapped to the shielreyah. "I am a *striker*, sworn to serve and protect my king. My motives are honorable and just. It is *your* intent that should be questioned!"

Rezkin glanced between the phantom and the striker as his temples began to throb. This was exactly the sort of outworlder drama he had hoped to avoid upon waking. Rezkin did not believe Shezar held ill intent; but, then again, the striker had been acting strangely, questioning Rezkin's decisions and insisting he be guarded every moment, day and night. Perhaps Shezar was not guarding Rezkin so much for his own safety as he was monitoring him. That made more sense. Rezkin did not need to be protected, but it was reasonable that people would feel threatened by him and desire to track his movements. The striker could seek to arrest control from Rezkin now that they had found a place of refuge.

A fiery red blade appeared between Rezkin and the striker as the shielreyah stood poised to strike.

"It attacks!" Shezar shouted as he immediately drew his own sword and jumped back beyond the *corveua.*

Wesson quickly formed a ward between Rezkin and the shielreyah, and Tam grasped Waylen's shoulder, jerking him back into the garden.

Rezkin shook his head to clear the fog that had taken hold. His temples throbbed, and he could tell, now, that he was not thinking clearly. Shezar was a man who, with little more than an ambiguous assignment of power by a dead king and the mere hope of serving someone less treacherous than the current king, chose to stand against Caydean and serve a mysterious dark warrior. Although Rezkin was certain Shezar had carried out terrible acts in service to his former liege, the striker's eagerness to believe in Rezkin's claim to the throne was proof of the man's desire for freedom and redemption from such tyranny.

Rezkin's eyes landed on the shielreyah, and the phantom abruptly retook his former non-threatening stance. He stepped past the specter, passing through Wesson's ward as he rejoined the others in the wild garden. Shezar was still on guard, ready to defend himself should the phantom attack. Tam and Waylen had also drawn their swords but appeared decidedly less confident.

"You may stand down," Rezkin stated. "He will not attack."

"Only because we are beyond his reach," Shezar muttered as he sheathed his sword.

Rezkin searched the striker's eyes for any hint of the man's thoughts. "So you believe him in this, at least?"

The striker shot the phantom a withering glare, although the wraith presumably could not see him. "I believe it about as much as I believe he serves your *will*. I hardly think you had intents on attacking me."

Rezkin cocked his head as he stared at the striker but did not refute the statement or provide assurance.

Catching the implication, Shezar's eyes turned to pained betrayal. "You *did* intend to attack me?" he exclaimed in disbelief.

With furrowed brow, Rezkin's face was a mask of concern and confusion. "I ... I am not certain. For a moment, my mind was as if in a fog ..."

He abruptly caught himself. He was not supposed to show such weakness. He could not confess to the striker that he had not been fully in control of his faculties. He shook his head and smiled broadly as he gripped the striker's shoulder in a sign of camaraderie.

"It is nothing, a momentary lapse in focus. The shielreyah must have mistaken a minor irritation for something more serious. We must return to the others now and get our explorations underway."

At that Rezkin, turned and proceeded back up the cobbled street toward the citadel. Shezar's hand whipped out and grasped Wesson's arm, momentarily preventing the mage from following the young king.

"Something is not right with the king," Shezar said. "It started when he touched that door. I do not believe he is recovered, and I fear these phantoms have something to do with it."

"You think he is under a spell?" Wesson asked. He had not noticed anything particularly strange that morning until the shielreyah drew its blade, but he was not accustomed to the practices of warriors.

"I've noticed it, too," Tam said. "He seems ... I don't know ... *hostile*."

"He did say that he had no desire to deal with people today," Waylen said. "Perhaps he did not sleep well."

The striker frowned in dismissal of the young lord, but Waylen was not to be deterred.

"Think about it," he insisted. "Rezkin is always on alert. You have seen what he does when he enters a room in which he intends to stay for a while. He searches the entire room for traps and poisons ... *every time* he enters ... even if he is only gone for a few minutes. I imagine being in this strange place with so many people depending on him is stressful. I would probably be a little grumpy, too."

"A little *grumpy*? That wraith nearly *attacked* me!" Shezar spat. Turning to Wesson, the striker said, "You need to keep an eye on him. Find a way to search him for spells or enchantments or whatever it is you do. Maybe he is ill or injured. I do not know, but you must figure it out."

Wesson's eyes widened. "I am not a healer, Striker Shezar. I am not the right person for the job."

Shezar shook his head. "It must be you. He trusts you, at least more than most of us. He will not let the other mages near, especially if those phantoms are influencing him in some way."

Wesson said, "Questioning the king in this way is close to treason, Striker."

Shezar gritted his teeth and argued, "I spent years serving a mad king. By the Grace of the Maker, I have been given a second chance, and I will not allow some dead *elves* to corrupt Rezkin's mind!"

Wesson, Tam, and Waylen glanced at each other and then nodded in acceptance. They all hurried up the path to catch up with the king, and much to their frustration, he was nowhere to be found.

16

The guards crossed paths before Adsden's eyes. "Mark," he said.
Fierdon made a note in the log. "That was twelve and fourteen, yes?"

"Correct."

"Can you see him?" Fierdon asked.

"Not yet."

A few minutes passed, and Adsden caught sight of a flash of light in an otherwise dark shadow cast by the tower's stubborn stand against the early afternoon sun.

"There," he said. "He is in position."

"Are you sure it was a good idea to trust the boy with this?"

"Benni is young, but he follows orders well."

Fierdon tisked. "His fighting skills are abysmal. If he is caught ..."

"He is a good sneak, better than most of my men. If no one sees him, he will not have to engage anyone. The other positions will almost definitely require combat. I would have preferred to do this one myself, but you know it is not an option."

"I know, I know. The strongest mages in the palace will be present. They would detect your *talent*."

"Miniscule as it is," Adsden muttered.

"Even so, it seems to have served you well. The fact that you have so little power demonstrates just how efficient you have become. You are capable of far more than I would have expected."

"You flatter me," Adsden said as he watched the next set of guards round the structure. "Mark—thirteen and fifteen."

"Are you sure?"

"Yes, why?"

Fierdon held the parchment up so that Adsden could see the map and watch the rotations at the same time.

"Here," he said, tapping the map over one section of the wall with his quill. "There is a gap in the patrol. Six and twelve should have crossed over here at station nine, but instead thirteen and fifteen crossed at eight. That leaves four open until the next rotation."

"Where are six and twelve, then?" Adsden mused.

Lowering the parchment, Fierdon pondered the puzzle. "Maybe they were pulled out for some reason."

"Or took a break," Adsden said. "Watch the wall for a moment. Let me see the map."

He examined the log of the patrol rounds for the past several hours. Finally, he said, "No. Every four circuits, the guards from station nine fail to show. They reappear during the next circuit over here at station ten. I think we are missing a station, perhaps inside. Maybe they are patrolling the transfer corridor."

"Wait, they reappear at ten?" Fierdon said. "Corridor *C* would be the most direct return route, which leaves corridor *A* clear." He paused, handing Adsden the quill. "Mark—seven and four."

Adsden made the note in the log and then checked the time dial they had managed to procure from a records office. It had been Fierdon's first acquisition of worth since joining the thieves. Although he was not a member of any specific guild, he now wore the Raven's mark with pride.

"Are you sure that is the corridor they would use?"

"Yes, I told you, when I was young ... before *this*"—he motioned to his face—"I was fostered for two winters at the palace. It was cold and dreary outside, so we spent most of our time exploring and playing in the corridors."

"You said these particular corridors lead to the dungeon. Why would you go there?"

"Mostly we hid from Caydean. Tieran Nirius was there as well. He and Thresson were of similar age, and Caydean made fun of me for spending time with the younger boys. I did not care for his forms of entertainment, though. Hespion, on the other hand, idolized Caydean. He followed him around like a puppy." Fierdon absently rubbed at the twisted flesh along one side of his face. "Perhaps I should have done more to prevent it, but Caydean was the prince. What was I to do? I never considered he would go this far."

"It is best to leave the past behind when there is nothing you can do about it," Adsden said. "You have a new family now, and your knowledge of the palace grounds and operations has been invaluable."

"Yes, I am sure that was the Raven's intent when he extended his invitation."

Adsden looked at him sideways. "It does not bother you, then—to be used like this?"

Fierdon grinned in his lopsided way. "Everyone gets used. It is how you are repaid that is important." He met Adsden's gaze and said, "Since joining you, I have been treated as a person, not the spawn of evil that my household seems to think I am."

Adsden chuckled. "I do not think you an evil man—wise and cunning but not evil."

"And what kind of man are you, Guildmaster Adsden?"

Adsden turned back to watch the guard rotation. "Mark, two and three." As Fierdon took the parchment to make the note, Adsden said, "I am a selfish man. I take what I want when I can." He turned and, as his eyes trailed the melted flesh of Fierdon's face, he said, "I would never do something so cruel and meaningless."

Fierdon huffed. "It was not meaningless to Hespion. He became heir to Atressian."

"Perhaps, but it would have been just as easy to kill you." He glanced at Fierdon. "Some might have thought it kinder."

"What makes you think he was not trying to kill me? It would have been *smarter*, not kinder. The fact that I am alive means I have a chance for justice —or vengeance. I am broken, but alive is better than dead. I walk a longer road to success, but still I walk."

Adsden's gaze traced the path of a hooded man crossing the street to where he stopped within the shadow of the building they had been surveilling.

"You are not broken, Fierdon," he said absently. "Only hidden behind an ugly mask." As his words echoed in his mind, he realized his error. Turning to the man beside him, he said, "Pardon me, Lord Fierdon ..."

"No," Fierdon said raising a hand, "kinder words have not been spoken. Please, just call me Fierdon."

Adsden nodded and then glanced back to the window just as the man from the shadow slipped around the corner of the building. "You are not concerned about turning your back on your family—possibly betraying them?"

"My brother betrayed our family long ago. Father will not be able to hold off the king's army indefinitely. Caydean has already bled our lands dry of workers and resources. We must join forces with the other dukes if we are to have a chance at survival, but Hespion does not see reason. He is no general. Without me to guide him, he will be lost. It is in his best interest for Father to live a long life, but Hespion is so eager to claim the title of Duke for himself.

"My betrayal may be the only hope House Mulnak has. It seems to me the Raven is more powerful and vicious than any of the dukes, and the fact that he supports the claim of this True King lends me hope that the kingdom may survive until the reign of a legitimate ruler once again. Perhaps if this True King hears of my loyalty, he will preserve House Mulnak in the new era."

Adsden shook his head. "You place much faith in a criminal overlord and unnamed claimant to the throne."

"*You* have faith in him—real faith. I have seen it in your eyes and in the eyes of the others, those who have met him—Attica, Rom, even Benni. A man does not garner that kind of loyalty through fear alone."

Adsden sighted the flash of light from the hooded man who had just reached his station atop the balustrade. "Blue two is in position." A couple of minutes passed, and he said, "It is difficult to explain. I do not fear many men, but I fear him. It is more than that, though. I am intrigued, enthralled, even drawn to him. He is sophisticated, eloquent, harsh, and deadly—like a master sword, a Sheyalin even—a piece of art. His plans—those he shares with me— are far-reaching and thorough. It would be easy to dismiss many of them as nonsensical or wasteful, and yet I know they are not. His every move is a thread in a tapestry so intricately woven and vast that I cannot fathom the pattern."

"But, to him, you are just a pawn."

"True, but a pawn personally chosen by the Maker is a pawn blessed. He cannot win the gambit without them."

"The Maker? You speak of him as if he were a god."

Adsden chuckled. "No, nothing so magnificent, although the slips seem to think so. I merely admire a brilliant player."

"Is that all you admire of him?" Fierdon asked.

With a sideways glance, Adsden grinned. "He has a presence."

Fierdon met his gaze and said, "One could dream of having such a following." He quickly glanced away and nodded toward the window. "Blue three has just arrived."

Adsden wondered if he had misjudged Fierdon. The man had spent as much time with Attica over the past couple of weeks, and he had thought for certain he was besotted. Fierdon had to be referring to the Raven's infamy and power, he thought. Surely he had not meant the words how they sounded to Adsden's ears. He shook his head to clear his thoughts, then rolled the parchment and placed it in the leather wrap.

"It is time to go. We will deliver the log to *red* and then take our positions in *yellow*."

The two men had been holed up on the top floor of a merchant house across from the palace grounds. From four stories up, they could see the top of most of the palace wall, the grand courtyard, the eastern tower, and the roof of the southeastern wing, below which the dungeon dwelled. The executions were to be held over the next several days in the grand courtyard itself. It was the first time in history that blood was to be spilled in this way in the palace courtyard. Previous executions had been carried out in the public square. Attica had suggested the king might have been concerned with security since those to be executed still held influence, but Adsden thought it more than that. It was a semipublic event, and attendance was not optional. All members of the new king's council and representatives from every major noble house were to be present. It was for this reason alone that the executions had been delayed for so long. People had been given time to travel so that they could watch their friends and former comrades die.

The Serpents and Diamond Claws of Justain were not the only guilds called upon to serve. The guilds of Kaibain were also involved, which included a second branch of the Diamond Claws, led by the half-Pruari named Groa; the Razor Edges, led by a man named Breck; and a few members of the Black Hall. Only one of the slips had provided a name, and Adsden was not sure it was his name in truth. A man named Briesh represented the assassins in the Raven's Council, the name they had bestowed upon themselves as the guildmasters and assassin who were charged with constructing and implementing the plan. There had been much dissent in the beginning, but all agreed on one thing—they had to succeed. Briesh had made the point that it would be better to die in the attempt than to live with failure. They had all met the Raven, and no one disagreed.

Adsden and Fierdon slinked across the street and slipped through the open gateway into the passage within the palace wall. The guards charged with watching the gate had been *replaced* by a slip and one of Groa's men. The corridor was dark, intermittently lit with torches and mage lamps, and was silent save for the patter of their footsteps. When they reached the exit that would release them into the courtyard, they discovered that their next man, Cobb, was not where he should have been. Adsden squinted as his eyes readjusted to the sunlight and then noticed a worn boot behind a stack of barrels and burlap sacks. He tugged one of the sacks to cover the evidence of Cobb's passing and then scanned the yard hoping to find him. A couple of minutes passed before Adsden caught sight of the man rounding the tower lugging two heavy pails. Cobb met Adsden's glare but pretended not to notice as one of the real palace guards began hollering.

"Do you have that water yet? What's taking you so long, damn it? You'll be back in training tomorrow if those buckets aren't in the courtyard before I need to scratch my arse!"

Adsden hoped, for Cobb's sake, that the guard had decent hygiene. Once Cobb and the guard had passed, Adsden and Fierdon began walking casually across the yard so as not to alert the sentries on the wall. The two intruders talked and laughed, seemingly without a care, but maintained a safe enough distance from anyone to avoid being called out. All kinds of workers were going about the palace grounds preparing for the bloody spectacle the king desired. Adsden and Fierdon trusted that if they stuck to their roles, they could avoid suspicion. Fierdon wore the robes of a priest of the Maker and hid his face beneath a wide-brimmed hat commonly worn by members of the priesthood, while Adsden was dressed to fill any number of laborious positions. He had smudged a bit of soot on his face, dirtied his hands, and also lugged a sack of tools over one shoulder.

When they reached the entrance to the southeastern wing, Fierdon turned and whispered, "What do we do? Cobb was not at his station."

"We will have to give it directly to Benni," Adsden said.

"Benni does not have the mind to put it together."

"Then write it down for him."

"Can he read?" Fierdon asked.

Adsden paused. He glanced around to see if Cobb had returned and then said, "I have been teaching him. Use small words."

Fierdon tisked. "You are going to entrust this with a boy who cannot read?"

"What choice do we have?" Adsden asked. "Neither you nor I can take his place because of our *talent*, and everyone else is already in position."

"Fine," Fierdon said as he took the quill out of the pouch that hung at his side. As a wind mage with a secondary affinity for water, he had a way with liquids. It had been no problem to force the ink into the feather so that they would not have to carry around an ink well. "Turn around," he said. He unrolled the parchment over Adsden's back and carefully scrawled a brief note that he hoped Benni would be able to read.

"How is he with his numbers," Fierdon asked.

"Good, he does not care to write them down but figures them well enough in his head."

"He is able to read them, though?"

"Yes, it will not be a problem. Can you get it to him?" Adsden asked.

"I believe so, but it will be more difficult since I cannot see him. Do we know where the guards are in their rounds?"

Adsden checked the time dial. "The way should be clear in about fifteen seconds. We will have to wait for the next rotation. That gives us almost eight minutes."

Fierdon finished his message, blew on the ink, and then cast a spell to make the stiff material more pliable. He then folded the parchment to resemble a bird, carefully placing the folds so that the tiny golem would be able to move.

"That is impressive," Adsden said. "How did you learn to do such a thing?"

"Most of my time was spent alone," Fierdon said in explanation. Then, returning to the task, he said, "There are wards around the perimeter. Wards are not one of my strengths, and this will require nearly all my attention. You said you are capable of manipulating them?"

Adsden stepped away from the building to examine the ward along the roofline. Now that they were closer, he could see how it had been constructed. It was weak, not designed to prevent passage, but it would alert the sentries if breached. Benni was hidden between a cistern and a structure the mages called a wind turbine, both of which were located approximately six paces from the edge of the roof. On the other side of the cistern was a trap door that opened to a stairwell leading into the building. The guards were stationed all over the palace roofs, most of them rotating in a well-timed circuit. Their attention was given to watching the courtyards and building entrances.

Adsden ducked back into the shadow of the building and said, "I am not strong enough to tear it, but I can bend the ward inward toward Benni. If you drop the parchment before the ward snaps back, your vimara will not be detected, and Benni can retrieve the note."

"Assuming he sees it," Fierdon said.

"He will be watching for the signal from Cobb. Surely he will notice a little bird made of parchment flying over the roof."

"Then let us hope he is quick. Once I release my vimara, it could be swept away by the wind."

Fierdon placed the bird on the ground and then began to wave his hands in the air. Adsden had never seen anyone performing magic in such a way. It was fluid and elegant, like the wind itself. The bird twitched and then twitched again. A wing flapped, and then it craned its neck as if to look at them. Fierdon muttered something under his breath, and the bird began flapping its wings in earnest. It took to the air as steadily as a natural-born chick on its first flight, but within seconds, its path became smooth and graceful.

"Okay, now," Fierdon said, but his attention was wholly on the bird.

Adsden checked the time dial and then began manipulating the ward along the perimeter of the roof. The bird fluttered upward, and he could barely see it as it swept over the edge. Adsden would have preferred to see what he was doing as he bent the ward, and he was certain Fierdon would have liked to watch the bird's path. For all they knew, they could have sent the golem straight into a guard's head.

"All right. I think it has gone far enough. I am going to drop it," Fierdon said.

Fierdon sighed and leaned heavily on the wall after releasing the fledgling's flight. The ward bounded back to its original position a little more quickly than Adsden would have preferred, but since they did not hear any shouts or tromping boots, he had to assume his transgression had gone undetected.

Fierdon was still composing himself when Adsden asked, "Was it really so taxing?"

"Normally, not so much. The closer in nature a material is to its desired use, the easier it is to animate. If the bird had been made of feathers, for example, it would have been quite easy. Parchment is made of reeds or wood, neither of which were meant to fly. More importantly, though, was the control. I had to keep it contained in the shadows as much as possible as I directed it to a specific location. Even paper birds wish to fly free."

"That is almost poetic," Adsden mused.

Fierdon said, "Many poems end in tragedy. Pray this one does not."

Adsden grinned. "Your prayers are fitting in that garb, but still I cannot see you as a priest."

Fierdon muffled his laughter. "My father tried to get me to join the Temple. He said it would look good for the family and maybe convince some of the critics that I was, in fact, not the spawn of a demon."

"You did not care for the idea, I take it."

"No, the Maker must have had a hand in this"—he stroked his face—"or he did not lift a finger to prevent it. Either way, I figure I have sacrificed enough."

Adsden checked the time dial again. "Some say the Maker punishes those who do evil. I have often wondered how he will take my measure."

"I did not think you a believer," Fierdon said. "Besides, Hespion has only benefited from his hatred and greed."

"I cannot say that I believe, but I do sometimes ponder these things. Perhaps the Maker intends to strike Hespion down, but he has raised his hand so far, the blow has not yet fallen."

Fierdon chuckled. "Then, I do not wish to get between the Maker's hand and his intended victim."

～

Rezkin had tried to sleep, but his head ached more and more as the colors swirled madly behind his closed eyes. When he delved into meditation, even the stone resting on his breast did not calm them. He was in such a state now, seeking the peaceful drift of mingling hues, hoping to hear the melody they sang as they pulsed and whispered in harmony. His people were all about the city, now, and he had this one place to himself. This was where he could rest. This was his sanctuary.

The settlers had spent the past few weeks exploring the mysterious city and palace. The refugees had either claimed or been assigned dwellings close to the central square, but a few desired more private accommodations on the outskirts. Some of the nobles took up residence in the palace, but several saw this as an opportunity to claim the larger estates. While most of the refugees considered their circumstances to be only temporary, some seized upon the chance for a new beginning. The more optimistic had dreams of a glorious future for the Kingdom of Cael and sought important roles within it.

The palace was a magnificent structure that seemed to defy the laws of nature. Corridors were far larger than those of Ashaiian buildings, and they twisted like the tangled roots of a marglow tree. Just when one thought to find himself back where he started, he would enter an entirely new hall on the level above or below. Even though the largest tower was at least nine stories above the ground, no one had found any stairs. While the corridors did not appear to be inclined, and even a cart would not roll away, every level could be accessed without ever ascending a flight. For this reason, the explorers were not exactly sure how many levels composed the palace, and their best estimates were based on the windows that could be seen from the outside.

Within the palace were a seemingly endless number of chambers for residences, offices, workshops, kitchens, and washrooms. There were some rooms for which no one had any practical explanation. In fact, the entire upper level consisted of such rooms. Twenty-seven chambers, each nearly as large as the receiving hall in the palace of Ashai, occupied the upper level. From the outside, the tower most definitely was not large enough to contain so many vast chambers. The walls, ceiling, and floor of each of the chambers were covered in crystals, although these crystals held no glowing power. While the perimeter of each chamber was level with the door, the floor swirled downward like a river eddy toward the center, ending at least ten feet below the starting position.

On other levels, strange rooms had gaping holes in the floor with matching holes in the ceiling. Some of these holes were merely hand width, while others were large enough to swallow a horse. Within the holes was naught but endless darkness. No matter how long the explorers peered into their depths, they could not see the levels above and below. Kai ordered these rooms blocked off to prevent anyone from accidentally falling into the black pits. In other rooms, what appeared to be extensive aqueducts twisted in serpentine form, at times rising to the ceiling before twirling back toward the floor and then terminating, with no obvious purpose, at a wall.

By far, the strangest room was the largest hall on the ground level. It appeared to be the throne room, although neither the nobles nor mages were entirely certain of this. After first encountering the hall, Rezkin had ordered everyone to stay out of the room for reasons he had not explained. He had even gone so far as to order the ghostly shielreyah to keep curious eyes and wandering feet from *accidentally* disobeying his orders. No one felt comfortable being in the presence of the wraiths, much less garnering their attention, so they stayed away.

"I do not care for the room you have claimed as your own," Kai grumped as he waited for his liege.

Rezkin roused. "Then it is good that this is *my* room and not yours," he retorted as he strapped on his sword belt.

"Indeed, but it is hardly fit for a king," Kai argued, glancing around the eerie space. "I am not sure for *what* it is fit. It is disturbing," he muttered as he ducked beneath a stone shaft that extended at a sharp angle from the floor to one of the walls.

As he straightened, he rocked back to avoid colliding with another of the odd structures. The entire room was filled with angular pillars that jutted from the ceiling, walls, and floor in random directions, each just barely missing the others. It looked as though someone had stabbed dozens of giant swords into a box from every side, and he was standing on the inside. Some of the monstrous spikes were composed of the same stone as the citadel, while others were massive clear crystals, each probably worth more than an entire kingdom.

"I like its unpredictability," Rezkin confessed. "No one can be certain of where in the room I will be. I could be over there on the floor beneath that pillar, or I could be up there on the ceiling."

"Yes, but it lacks any comforts," Kai said.

Rezkin shook his head. "Not true. Tam provided me with several blankets and soft padding. There is a garderobe ... at least, I think it is a garderobe ..."

Rezkin paused as he considered the small chamber.

"*Spirétua Syek-lyé*, how may I be of service?" the shielreyah asked from directly behind the striker.

Kai leapt away, striking his head on a pillar he was certain had not been there a moment ago. He scowled and rubbed the quickly forming lump while glaring at the wraith. He did not recognize this one, and that also irritated him.

"Shielreyah Manaua, is that a garderobe?" Rezkin asked as he pointed to the doorless chamber.

The phantom warrior paused, presumably to consider the translation.

Rezkin had the feeling the wraith was searching his mind for the information it needed to fill in the blanks in its vocabulary. The specter inclined its head. "Yes, *Spirétua*, it is used for such a purpose."

"Thank you, Manaua. That will be all," Rezkin said, and the specter disappeared. He turned back to the striker with a grin. "So, I have the luxury of my own personal garderobe and plenty of fresh water."

Kai eyed the *other* feature in the room, the one he had pointedly avoided. He considered it to be even more disturbing than the stone blades that pierced the chamber. Down one entire wall flowed a curtain of water from the ceiling to the floor. That in itself would not have been so disconcerting except that the water seemed to appear from nowhere and then disappeared just as mysteriously, much like the shielreyah. None of the stones around the water were dampened by its flow or spray, yet Rezkin had no problem washing in the phantom water. Additionally, the water had not been present when they first discovered the room. It had not appeared until Rezkin had taken up residence in the chamber.

"Are you certain it is safe to drink and bathe in that water? If it really *is* water," the striker muttered.

"It is water, Kai, and it is clean and fresh. You are welcome to try it for yourself," Rezkin said with a pleasant smile.

Kai noticed that Rezkin had been smiling often, *too* often. The smile never reached his eyes and was even less convincing than the one he donned when playing the role of the pompous courtier. That one, at least, had been believable—unless you really knew the man. Kai and Shezar had been keeping close watch over their king, and both had seen fleeting moments when the young warrior appeared pained. It was particularly worrisome because they had been witness to recent *training* incidents when Rezkin had endured brutal injuries without a flinch.

The so-called training was far more intense and, quite frankly, *insane* than anything either of the strikers had endured. The young man did not give up until he looked like the walking dead, and he *never* reacted to the pain. Persistent in his *Rules*, Rezkin claimed doing so would expose weakness and vulnerability. Kai and Shezar both openly applauded the young warrior's fortitude, but the healers were always disgruntled. Rezkin's injuries were invariably far more serious than they appeared. The healers complained that they could not effectively treat a patient who would not admit his injuries. The strikers and

Rezkin's closest friends were concerned the same was true with sicknesses of the mind.

Rezkin dropped to the floor from his perch on a crystal beam above Kai's head, and both men departed the chamber. Just after they crossed the threshold, a stone slab appeared in the previously empty doorway, sealing the room. Kai knew that no one would be able to enter the room without Rezkin—at least, no one in *their* party. The striker was still not convinced the dead city was safe *or* unoccupied. They were already aware of the presence of seventeen elven wraiths. Who knew what other insidious creatures lay in wait?

The two men strode on silent feet toward the dining hall.

Rezkin said, "Have they been found?"

Kai said, "No, even with the mages' help we have discovered no trace of them."

"Make this our number one priority," Rezkin replied. "Three people have disappeared, and we have no idea how, when, or to where."

Kai cleared his throat. "Four."

"What?"

"A fourth has gone missing, just a little while ago. We do not know that she has disappeared, though. She could be lost or forgot the time."

"From where?" Rezkin said.

"Like the others, we do not know. Her parents thought she had gone to visit a friend. The friend thought she had changed her mind and stayed home. The last anyone saw of her was about an hour after dawn when the family finished breakfast."

"Also one of the passengers who boarded in Serret?"

"Yes, just like the others," Kai said.

Rezkin's head pounded harder, and his eyes squeezed shut of their own accord. When he opened them again, he realized he had stopped walking, and Kai was looking at him with concern. Rezkin shook his head and said, "Reiterate my orders that no one is to travel alone. Perhaps we should assign everyone partners."

"That would be difficult. These are not soldiers. They have personal lives and tasks to perform. I doubt many would comply if we tried to force them to stay in assigned pairs at all times."

"Outworlders make no sense," Rezkin muttered. "They will not do the simplest things to keep themselves safe. It is like they do not *want* to survive."

"Unlike *you*," Kai said, "who could go missing, and none of us would be the wiser. You disappear regularly and practically right in front of us. You refuse to stay with your guards, and you explore unmapped chambers alone."

"The shielreyah watch over me," Rezkin said.

Kai growled, "Have you considered that they may be the ones *taking* the people?"

"They have denied any involvement," Rezkin said.

"I do not know why you place so much faith in them. You probably think it more likely that *I* am taking the people."

"Are you?" Rezkin asked as a knife stabbed his brain.

Kai said, "I am going to pretend you did not just ask me if I am kidnapping people."

Rezkin abruptly changed the subject. "What are we eating today?"

Thrown, Kai said, "What? We were just talking about missing people, and now you are asking about the meal?"

Rezkin's stomach grumbled for what felt like the hundredth time since breakfast. He said, "Talking about them is not going to bring them back, and I am hungry."

Kai looked at Rezkin with narrowed eyes, "Since when are you concerned about what is being served."

"I am not, so long as it is edible," Rezkin said.

"Then why did you ask?"

Rezkin almost winced at the pain in his head, but knowing Kai was watching, he managed to hold back. He said, "Because outworlders discuss these things. Tam is always asking about what we are having for the next meal. He knows there are only a handful of ingredients on the island, yet he asks every day as though the answer will be different. It seems prudent to try to behave as they do."

"And you are using Tamarin Blackwater as your example?"

After following the same curvy corridor and never descending any stairs or ramps, they finally made it to the dining hall that was estimated to be two levels below Rezkin's quarters and on the opposite side of the building from the direction they had traveled. This room, at least, had reasonable accommodations, as far as furniture was concerned. The long tables and benches were carved from stone, so they had survived the test of time. Also, many of the clay and stone vessels in the kitchen were serviceable, and there were supplies from the ship to sustain the settlers.

Rezkin had managed to start the flow of water in the kitchen and bathing chambers, although even the water mages were stumped as to how it was accomplished. Not only the palace, but presumably all the buildings in Caellurum, had the potential for water to flow directly into the dwellings through small conduits. No one knew where the water came from or what forced it to flow, but Rezkin assured everyone it was perfectly reasonable. Since water was essential and the convenience so much better than lugging pails from a well, few complained.

Small hunting and reconnaissance parties were dispatched in an ever-widening array beyond the city limits, but so far, none had returned with anything larger than a fox. While the life mages had managed to cultivate several small garden plots within the city, without seeds to plant, the variety of produce left much to be desired. Fish, fowl, beans, potatoes, and cabbage were the primary staples, and everyone was ready for something more interesting to grace their plates. Still, it was better than being stuck on the ship.

It had been several days since Tam and Captain Jimson had embarked on a journey to Uthrel to resupply and catch up on the news. Although Rezkin had wanted to send one of the strikers for reconnaissance, the security of their new island home was his top priority.

Contrary to what everyone believed, Rezkin was *not* completely convinced of the shielreyahs' assurances. The cool, soothing effect he had experienced in the citadel was present throughout the entire city. It was more concerning to him than the long-dead phantom elven warriors, particularly since no one else seemed to be affected.

The power of the citadel seeped into him, and if ever Rezkin removed the stone pendant he wore against his skin, the pacification of his mind and body became unbearable. He could not afford to lose his battle edge. He needed to remain alert and in a constant state of vigilance. Even a single moment of complacency could lead to his demise should that same moment be exploited by an opponent.

Rezkin had considered discussing the soothing phenomenon with the mages. His natural inclination was to discover as much as possible about the unknown and potentially hazardous effect, but to do so would also expose a severe weakness. Thus far, the small stone that rested upon his breast was the only item he knew of that could enable him to stay sharp. He could not afford for a potential enemy to discover this liability.

Rezkin took his seat at the head of the table and glanced over at Journeyman Wesson who was sitting to his right. The mage had been dependable thus far, and of all the mages present, Rezkin trusted him the most. He thought perhaps he could at least broach the subject with Wesson. The young mage was quite knowledgeable. Wesson joined the other mages on occasion, but Rezkin could tell that he never seemed to fit in with them. Most of Wesson's free time was spent doing his own research in the city, performing magical experiments, or going about in the company of Waylen. Being of similar age and interests, although from different backgrounds, the two had become friends during their travels.

The one activity Wesson undertook more than anything else, though, was following Rezkin. Between Wesson, Kai, and Shezar, he was almost never alone. He knew the three conspired to monitor him. They thought his mind addled or that, somehow, he was being corrupted by the wraiths. The prospect was not altogether ridiculous, and Rezkin had even wondered fleetingly about it. Sometimes his mind was filled with thoughts and feelings that did not seem reasonable. At first, he had been overcome for brief moments with the sensation of being tossed into a bottomless pond of emotions. As the days passed, he was growing accustomed to the occurrences. The hardest part had been hiding the internal flood from those around him. The emotions, which had led to uncomfortable incidents between his friends and the shielreyah, no longer consumed his mind as often as they once had.

Rezkin rubbed at his temples and caught himself, hopefully before anyone noticed. The pain was excruciating. It had been growing in intensity ever since arriving on the island. He was going to have to confide in the mage, if for nothing more than the hope of finding relief from the blinding, persistent headache. He had to fight through the pain just to appear reasonable, and he was constantly second-guessing his own decisions. His training had taught him that people could lose their minds and make poor choices when subjected to pain of extreme intensity or duration. Rezkin was experiencing both, and he did not want others to suffer for his mistakes. It would be better to confess the vulnerability to the mage than to have an enemy discover it by chance.

"May I assist you with something, Your Majesty?" Wesson anxiously asked.

Rezkin blinked. He realized he had been staring at Wesson for several minutes, minutes in which he had been completely lost. It was confirmed. He would need to talk with the mage.

"Yes, Journeyman, there is. We will discuss it in my chambers later," Rezkin said as he drew his eyes away to survey the dining hall.

Frisha was seated to his left. The young woman was polite but reserved, and she never met his gaze or started a conversation with him. She seemed to have forgiven Wesson for *his* part in Rezkin's deception. While her smiles and conversation were sincere and friendly toward the mage, she never once graced Rezkin with the same warmth. Rezkin had not set out to deceive her, but he had concealed many important facts about himself. He was frustrated with her coolness toward him, though, since he *had* told her he was keeping secrets from her for her own good. Worse was the fact that Frisha had discovered only a single new facet of his existence, and already she was having trouble accepting him. How would she react if she knew all that he truly was?

Rezkin did not focus on Frisha for long. Many were present who posed far greater risk. He chided himself for the errant thought. He should not disregard the very real threat his *friends* posed. History was filled with examples of great men who had fallen under a brother's traitorous blow or a lover's poison. In fact, he was more likely to die at the hands of one he trusted than a stranger. Still, those who were closest to him were unlikely to strike during such a tumultuous time. They would wait until they felt safe and comfortable with their new lives.

He looked past Wesson and Frisha to the remainder of his guests. Everyone but Rezkin seemed to care who sat where, and proper seating arrangements were particularly difficult considering the hodgepodge of nobles, mages, foreigners, and displaced Ashaiians that were present. Any who cared finally agreed to a rotating schedule for those who were to have the honor of sitting at the king's table. At first, the placement of Wesson, a mere journeyman mage, at the king's right hand caused such a ruckus that the young journeyman was ready to flee to the kitchens for his supper. One word from Rezkin had put an end to the dissent.

Wesson and Frisha were to be seated at his sides, no matter what, and Tam, too, if he was present. Rezkin knew the protocols, and he knew proper dining and court etiquette, but he simply did not care. This was *his* kingdom, and his head hurt, and he did not want virtual strangers flanking him. He wanted the people he trusted most at his sides, both because it was easier to protect them and because it reduced the likelihood of being attacked or poisoned. One of the strikers was always at his back during meal times, which was more concerning than comforting; and occasionally, when Rezkin was overcome by one of the mental *episodes*, as he had taken to calling them, the shielreyah would pop in on the diners and send everyone into a tizzy. Rezkin never provided an explanation for the phantoms' appearances.

Shielreyah Elry suddenly appeared at Rezkin's side, and he thought at first that he had inadvertently summoned the phantom again. Frisha jumped at the abrupt appearance of the specter beside her, dropping her spoon in her dish with a loud clink, and the *schlik* of drawn swords reverberated around the open hall.

Ignoring the titters and grumblings of the diners and the ever so eloquent Kai, Shielreyah Elry announced, "*Spirétua, Stargazer* has returned. A second ship follows."

Rezkin excused himself from the table, although excuses were hardly necessary when everyone was eager to know what was happening. The prospect of news and supplies was excitement enough, but the gabblers were quick to conjecture about the nature of the second ship. Passing through the winding corridors, Rezkin slipped into the rear passage that led directly from the palace to the dockside warehouse with Kai, Wesson, and several guards on his heels.

Rezkin began barking orders. "Drascon, to the seawall. Alert the lookouts and organize any resistance. Activate the alarm runes if necessary."

Drascon took off at a sprint, his weapons and light armor jingling in concert with the thud of his boots. Rezkin made a mental note to include *Introductory Stealth Skills* in the minimum training regimen, especially for the officers. He had been taught that silence was a virtue, and in this, he was a true believer.

As he and his guards descended the grand stairs to the warehouse, they could hear footfalls approaching from behind. Although the refugees were few, most of them were skilled fighters or mages. Their standing orders were to take up arms and report to the citadel upon arrival of any ships. The incomplete form of a shielreyah appeared as a blue wisp several paces ahead of Rezkin.

"*Spirétua, Stargazer* has entered the causeway. The second ship is stalled beyond the *corveua*."

The specter disappeared as Rezkin stepped through the space it had just occupied.

"Thank you, Shielreyah Manaua," Rezkin replied into the emptiness. "Inform the guard that they are to take up tactical positions."

The specter puffed into existence for only a momentary bow and said, "Yes, *Spirétua*. As you wish."

"You know you do not have to speak to them aloud," Wesson huffed as he trotted beside Rezkin, his shorter legs unable to keep stride with the taller warrior's own.

"It is for the benefit of the others," Rezkin explained. "You will take up position in the rear, Journeyman. Prepare yourself for battle."

"Battle, Sire?" Wesson sputtered. "What battle? I am not prepared for battle!"

"We do not yet know the intent of the other ship. For all we know, *Stargazer* could have been hijacked. You are a battle mage, Wesson. You will act as such."

"You said I would not have to kill!" the mage protested.

"And you do not. I stand by my word. Our numbers are not so great that those with useful skills may sit idly while the others fight for survival. You will participate in any battles where you are needed. *How* you participate is up to you. Whether you kill our enemies, subdue them, or guard and protect our own is your prerogative."

"Well, of course I will," Wesson huffed in indignation. "I would not just sit by and watch people die."

"Then what is your problem, Journeyman?" Rezkin said as he came to a stop on the dock.

Wesson shrugged uncomfortably and said, "Nothing, I suppose. I guess I was just hoping it would not come to violence. At least, not *here*. Not for a while, anyway."

"I understand," Rezkin said, attempting to appear consoling and empathetic.

With Wesson's extensive knowledge and maturity, it was easy to forget how young and guarded the journeyman battle mage was. Although Wesson was less than a year younger than Rezkin, it sometimes seemed like decades lay between them.

"You have come to see this place as one of safety, a refuge," Rezkin said. "You must remember, though, Journeyman, that we are at war. Enemies may come from all sides at any time. They may even come from within."

The mage glanced around to see Kai directing the guards to their stations on the docks and within the warehouse. "No, I understand. Sorry. I just hate the violence and destruction," he said with a haunted look.

Rezkin nodded and then donned his black mask, determined to present his most imposing visage to potential enemies. He spied the journeyman mage out of the corner of his eye as he waited for the ship's arrival. Not for the first time, Rezkin wondered about the young mage's past. Wesson was largely a mystery. Nobody on the island had heard of the journeyman prior to meeting him, not even the other mages. Rezkin did not think the young man withheld anything out of deceit, but Wesson rarely shared openly or expounded on the details of his past without prompting.

Rezkin wished he had more information on many of the people who now resided on the island, but he presently had no access to such intelligence without asking them directly. Even if he could contact his spy network in Ashai, he would not request information on Wesson. Unlike the strikers, the thieves' loyalties were held loosely through fear. Any lack of knowledge on Rezkin's part could be seen as a vulnerability to be exploited. It was common knowledge among the refugees that Wesson held the king's confidence, and Rezkin did not wish for others to discover that he actually knew very little about the mage. He was better off if people believed he knew far more than he did.

Jimson and Tam were both standing next to the railing on the deck of *Stargazer* as it pulled alongside the dock. Nothing about the ship appeared amiss, and neither man looked the worse for wear. In fact, both men were smiling. Tam's gaze darted around everywhere, making it obvious he was just glad to have returned. Jimson, however, was singularly focused. Rezkin followed the captain's gaze and found Reaylin at the other end. The young woman was holding her ground with the rest of the able-bodied fighters, but she had strategically placed herself behind a pillar that stood in Rezkin's direct line of sight. Although Rezkin was irritated that the young woman had disobeyed his command to stay within the citadel, she was ideally placed to provide both defensive backup and emergency healing should things turn foul on the docks. Rezkin caught the young woman's gaze to make sure she knew she had been seen and then turned his attention back to the ship.

Jimson had already given the signal indicating the ship was secure, and as soon as the gangplank hit the stone, Kai was aboard. Jimson and Tam disembarked first. Jimson was dressed splendidly in polished armor with a black tabard bearing a green lightning bolt. Tam wore the same tabard but without the armor, giving him the appearance of a servant of high standing. They were followed by two men Rezkin recognized, one of whom he might have to kill in the next few minutes. Tam bowed low in the manner of servants, while Jimson gave the formal salute and bow of a soldier.

Rezkin had never assigned anyone an official position within the royal household's hierarchy, yet his friends and followers had taken it upon themselves to fill their roles properly. He did not think the refugees' eagerness to serve was out of any sense of dedication to *him*. These outworlders were conditioned to believe that each person had a role in society, and that role was the only one he or she was suited to fill. Rezkin held no such notions, as he had been trained to fill any number of roles, from a blacksmith or soldier to his present role as king. Still, none of them were real. Rezkin held no delusions that he was truly meant to be king. No one who spent his days upon a throne or behind a council table would need his specific set of talents. He was fairly certain that he was intended to dethrone Caydean, but beyond that, he had no idea what he was supposed to do. He wondered if he was not meant to survive at all.

The two new arrivals held back several paces behind Jimson and Tam until they had finished their greetings and stepped aside. Jimson motioned the first man forward, and he complied with only a slight hesitation.

The older man gave a formal salute and said, "Your Majesty, I am …"

"LeukSergeant Yail Stratus," Dark Tidings finished.

Yail's mouth gaped in surprise. "You know me?"

Dark Tidings tilted his head and said, "Former Third Tier Champion of the King's Tournament. You were an official at this year's event."

"Quite so, Your Majesty, although some might refer to it as a catastrophe," he added with disdain.

"Indeed," Dark Tidings intoned, his eerie, enchanted voice seeming to drop several octaves. "You are a citizen of Ashai in good standing, LeukSergeant. What brings you to my kingdom?"

Yail nodded to Striker Shezar who was standing several paces behind Rezkin and then to Kai, who had closed in on the second man waiting for an introduction. The striker was suspicious and for good reason, Rezkin thought.

"The strikers believe *Ashai* is your kingdom, and I am inclined to believe them," the army veteran replied. With a heavy sigh, he said, "But mostly it is because of my wife, Sire. She is Sandean. We've lived in Skutton for the past ten years, since I retired from the army. We were in the stands together when we heard the striker's announcement that they were rounding up all the foreigners. I gathered my wife and son and a few of our friends, and we fought our way past the soldiers. Master Cormack, here, was very helpful in getting us through the crowd," Yail said, indicating the man behind him. "He's a good man to have at your back in a fight."

"I am sure," Dark Tidings drawled.

Yail paused at what he thought sounded like amusement in the dark wraith's tone. He turned to see that Master Cormack was holding Dark Tidings's black gaze without blinking. Finally, Cormack's eyes shifted to survey his surroundings, but Yail could tell that his focus never truly left the dark wraith.

At a nod from the king, Yail continued. "We managed to avoid the patrols and made it home for a few supplies and personal possessions. Then, we headed for a small cove where Master Cormack kept his fishing boat. We loaded on as many people as we could. It's not a big boat, so we were able to slip past the navy patrols in the dark. We didn't really have a plan, but Master Cormack suggested we make for Channería. We hugged the coastline until we got to Serret. I thought we would seek asylum there, but some priests on the pier warned us against it. They told us that you and your refugees were headed for the Yeltin Isles.

"Master Cormack convinced us that we should seek you out in Uthrel. He seems to think you have a plan to take back Ashai. He said we could serve the True King and help reclaim our home. I don't know how they heard about it, but by the time we found a ship big enough to brave the open sea, we had more than a hundred others who wanted to go with us. We weren't the only ones who made it out of Ashai, and still people are fleeing over the borders into the neighboring kingdoms. Most of them are looking for *you*."

Dark Tidings gave no indication that he was surprised … or even *alive*, for that matter. He stood as a statue carved in ebony, utterly still, just as he had during the tournament. Yail knew the man, or *wraith*, or whatever he was, could snap into motion in a breath and probably kill everyone on the docks without breaking a sweat. Or maybe that was just his fear-filled imagination running away with him. Probably not. The dark warrior wore the infamous black sword across his back but now had two other swords at his hips. Something about that tickled the back of Yail's mind. Yail did not care to meet any of those swords.

Dark Tidings made no reply, so Yail continued. "Once we got to Uthrel, nobody knew your whereabouts. I started to think we made a mistake when your ship finally came into port for supplies. I don't know how, but Master

Cormack knew it was yours. He arranged things with Captain Jimson to bring the refugees here. We also picked up a few more escapees who managed to make it to Uthrel on their own, as well as a few merchants and other businessmen claiming an eagerness to make deals. We have nearly two hundred people on the second ship awaiting authorization to enter the channel."

Dark Tidings abruptly asked, "Have you known Master Cormack for long?"

Yail paused. Of everything he had said, that did not seem to be a significant detail. "No, Your Majesty. I never met the man until we fled the arena together. We wouldn't have made it out of Skutton but for him. I would be dead and my wife and son, slaves. We owe him a debt that cannot be paid, and we thank the Maker for our luck in finding you."

"It was not luck that brought you to my shores, LeukSergeant," Dark Tidings said before turning his attention to the second man.

Captain Jimson noted the change in the king's focus and said, "This is Master Gillis Cormack, Your Majesty. As you heard, he and LeukSergeant Stratus have been instrumental in bringing refugees to safety."

"Cormack? Is that what you are going by now?" Dark Tidings asked with little interest.

He was studying the man's eyes and nearly imperceptible ticks. Having sensed something off about the man, Kai had moved in with his hands hovering over his weapons.

Cormack shrugged and said, "It is as good a name as any."

"And yet so many develop an unhealthy fixation with their names," Dark Tidings said, thinking about all the pompous nobles who flaunted their names as though a name alone could hold the power of the Maker.

"I do hope this disguise is not for *my* benefit," Dark Tidings remarked while looking the man over.

Cormack wore plain, unkempt, homespun clothes, his shoulders were stooped, and his beard and hair were grown long and shaggy. Rezkin could never have mistaken the man for anyone but who he was, though.

Cormack huffed at the absurdity. "It was for their benefit," he said as he tilted his head at Kai, who was no longer bothering to hide his suspicions. Cormack held his hands steady at his sides and tilted his chin at Shezar. "That one is too young to know me, but Zankai would never have allowed me this close had he known."

Their hackles raised, Shezar and Kai both drew their swords. Jimson made to follow their lead, but his hand was stayed by Rezkin's firm grip. A feminine yelp sounded from farther back in the warehouse, and somehow Rezkin just knew it was Frisha. The woman had apparently disobeyed his orders to stay in the secured wing of the palace so that she could see the excitement on the docks.

"You did not come here to kill me—not yet, at least." Dark Tidings said. "Why are you here?"

Cormack smiled, white teeth gleaming behind a bushy beard. "Someone had to assist your refugees and bring them to you. I doubt they would have found you on their own."

The unnatural voice emanating from the masked wraith sounded like a growl as Dark Tidings responded. "I may be convinced that you are dedicated to Ashai. I may even be convinced that you are concerned for the welfare of the refugees. You will never convince me, however, that you believe they are in better hands with *me*."

Cormack's smile dropped as he bitterly spat. "True, I have probably brought them to a painful death—lambs to the sacrifice."

Yail turned with wide eyes to the man he had trusted to lead him and his family to safety, but Cormack did not offer the leuksergeant so much as an apologetic glance.

"What about this man? Why him?" Dark Tidings asked, as though reading Yail's thoughts.

Cormack shrugged. "You were familiar with him, having had a past, albeit brief, interaction. I gambled that he might be able to get closer to you before you struck him down. Also, he was a tournament official, so it was easier to get past some of the guards with him during our escape. He and a few of his friends are former soldiers, so they would be useful to you. Basically, he was the best I could do in a short time."

Yail again looked at Cormack, this time with scorn and betrayal in his eyes. He could not believe the pleasant man who had preached so passionately about serving the True King was naught but a self-serving deceiver. Aside from that, the man's logic was flawed. Yail had not worked the fifth tier competition or the melee, and he would have remembered any amount of interaction with the infamous dark warrior.

"Why did you really bring them all here?" asked the dark wraith.

Cormack sighed. "A peace offering. You have no reason to kill me, and you have something I want."

"I need no reason to kill *you*," Dark Tidings retorted, and he heard another gasp from the warehouse.

Kai narrowed his eyes as he carefully studied the stranger's sun-darkened face behind the jungle of hair. Suddenly his eyes widened in recognition.

"Farson!" Kai exclaimed in dismay.

In this man, Kai saw a ghost from the past, a colleague he had admired in his youth, a man long thought dead. A small measure of reality came crashing down on the striker. Until that moment, he had managed to reserve a reasonable doubt in the back of his mind about Rezkin's assertions of his past, his claim to have been raised and trained by so many strikers and then to have killed them all. It struck him, for the first time, that Farson's very existence and presence on that dock was proof that Rezkin's claims were probably true. Kai's inner turmoil was interrupted by the dark wraith himself.

"You would bargain in blood for peace with *me*?"

Farson grumbled through gritted teeth, "Obviously *not*, you being the antithesis of peace. A trade, then. You seem to place some value in these refugees, although I have not yet divined your true motives. You desire those with strength. A good number of these that I brought are fighters, *talented*, or skilled craftsmen. Just release her, and you can have them all."

Yail wanted to rail at the man for bargaining to *sell* him and his fellow refugees to a man that Cormack, or Farson, or whoever he was, obviously thought to be a murderous demon.

"What is she to you?" Dark Tidings asked.

Farson shifted, unwilling to answer.

"You know I will find out one way or another," Dark Tidings stated blandly.

With a heavy sigh, Cormack said, "She is my niece, the last of my kin."

Rezkin was not sure why, but he was angered that Farson held such a low opinion of him. He persistently endured an endless struggle to follow the *Rules* the strikers had taught to him, and he continued to maintain mastery of the *Skills*, yet his trainer hated him for it.

Dark Tidings took a step forward, his eerie voice erupting in a hiss. "Except now I have you … *and* them … *and* your niece. Why should I give you *anything*?"

Sadness flashed in the striker's eyes for only a moment, and then it was replaced with resolve. He pulled himself to attention, and his eyes lost their light, the spark replaced by the emptiness of duty. "Release her, and I will serve you."

Rezkin had had enough. "I do not want your service, Farson. You may go or you may stay. I care not so long as you do not get in my way."

He knew he should kill the striker. It was obvious Farson would never support him, which meant he was an enemy. It was folly to leave an enemy at his back. But, for some reason, he could not bring himself to end Farson without provocation. When he thought of killing the man, it felt as though he were killing all his trainers again, and his chest tightened painfully.

Farson gaped in surprise. Death was letting him slip away *again*. "My niece …"

Rezkin snapped, "I did not *take* her, Farson. She came of her own free will, and she has ever since been attempting hide her presence from me—very poorly, I might add. If she wishes to leave, then she may leave, but you will not take her against her will." He thumbed the hilt of his sword, a message of warning. "It was my belief that you likely sent the woman here for your own devices. It is a belief I am not prepared to discount. Was it a clever ploy to gain access to the island, to *me*?"

Farson fisted his hands and struggled to remain steady knowing any advancement or hostile actions could lead to a swift death. "I would never intentionally place her in danger, and I cannot fathom anywhere more dangerous than with *you*."

Dark Tidings tilted his head and replied, "Really, Farson? You think I would place any stock in such touching sentiments?"

Farson's inscrutable gaze reminded Rezkin of the countless hours spent both learning to read his opponent and conveying, in his own eyes, only the messages he *wanted* delivered. After years of training with the striker, Rezkin was certain only that he could never know the mind or heart of Striker Farson in truth. It seemed the striker felt the same way about *him*.

"No, I would never expect *you* to understand what it means to care about someone," Farson spat.

"Oh, I understand," Rezkin retorted. "She is a young, attractive female who is highly intelligent and possesses an unusual combination of elemental mage affinities. She is a valuable resource that anyone would be distressed to lose."

"She is not a resource!" Farson snapped. "She is my niece, and I will die protecting her because she is family and I care about her."

"An outworlder sentiment that does not suit you, Farson."

"I *am* an *outworlder!*" Farson barked. "We are *all* outworlders, except *you*! *You* are the one that cannot relate because you do not belong among us! You belong in the darkness, slipping between shadows or bathing in blood on the battlefield. You were never meant to be *here*," he said, pointing at the ground.

His meaning was clear, though. Rezkin was never meant to walk among the outworlders. He was never meant to be known. He was supposed to always remain in the shadows.

"Mage Threll!" Dark Tidings said, his disturbing voice reverberating around the docks and through the massive warehouse.

Nanessy peeked around a pillar. She had accompanied Lady Frisha to the warehouse to see the new arrivals. She was *supposed* to be protecting the lady and other important residents on the second level, but Lady Frisha had insisted on coming down to the docks. Knowing the king would be furious if anything happened to his future wife, the elemental mage felt obliged to follow. The two women had grown acquainted on the journey to Cael, and Nanessy had been disappointed to find that she actually liked the younger woman. She wanted to hate Frisha, mostly out of jealousy. The mage begrudgingly admitted to herself, though, that she admired the young woman's courage and determination.

Taking a deep breath, Nanessy glided forward with her head held high. She was a mage, after all, and mages were respected for their *talent* and education. Nanessy had always been an overachiever, which was why, despite her youth, she had been selected to officiate at the King's Tournament. After an embarrassed glance toward her uncle, she gave her full attention to the king. She bowed and then stood with a confidence she truly did not feel at that moment.

Her reaction to the shadowy leader was a mystery to her. Since their first encounter, she had been drawn to both Dark Tidings *and* Lord Rezkin. Her blood rushed in their presence, and she had developed an almost unhealthy obsession with both of them. She did not, however, understand *why* she had the reaction. She knew the cause had to be important and that it was *real*, not a simple emotional or physical attraction. She had experienced the sensation for the man in both his personas, even though she had not known they were the same person. She felt the effects strongly in that very moment as she stood before him. She knew her face was flushing and not from the embarrassment of being found in Rezkin's presence by her uncle, who had strictly forbidden it, or from being caught away from her assigned station by the king himself.

Dark Tidings spoke to her in his eerie, unfamiliar voice. "Mage Threll, you are not at your post. Do you make a habit of defying orders?"

Nanessy tipped her head in an apologetic bow and replied, "No, Sire. I sought only to protect the Lady Frisha."

Dark Tidings's intimidating visage turned toward Frisha, and he drawled, "Yes, she is *also* not where she is supposed to be." Frisha lifted her chin stubbornly, and he abruptly changed the subject. "Your kinsman has arrived, Mage Threll. You will assist him in finding suitable quarters in the palace. You may both leave on the next ship, if you wish, or you may stay and be productive members of our community. *But*, if either of you causes me problems, you will *both* be executed. Do you understand?"

Nanessy's mouth went dry as she met Dark Tidings's bottomless black gaze, and a shudder passed through her.

The wraith tilted his head to the side. "You may reject his claim of kinship and secure your own safety if you wish. He will be held in the cells until the next ship departs."

Rezkin had given her an out. In her mind, she never thought of him as *king*. He was always just Rezkin, and he had never been so harsh with her in her imaginings. She was an intelligent woman, though, and she understood his misgivings. Her uncle *hated* Rezkin and had likened the man to a demon on more than one occasion. Uncle Farson had never told her *why* he hated Rezkin, but she could see the deep-seated fear behind her uncle's warrior gaze. It was not a look she was comfortable seeing in the eyes of any striker, much less her uncle. There was a very real chance that Uncle Farson would strive to cause problems for Rezkin, maybe even kill him. Rezkin was offering her a chance to save herself by rejecting any association with her uncle.

Nanessy's mother, now deceased, was Farson's younger sister. Her uncle had visited them periodically until she was about nine-years-old. Then, one day, the family received notice of Farson's death in service to the king. Nanessy's father died a few years later, just after Nanessy moved to the Mage Academy. Now, seemingly back from the dead, Farson was the only family she had left. He was the only reminder of her past, the past she shared with her mother and father. Farson had come here for *her*. After their rooftop encounter with the frightening dark warrior in Skutton, her uncle had told her that Rezkin would kill him if he ever saw him again. Nanessy had been grown and alone for a long time, though, and had not thought that Farson would follow her to this place. She had not thought that Farson would face what was perhaps his only fear for *her*.

"No, of course, he is kin," she said quietly. With a glance to her uncle, she said, "I will find accommodations for him near my own quarters." Farson looked both relieved and saddened. Turning back to the frightening mask, she said, "Thank you, Your Majesty."

Rezkin looked to Farson and asked, "Do you understand the potential consequences of your actions?"

The striker drew his gaze away from his sweet niece and snapped, "I am not an idiot."

"I did not think you were," Dark Tidings replied, his meaning clear. "You are dismissed."

Nanessy took Farson's hand and led him into the warehouse. Rezkin put the striker from his mind, for the time being, to focus on the other tasks.

"LeukSergeant, you arrived in ill company," he said.

Yail appeared angry and mystified. "So I see. I apologize, Your Majesty. I had no idea he was such a man."

"No, I am sure you did not," Dark Tidings said as he stared up at the ship and the waiting faces.

The leuksergeant cleared his throat and ventured, "You seem to be familiar with him, though. I hope you understand that we were deceived, and neither I nor any of my family mean you any ill will."

Dark Tidings's black gaze beheld the retired soldier. "I do not hold you accountable for Striker Farson's behavior or actions. He is a Master of Deception."

Yail's eyes widened. "Striker? Then he is one of Caydean's?"

"I think not," he replied.

Farson had appeared lost, without purpose. Truly, Rezkin could relate. But the striker was allowing his emotions to guide his actions. He was breaking the *Rules*, and it was likely to be his downfall.

Rezkin dismissed Yail and directed the others to begin unloading the ship, and, with merely a thought, he silently instructed the shielreyah to allow the second ship to pass the *corveua*. Rezkin examined each person as he or she disembarked to make sure there were no more surprises. Farson had been ambitious in presenting himself up front, but the striker had a clear objective and knew it could not be accomplished through subterfuge. Others might not be so transparent.

Kai approached his king and quietly beseeched him, "Sire, about Farson …"

"We will not discuss this now," Rezkin said.

"But we should kill him now," Kai quietly pressed. "He is an openly hostile threat. By your own testimony, he wants you dead for good reason. At the very least, he will sow dissent and undermine your rule. We cannot allow this man to roam free."

"And you, Shezar? Do you concur?" Rezkin asked when he noted the second striker had wandered within hearing distance.

Shezar appeared troubled as he studied the ground at his feet. He finally looked up and said, "I do not know Farson, and I know little of your history with him. I must admit that he is extremely hostile toward you. He is definitely a threat. You do not believe he serves Caydean, though, so I must believe there is a chance he could work toward the advancement of our cause. I do not relish the thought of watching more of my brethren die. The strikers are strong because we are united in our purpose. We are dedicated to our king and to each other. He may behave himself if he is reminded of this honor, especially now that his niece's life is at stake."

Shezar shook his head and sighed as he continued. "He is Master of Deception, though. Farson's feelings for his niece, if she really *is* his niece, seem genuine, but who can say? Maintaining compliance through coercion is dishonorable and rarely effective in the long term. Still, I would not be so hasty to dismiss our brother outright."

A frustrated Kai grumbled, "It must be done now, before he has had time to sink his talons into someone or poison the well, so to speak."

Rezkin's gaze travelled over each man's face, their respective convictions clear. Finally, he said, "I value your assessment, Kai, and I agree with you. It would be prudent to terminate the infestation before it spreads. A rule guided by fear is not a good foundation for a new kingdom, though."

"It is not *fear*, Rezkin. It is common sense. The man has spoken openly against you on at least two occasions."

"True, but he has never acted on those threats. He did not even fight in the initial battle at the northern fortress," Rezkin said as his thoughts roamed back to the bloody carnage that saw everyone he had ever known dead … mostly by his own hand.

"Only because he is waiting for an opening," Kai retorted. "He waits for you to show weakness."

"Perhaps, or maybe he does not actually wish to kill me," Rezkin mused. With the tiny flutter of hope in his chest, he realized he sincerely wished the sentiment were true. He raised a hand to hold off Kai's continued grumbling and said, "This discussion is over. We will wait, but we will keep a *very* close eye on him."

Kai saluted and then stormed off, barking angrily at the men and women unloading supplies from the ships. Rezkin became uncomfortable when he realized Shezar was staring at him with an odd expression.

"What is it, Shezar?"

The striker's dark brown eyes appeared thoughtful and perhaps a little surprised. "Striker Farson has given you every reason to doubt him, and you would be perfectly justified in demanding his head; yet, you stay your hand in hopes that he will prove himself to be a better man than, I think, he believes himself to be. It may not be the most responsible course of action, but I believe it to be the honorable one." He bowed deeply and said, "I am reminded that it is an *honor* to serve *you*, King Rezkin."

Rezkin shook his head. "There was no room for honor in my training."

Shezar's smile fell. "Perhaps not, but there was in *ours*."

He turned to leave, but Rezkin stopped him.

"What did you mean that Farson would be a better man than he believes himself to be?"

Shezar's brow furrowed as he considered how to answer his liege's question without its resulting in the removal of his head. To any other king, his next words would cause high offense. Rezkin was no such king, however, and Shezar was inclined toward honesty in this matter. Rezkin was confident and even ruthless, but he was also practical, with no apparent ego. Shezar was fairly confident that Rezkin would not waste a valuable *resource* like a striker for an offensive truth.

"It is clear that he thinks very poorly of you, but not due to any lack of skill or dedication on your part. He believes you are a threat … to *everyone*. He may even have good reason to think so."

Shezar knew he was testing his limits with the observation, but Rezkin showed no sign that he had taken offense. Then again, he could rarely read Rezkin when he was *not* wearing the inhuman mask. He thought the mask a bit redundant since Rezkin barely seemed human without it.

When Rezkin did not protest, Shezar continued, "Farson was one of your trainers, for a long time it would seem. I believe he may blame himself for what you are ... or, at least, what he perceives you to be. No matter his terrible opinion of you, he must think worse of himself."

A moment passed before Rezkin said, "Thank you for your assessment. I will consider your words. For now, I want you and Kai to keep an eye on him." As the striker bowed and turned away, he added, "Shezar, Farson was chosen to be one of my trainers for a reason. Do not underestimate him."

Shezar tilted his head and then disappeared into the shadows of the warehouse. Rezkin still could not understand why Farson hated him so much, aside from the fact that he had been ordered to kill the man. If Shezar was correct, though, then Farson believed something was wrong with Rezkin's training. He could not believe that nearly two dozen masters had spent almost twenty years forging him into a weapon, most likely at the king's behest, and it had all been *wrong*. No, the most logical explanation was that he was failing in some way. Since there were only two *Rules* he did not completely comprehend, his error must lie with those. Perhaps he had acquired his friends incorrectly.

Benni intently watched the wall across the yard for the signal. He thought it was past time, and he was beginning to worry that he had missed it. A white blur was suddenly thrust over the wall. No, it was flying. It appeared to be a small white bird, but as it flapped its tiny wings, he decided it was unlike any bird he had ever seen. It flew to within five feet of him before it abruptly dropped out of the sky, lifeless. It did not hit the roof with a thud as he would have expected of a bird. It crackled, like dried leaves. He squinted at it for a minute before realizing it was not a bird at all. It was a paper construct.

The bird began to move again, but its movements were awkward, like it was being pulled. It skittered across the rooftop toward the wind turbine, and he realized he was about to lose the strange object to the even stranger rotating blades. Benni quickly glanced around for guards before darting out of his hiding place. He hoped the sentries on the wall were not looking in his direction, but he knew most of them were preoccupied with surveying the larger threats below in the yard and outside the palace grounds. He snatched up the paper bird just before it would have been sucked into the contraption and nearly lost part of his shirt in exchange. He bounded back to his hiding place where he was safe from detection. It was cramped between the cistern and the turbine, but at least he was saved from the afternoon heat. As the turbine sucked air across the water, it became chilled before being swept down into the building. He wondered if this was the intended purpose of the device.

He unfolded the little bird, sorry to see the fine work destroyed. The parchment held a map and a list of words and numbers. Benni realized this was probably the information Cobb was supposed to have interpreted and relayed to him through the signals. This was not good. Something had obviously happened to Cobb, and Benni had no idea what to do with any of it. His brow broke into a cold sweat, and his heart thudded furiously in his chest. He was not supposed to have this responsibility. Adsden would be furious that someone had messed up his plan, not that it would matter to Benni because he would probably be dead. He could not stay on the roof forever, and escaping unnoticed would be difficult without the assistance that had gotten him there in the first place.

Benni wiped at his brow and then turned the parchment over to see what was written on the other side. It looked like a hastily scrawled note. He had begun reading lessons only since Adsden had taken him as an apprentice, but one of the first words he had learned was written across the top: B-e-n-n-i. He recognized his name and knew this message was meant for him. He swallowed the bile that threatened to spill from his lips and took a deep breath. Finally, he looked at the letters below his name. After deciphering the first three words, he began to gain confidence. A thrill ran through him. He was reading. He was actually reading, and it was something important—something that could save lives.

The clink of metal accompanied by thundering footsteps broke through his deep concentration, and he realized he had been quietly muttering the sounds of the letters aloud. He peered through a gap in his shelter to see the guards tromping by at their usual steady pace. Luckily, the sound of their own passing had drowned out his whispers, and he had not been overheard.

After finishing the four-line message, Benni turned the parchment back over to examine the map. He knew that in Justain criminals were held in a tower until they had served their sentences or were executed. In fact, one of his friends, a young man named Oben, had met his fate in the tower during the past winter. There was no escaping from the tower, except perhaps by plummeting to one's death. It did not stop people from telling stories about fantastic and sometimes failed attempts at escape, though, which had given rise to commonly used phrases like *he took a long flight from the tower*, meaning a person did something that resulted in his own death, or *he flew from the tower on a wing*, meaning that someone had managed to escape a terrible fate or death by pure luck. Benni looked down at folds in the parchment and wondered if someone might be able to create a giant parchment bird to carry him from the tower to safety. He liked the thought of Oben flying on a giant bird.

In Kaibain, though, the dungeon was in a cavern beneath the palace, one that he had heard tended to flood during periods of high rain. Benni had never desired to visit the tower, and he had even less desire to be trapped underground in the palace dungeon. The others in his party all had jobs, though. They were to create distractions, eliminate guards, and otherwise clear the way for his entrance and exit. Benni was supposed to lead the escapees to freedom via the route given to him by people who were far smarter than he. He had been assured that if all went well, he would not have to fight. They had called his position the hinge—the hinge that connected the two major pieces. He knew, though, that if the hinge broke, the entire mechanism would fail.

The corridors, guard stations, and patrols were designated by single letters and numbers, so reading the map was not difficult. He had no time dial, though, so he was going to have to figure out at which point in the guard rotation they currently were. The other teams would not be happy about the delay. They had wanted to get the prisoners free and be gone from the palace long before the executions were set to begin. The closer they got to the event, the more people would be around to interfere.

Once he was reasonably sure he knew what was happening, he stretched his legs and prepared to make a run for the trap door. It lay open, and he hoped that the *red* team had already taken care of the guards at the bottom of the stairs. If it had been easy to get their people into the dungeons, his position would not have been necessary. As it was, the other teams had to lure the guards away from their posts or take them out as they changed shifts. He knew already of one kink in the plan, and he hoped it would be the only one.

Trying to keep the sound of his steps to a minimum, he ran for the trap door. Just as he was closing in on the dark recess, a set of guards rounded a corner. He dropped into the hole without looking, crashing into the steps before tumbling uncontrollably down the stone staircase. He crumpled to a halt at the bottom and bit into an already bloodied lip to keep from groaning. He inhaled and exhaled in short bursts as scorching pain rippled up and down his body, the sensation so new and intense that he was not sure what was injured. When his head stopped spinning and his stomach was under control, he began testing each part of his body, starting at the toes. He finally decided that nothing was seriously broken, but he would certainly be covered in bruises the next day. He got to his feet but nearly buckled to the floor again when he put his weight down on his right foot.

Panic began to swell in his chest again. He was already behind schedule, and he had been wrong about the guards. He had thought they were in the third rotation of the second circuit, but since those guards had appeared unexpectedly, he now knew they were already into the third circuit. That meant he had less than two circuits to get the prisoners out of the dungeon so they could take advantage of the gap in the guards' schedule.

Slowly, he lowered his foot to the ground and tested his weight again. The pain was severe, but he would have to deal with it. He needed to get to the cells. The corridor was dark, the natural cavern floor had not been smoothed, and as he got farther from the wind turbine, the air became damp and musty. He checked for guards at the next turn and then limped toward his destination. When he was about halfway down the passage, he heard the jingling of the guards' buckles from down the corridor behind him. He could not yet see them, which meant they probably could not see him either. He glanced around for a place to hide but found nothing. Spikes of pain shot up his leg as he forced his injured ankle to take too much of his weight too quickly. Still, the guards were closing on him at a steady pace. Suddenly, strong arms wrapped around him and a hand covered his mouth as he was yanked into a dark recess that he had not seen.

"Sshhh," the man hissed into his ear.

Neither moved as the guards approached. Benni did not even breath until they had passed beyond the torchlight. The assailant's grip loosened, and Benni reeled away into the passage. The hooded man stepped out of the alcove behind him, raised a finger to his lips, and then slithered after the guards on silent feet. Benni swallowed hard. He had recognized the man from the meetings he had attended with Adsden. It was Briesh, a master assassin of the Black Hall. Benni was glad they were on the same side—for the time being.

He limped and shuffled the rest of the way, careful to avoid the guards who were still patrolling the corridors. He had taken the long way around to the cells because that was what the map and note had indicated he needed to do to avoid the patrols, and it had been right for the most part. When he got there, three guards were in the walk taunting the prisoners. These guards were not supposed to be there, though. They should have been cleared out before he got there. Nothing ever went to plan, he thought.

Benni could never take down three men on his own, and he considered turning around and trying to get out of the palace on his own at that point. People were depending on him, though. It was an odd feeling. For most of his life, he had only to think about himself, since starvation was a real possibility if he did otherwise. Benni had no desire to leave those people to die, but neither did he know them. Truly, he did not wish to let Adsden and Attica down. He did not want to let the Raven down. He had a feeling he was about to take a long flight from the tower himself. He waited for the men to leave, but it became apparent that they had nothing better to do than taunt and snicker at people who were about to die.

With anger stirring in his gut, Benni wished more than ever that he could be like the Raven, like Adsden or Briesh. He wanted to kill those men, and he wanted them to know it was coming. The prisoners were suffering from torture, starvation, and fear, yet these guards found humor in their terror. Some of the male prisoners held women as they cried, some of the women held their men while *they* cried, and Benni felt like crying because there was nothing he could do to stop it. Then he decided to do something stupid.

He pulled his belt knife from its sheath and held it in a reverse grip hidden along his forearm. He limped forward with determination, hoping that anger simmered in his eyes. He was already through the door of the cell block before the guards noticed, so busy were they in their jeering.

"Hey! Who are you?" the tallest guard said.

"I was sent down to give you a message."

"A'right, give it, then, an' get outta here," said a guard with a ginger beard.

Benni strode straight up to the guard with the ginger beard and lunged with his dagger. He was pretty good with daggers. At least he had thought he was. It did not work out the way he had hoped. These men were not street thugs. The ginger dodged his strike and knocked Benni's arm away. The next thing Benni knew, he was staring at the planks of the ceiling. His eyes widened in alarm, and he rolled to the side just as a heavy boot came down where his head had been. His jaw throbbed, and he fell into the bars of a cell to the side as he tried to regain his feet. Someone reached out from the cell grabbing at his shirt, and he struggled to knock the hands away. The guards laughed, and Benni spun as he managed to free himself. The third guard grabbed him by the tunic, and Benni brought his knee up into the man's groin. The guard released him as he doubled over, and Benni remembered enough of his training to bring his elbow down on the back of the man's head. The guard fell, smashing his face into the ground, but Benni's victory was short-lived. He was yanked backward just as he felt a sharp, searing pain beneath his ribs. He called out, and stars twinkled in his eyes.

Then he was falling. Benni knelt on his hands and knees as he struggled to breathe. He could hear a commotion around him. A man's shout was cut short, metal clashed with metal, and then silence. Benni gasped as silence and darkness closed in on him. Then a rough hand pounded on his back. His head was yanked upward by the hair, and his disjointed gaze beheld cold, grey eyes. The mouth moved. The face was speaking to him. Benni blinked, and then he felt a hard slap to his face. The sounds that had previously eluded him suddenly snapped back with crisp clarity.

"Boy," said the gruff voice. "Boy, you snap out of it or I'm gonna leave you here."

Benni coughed and then sucked in a deep breath. His back ached, but with each breath he regained some of his senses. "I-I'm 'ere. I'm 'ere, don't leave me."

Briesh hummed under his breath as he dropped Benni's head. "Hmm, I shoulda just let you die for your stupidity. What were you thinking, taking on three men by yourself?"

"They weren't s'posed to be 'ere," Benni said.

"So you thought you'd take them on your own," Briesh said.

"I killed men before," Benni snapped.

"Get up," the assassin said. "We need to get these people outta here."

Benni started to straighten, but his back screamed in pain. "My back hurts. What happened?"

"You got stabbed," Briesh said as he took the key ring from the tall guard's belt. "Your heart's still beating, and you ain't got blood pouring from your mouth, so you'll probably live if you get to a healer. That means you gotta get outta here, so move it." Briesh took out a knife, used it to cut away one of the guard's pant legs, and then cut it again into wide strips.

"What are you doing?" Benni asked.

Briesh came toward him, and Benni instinctually backed away.

"Stop moving, you idiot. You got stabbed. Why do I gotta repeat myself? Now, come here so I can bandage it, or you'll bleed to death."

Benni allowed the master assassin to wrap the bandage about his torso as he spied the curious, pleading faces peering through the bars. They were all silent now, probably worried that words might dash their hopes. They were strange looking people. The women wore gowns that had once been worth more money than Benni had seen in his entire lifetime, but now they were filthy, stained, and torn. By their appearances alone, he could not tell how they were any better than the street whores. Worse, in fact. The men's breeches and blouses were equally worn, and most of them had disposed of their fancy doublets. Their clothes hung loosely, and their eyes appeared dark in their hollow faces.

Briesh finished his wrap with a painful tug and then handed Benni the keys. "Go, finish your job. I'll make sure the way is clear." Then the assassin was looking at the map Benni had kept in his pocket.

"How did you—"

"Go," Briesh said, checking his time dial. "You got about five minutes to get everyone out."

"Wait," Benni pleaded, "you gotta stay and help me."

"Look, Boy, saving people ain't my job. It's yours." Then he was gone.

Benni turned with keys in hand and, in that moment, witnessed sparks igniting in the prisoners' eyes. "C-Count Jebai," he said. "Where's Count Jebai?"

"Here," a man rasped from a few cells down, and a thin arm reached out from between the bars.

"Hey, what about us!" another man called, and others joined the chorus.

"Quiet!" Benni shouted as loudly as he dared. "I'll get to you, but I gotta do this in order. That's what I was told, and that's what I'm gonna do. If you start hollerin' none of us'll be gettin' out." Benni had no idea how many he would be able to save, but he would make sure the Raven's priorities were met.

Benni shuffled to the cell, which somehow smelled worse than the rest of the dungeon, and then flipped through the keys until he found the one marked with the same rune that was on the cell door. Before slipping the key into the lock, he peered into the dark recess. The man who had called out stood a few paces back clutching a woman of similar age. Their raggedy finery was all that hinted at their former stations. Both had pale faces with sunken cheeks and dark eyes, and the man had practically been swallowed by unruly facial hair. Four other people shared the cell with them, one of whom had not bothered to rise with the hope of freedom.

He nodded to the prone form. "What about him?"

Count Jebai glanced back and said, "He died a few days ago."

"That explains the smell," Benni muttered. "A'right, 'ere's what's gonna happen. I know most of you are nobles and the sort, but you're gonna have to follow my orders if ya wanna get outta here. We got a plan, and if you all go doin' your own thing, you're gonna mess up the plan. Got it?"

The prisoners nodded, and Benni braced himself for the rush as the cell door creaked open, but no one moved. Lady Jebai looked up at her husband. Finally, they plodded toward the exit, and Benni could not tell which of them was holding up the other. Once they and the other three had vacated the cell, they stood staring at him. Benni wondered if they were using all their remaining energy just to continue standing.

Benni softened his voice and said, "Lord Jebai, I been told to get your help in identifyin' the others on the list." He glanced around the cells and said a little louder, "We'll get everyone,"—then looking back to the count—"but we gotta be sure we get these."

The count took the list and asked, "Why me?" He cleared his throat and said a little louder, "There are several others of higher station. Why am I at the top?"

Benni shrugged and then regretted the minor motion. His back burned fiercely, and he was glad he could not see the bandage that was probably soaked in blood. "I didn't make the list. What about this one?" he asked.

"He is a mage. They keep them locked in there," the count said, pointing to a stone door covered in runes. "It would take several powerful mages to breach the ward, and they are also chained in special shackles that mute their powers. Do you have a plan to get them out?"

"Oh, right, yeah. I'm s'posed to use this," Benni said, drawing a small wooden box from his pocket. Within the box was a tiny glass sphere filled with what looked like pitch-black smoke.

Count Jebai's eyes widened. "Where did you get that?"

Benni rolled the sphere between his fingers. "They said it'd help me get through the wards."

"More than that," said Count Jebai. "In that sphere exists pure destructive magic. The darker, the more powerful the spell. I have only ever seen one, and it was merely grey."

Benni said, "I guess the mage who made it must be pretty powerful, then."

"Impossible. It had to have been created by multiple battle mages wielding nocent power. They are illegal to make and to own without a permit. It will destroy *any* spell or enchantment within a given radius. How did you get it? That sphere is probably worth half my fortune."

Benni gripped the marble in his palm and studied it again. Every so often, the swirling smoke arranged itself into complex designs. He met the count's eyes. "Is it worth your lives?"

Knowing time was limited, he hobbled awkwardly toward the stone door, every step tweaking his back and shooting pain up his leg. Without hesitation, he smashed the black orb onto the floor. Snaps and pops filled the air around him, and the surface of the door seemed to ripple as the runes cracked and melted. He pulled on the handle, opening the door with ease. Empty shackles lay across the floor, and the people within hid their eyes from the meager light that infiltrated the room.

"A'right," he said. "You can come out."

17

T am grinned as he executed a celebratory bow. While his back was turned, Brandt regained his feet and swiped Tam's legs out from under him. Tam struck the dirt with a *whomp* and coughed as he struggled to recapture his breath. Dazed, he blinked away dust as a dark figure eclipsed the overhead sun.

"Well?" Rezkin said.

"Um"—Tam wheezed—"*Rule 14?*"

"Which states?"

"Do not revel in success," Tam muttered. He groaned as he rolled to his knees."

"And?"

Tam hesitated. "*8, 9, 24,* and … *123?*"

"Also *Rule 87,*" Rezkin added.

Tam pushed to his feet and shook his head. "I don't think I know that one."

"Never assume victory," Rezkin said. "Unless you have confirmed that your opponent is dead, you should not assume you have won."

Tam scoffed. "It's not like I'm going to kill Brandt."

Rezkin looked at him pointedly. "Then you should not assume he is finished and turn your back on him."

"Right," Brandt said with a smirk as he slapped Tam on the back a little too hard. "I could have been faking getting my hide handed to me."

Brandt retrieved his shirt and then swaggered out of the courtyard with a cheeky grin for the women who were passing by the gate. Tam scowled at the retreating figure, but to Rezkin it looked like a pout on his friend's innocent face. When he looked upon Tam, he saw a young man filled with hope and eagerness for adventure. Despite the trials he had experienced over the past few months, Tam did not carry the weight of a mind burdened by darkness. Although their feet trod the same ground, Tam did not live in Rezkin's world.

Tam finally accepted defeat and said, "I guess I should add *Rule 258* to the list."

Rezkin looked at Tam quizzically. He had been teaching Tam for some time now, but he had never thought of himself as the master.

"I don't get it," Tam said. "How can you remember *all* these rules *all* the time and expect to actually follow them? There are so many."

"I have lived the *Rules* my entire life, Tam. You are only just learning. In time, many of them will become second nature to you. I do not expect that you will ever be consistent in all of them."

"But you said we must follow all the rules to survive."

"That is true for *me*, Tam. The *Rules* will benefit anyone who chooses to follow them, but I have come to understand that they are specifically designed to improve the chances of surviving the kinds of ... *activities* ... in which I participate," Rezkin explained. "You are not training as I did. The conse-quences of failure during my training were extreme."

"Why don't you train me the same way you learned?" Tam asked. He almost appeared offended that he might be receiving an inferior education.

Rezkin stared at Tam. The answer was one that had been haunting him of late, a reality that even he had been trying to avoid. A weight settled in his chest just behind his sternum. Tam began to shift awkwardly under Rezkin's lingering gaze.

"I am not training you to be like me, Tam," he said almost regretfully.

"But why not? You're amazing! You can beat anyone."

"I have said it before. I am not infallible. One day I will not prevail, and on that day, I will likely die. I am reminded daily that I do not belong in this world. I do not belong in *your* world. If you train to be like me, then you will not belong either. You have many who care for you, and you have much to offer just as you are." Rezkin did not care for the look on Tam's face. In that expression of disbelief was insufferable *pity*.

"People care about you, too, Rez," Tam said weakly. "You are our friend, and you are the king! But, if you really think you don't belong, you can always change. You can learn to be ... well, whatever you want."

Rezkin surveyed the length of the walls and peered into the shadows. He envisioned escape routes, tactical positions, and hiding places both for him and potential assailants. He saw defensive and offensive strengths and weaknesses, and he estimated the time and energy it would take to execute a variety of maneuvers. He did all of this within a few breaths, and Tam still looked at him expectantly. Rezkin knew Tam saw none of this. Tam saw a mighty, magical kingdom with an unbeatable monarch.

Rezkin's voice was firm as he said, "I serve a purpose, as do you. I have been trained to serve my purpose efficiently and effectively. I would be ill suited for any other. Even if I could change, I would not. Society needs all sorts of people. Some of them are more specialized than others. I am one of those people."

"Specialized?" Tam said with disbelief. "I don't know what kind of *specialized* you think you are. You seem to be good at everything. You could become anything, any*one*."

Rezkin smiled. It was a genuine smile, but it lacked humor. Tam did not realize how astute his observation was. "Thank you, Tam, for your confidence. Frisha will be looking for you soon. I believe the two of you have a standing reservation. What is it you do, anyway?"

"Don't worry, Rez. You know it's nothing like that. Mostly we just talk, usually about Cheswick and our friends. She talks about her parents, and I tell stories about my brothers' crazy antics. She knows most of them already, but she likes hearing them, and I like telling them."

"Does that help you in some way?"

Tam grinned. "Yeah, it helps to relive old times—you know, when things were normal. We get to laughing, and it feels better—for a while, anyway. Sometimes we just sit and don't say anything at all." He looked away and rubbed the back of his neck. "Have you, ah, thought about talking to him? Your trainer? Since you decided not to kill him and all—he's the closest thing you've got to family, right?"

Rezkin gripped Tam's shoulder and caught his gaze. "Make no mistake, Tam. Farson is dangerous, and I have not decided to spare his life. Think of it as a temporary stay of execution."

"But you don't know that he's done anything wrong," Tam exclaimed.

"You said he's the only person left who really knows you, Rez. That has to count for something."

Did it? Rezkin had not only neglected to kill the man, despite his orders, but they were now living under the same roof—albeit a very large roof. Farson claimed to have followed him to the island to save his niece, but Rezkin wondered if he had an ulterior motive.

"Perhaps it does," he said, unable to extract any semblance of order from his swirling thoughts. When it came to Farson, he was plagued with an unfamiliar feeling—doubt. He said, "It does not change the fact that someone with far more knowledge of the circumstances decided that he needed to be killed. In addition, I do not believe he would hesitate to kill me if he thought he had a chance at succeeding. Although I am inexperienced in such matters, I do not believe those to be the ideal circumstances for developing a familial relationship."

Tam's lips slowly slid into a mischievous grin. "I think I have to disagree. I'm pretty sure my brothers and I have been competing for the chance to kill each other all our lives." Then more seriously, he said, "I'm sorry, Rez. I know it's pretty messed up, but I still think you should at least talk to the guy. I don't see that it could hurt—ah, unless one of you kills the other, that is." His face drained of color. "Maybe it isn't such a good idea. If you get killed, I think we're all lost."

Frisha paced the courtyard as she waited for Tam. She knew he was practicing with Rezkin, and that bothered her even more. No one *practiced* with Rezkin. He was either teaching them or pummeling them. She knew it now. Rezkin was dangerous, and everyone was afraid of him—even the strikers. They would never show it, of course. They were strikers after all, but their deference toward him was about far more than the piece of paper they all seemed to worship. She had not seen the document, herself, but she knew it contained information that others seemed to think made Rezkin king. She wondered, now, if Uncle Marcum had known it. She was sure it was the same note that had changed her uncle's tone on that day two months ago.

Nobody on the island questioned Rezkin, although he had not really given them a choice. She wondered what he would do to someone who truly resisted his authority. So far, the only person on the island who had done so was Striker Farson, and he and Rezkin had history. That was not quite fair, though. She had not seen Rezkin threaten anyone. The only other people that she had seen reject his authority were the strikers at the tournament. Rezkin killed them all. He killed them, all five of them, right in front of everyone—thousands of people—and no one had stopped him. The strikers had been trying to arrest him on behalf of the mad king, though, so it was not as if they were innocent.

He had killed the Sandman, too—chopped him into pieces. And everyone had cheered. She carried guilt for the part she had played in that slaughter. She had not known Rezkin was *Dark Tidings,* and she had scolded him for not punishing the man for poor Parker Farmer's murder. Was it her fault? Would Rezkin have gone so far if she had not berated him for his failure to bring the Sandman to justice?

It had not been the first time she had seen him kill. She had witnessed it before when he had saved Reaylin from the bandit. Even then, she had known something was not right. He had been cold and empty when he executed that man, but she had managed to convince herself it was her imagination. But she had told herself that Rezkin had been defending them and was caught up in the moment. Tam had even tried to warn her on the ship when he told her that Rezkin had killed people for the king. He had called Rezkin an executioner. It was apparent, now, that *executioner* might have been an understatement. Rezkin was not just an innocent man carrying out the king's justice. He was not the kind of man that felt burdened by a guilty profession. She had not seen a single sign of remorse from him, and that made her question everything she thought she knew about him.

"You are not supposed to be alone," said a gruff voice from behind her.

Frisha spun, and her heart leapt again when her gaze landed on its owner. "Striker Farson"—she gulped—"you should not be here."

"You are probably right," he replied with a mirthless smile. He was sitting on a stone bench, reclining against the wall with one foot propped on the seat. "Perhaps he will kill me for it."

Frisha shuddered at the thought.

"Does that bother you?" Farson asked.

"What? That he might kill you?" she asked uncertainly. "It is none of my business."

"But?"

Frisha glanced away. "But I don't condone killing people—unless it's really necessary. I mean, if they're guilty ..."

Farson laughed. It was a hearty laugh that made her cringe. "Yet you would bind yourself to *him*." He laughed again, and Frisha's face heated. "Foolish girl. You have no idea what he is, what he is capable of, what he is *willing* to do. No, a girl like you does not even have nightmares about the things he has done."

Frisha's eyes began to sting, and she realized she had forgotten to blink. "What do you mean? What do you know?"

"Whatever you think he is, I assure you, he is not. There is no benefit for you in being with him," Farson said.

"You don't know anything about us," she said, but her protest sounded weak even to her own ears.

"I know everything about *him*. Why do you want him? Do you want to be queen?" he asked mockingly.

"Of course not! I didn't even know anything about this *True King* business when we started courting. But, even if I had, it would be a benefit enough, don't you think?"

"Do you really think he will make you queen? Queen of what? *Cael*? Ashai? He will never be king. There will be no kingdom left. He and Caydean will see to that."

Frisha lifted her chin. "He will defeat Caydean. He will make Ashai great again."

"No"—Farson shook his head—"he will not. He is destruction. Without the shackles to bind him, he is free to rain darkness down on us all. Mark my words—chaos will rule all that he touches."

"You are horrible!" she said. Frisha was swept away by anger, even though she was not confident that what Farson said was untrue. "Rezkin has killed people, yes, but as far as I know, they were all guilty of something. He is good and noble, and he is the smartest person I've ever met. If there's anyone capable of building a kingdom, it is he."

The striker was suddenly standing right in front of her. She had only ever seen Rezkin move so quickly. She said, "H-how did you do that?"

A sardonic smile played at his lips. "An occupational necessity. I had to get faster—to survive *him*." His gaze was calculating. Finally, he tilted his head back and said, "Perhaps you do *perceive* some benefits to being with him." He smirked. "You may even have convinced yourself that you love him. But why do you suppose *he* wants *you*?"

Frisha tried to appear confident, but her voice wavered as she answered. "H-he loves me."

The striker shook his head slowly. "Rezkin does not love you. He does not know the meaning of love. He feels nothing … for anyone … ever." His voice was laced with sadness, but Frisha was unconvinced.

"I don't believe you."

"Has he told you that he loves you?" Farson asked.

She shifted uncomfortably. "Well, no, not exactly."

"But the romance must be overwhelming …"

Frisha's face flushed, but she said nothing.

Farson chuckled. "The boy can recite the prose of a hundred love-struck poets, sing ballads of star-crossed lovers, and create works of art so delicate they were surely wrought of the soul. Yet he has done nothing to gain your favor?"

Flustered, she said, "It's the little things …"

"Right, the *little things*."

Frisha huffed. "If he doesn't love me, then why would he ask me to marry him?"

He chuckled and said, "I honestly have no idea, but he no doubt has a reason. Perhaps it was a matter of convenience. Whatever his plan, it is beyond me at the moment, but I am sure your well-being has nothing to do with it." He gazed knowingly into her eyes. "He could have played you in so many ways. If you are pertinent to his plan, then he will lie. If not, he might be truthful. Why don't you ask him?"

"Ask him what?"

"Ask Rezkin if he loves you."

"What good would that do?" Frisha said. "Just now, you said that if he doesn't love me he would lie, so what would it prove?"

Farson shrugged. "Perhaps nothing. It is worth a try."

Frisha narrowed her eyes and snapped, "Why are you so determined to turn me against him?"

The striker growled, "This is not about him! He is what he is, and that cannot be changed. This is about *you*. I am trying to protect you, *girl*, and not just because I respect your uncle. I see an innocent young woman in the clutches of a demon."

"He is not a demon!"

"He may have been born with a soul, but it was surely destroyed long ago. There is nothing left inside him to love you. If you stay with him, you will drown in his darkness."

"You are wrong"—she balled her fists and took a step toward the offensive striker—"You think you know him, but you are wrong."

Just then, Striker Shezar strode through the gate, and Frisha was relieved. At first, she had been startled but curious about Farson's presence. She had wanted to question the man about Rezkin's upbringing. She had known that Rezkin had been looking for him but had no idea their relationship was so volatile. As she spoke with him, Farson's unrelenting hatred and contempt had begun to scare her.

"Lady Frisha, is this man bothering you? Are you well?" Shezar asked, his voice carrying no hint of concern.

Frisha crossed her arms and said, "I don't care for his words, but he hasn't harmed me, if that's what you're asking."

"Let us hope he has no such intentions," Shezar said as he came to stand beside them. "Do not listen to him, Lady Frisha. He knows not of what he speaks."

"Of course. It is already forgotten," she said. She tried for more confidence than she felt, but she was not going to let this stranger get to her. She was already plagued by enough doubts. "There's Tam, now" she said as she spied her friend approaching the gate. "Excuse me."

Frisha hurried to intercept Tam before he, too, got drawn into the drama. Whatever curiosities she had about Rezkin's past would not be satisfied by speaking with Farson. She hoped that not everyone at the mysterious fort where he grew up had been so terrible.

He watched as the woman scurried away like a mouse escaping the cupboard. Once she and her friend were gone, Farson turned on the younger Striker Shezar. "I have no desire to harm the girl. I am a striker, not a common criminal. Perhaps you slough the virtue of honor like you did the bonds of brotherhood. I hear you did not stand with them when they faced the enemy."

"That *enemy* is the rightful king, a truth they failed to acknowledge. From what I am told, though, you failed to stand with your brothers when facing the very same enemy. You ran while they died."

Inhaling deeply through his nose, Farson spat, "It was a battle that could not be won."

"There were *fifteen* of you!"

"And fourteen of them died! It was my *duty* to escape in hopes that I could find a way to bring an end to the madness that was sure to ensue."

Shezar asked, "Is that what you are doing here, Farson? Are you trying to end it—to end *him*? Would you harm this young woman just to get at him?"

"I would find no pleasure in taking an innocent captive *or* by harming her, but if I thought it could bring him to heel, I would, and so should you. I know the truth, though. He does not care for her any more than he cares for the rest of you. Taking her would only further soil my already sullied soul."

Farson's attention was drown to a movement from a shadow beneath an eave so subtle it might have been his imagination. His instincts were honed by too many years of training Rezkin, though, and he knew they were being watched. He gestured to Shezar so that his warning could not have been seen by the intruder. Then, surprisingly, the shadowed figure fell from his perch—or rather, he was pushed from it. Another dark silhouette loomed in the vacated space, and this one, Farson knew better than any other.

The displaced spy rolled as he struck the ground, then regained his feet with graceful ease. Farson recognized the man as Lus, Princess Ilanet's guard. At least, that was what they were telling people.

Rezkin followed Lus to the ground in a more controlled manner. He gave each of them a penetrating stare and then said, "Shezar, your presence is required in the war room. Bring Tam."

Saying nothing further, Rezkin turned and left the courtyard. No matter how hard he tried, Farson could not discern his former pupil's motives. Rezkin had caught Lus spying and had surely heard at least some of the denigrating remarks Farson had made about him to Shezar, yet he said nothing—did nothing. Farson felt like the moment the shackles of *Rule 258* had been released, Rezkin had sprinted away, his influence spreading like a plague, and his designs inconceivable to anyone but him.

Shezar tore his eyes from Lus and looked to Farson. "Take care of this, *Striker*."

As Shezar left the courtyard, Farson turned his attention to the so-called guard. This was the first time in months that anyone had tasked him as a true striker. He did not know the younger striker, Shezar, but the man was a brother nonetheless.

"Does Rez know who you really are?" Farson asked.

Lus grinned unashamedly. Instead of answering, he asked, "Do you know who *he* really is?"

"I trained him. I know what he is."

Lus's face sobered. "Why would you do that?"

Farson gritted his teeth. "So many times have I pondered that question. We were ordered to teach him everything we could. We did not expect him to learn it all. What do you care? You are in *his* kingdom now, and it is to your benefit to have a strong king."

Lus's gaze hardened. "It is the same for you, yet you speak openly of your desire for his death. You would kill him if you could."

"Something tells me you would do the same."

Lus smirked. "That is between him and me. Nevertheless, I am bound to serve and protect him at any cost. Know that his strength has grown beyond the limits of his body. His spirit now possesses the blades of many."

Farson narrowed his eyes. "You do not look like a follower of the Temple yet you speak of spirits."

Lus grinned in a boyish manner that was contradictory to his otherwise predatory demeanor. "There are many kinds of spirits, as we all have seen since coming to this place."

Farson's hackles rose. "I have doubts, for certain, but at least I know him. *You* and whatever agenda you harbor, I do not trust. I will not stand idly if you turn against him."

Lus grinned again. "Then we are in agreement."

Benni paused as he attempted to catch the breath stolen by the returning pain in his back. It had been coming and going ever since they had left the cells, and for the past several minutes, he had felt nothing—literally. His body was becoming numb and his head woozy, not unlike those moments before he lost consciousness prior to the arrival of the Raven, the times when he had suffered through the persistent ache of an empty belly. The pain was not in his stomach now, though. It was in his back, and it felt like he was being stabbed all over again. He wondered if it was a good sign or bad that he could feel again.

He blinked away the sweat dripping into his eye, and then his body rocked with a violent shiver. At the end of the corridor, light streamed in through the doorway that was strangely tilted at an angle. Someone grabbed his arm and shoved him roughly against the wall. A man hovered in front of him. Benni blinked again. The man was saying something. He thought he should know the man's name, but it eluded him.

"W-what?" he mumbled.

The man spoke again, but the sounds made no sense. Benni shook his head and wiped the sweat from his brow. He peered down the corridor again and was glad to see that the exit had righted itself. He inhaled deeply as the pain receded, and then he understood the man's words.

"Yes, Count Jebai. I'm okay. We're goin' through that doorway there. If all's good to plan, the way'll be clear. If not, we'll have to fight."

"You do not appear in any condition to fight," said the count.

"No less than you," Benni muttered.

"Under different circumstances, I would have you flogged for that."

Benni wheezed a chuckle. "Under different circumstances, I'd have run off with that orb and lived a comfortable life."

The count shook his head. "Fair enough. Why did you not?"

"Besides saving your lives?" Benni asked. The count gave him a dubious look. Benni shook his head, partly in answer and partially to clear the fog. "No one crosses the Raven."

A flag fluttered into view through the doorway. "There's the signal. Don't forget, someone'll grab you. You gotta go with 'em. Each group's goin' somewhere else to be hid. No one knows where the other groups are goin' so no one can give anyone up if they're caught. Jebais're with me." The count gave him the same doubtful look, but Benni ignored it. "Let's go."

The group shuffled along, most leaning on the wall or each other. Benni gripped his knives and hoped it would not come to a fight. His hopes were dashed the moment they entered the yard.

A broken body fell to the ground, missing him by an inch. Two more sailed over the roof in a tussle, striking the hard-packed dirt with a stomach churning crunch. Only one of them regained his feet. Luckily, he was not wearing the uniform of a palace guard. It was the master assassin Briesh. Benni had never thought he would be so glad to encounter a slip. An alarm sounded from somewhere beyond the building, and then guards came dashing around each side. One came at him, and Benni's first instinct was to throw his dagger to keep the man away, but Guildmaster Adsden had instructed him never to throw away his only weapons. Now that he could barely move, he wished he had a longer blade.

A beam of light suddenly shot past Benni's head and struck the guard in the forehead. When it ceased, he could see clear through the man's skull to the guard behind him, and that man fell over dead as well. Benni glanced back to see one of the rescued mages collapse onto the ground. The other escapees helped him to his feet, and Benni motioned for everyone to move forward. He had to get the prisoners through the gate before they lost control of it. He ducked low so the next guard's sword swept over his head and then struck at the man's side, only to score a glancing blow and wrench his injured back in the process. He sucked in a deep breath as he tried to stab again with his other dagger, but he was too slow. Just as the man's blade would have taken his head, the sword was deflected, and a deep, bloody gash appeared across the guard's torso just before he collapsed. At Benni's side, Count Jebai leaned heavily on the sword he had procured from a dead soldier and then brought his blade back up to meet another attack.

Benni regained his feet, but with the ground swaying around as it was, he was having difficulty determining which direction he should go. Two graceful figures danced into view. They spun and slashed and cut men down with ease. He recognized them. One he knew to be a sophisticated scholar dressed as a peasant and the other was a hideous priest. As the world grew dark around him, though, they were the most wondrous sight he had seen. Benni blinked several times and noticed that many others loyal to the Raven had joined the fray, in addition to some of the prisoners. Bodies littered the ground, and not all of them wore uniforms. Some of the Raven's men would not be escaping. As the light winked out, he suddenly realized he was one of them.

Yserria rounded the corner and came up short. Minder Thoran was standing in the corridor as if he had been awaiting her arrival.

"Greetings, Minder," she said.

"Greetings, young lady. Might I have a moment of your time?" the priest asked.

"I am set to a task by the king," she said, glancing at Ilanet who followed in her footsteps.

Minder Thoran bowed and said, "Greetings, Princess. I am glad to see you well."

Ilanet glanced between them uncertainly. "Greetings, Minder. Is there some reason I might not be well?"

The minder spread his hands and said, "Who can say? I heard a fifth has gone missing. I continue to pray, but I fear the Maker cannot hear us in this cursed place. If you do not mind, Princess, I wished to have a word with Knight Yserria."

Yserria said, "I have already visited the chapel once this week. I will do so again tomorrow."

"Yes, I am aware of your kind devotion. It is reassuring in this place to have some who dedicate themselves to the Maker, unlike your king."

Yserria shifted uncomfortably and noticed that Ilanet's gaze had dropped to the floor. She said, "He may not recognize it, but he does the Maker's work."

Thoran looked at her knowingly. "Tell me, child. What has this man done to gain such devotion? For certain he has proven himself to be a great warrior, but a great king?"

Yserria lifted her chin and replied, "He gave me justice for my father's murder. He did everything he promised he would. I neither expected nor wanted for anything more."

"Was it justice or vengeance?" Thoran asked.

"What difference does it make? The result is the same, and for that he has my loyalty."

"I do not believe that vengeance is a sustainable foundation for loyalty, and neither is it a good reason to sacrifice your independence," the priest replied.

"What makes you think I've given up my independence?"

"I understand you were born and raised in Ashai, but you seem to identify with the values of Lon Lerésh. No Leréshi woman would ever swear fealty to a man."

Yserria glanced at Ilanet, who still seemed satisfied to stay out of the conversation. She said, "You don't seem to understand. My father wasn't murdered by some street thief. It was a *duke*. He was powerful, untouchable. I never imagined that I would have the satisfaction of seeing his demise, much less the honor of carrying out the deed."

Thoran looked upon the young woman with sad eyes. "He has defeated many a foe. I have heard the tales. I am assured of their validity no matter how farfetched they sound. The battles in the arena and then later in your escape were far from his first, I am sure. He chooses to appear as a demon—a dark wraith, they call him. All I have heard of him involves destruction and death. These are not the actions of a good man. He draws to him the young and impressionable, the desperate and bitter, and encourages them to follow his lead. Would you ever have killed anyone if not for him?"

"I might have if I'd had the chance," Yserria replied with less conviction.

"We will never know," the priest mused.

Yserria glanced at the emblem of the Maker hanging from the chain about the priest's neck. "You've heard of what he can do. People say it's impossible. I would've said the same if I hadn't seen it for myself. How do you know he isn't favored by the Maker?"

Thoran tilted his head and said, "That is why I am here."

"What are we doing here?" Malcius exclaimed.

Rezkin, Kai, and Shezar had been poring over a map spread upon the stone table that occupied one of the many chambers on the first level of the palace. They had designated this the war room. Tam and a couple of the other men who had skill with wood had whittled the rough figures that rested upon the broad length of vellum. The blue figures represented estimated troop numbers in the various forts and outposts of Ashai. Smaller figures stained red showed the last known stations of strikers in and out of the kingdom. The estimates were the combined knowledge of the strikers and the few military men who had escaped with them. Rezkin's understanding of troop movements was the most recent and most extensive, leading the others to regard him with both skepticism and suspicion. He declined to explain how he had acquired the information. Rezkin and the strikers' attention was not on Ashai at that moment, though.

Tam and Tieran's presence had been required, but Rezkin had indulged Malcius and Brandt's curiosity. They had been watching quietly until Malcius's abrupt outburst.

"What is it, Malcius?" Rezkin asked as he and the two strikers regarded the young lord.

"This!" he said, slapping his down on the table in frustration. "Ashai is falling, and you are talking about Gendishen. We should be fighting back! Why do we not return to Ashai *now*?"

"And do what?" Kai asked. "What troops do we have? A few hundred refugees, a third of whom have no skills or *talent* with which to fight. Even if we made it past the navy, we would not make it to the first city."

"Why do we need troops?" Malcius asked. "You are strikers, and he is"—he motioned toward Rezkin—"well, whatever he is. You can just sneak into the palace and kill the king. Make it look like an accident or something. Rezkin shows his papers, the Council must accept him, and then he becomes king. The end. Done."

"Bah," Kai scoffed. "You know it is not that simple. First, you must remember that Caydean is a mage, a very powerful one, and he has been secretive about it. We do not even know his affinities. He will not be so easily defeated. Second, he surrounds himself with supporters and has filled the military command with loyalists. Third, we have more immediate concerns."

Malcius's eyes flashed with anger. "What could be more immediate than taking our home back and avenging Palis? What about our families? As far as we know, they could still be alive, rotting in the dungeons."

Rezkin intruded before Kai could respond. "Malcius, we *will* return to Ashai but not until we have the resources to succeed. We cannot even determine what those necessities are at this point. We need more information. We need supplies, and we need to contact our allies. None of that is our top priority, though. Right now, our biggest problem is not Ashai. It is everyone else."

"What do you mean?" Malcius said. He appeared suspicious and not yet ready to concede.

Rezkin waved a hand over the map of Ashai and the surrounding kingdoms. "Everyone is angry. It is almost certain that every one of these kingdoms sees what happened at the tournament as an act of war. They will all want recompense and, in some cases, revenge. Sandea and Jerea have desired an excuse to invade for decades. Torrel has been essentially neutral regarding Ashai, and we have historically engaged in decent trade with them, but their long-standing feud with Channería has been a point of contention. Channería is our closest ally, but even before the tournament, political and economic tensions were testing those bonds. As you know, trade with Verril collapsed months ago, and our relationships with the other kingdoms was also dependent on trade."

Shezar added, "Even during King Bordran's reign, interkingdom relationships were tenuous at best. Organization of the King's Tournament and enlisting the participation and cooperation of the other kingdoms was one of the greatest accomplishments in Ashaiian history, and it was destroyed by one act of unexplained savagery."

"One in which you were perfectly willing to participate," Malcius said.

Brandt jabbed him in the ribs with an elbow. In a forced whisper, he said, "Shut up, Malcius. You forget he is a striker!"

"No, he has a right to be angry," Shezar said. Capturing Malcius's gaze, he added, "I did not know your brother, but from what I have heard, he was a good man and a talented swordsman. His death was a great loss for your family and to Ashai. For what it is worth, I never agreed with what happened at the tournament. I could not see any way to prevent it, however." He glanced at Rezkin and then back to Malcius. "I took the first viable alternative that presented itself. Unfortunately, many of my brothers were not prepared to do the same."

Malcius was not appeased. As he opened his mouth to retort, Rezkin interrupted. "Back to your original question, Malcius. Look at the way the troops are arrayed." He pointed to the clusters of wooden figures at various points across Ashai. "What do you notice about their positions?"

Angrily tearing his gaze from the striker, Malcius studied the map. "The groups near the capital cities are small. The largest number is gathered here in the central hills."

"Exactly. So, who is protecting the borders?" Rezkin asked.

Malcius looked back to the map. "What are you saying?"

Kai huffed. "What he is saying is that Caydean kicked the hornets' nest and then left Ashai completely open to attack."

"But why would he do that?" Brandt exclaimed.

Tam muttered, "He's taunting them."

"What was that?" Kai asked.

Tam looked up from the map and was startled to see everyone staring at him. "I, ah, said he's taunting them." His face heated under their gazes, so he turned his attention to the map. "He's trying to get them to attack. I mean, I'm no expert in warfare, but it doesn't look like there are enough troops there,"—he pointed to the figures amassed near each of the Ashaiian capital cities—"to fight off an attack. I'd guess those soldiers are only there to keep the people in line. And I don't think these here are enough to actually win against the dukes' forces," he said, pointing to the small clumps near the three remaining dukes' estates. It seems like he's got the whole army stuck in the hills, and I don't think they're going to do any good out there. I've never been to the hill country, but I've read about it, and it sounds like a rough hike. I'm pretty sure that if an attack came, the army couldn't get from the hill country to *anywhere* in time to help. Not even to Kaibain."

"That is absurd," Malcius protested. "Caydean has been preparing for war for months, maybe years. What about the muster? He has probably doubled the size of the army by now. Why would he put them all where they would be useless?"

Tam stared at Malcius blankly, and then a thought struck him. "To get them out of the cities."

"What?" Malcius breathed in dismay.

"It's like in my book. Here," Tam said, as he pulled the text from where it had been tucked into the back of his belt. The leather cover was worn, and the book flexed as he flipped through the pages. He stopped about halfway through and pointed to the title of one of the stories while holding it up for the others to see.

"It's like in 'The Harrowing of House Lorack.' You see, the Shadow Knight was given two major tasks to complete in a very short time. He was supposed to cause the fall of House Lorack *and* take down a rogue general whose troops had been marauding over the peninsula for months. Well, he wasn't really a general, only a major, but he called himself a general. Anyway, a lot of men were loyal to him, so he was constantly surrounded by his people. They kept moving all the time, and the Rez—or Shadow Knight—was having trouble getting to the man."

"What does this have to do with Caydean and Ashai?" Malcius asked impatiently. "We do not have time for stories."

"Ah sorry, Lord Malcius," Tam mumbled, shoving the book back into his belt.

"Go on, Tam," Rezkin said as he casually leaned back against the wall.

Tam's gaze darted between his king and Lord Malcius. Rezkin did not appear to be in any hurry, which seemed to frustrate Malcius even more. Before Palis died, Malcius had been level-headed and fairly gracious, as far as lords went. He had even taken the time to speak with Tam, and his words had been a great help. Malcius no longer seemed to care about anything but getting vengeance for Palis's death.

Tam looked back to Rezkin who nodded for him to continue. He knew Rezkin had already read the book and probably knew where he was going with the story, but for some reason, he wanted Tam to tell it anyway.

"Right, well, the Rez decided to take care of both problems at once. He went to the taverns in the areas where the general's men were known to gather and spread stories about the hidden wealth and poor security of House Lorack.

Then, he made sure that reports of the marauders attacking villages on Lorack lands got back to Baron Lorack. The baron sent his guard and most of the able-bodied men to deal with the false attacks, so the castle was empty when the general and his men arrived. They swept in and killed everyone, including the baron. After that, it was easy for the Rez to get to the general since he was already waiting in the castle."

When it was clear that Tam was finished, Shezar said, "There are a few problems with your analogy. For one, Caydean is not the Rez in this scenario. He is the baron—the one that was *killed*, and Ashai is the castle that was over-run. Since Caydean is the one setting everything in motion, your analogy would lead us to the conclusion that the king wants Ashai to be destroyed."

"Ah ... right," Tam muttered, his confidence dashed.

Rezkin pushed away from the wall and said, "Although I cannot conceive of Caydean's motives, I believe that Tam's assessment is accurate." Tam brightened, but then reality struck. If he was right, Ashai would be destroyed.

After a moment of silence, Brandt said, "So what is this about Gendishen?"

"We need to secure our sanctuary," Shezar answered. "Cael technically belongs to Gendishen. If we want to stay here and trade for supplies, we need to work out something with King Privoth."

"And then we go to Ashai?" Malcius asked.

"No," Rezkin answered. "Every kingdom is preparing for war against Ashai. Already they are fighting over the pieces. Caydean has complete control, so there is little chance he will do worse to the people than he already has."

"You are assuming him to be a sane and reasonable man. I think he has already proven otherwise," Shezar retorted.

Rezkin inclined his head. "Still, Ashai is likely better off in his hands than with half a dozen or more kingdoms picking at its bones. Before we can save Ashai from Caydean, we must save it from everyone else. We must convince the other kingdoms not to attack, even though Caydean has done a masterful job of antagonizing them."

"An impossible task," Shezar replied.

"Perhaps, but we must minimize the damage. Since we are here, we will start with Gendishen. It has a sizable navy and a number of trade ships oper-ated by the crown."

Kai laughed mirthlessly. "So we will not only be demanding they relinquish claim to their land, but we will also be asking them to stand down and not pursue justice for their people who were abducted and slaughtered, an action officially sanctioned by the crown."

"Yes, that is correct," Rezkin said.

Malcius buried his head in his hands on the table.

"So what are we going to do?" Tam asked.

"First, you are going to set up a monitoring station in Uthrel. With all the trade ships and navy personnel passing through there, it is the ideal location for reconnaissance."

"Wait, *me*?" Tam asked, already shaking his head.

"You are not up to the task?"

"I don't know," Tam sputtered. "Why me?"

"You said you wanted to be involved. You have already been there, so you are more familiar with the city than most of our people. You are a commoner with commoner tendencies; therefore, you are less likely to attract attention than one of the strikers or soldiers. You have also made remarkable progress in both weapons and hand-to-hand combat."

"Whoa, I'm still not very good," Tam argued.

"Nonsense," Kai said. "You are far from mastery, but you are more skilled than the average swordsmen. You are certainly better than the regular soldiers."

Tam was bewildered. "Seriously? But I've only been practicing for three months."

Kai grunted. "You have a brutal teacher. Do not forget he is also the best swordsman in Ashai and possibly anywhere else."

Rezkin said, "I doubt the best swordsmen entered the tournament, Kai. True masters feel no need to prove themselves."

"You think I could've made it into the tournament?" Tam asked.

Rezkin said, "Not at the time, but with your current skills, you may have done well in the first tier. If you continue to improve at this rate, by year's end, you might have made it into the second. I believe you have a natural talent for the sword." With a smirk, he added, "It is a good skill to have for someone already talented in adventuring."

Light. It was his first and only thought. Light was all around him and nothing else. He stared into the illumination not really understanding what it was. As the moments passed, he began to see that there was more than just light. He was in a room. People were talking.

"You will save him. Do what you must!"

"Watch your tongue, Count Jebai."

"My apologies, Lord Fierdon. I meant no offense, but he saved our lives."

"Many men and women were involved in saving your lives. He was only one. Why is this so important to you? I have never known you to care as much for a commoner, much less a thief."

"I ... I do not know. I suppose he reminds me of my son."

"Malcius?"

"No, Palis. Caydean questioned me about them. He thinks I know where they are, but I do not." The man's voice grew angry as he said, "I know not where my sons and daughter are, Lord Fierdon, and I fear I am going mad with worry. Have you heard anything?"

"Not much. Rumor has it that they were last seen escaping the tournament in the company of the champion Dark Tidings."

"That is the one they are calling the True King?"

"So they say."

"Who is he?"

"No one with whom I have spoken seems to have any idea."

"I suppose I should be grateful, then, that they were not captured. Marcum had to have known something was happening. I thought it odd that he would place our family's children in the hands of a complete stranger, at least to me, but I trusted in his judgment."

"You knew your children were with Dark Tidings?"

"I know nothing about any Dark Tidings. Marcum spoke for the man who was to escort them—a Lord Rezkin. Do you know of him?"

"No, the name does not sound familiar."

"Are you certain? Marcum spoke highly of him. He said Lord Rezkin was of the highest standing and that if anyone could keep my children safe, it would be he."

"If he is in high standing, then it is not in *this* kingdom. I have never heard of him. Perhaps General Marcum was working with the rebels or a foreign faction."

"Marcum would never. He is a king's man."

"Obviously no longer. The general somehow managed to escape, and with his departure, hundreds of soldiers abandoned their posts. I expect more to do so when he reveals his location. By royal decree, any deserters who are captured are to be hanged, drawn, and quartered in the nearest public square, and their remains are to be left on display until the ravens have picked them clean."

"And my children? If they are captured, what of them?"

"Same as was expected for you, I suppose. Now that you have escaped, it is probably safe to say that Caydean will use them to force your surrender."

"What of your father? What are his intentions?"

"The duchy is under siege. I was sent to retrieve Hespion, but he chose his own way home."

"And now you serve this Raven? You were once heir to Atressian. Have you stooped so low as to serve a notorious criminal?"

"Do not forget, Count Jebai, that it was that criminal who saved your life … and mine. He has declared support for the True King—the one who, we may hope, harbors your children."

"Why would he support the True King?"

"I have not met the Raven and cannot speak to his intentions, but Guildmaster Adsden says the Raven is a farsighted and cunning man. To help claim a kingdom, to put a man on the throne—I imagine that would gain him great favor with the new king."

"With his resources and the turmoil already infesting the kingdom, he could join with the rebels and claim the throne for himself."

"It would not be a legitimate claim, which, it is said, the True King bears."

"Truly?"

"Two strikers swore fealty to him right there in the arena."

"You do not think he is Prince Thresson?"

"No, not possible. I sparred with Thresson many times. He was good with a blade, but not *that* good, and he lacked conviction. To him, it was a game, an *art*. From what I hear, Dark Tidings did not have that problem."

"You speak of Thresson as if he is dead."

"I have no reason to believe otherwise. Given present circumstances, it is a reasonable assumption."

"Are you awake?"

The female voice was loud beside Benni's head. He winced.

"He's awake," the voice announced, and he recognized it as belonging to Attica.

He closed his eyes and inhaled but abruptly stopped as his body erupted in pain. When he opened them again, Lord Fierdon was staring down at him.

"I-I'm alive?" Benni rasped. His mouth was dry, and his head was beginning to throb.

"I have no healing ability," Lord Fierdon said, "but I do have an affinity for water. I stopped your body from leaking, but the damage remains. I cannot replace the blood you lost. We sent for a healer, but we must be careful. We risk discovery by doing so."

"Why would you do that for me?"

"You have the Raven's favor ... and ours."

Choking back his emotions, Benni asked, "How many escaped?"

"We got most of the prisoners but lost more of ours than we had anticipated. A few were captured, but the slips made sure they could not give us away."

A knock sounded at the door, and Benni managed to turn his head enough to see a young man in healer's robes being forcefully shoved through the doorway.

"What are you doing?" Adsden snapped.

"What, boss? He didn't wanna come," said a rough man Benni did not recognize.

The healer straightened and tugged at his robes. He said, "You might as well release me. I do not treat criminals."

Adsden performed a courteous bow and said, "I apologize for the rough treatment, Healer Yerwey. We had orders to contact only you if it became necessary."

"How did I make the list? Everyone who knows me knows that I don't treat criminals."

"Healer Yerwey," Fierdon said. "Do you know me?"

The healer's eyes widened. "Ah, y-yes, Lord Fierdon. We, uh, studied your ... *condition* ... at the academy." Yerwey glanced around the room at the others, and his gaze paused again. "You're Count Jebai, are you not?"

"Yes," said the older man, "and I would appreciate it if you would see to this young man, here, who saved my life."

18

Rezkin stood before the throne room that had previously been blockaded. After his meeting, he had somehow ended up here instead of his destination. Every corridor he took led him back to this point. He had even tried backtracking several times, and still he arrived here. He glanced over to the window and wondered if he would somehow fall back to this spot if he jumped out of it.

Before this moment, crates had been stacked in front of the doors that now stood clear. The stone monstrosities had opened of their own accord the first time he had reached this location, and he was hesitant to try closing them. He wondered if this was how the others had gone missing. Had they started down a passageway and found themselves in an infinite loop? Were they still somewhere wandering and dying of thirst and starvation?

"Shielreyah," he said, his voice echoing through the empty corridor.

The phantoms did not respond for the first time since he had awakened them. He focused past his throbbing headache and *willed* them to appear. Still they did not answer his call. Rezkin did not want to enter the throne room. He had seen it from the threshold once during his initial exploration of the palace but had not entered. He had immediately ordered the room sealed and guarded so no one else would wander into it. But now it stood open, and the crates were gone.

He reached for Kingslayer and realized he did not have his swords. He patted his arms, legs, and torso and found that he was completely unarmed. Aside from when he was bathing and the occasional unarmed combat training exercise, he could not remember the last time he was without some sort of weapon. It was no matter, though. *He* was the weapon. All the others were only tools. At least he had the stone that hung from the lace around his neck.

He still did not want to enter that room. What he wanted apparently meant nothing, though. The power of the citadel desired his presence, and it seemed that it would not permit him to avoid the task any longer. He put one foot across the threshold and then followed with the rest of his body. When nothing assailed him, he took several more steps toward the room's center. A short pedestal, barely wide enough for a man to stand on, occupied the space. While the rest of the room was dark, the pedestal was illuminated like a beacon. As Rezkin walked toward it, crystals on the floor lit with his every step and then darkened again once he had passed. He took a deep breath. As he stepped onto the pedestal, he looked around the room. An errant thought crossed his mind that this was not a throne room so much as it was a mausoleum.

Around the pedestal were seventeen chairs carved from stone and backed with assemblages of crystals, each prism as thick as his arm and twice as tall as he. The crystals glowed as though topaz lightning was trapped within them. The chairs did not touch the ground, and their occupants did not seem to mind that they hovered in the air. Seventeen elven warriors stared at him. These were not the wispy specters to whom he had grown accustomed. These were mummified corpses, bodies of the eihelvanan, each dressed in the full regalia of a Knight of Rheina. Their skin was leathery, devoid of any moisture and stretched tight across their skeletons. Straw-like hair arranged in intricate braids clung to their scalps, and their mouths gaped as though to consume wandering souls. Within the eye sockets glowed topaz orbs, and he sensed that a hostile presence watched from within them.

One of the mummies raised a crooked finger and said, "You must be tested."

A second, that he thought might once have been Manaua, said, "You did not come for them."

Another said, "But now a sixth has been claimed."

"And you came for *her*," said another.

"A sixth? What sixth?" Rezkin said.

"You already know."

He said, "How can I know? You have not told me."

"We have," they said in unison, "but you do not listen."

Rezkin's head throbbed as though a hammer was pounding on his brain.

"Tell me," he said.

"The knowledge is there," said the first that had spoken, still pointing at him. He decided by the hairstyle that it must be Elry. "And you heeded our call. Even though you have not listened, you know."

Again, his head pounded with immense pain, a pain so sharp it took him to his knees, and he nearly fell from the pedestal. Grabbing his head, he struggled just to take a breath.

"*Listen ...*" a disembodied voice hissed.

Rezkin focused on the pain, and he tried to listen, but it was getting him nowhere. He listened harder. He tried to hear their voices, a sound, any sound. Something within his mind burst.

Then he heard water. It sounded like the rushing water that was in his room —water that came from nowhere and went nowhere. He felt a tug at his hair, and he jerked his eyes open. He lay on the floor in his chambers, curled in a ball and clutching his head. He patted the cat that was licking his hair and realized his head no longer hurt. For the first time in weeks, he could think without experiencing the stabbing pain, and he *knew*.

Rezkin leapt to his feet and grabbed his sword belt. Unlike in his dream, he was already dressed with knives and other small weapons secreted about his person. He strapped his Sheyalins to his hips and the black sword across his back and rushed out the door. He did not stop to greet the people he passed on the way. He made his way to the wing where the women were staying. He had given orders for everyone to stay in pairs, so although the palace afforded plenty of space, they shared rooms. He pounded on the door that had recently been installed, but after several attempts, no one answered. He went to the next door and banged on it until it opened.

Frisha said, "Rezkin? What is it? Is something wrong?"

"Have you seen Yserria?" he said in a rush.

"Um, no, not for a while. She was to escort Ilanet to the garden."

"Then you have not seen Ilanet either?"

Frisha was finally overcome with alarm. "No, what's wrong? Are they missing?"

"Just ... who is with you?" Rezkin asked.

She stood to one side so that he could see past her. Shiela, Malcius, and Brandt were all in the room watching them with pensive expressions.

"Good, you all stay here. I will send for you if your assistance is required."

Kai and Shezar rounded the corner in a hurry.

"What is wrong?" Kai asked. "The phantoms said you needed us."

"Shielreyah!" Rezkin called. They did not appear. "They came to you?" he said.

Kai nodded. "Yes, it was Elry, I think."

"Yeshri came to me," Shezar said.

"They do not respond to my summons," Rezkin said. "Have either of you seen Yserria or Ilanet?"

"Yes," said Shezar. "I just left Ilanet. She was watching the life mage class in the garden."

"What of Yserria?" Rezkin said.

Both men shook their heads.

He finally said, "Yserria has disappeared."

Everyone gasped and began talking at once. He had a sudden thought. He caught Frisha's attention and said, "Where is the tree?"

"Um, what tree?" she asked, still distracted by the upsetting news.

"The little tree—the one from the ship," he said. "Where is it?"

Frisha shook her head, looking at him as if he had lost his mind. "I don't know, Rez. I haven't seen it since we got here. Shouldn't we go look for Yserria?"

Rezkin turned and strode down the corridor toward the throne room. He needed to find out what was happening to the missing people. Until now, all of those missing had been people who had joined their party or arrived on the island *after* Serret—after he had made the deal with the katerghen. He had no idea if that made a difference, but he knew that if something happened to Yserria, Bilior would have a problem. He needed to speak with the little ancient, but he had no idea where to find him. Like Frisha, he had not seen the creature since they had arrived.

As soon as he got to the throne room, he started shoving crates aside. Everyone had apparently followed in his wake, even Shiela, and most of them started doing the same. Once the crates were out of the way, Rezkin opened the chamber doors. Just as in the dream, he felt a sense of foreboding about entering the hallowed place. Also like in the dream, the vast chamber was mostly dark. He could not see the far walls or the ceiling, but in the center glowed the pedestal, lit by an unknown overhead source.

He stepped into the room, and the floor around his feet glowed. The light followed him as he moved toward the pedestal, his gut tightening with each step. A familiar melody began to play in his mind. It was the soothing sound that sometimes accompanied his deepest state of meditation. The tenseness in his shoulders began to ease, and he worried that something was trying to steal his acuity.

"Rez?" came a hesitant call from the doorway.

He glanced back to see that one of the shielreyah was preventing his companions from entering the room. He did not know if the wraith was simply following his standing orders or if it wanted him alone. He shook his head at Frisha's anxious gaze and then turned back to the pedestal. Before stepping upon it, he surveyed the chairs around him. Each one would have been a magnificent throne in any other kingdom, but in this place, there were seventeen, and they hovered above the ground as if suspended by invisible cords. Unlike in his dream, the crystals on the backs of the chairs did not glow with the topaz lightning, and no corpses occupied the seats. Although the evidence of death was absent, somehow the room felt less alive without the mummies.

Remembering his purpose, Rezkin's renewed sense of urgency pressed him to take his place. He stepped upon the pedestal and rocked as it unexpectedly began to rise. It ascended high enough that if he fell, it would be to his death. He looked down at his friends who were gathered at the threshold looking up at him. They appeared small, yet still he could see the dread on their upturned faces. Around him, small points of light began to glow in the gloom. They grew larger as they moved toward him. Then each erupted into a swirling chaos of colors that seemed to fill the vast emptiness of the chamber. An icy tendril snaked toward him, lashing him in the chest. Another struck from the side and then another. A face appeared in the mass of vapors, and it sailed at him with a shriek.

He resolved to hold his ground and met the wraith with determined focus. He envisioned himself smashing through the phantom, a stronghold against the storm, dispelling its wispy vapors with ease. His efforts were in vain. As the wraith struck, an icy spear seized his will and struck at his core. Rezkin was thrown from the pedestal, and he heard his friends scream as he toppled to the ground. He landed on his back with a crunch as dust was tossed into the air around him. The searing pain of crushed bones did not assail him as he had anticipated. His mind spun as he tried to determine how the hard stone of the throne room could have cushioned his fall. A sense of stillness enveloped him as his eyes tried to focus on the darkness above. Tiny specks twinkled over him, and dark, shadowy tendrils threatened to block out their light. He blinked several times trying to make sense of the vision. His chest began to burn, and he realized he had not taken a breath since striking the ground. The muscles surrounding his lungs refused to heed his call, and he struggled to gain control before, finally, they released and sweet air was sucked into the vacant vessels.

He rolled to his side as he coughed and choked on the new sensation of breath, his fingers digging into the earth beneath him. His vision swam and his eyes watered, but when he could finally see again, he realized what the terrible crunch upon landing had been. He lay on a rich soil covered in detritus, the sticks and leaves beneath him crushed. Turning his gaze upward, he saw that the tiny specks were stars and the black tendrils, branches swaying in the breeze.

Lurching to his feet, he drew his swords in preparation for attack. He was surrounded by towering sentries, but none were likely to move. The trees were massive and gnarled, appearing as ancient as the citadel he now called home. That citadel was gone, now, and he was surrounded by thick forest. In the depths of darkness, he could feel a presence, but he could not place it. The sensation was everywhere, all around him, yet nothing stirred save the wind through the trees.

Then, he saw it—the silvery-red glow of moonlight reflected off animalistic eyes. First one set, then another, and another. They appeared everywhere, and they were advancing. Something seemed off, but he was struggling to find the pieces that were missing. His mind racing, a vision came to the forefront of his memory. A black sky with tiny specks of light and dark tendrils. There was no moon that night. From where was the light of the creatures' eyes emanating. It seemed an insignificant detail, and yet he felt it was important. He risked removing his gaze from the advancing creatures for only a second to investigate. It was *him*. He was the source of light. Not his weapons or any other possession, but his very person was radiating energy.

Rezkin's eyes lifted just in time to catch a glimpse of the first creature to strike him. It was roughly the size and shape of a human small-one, completely hairless, its skin pure white and wrinkled with black eyes and red lips, behind which sharp, serrated teeth dripped with saliva. Its black nails dug into his armor as it tried to sink its teeth into his throat. Its hisses were joined by the hisses of dozens more. It collided with three others as he thrust the first away from him. He felt the throbbing jab of tiny teeth in the back of his neck, and claws slashed at his hands where he gripped his swords. He spun to throw the creature from his back, but it clung to him. His swords slashed through two more with ease, spraying blood across the others.

The creatures were unnaturally fast, faster than anything he had previously fought; but unlike the drauglics he had encountered during his training, these creatures' skin could not withstand the razor edge and strength of steel. He sliced through the attackers as he backed his way toward a tree and then drove himself into its trunk. A terrible crunch reverberated through his torso as the creature on his back was crushed against the sturdy, old wood. It released his neck as it shrieked with its last breath. Now that he was free, he moved faster, hoping to at least match the frantic speed of the creatures. He thrust, sliced, kicked, and stomped the fiends until no more assailed him. He breathed heavily as he appraised the carnage. White flesh, crushed bone, and crimson blood littered the ground. Some of the creatures continued to twitch and grasp even after having lost half of their bodies.

Rezkin scanned the forest and sky for any clues as to where he might be or in which direction he was supposed to travel. He knew that, somehow, this had to do with Yserria and the others' disappearance, so he wondered if these creatures were involved. While the others who had disappeared were vulnerable, he could not imagine their easily taking Yserria. If they had swarmed her with so many, though, she might have succumbed. Still, some evidence should have been left for his people to investigate.

He circled the area using the light of his own body to search for clues. The creatures seemed to have come from every direction, but one held the largest concentration of tracks and broken branches. He followed the trail through the dark, ever cognizant that other *things* could be stalking him. Strange sounds began to reach his ears. Yips and hollers and cackling hisses. A woman screamed, a blood-curdling wail, and a cacophony of growls and gaggling chirps followed. A yellow glow seeped through the gloom, and a dance of shadows played in the firelight.

Rezkin edged closer to the clearing that smelled of putrid, rotting flesh. A breeze swept the heat of the fire over his face, and the scent was mixed with a noxious odor of burning hair and bone that threatened to choke him. Concerned that his enemies might see the light that filled the air around him, he crouched low behind the underbrush. He doubted it would do much good if any looked his way. He glowed like a beacon, beckoning the hostiles to attack. By the way the shadows stretched up the cliff across the clearing, he realized the fire had to be coming from somewhere below. He sheathed Bladesunder and gripped Kingslayer as he crawled forward on his belly, frustrated each time one of his sword hilts caught on the branches, roots, and rocks. His head came free of a particularly thick tangle of limbs, and he nearly dived over the edge of a steep drop.

Thirty feet below, in a chasm, was a pool of black water, from the center of which erupted a slab of rock bearing a flaming pyre. Surrounding the pyre were six monoliths, each possessing one of the missing people from the citadel standing and trussed by thick ropes. Although they suffered no obvious signs of serious injury, a few looked half dead already, probably from days without food or water. On the far side, Rezkin spied Yserria. She appeared to be unconscious, her head hanging forward, painted with partially dried blood that had spilled down one side of her face and neck.

Of the raucous enemies that were making such disturbing and unrelenting sounds, he saw no sign. Still he heard the wail and chitters, but the source eluded him. He backed away from the edge and skirted the perimeter, peeking down into the chasm every so often to survey it from different vantages. When he reached the side where Yserria was bound, he was nearly to the mountain-side cliff, and still he could not see the creatures making the noises. Then a glow came toward the pool from a shadow in the cliff below where he had been hiding. A moment later, a torch came into view, carried by a figure in a dark, hooded robe. Rezkin realized that the cloaked figure was emerging from a cave. It was from there that the noises were originating, and then they echoed off the walls of the chasm to sound as if coming from everywhere.

Rezkin now saw a small path that led from the cave to the stone slab and another that passed around the pool at the base of the cliff. The figure took the second path toward the opposite end of the chasm and past the pool where he disappeared into the dark. Rezkin wanted to follow the figure, but the prisoners were his priority. He did not know if the mysterious figure would be returning soon or how many more were down in the cave, so he had to move quickly. He had another problem, though. Once he had freed the people, what would he do with them. A few looked like they would not be able to walk, and Yserria had not shown any signs of rousing. In addition, he had no idea how to get back to the citadel. He did not even know if he was still on the island.

Rezkin backed away from the edge intending to return to where he could climb down onto the walkway, when suddenly he fell backward ... and kept falling. His breath was once again dispelled from his lungs as he slammed into hard stone. Kingslayer went sliding across the ground as it was forced from his grip. Knowing, now, that there was a good possibility of immediate attack, he had drawn a dagger and rolled to his feet before even managing to catch a breath. He blinked several times to clear his blurred vision and then spied several indistinct figures running at him. He heard shouts and the thunder of footsteps, and he prepared to defend himself as his mind worked to catch up to the present.

"Rezkin, Rezkin, can you hear me?" someone was saying.

The voice sounded familiar and concerned, so he did not attack when he was jostled.

"Step back!" said a deep, male voice. "He is not yet cognizant of his surroundings."

Rezkin recognized the voices and was somewhat confident they would not take advantage of his momentary vulnerability, but he was still hesitant to put away his weapon. He inhaled deeply and blinked several more times as the world began to right itself. Finally, he recognized the faces of his friends, looking at him with trepidation.

"I am well," he muttered.

He surveyed the thrones, all of which were currently occupied by misty blue wraiths that stared at him expectantly. The others followed his gaze but did not seem surprised. His friends had joined him in the middle of the throne room, apparently having been allowed to enter when the shielreyah took their seats.

"He lives," said Manaua.

"The gates are open to him," Opohl intoned.

"His strength is sufficient," Elry said.

Then they all disappeared, and the entire room was cast in darkness save for the light of the pedestal that had returned to its original position.

"Rezkin," Frisha said, as she clutched at his arms looking for something. "Are you hurt? Did you break anything?"

"No," he said. "I am not broken. The leaves and dirt broke my fall."

She furrowed her brow. "Rezkin, did you hit your head? There are no leaves and dirt here."

"No," said Brandt as he pulled a twig from Rezkin's hair, "but there are on *him*."

"Are these scratches?" Frisha said, examining his hands.

"They look more like claw marks," said Kai as he circled Rezkin. He tugged at Rezkin's collar. "Is this a bite mark? It looks nasty. We need to get that cleaned."

"What happened? Where did you get all this?" Frisha asked as she studied the livid, bleeding marks.

He finally turned to her and said, "What did you see?"

"What do you mean? We saw you fall from up there," she said, pointing toward the ceiling.

"That is all? I just fell?"

"Yes," said Brandt, "and then you smacked into the floor. I thought for sure you would be dead."

Malcius stood behind them glaring at him, although Rezkin did not know the reason for his hostility. Shiela appeared pale and clung to Shezar's arm as though he might save *her* from falling. Rezkin glanced one more time at the pedestal and the now vacant thrones.

"Let us reconvene in the war room. Prepare the troops—all of them, including the mages. We must make haste."

With his officers and mages gathered in the war room, Rezkin perused the map they had been making of the island from their explorations. It was far from complete, but he could at least narrow down possible locations.

"Have any of the patrols reported a chasm near the mountains? One that is filled with water and has a stone slab in the center."

Chieftain Gurrell stepped forward. "We have been seeing this place at the foot of the northeastern slope of the bowl." He pointed to the spot on the map and said, "We did hike to it in two or three hours."

Rezkin nodded and said, "That is our destination. The people that have gone missing are there. They have been captured and are in immediate danger."

"How do you know this?" Shezar asked.

"When I fell from the pedestal, I did not strike the ground—at least, not *here*. Somehow, I landed in the forest. I was attacked by a few dozen creatures I could not identify. After I slew them, I followed their trail to this place. The missing people were in the chasm tied to stone pillars around a bonfire on the rock slab in the center. There is a cave under the ground on this side opposite the mountain. There is no telling the range of the cave system. It could even extend under this city. I believe the cave is inhabited by a large population of *something*, but I did not see what. Someone else was there, though. Presumably human. He or she was dressed in a hooded robe."

Brandt said, "So someone stole the people and took them to this place, but for what purpose?"

Wesson spoke from where he had practically been hiding in the corner. "It sounds like a ritual."

Rezkin waved to him, "Come here, Journeyman. Explain."

Wesson shuffled forward, obviously uncomfortable with the full attention of the soldiers, nobles, and mages. He turned and spoke directly to Rezkin.

"There are forms of spell casting that depend on rituals. Ritual spells are useful because certain artifacts or runes used in the ritual store much of the energy expended while performing the different parts. They can be executed over an extended period, so the caster does not need to be very powerful or risk depleting his energy all at once, as is a concern with traditional spells. Some rituals can even be performed by mundanes. In times past, it is said that rituals were used to commune with or make deals with the fae. But, there are darker forms as well. Obviously, I have never performed any, and I would not even know how, but I have heard that they involve demon worship."

Rezkin glanced at the mages. "Do any of you know how to summon a fae?"

The mages glanced at each other, and then Nanessy said, "It is not something that is taught at the academy. While not exactly illegal, it is strongly discouraged. Some of the researchers summon minor fae to study under strictly controlled conditions, but one should never seek the higher fae, especially on their terms. Nothing good can come of it."

Rezkin might have laughed if the situation was not so dire. None of them would be standing in their new refuge without his deal with the ancient. Then again, they also would not be in this predicament.

He said, "Alright, if we assume someone is performing a dark ritual, how do we disrupt it and rescue our people?"

Wesson said, "It depends on how far they have gotten in the ritual. If it just starting, it is no problem. The pillars around the pyre—did they all have people tied to them?"

"Yes, is that significant?" Rezkin asked.

"Well, if it is a demon ritual, then based on what you described, it probably requires human sacrifice, and the pillars were likely arranged for the correct number of people. Therefore, it is reasonable to assume the ritual is in the advanced stages. The pyre in the center was lit. It could serve only to stave off the chill and provide light, *or* it could be a trigger."

Elemental Mage Morgessa added, "Someone could potentially store ritual power in the fire. If we douse the fire, the ritual could be disrupted."

Rezkin said, "What happens if we take the people without interfering in the ritual?"

Morgessa narrowed her eyes at Wesson as though she might pull the information from his mind. "Perhaps nothing," she murmured, her mind absorbed in her thoughts. "If the ritual is tied to their life forces, though, it could kill them. I do not know much about demons, assuming they are real, but the tales suggest they need bodies to host them in this realm. If someone *is* performing a demon ritual, it could be that he or she intends for whatever is invoked to possess the bodies of the captives. If this is the case, there is a good chance their life forces have already been tied to the ritual."

Rezkin said, "If their life forces are tied to the ritual, and the ritual is triggered by the fire, will dousing the fire kill them?"

Morgessa pinched her lower lip in what appeared to be an absent-minded habit. "Perhaps. I cannot say for sure."

Rezkin said, "So if we take the people, we may kill them. If we disrupt the ritual, we may kill them. How do we disconnect their life forces from the ritual?"

Wesson said, "Remember, this is all conjecture. We do not know that someone is trying to summon demons."

"I have reason to believe that is exactly what they are doing, so let us assume it is true. How do we proceed?"

Life Mage Ondrus said, "We could reattach the ritual to something else, but it would have to be something living."

Wesson shook his head, "No, no. Who knows what the ritual might summon if we change the parameters."

Apprentice Life Mage Aplin said, "What if we capture the fire?"

Rezkin looked at the apprentice who was a few years older than he. "What do you mean?"

Aplin glanced at the other mages. Upon seeing Mage Morgessa nodding thoughtfully, he seemed to gain the confidence to continue speaking.

"If we have a vessel that can store energy, something made from a mage material or possibly some of these crystals, we could capture the energy of the fire. The link to the prisoners would not be broken, but the ritual could not be completed because the energy would be trapped. We would still have to figure out a way to disconnect the captives from the fire, but we can figure that out after they are safe."

Morgessa said, "Yes, that would work, assuming the fire is the trigger."

Rezkin said, "Very well. Since we have little time, we will go with that plan. How many vessels do we need?"

"I would suggest one for each captive, just to be safe," said Morgessa.

"Can you capture fire in these crystals?" Rezkin asked.

The mages all glanced at the crystals on the walls. Morgessa shook her head. "We have tried. We cannot work with the crystals. They do not respond to us." She looked at him knowingly.

Rezkin said, "What other viable materials do we have?"

Wesson ventured, "Perhaps *you* could try?"

Rezkin frowned. "I am not a mage. What do you think I can do?"

"I think there is enough evidence to warrant discourse on that subject," Wesson said cautiously to the nods of his peers. "But putting that aside, maybe you do not need to be a mage. For whatever reason, the citadel responds to you. Maybe the power is within the crystals, and they will heed your *will* as well."

Rezkin shook his head. "We do not have time for this, Journeyman."

Wesson pulled a clear crystal from the pocket of his robes and placed it on the table in front of Rezkin. It was about the size of his pinky nail. Wesson opened his palm, and a ball of flame erupted in the air above it. Rezkin looked at the crystal and then back at Wesson.

"This is a waste of time," he said. "We should find another material with which the rest of you can work."

Wesson shook his head. "We do not have six vessels made of mage material that could contain fire. We do this, or we come up with a new plan."

The other mages glanced between Wesson and Rezkin with looks varying between trepidation and awe. They all knew Rezkin favored the battle mage, but Wesson was generally reserved, at least in front of them.

Rezkin sighed and picked up the crystal. "What do I do?"

"Whatever you did to light the crystals and open the doors," Wesson said. "Only this time, focus your *will* on your intent for the crystal to capture the energy of the fire. Normally, it is impossible to capture an element like fire within another element like stone without changing the nature of the material, but it appears this is not a problem with these crystals."

"Except that you cannot do it yourself," Rezkin said.

Wesson smiled shamelessly. "Exactly."

Holding the crystal between his thumb and forefinger, Rezkin watched the fire swirl over Wesson's hand. He thought about his desire for the fire to be inside the crystal. After an intense effort, he decided it was not going to work. Then, he thought maybe he had erred in his approach. He was not supposed to try to make the fire do anything. He was supposed to focus on the crystal. In his mind, he told the crystal of his intent for it to exist *around* the fire.

And then he was falling. It was as though the crystal had opened, inviting him in, beckoning him to join with it. Inside, the crystal was massive. It was a dark world surrounded by facets that reflected and refracted the light around him. Above, he could see the sun shining brightly, swirling with powerful flaming eddies, but it was too large. Rezkin realized it was not the sun. It was Wesson's ball of fire. He looked down at himself, or at least, where he should have been, but he had no body. He also heard voices. They were all around, but they were too large, too vast to understand. Then, one came through. It was a whisper, but it was clear as a bell.

"*Iréshke cadue, Spirétua pritehwa. Casue rienau flieska fontris mes.*"

Rezkin did not understand. The voice sounded patient but urgent.

"*Caheileian.*"

Again, he was at a loss.

"*Caheileian,*" the voice repeated.

It proceeded to repeat the word several more times, and although he did not know the meaning, he felt as though it was beckoning to him. He realized that he had made a mistake. He had allowed the crystal to swallow him instead of the fire. He gathered his *will* and drew his mind out of the crystal.

"Are you okay?" Wesson said from beside him. "Rezkin? Can you hear me?"

"Yes," he said. "I can hear you now."

Rezkin glanced up and nearly dropped the crystal when he saw one of the shielreyah hovering inches from his face.

Elry said, "*Casue rienau flieska fontris mes, Spirétua Syek-lyé.*"

He stared at the shielreyah and willed it to speak Ashaiian. Elry grimaced and said, "It is dangerous for you in the crystal vessel, *Spirétua Syek-lyé.* You must remain on the outside, or you may never leave."

The shielreyah's wisps seemed to separate into strands and then were sucked into themselves as he vanished.

"How long was I gone?" Rezkin said.

"Gone?" Wesson said. "It was less than a minute, but we were concerned when the shielreyah showed up, and then you did not respond to our calls. What happened?"

Rezkin looked at the mage and said, "I fell in. I was inside the crystal, looking out through the facets. I could not hear you, but I could hear *him*." He frowned and looked back at the crystal. "Unfortunately, he was speaking Fersheya, so I could not understand what he was saying. I need to reserve some time to learn the language."

"Should we come up with another plan?" Wesson said, absently bobbing the fireball up and down as if playing with a toy.

Rezkin looked back at the crystal. What he did know about the crystal was that it had been empty. It was not a solid structure like a normal crystal. Inside was a vast chamber waiting to be filled. He also knew that the power was not within the crystal, but it was willing to take instructions from him.

"I will try again," he said.

This time when he experienced the falling sensation, he held back. He refused to enter the vacant chamber, and instead *willed* it to absorb the energy of the fireball. He felt a tug, and then a spark blinked into existence. A trail of energy began to flow from Wesson's fireball into the crystal. As the fireball shrank, the luminosity of the crystal intensified. Eventually, the fire in Wesson's palm winked out of existence. Peering into the tiny glowing crystal with his mind's eye, Rezkin saw a blazing inferno filling the chamber.

Satisfied with the results, Rezkin looked at the mages and said, "It worked. This crystal is too small to contain the pyre that I saw, though. The crystals we use need to be larger, perhaps the width of a thumb, at least."

Wesson and the other mages said nothing as they glanced between him and the crystal.

"You know, the coin?" he said.

Wesson said, "Yes, we know what a thump is. It is just that I did not really expect it to work. I have never seen fire held inside a crystal before, and I felt no use of power when you did it."

The other mages nodded in agreement.

"You were right about the crystals being different," Rezkin said. "I have seen the insides of other crystals, and they are solid. Inside this one is a vast chamber ready to be filled."

Wesson shook his head. "We have cut and crushed them. Physically, they are as solid as any other. You must have found some kind of vimaral reservoir."

Rezkin rubbed at his chest, adjusting the little stone that had heated uncomfortably against his skin. He glanced at the mages and then took in the others in the room. The strikers, army officers, a few of the swordmasters, and the Eastern Mountains chieftain and his second were present. Malcius, Brandt, Tieran, and Tam had also joined them, mostly because Rezkin indulged their curiosity and willingness to learn new skills.

He said, "Alright, here is what we are going to do."

19

"Are you sure it's okay that I'm here?" Benni asked.

"No, but you are here nevertheless," Adsden said. He looked at the anxious young man and then returned his gaze to the sentries. "The Raven favors you and so do Lord Fierdon and Count Jebai."

"Don't see why," Benni muttered.

"You are the likeable sort," Adsden said absently as he searched the faces of the few people he could see. He sighed heavily and said, "We need to know if he is there. We cannot afford any misunderstandings."

Benni said, "I don't like it. It don't make any sense. We're thieves, but we're gonna go in here and hand ourselves over to the army?"

"We have instructions to deliver the count and countess to this fortress," Adsden replied.

Benni said, "Now that we're here, why don't we just tell 'em to walk in on their own, and we can leave with our heads?"

"Count Jebai has said he will speak for us," Adsden replied.

"And you believe him?"

"I believe that if we do not do as the Raven commands, it will not matter what the army does. It is better to take our chances with the count."

"Right," Benni said soberly. "It's like—maybe death or definitely death."

"Precisely," Adsden said as he turned and strode back down the path to where Lord and Lady Jebai were waiting with the horses.

"So?" Simeon said.

Adsden sighed. "I did not recognize anyone, but it was an unlikely chance. I do not make a habit of spending time with guards and soldiers—at least, not unless they are in my purse."

Simeon gave him a disapproving frown, which Adsden returned with a smile.

He added, "Most of them are wearing uniforms. Some appear to be city or private guards, others are regular army. I would say it is obvious they are a conglomerate of deserters and rebels."

"Then they are most likely on our side," Simeon said.

"What side is that?" said Adsden.

Simeon paused, his inner conflict playing across his face. Finally, he said, "I suppose we are all working toward Caydean's downfall, for now. We can figure out the rest afterward."

Adsden shook his head. "That does not sound like a plan for long-term survival."

"No," Simeon grumbled. "We are just trying to survive today. I told you, unless I see proof that this Dark Tidings has a legitimate claim to the throne, I intend to support Wellinven. We should have gone there."

"You know we would never have made it through. Wellinven, like the other duchies, has been under siege for two months. The army is not going anywhere. They are trying to starve them out. Here is a manned fort that has somehow been overlooked. These do not look like the king's forces, but I cannot say that they are friendly either."

Count Jebai looked up at the spires that could just barely be seen through the trees. "How is it that this Raven could have a fortress the size of the palace and no one knows about it?"

Adsden said, "I do not know. The Raven is a mystery in every regard. He is a man of many means, but perhaps it belongs to Dark Tidings. I suppose we will find out when we get there."

Adsden pulled up his hood and ordered Benni to do the same. He rode at the front with Simeon and Lady Jebai side by side in the center, hoods down, and Benni in the rear. It had been a conundrum trying to figure out how to approach without getting shot through with arrows before they reached the gate. Four people could hardly be considered an immediate threat, but emotions ran high where treason was concerned, and frightened people some-times acted rashly.

As they approached, the wall patrols raised their bows, and a gate guard called, "Halt. Who goes there? Identify yourselves."

Adsden said, "Count Jebai and his lady seek refuge in the northern fortress."

The wall guard conferred with a comrade while they waited, and then a boy of perhaps twelve took to the steps at a sprint. After a short while, an older man wearing the splendid regalia of an army general appeared on the wall.

"Simeon? Is that you?" the man called.

Simeon's withered face turned up, and he smiled keenly. "Greetings, Marcum. I did not expect to find you here—or anywhere for that matter."

The gates were opened immediately, and Marcum met them in the bailey. Simeon struggled to dismount after having spent so much time in the saddle at his age and in his condition. The month spent in the palace dungeons had not been kind. He turned to Marcum with a brotherly embrace, and the stout men had tears in their eyes.

"It is good to see you, Brother," Marcum said. "I had thought you dead."

"And I you," Simeon said.

Marcum grinned broadly. "I am not so easily defeated."

"No, I should have known," Simeon said, suddenly looking much older than he had. "Adelina?"

"She is well," Marcum said. "She will be glad to see you both."

Marcum and Simeon turned to help Simeon's wife Pethela from her horse. After a tearful greeting, Marcum bade them join him in his quarters to rest and catch up on the news.

A few soldiers came to take their horses, and Adsden and Benni waited silently to be either invited or forgotten. Adsden almost hoped for the latter, but he had orders. His hopes were dashed when Count Jebai turned and motioned for him and Benni to join them. He and Benni shared a look and then followed the nobles into the fortress.

After several turns and staircases, Simeon said, "This place seems familiar."

"I was thinking the same," Pethela said.

Marcum grunted. He did not sound pleased when he said, "Yes, although it lacks the accoutrements, the interior is the exact layout of the palace in Kaibain."

Simeon turned to him with surprise, "Have you been hiding a palace from the king?"

"Not I," said Marcum. "This place was unknown to me until a few months ago when Caydean's men came for me."

"How did you get away?" Simeon asked.

Marcum's said, "We shall discuss that once we are in closed quarters."

A few minutes later, they reached Marcum's office suite. It was grand, fit for a king, and Adsden knew now that it probably had been designed for one. A man at the door took their cloaks and hung them on a rack. While they were making themselves comfortable, two young women arrived, one with a tray containing moist towels and a teapot with matching cups and saucers, and the other bearing a platter mounded with breads, cheeses, and thinly sliced meat rolled into little tubes around pickled vegetables.

Benni reached for the tray, but Adsden stopped him before he offended someone.

"Let the boy eat," Simeon said. "We have all had a hard time of it, and he deserves whatever thanks we can give him."

Benni smiled, grabbed a plateful, and then proceeded to shove the food into his mouth as quickly as possible.

"You too," Simeon said, waving to the platter.

Adsden generally did his best to imitate the refinement of the nobles that he had observed throughout his time as a thief, but he had never been invited to sit at their table. He was uncertain and did not want to expose himself for the common street thief that he was. He glanced at Benni and then looked back to Simeon uncomfortably. Pethela smiled at him and then handed him a towel before graciously pouring him a cup of tea. She then stacked several of the food items onto a plate and passed them over.

He said, "Thank you, Lady Jebai. I had never thought to be served by a countess."

"It is my pleasure," she said. "If Adelina were here, I am sure she would do the same." She turned to Marcum and said, "Where is Adelina, dear? You said she is well."

Marcum waved and said, "Oh, she will be here momentarily. She spends most of her time in the sewing room or the solar these days. She does not like to be around the soldiers. She says it upsets her to think about them dying in the coming war. Sometimes I wonder how I ended up with such a soft-hearted woman."

"Perhaps a hardened man needs a soft woman," Pethela said.

"You may be right, but although she is soft, she is strong. I doubt I could have reached my position had it not been for her support."

A woman's voice came from the doorway. "I am pleased to hear you understand that, Marcum."

Pethela rose, so the men rose with her, and the two women embraced each other as though they might be lost if they let go.

Adelina said, "Oh, Pethela, you have been through so much. Please, sit and enjoy some comforts."

Simeon embraced Adelina and then everyone sat facing each other around a coffee table. Adsden felt awkward, as if he had intruded on the family's private business, but Benni was happy to continue scarfing the food as he watched with wide-eyed interest.

General Marcum broke the silence. "Who are your friends, Simeon?"

Simeon glanced at Adsden and Benni. He cleared his throat as if to speak and then perched at the edge of his seat to collect a cup of tea. He said, "Well" —he paused to stir in a pinch of sugar—"they, ah,"—he paused again to sip— "they are responsible for freeing Pethela and me from the dungeon, along with many others who were to share our fate."

Marcum said, "Oh? And the names of these heroes?"

Simeon wiped his mouth and cleared his throat again, as if stalling might change the answer. Adsden's resolve hardened. He held a position of influence, one of prominence. He had worked hard to acquire it and had started with far less than these people had. He was not a common urchin. His task here was to represent the guild, to further the Raven's interests.

He stood and, with a courteous bow, said, "Greetings, General Marcum and Lady Marcum. I am Adsden Vesti, guildmaster of the Serpent Guild of Justain. This is my apprentice Benni."

Marcum stared at him with a calculating gaze. "I see, Guildmaster. You may take your seat." Once Adsden was settled, Marcum said, "I doubt you took to rescuing people from the castle dungeons out of the graciousness of your heart. What is it you want? Are you here for a reward?"

Adsden smiled cordially and said, "I doubt it would be in my best interest to walk freely into your fortress and demand payment."

Marcum glanced at his brother who was preoccupied with his tea and then returned his studious gaze to Adsden. "Unless you are keeping others hostage. Are these two here as a show of good faith?"

Adsden sipped his own tea and then relaxed into his chair. "I cannot take credit for the design, only for the delivery. I serve the will of another. Perhaps you have heard of him."

"The Raven," Marcum said with disgust.

"Quite so," Adsden said, "and it is a service for which you should be thankful. Lord and Lady Jebai were his top priority."

"Why?"

Adsden shrugged. "I cannot say. I cannot even begin to presume why he would choose them. On the larger scope, I figure it must have something to do with his support of the True King."

Marcum nodded. "Yes, I received reports of rumors regarding this True King. He calls himself Dark Tidings. He made quite the spectacle at the tournament, I hear. Who is he?"

Adsden shrugged. "Again, I do not have that answer, but you should not disregard him. From what I have been told, your missing kin are in his company."

Marcum turned to Simeon. "Is this true?"

Simeon rubbed his brow and said, "I know only what they have told me. I pray it is so. It seems the safest place for them under the circumstances."

"News is slow to come here," Marcum said. "We do not have a mage relay. Do you know where they are?"

Simeon raised a hand toward Adsden and then dropped it. "Again, all of my knowledge is gifted to me by Adsden and his people. You must ask him."

Marcum's face darkened as he turned back to Adsden. "Do you know where they are?"

Adsden inclined his head. "The latest is a few weeks old. It seems Dark Tidings made a bold stand in Channería. He walked away from his meeting with King Ionius bearing a treaty for a new island kingdom *and* the princess. It appears he was headed to his new capital on the island of Cael."

With furrowed brow, Marcum said, "*Cael*? What capital? Cael is a barren rock."

Adsden sipped his tea. "Well, it is a barren rock free of Caydean's tyranny."

"And this is where he has taken my nephews and nieces?" Marcum said.

"That is what I was told," Adsden replied. "He left with a large group of escapees from the tournament, including the blood heir to the throne."

"Nirius?" Marcum said. "So he has kidnapped the legitimate heir?"

Adsden shrugged. "I know nothing of Dark Tidings's motives, only that the Raven has endorsed his claim, and so I do as well."

Marcum growled, "Forgive me if I place little value in the endorsement of a bunch of criminals."

Adsden said, "According to the king, we are all criminals."

"You know what I mean," said Marcum. "*We* do not murder and steal from innocent people."

"Where do you draw the line, General Marcum? Lies, collusion, assassination"—he raised a brow—"or *treason*? Some would say you are the worst kind of criminal, a traitor, and your men deserters. We are all guilty of sedition, and should we be caught, we will all die miserably. You and I will share the same fate."

"Maybe," said Marcum, "but it is not the fate of our lives that discriminate between you and me but the fate of our souls."

Adsden nodded slowly. "That is a valid point. Perhaps, then, we should set aside our differences for the sake of our lives, and let the Maker worry about our souls."

Marcum sat back in his chair, drumming his fingers on the arm. "You are either wise for a thief or you speak with a serpent tongue."

Adsden said, "The enemy of my enemy—"

"Is still my enemy," Marcum snapped. "But unlike the youths that fill our ranks, I have experience in war. War is the time and place where the Hells spew onto the earth, and there is no line between the deeds of good and evil men. Blood shed in the name of right and blood shed in malice all looks the same. Whether our hearts are filled with light or dark makes no difference. We all hope that most of the blood spilled is that of our enemies, and we take no account of what resides in their hearts when we draw it from them."

The general's sight had wandered to some other place as he spoke, but his gaze was sharp when he returned it to Adsden. "So long as your blade is pointed at *them* and not me, I will not stand in your way."

Adsden tilted his head in acceptance, and Marcum nodded once as if finished with the subject and with *him*.

Marcum turned to Simeon and said, "How did you find me?"

"We did not set out to find *you*." Simeon glanced at Adsden. "Apparently, the Raven gave him instructions to bring us here."

Marcum narrowed his eyes as he turned his attention once again to Adsden. "The Raven knew of this place?"

Adsden nodded. "It was a coded message regarding a fortress in the north and its location. I am the only person with the key to that particular code, and I was given strict instructions to tell no one else." He glanced at Benni who was happily helping himself to seconds. "I may have stretched the rules in bringing him. The message said nothing of your presence here."

Marcum's gaze was intense as he leaned forward and said, "Tell me, Guildmaster. What does this Raven look like?"

Adsden donned an apologetic smile and said, "It is interesting you should ask. I do not know. He seems to bear some power that makes one forget. None of my associates who have met him remember either."

"That is a very convenient *talent* for a criminal overlord," Marcum grumbled.

With his mouth filled and his face practically in his plate, Benni said, "He's cold."

They all looked at him, probably out of surprise that he would stop inhaling food long enough to speak.

"What do you mean?" Adsden asked.

Benni looked up and said, "That's what I remember. He was cold. Every time I was with him, it felt like my insides were freezing. Like ... like death walked through me. I could see it in his eyes. But, I can't exactly remember what they looked like. Just ice. But ... I guess ... maybe I was just scared."

Rezkin slipped through the silent, inky blackness. He kicked and pulled, and the silky chill swept around him. Slowly, he moved toward the orange glow that suffused the murky water from above. He stared up at it, the silvery ripples causing his visions to shift and twist into unnatural forms. From his angle, the little creature was milky white dashed by the orange of the firelight on one side, and eclipsed in black on the other. Several others scurried around the platform, clearly defined one moment and like little white blobs the next, as the water's surface was disrupted.

One of the creatures slinked over to a woman who had gone missing two days prior. His bald head barely reached her waist, but he used his claws to dig into her dress and flesh as he climbed up to her face. He sniffed at her and then licked her neck, and she cried in terror. The sound reached Rezkin's ears in the water as a distorted yowl. The scream drew the other creatures' attention, and they jumped and skittered around her. One unfortunate little beast stood too close to the edge, its attention captivated by the hysteria.

Rezkin reached out of the water and snagged the thing by its pasty-white ankle. He yanked it into the black water and held it there as it writhed against his grip. Its claws raked his armor, and its sickle-like teeth gnashed as it struggled for air—a problem Rezkin did not have thanks to his enchanted mask. Once its thrashing ceased, he released it to float to the surface, a white corpse bobbing in an ink well.

One of the beast's brethren turned to see the floating carcass and scurried over to inspect. Stirred by the vision, its kin followed. They stroked the water to draw the body closer and then sunk their claws into its hide to fish it out of the pool. Rezkin was surprised that the beasts would concern themselves with the welfare of another, but his initial assessment was satisfied a moment later when they began ripping it to shreds to eat its flesh in ravenous pandemonium. Another crashed into the water with an arrow through its eye.

That was the signal. Rezkin rose from the water, pulling himself onto the slab. Within seconds, he had scythed through the five creatures that occupied the platform and then knelt to inspect the fire.

"Rezkin?" came a scratchy voice.

He turned to spy Yserria blinking at him, her face still crusted with dried blood, although some fresher scratches were now evident. Others of his people were hurrying down the narrow path, led by Shezar and Farson, when the little creatures began swarming out of the cave. Archers high on the surrounding cliff shot down the first several creatures that emerged, and then a fireball smacked into a larger horde as the creatures appeared en masse. Although the intensity of the blast threw them in every direction, some slamming into the cave walls with terrible force, their skin did not burn.

Rezkin removed his mask, hooked it to his belt, and then checked Yserria. He dabbed a bit of blood from her head wound and used his thumb to smear it onto one of the crystals. Then, he moved to the next prisoner.

"Untie me," she said. "I will fight."

"I cannot," Rezkin replied, "not yet. You are most likely entwined in a ritual. I must first contend with the spell before you can be released."

He laid the six clear, bloodied crystals on the ground in front of him, glanced back at the commotion where his people were fending of the flood of little white creatures, and then looked to Wesson who was at the edge of the cliff watching over him. With a nod from the mage, Rezkin took a deep breath and dove into the first crystal.

Wesson kept a close eye on Rezkin while he was preoccupied with the crystals. It was his job to make sure nothing got to the king while he was distracted. He knew Rezkin did not often place his trust in people, so he had been surprised when he had been asked to perform the vital role. It was one that would challenge him. There were more of the little white creatures than he had expected. They flowed out of the cave in a seemingly endless swarm, and by the thunderous chorus that rumbled from the caverns beneath his feet, it sounded like many more were to come.

"They're here," Tam shouted from behind him.

Wesson did not glance back as he erected a web of lightning across the narrow land bridge that led to the island. He heard the squelch of steel through flesh and a shriek as some foul thing died. Meanwhile, three of the little white beasts ran straight into his lightning web. One appeared as if it would scale the blazing bolts just before they crackled through its pasty body. The creatures were thrown, their bodies bursting from the force, but the malodorous wisp of burnt flesh on the breeze was not forthcoming.

He released the lightning web and thrust a blinding javelin of power at a mass of creatures that threatened to overtake Malcius and Jimson where they fought at the mouth of the cave. The strikers, Mage Morgessa, a few of the mountain men, Sir Marlis Tomwell, and LeukSergeant Yail Stratus had led a few others down the narrow path. The remainder of the troops, like he and Tam, were at the surface fending off the creatures that emerged from the gloom. He and Mage Nanessy had set several small blazes throughout the vicinity to light the battle field, but they had not seen any of the little beasts above ground until now.

Tam grunted as he clashed with another of the pale beasts. He called over his shoulder, "There must be another entrance to the caverns nearby. There is no way this many could have hidden without our noticing."

Wesson did not respond, although he was glad to hear Tam speak since he could not look back to check on him. Tam's assignment was to protect *him* while he tended to other needs. The ward around Wesson was weak since he could not maintain a stronger one around himself while also maintaining one at a distance around Rezkin *and* casting offensive spells. Some were spells he had sworn to himself he would never use, although he was now glad his master had insisted he learn them. He had not trained at the battle mage academy, though, so many of his spells had been designed for other functions, and he had modified them for present needs. After realizing that fire did not affect the creatures, he had needed to get creative.

Tam hollered, and Wesson heard branches crack as something heavy thudded to the ground. Wesson turned just in time to see that Tam had been pulled down when four of the creatures had attacked at once. He whipped his hands forward using a sloppy kinetic spell to fling debris into the fray, hoping that Tam's armor and the blanket of creatures would prevent him from enduring much of the assault. The creatures screamed and hissed, and two of them fell back having been impaled by branches and rocks. Tam thrust a knife under one beast's ribs and then spun, smashing his elbow into the other's jaw just as it tried to latch its razor teeth onto his arm.

Wesson returned his gaze to the king and was shot through with alarm as he saw one of the creatures bearing down on Rezkin, having managed to get through his weakened ward when he had lost his focus. Before he could release a spell, an arrow streaked through the air to sail clean through the creature's throat. Another followed, striking the little beast's chest, causing it to fall from the platform into the black water. Wesson glanced to the ledge opposite him to see Xa, or *Lus*, as most of the others knew him, releasing arrows into the stream of creatures. For the first time, he was thankful to have a master assassin in his midst. He glanced back at Rezkin and wondered if he should revise that to *two* assassins.

Rezkin did not like losing focus on his surroundings during the best of times. Doing so intentionally during a battle was something he would not even have considered when he left the fortress only months ago. Now he was dependent on others to make sure he survived while he worked to save people he barely knew, some of whom were complete strangers. But now he hovered over a dark and vast chamber within a crystal no larger than his thumb. The faces of the crystal were sharp and clear, and he could see the light of the flame from the outside. Some monstrosity was beyond his focus, but he knew that it was his own body.

He turned to peer out of an opposite facet. In his mind, he was the chamber, and he beckoned to the wild energy that radiated from the pyre. A spark lit in the center of the chamber and then a second. He watched in fascination as the two sparks elongated and then grew human-like appendages. On each, the waves of flame morphed into the semblance of a face. They danced gleefully, spinning about each other. They raised the tongues of flames that were their arms, and he felt a power burst through the chamber unlike any he had previously felt. A rush of wind whipped around him, encouraging the flames to grow. The little fire people ceased their dance to look at him, and in their golden gazes he saw an aged intelligence. The wind rustled the flickering flames, and the air and fire sang a melodic cadence that almost sounded like speech, but it was in a language he could not comprehend.

Although these beings were foreign to him, not once did he consider that they might be demons. They felt ancient and wild, and while his instincts warned of danger, he did not feel from them a sense of malicious chaos he might have anticipated from a demon. To his knowledge, though, he had never met a demon, so he accepted that his expectations might have been flawed. After crackling and hissing at him for a moment, the fire people gleefully danced a merry jig. As the wind died, their forms blurred until only a normal flame burned in their place. While he was confused and disturbed by the event, he knew a battle waged outside where his body was bent over the structure. Rezkin finished drawing as much fire as he could into the chamber and then left it to fill the next one.

"I wish we had some way of communicating with them," Tieran said.

"I am sure they are fine," Frisha replied anxiously. She rubbed her clammy hands on her pants and said, "Rezkin will win. He always wins."

Tieran stopped to stare at her then shook his head as he took up his pacing again. "He is not a god, Frisha."

She scowled at him. "I know that, but if anyone could survive and bring back our people, it would be Rezkin." Then, more to herself, she said, "He won't let anything happen to Tam and Malcius."

"Or Palis?" said Tieran.

She dug her fingers into her thighs. "Palis made his own choice."

"And Malcius and Tam will do the same," he said as he plopped into a chair across from Ilanet who was quietly observing their conversation.

He regretted his disregard for proper behavior when his rear reminded him that this chair was carved from stone and held only a small cushion to soften the seat.

"But you are right," he added. "Rezkin will probably return, even if the others do not."

"Don't speak like that," she snapped. "I didn't see you volunteering to go."

He growled, "I was told to stay here and guard the citadel—to guard *you*. He would not let me go. He said that, as his heir, I had to stay here where it was safer."

"If it is so safe, why are you guarding us?"

"Because we do not know if there are any underground chambers leading from the cave system into the citadel. What if they kidnapped those people to draw out our troops so they could attack from within?"

Ilanet said, "It is a common ... um ... *tactic*, from what I have read."

"Surely the shielreyah would take care of them," Frisha said with little confidence.

Tieran huffed. "I, for one, do not place faith in ghosts to protect my life."

"Will you please be quiet. I am trying to read," said Shiela from her place on a pile of cushions in one corner of the room.

Frisha and Tieran both looked at her in dismay.

Frisha said, "How can you be reading at a time like this, and what, in this place, could possibly be so interesting?"

Shiela pursed her lips as she glanced at her cousin. "I did not say it was interesting. In fact, I do not know what it is because you two are making enough noise to distract the dead."

Tieran said, "That is not funny when we are in a place where the dead literally roam the halls."

"It was not supposed to be funny," Shiela replied. "But if the dead are supposed to be protecting us, then you had best not distract them. Besides, what could *you* do against a horde of enemies."

Tieran raised his chin. "Your tongue betrays you again, Lady Shiela. Your impertinence has nearly drained me of patience. Besides, I did well enough in the tournament, and my skills have improved dramatically since training with Rezkin and the strikers. As for the horde, everyone who did not go with Rezkin is prepared to fight. Believe me, Striker Kai was not happy to be left behind."

"That *was* odd," Frisha said. "Of the strikers, Rezkin seems to trust Kai the most. I would think he would prefer Kai at his side in battle."

Tieran said, "I think he believes it is safer to leave *us* with Kai. He is protecting his queen."

Frisha flushed. "I am not a queen."

Tieran waved his hand and said, "It is only a matter of time."

The stone door opened permitting previously unheard shrieks and shouts that were assailing the corridor. Healer Aelis stepped into the room and waved for them to hurry.

"Come," he said. "We must go. The beasts have breached the palace and are nearly here."

Tieran drew his rapier as he rushed toward the opening.

"But Kai told us to stay here," said Frisha.

Aelis replied, "He did not anticipate they would make it this far into the palace. We must get to a more secure location."

"What about the others?" she said, thinking of all the people who were not fighters.

Anyone who was not prepared to pick up a sword or wield the *talent* had been told to remain in assigned rooms in the palace.

Healer Aelis said, "Most are secure in their rooms. These things seem to be heading straight for you, though. It is as if they somehow know where you are."

"But maybe they can't get past the door," Frisha said. "I think we should stay where Kai can find us."

"Come on, Frisha," said Tieran. "We cannot trust in these doors to keep out the beasts. If they have made it this far, it is likely they can get past the doors."

Rezkin had been told to fill the crystals for each person in the reverse order they had been added to the ritual, so after divvying the fire into six parts, as the mages had instructed, he filled Yserria's first. The crystal turned a deep crimson once it was filled, and he wrapped a leather thong around it before shoving it into a pouch at his waist. The next crystal turned yellow, the third green, and the fourth blue. He tied leather laces around each of them, as he had the first, and put them in the pouch. By the time he was done with the fourth crystal, though, the fire had been consumed. Rezkin knew he had separated it properly before starting, so he was still searching for the answer in the ashes when Yserria shouted.

"Look out!"

Two of the captives, a woman and an unrelated small-woman—the first two to be taken—were free. The younger started throwing rocks at him, while the older ran forward to claw at his face.

"I am trying to save you," he said as he pushed the grown woman away.

She collided with the small-woman who fell into the water and then came at him again. Before she had covered half the distance, she abruptly stopped. Her pupils expanded to consume her irises, and she donned a malicious grin. The woman snapped her hands through the air, and streamers of black smoked jettisoned toward him. Rezkin dodged to the side, and the black smoke struck a man who was tied to one of the other posts. The man's wail was enough to weaken the stoutest resolve, although it did not last long. His skin began to blacken and bubble as it was sloughed off and fell to the ground, exposing his muscles and tendons. Those followed in the same manner, and within seconds, all that was left was a pile of charred bones.

Rezkin dodged another stream of black smoke just as three arrows struck the woman through the back. She did not fall, though. Although her body struggled for function, she did not seem to notice the pain. He had never heard of a power like this, and the woman was not supposed to be a mage. She grinned at him and then raised her hands toward Yserria. Rezkin drew the black blade from his back, and with one leap, the longer blade fell, cleaving the woman in two. The pieces of her body struck the ground, and the one good eye that he could see returned to its normal, soft brown. Instead of the vibrant green lightning that normally filled the black blade, it now crackled a brilliant red.

Several more arrows flew by him as the little white creatures threatened to swarm the platform. Most of his people had retreated a short way up the path, but Farson and Shezar held the land bridge. The small-woman, a *child* of eleven years, was pulling herself from the water as she stared at him with black eyes and a twisted scowl. She cackled as inky-black ribbons began slipping over her skin to snake into the air around her. The ribbons appeared to hiss and strike at the air like snakes. Rezkin did not want to snuff the potential from this small-woman, but to him, the small-one that she had been was gone. The ritual had apparently already claimed her as its victim, replacing her soul with a demon. He now understood why the last two crystals had been empty. These two had no life force left.

Rezkin strode toward the small-woman, raising his blade to strike, when he was suddenly splattered with bloody gore. An arrow protruded from a mass of flesh where her face had been, and she fell dead at his feet. He looked to the ledge above to see Xa knocking another arrow. The assassin did not look his way as he continued putting arrows through the seemingly infinite sea of little white creatures.

Tieran brought up the rear as Frisha, Ilanet, and Shiela followed Healer Aelis through winding corridors and strange rooms. When they came to a room that appeared more like a cave than a building, they paused. From the ceiling hung dripping stalactites, and pools of water were illuminated by colorful, radiant crystals from beneath.

Healer Aelis hurried across the room toward a dark passage. "Come," he beckoned. "We must make haste."

Frisha's feet refused to move one step farther. "I don't like this. Are we underground? Aren't these things coming from underground?"

Aelis abruptly turned and spewed a stream of black tendrils toward them. Tieran leapt in front of the women as he lobbed a handful of seeds into the air. The seeds exploded into a mass of vines that created a wall between them and the healer. The black tendrils struck the wall, and the vines immediately began to blacken and curl into withered chunks and dust.

"Get back!" Tieran said.

The women turned for the exit, but the entire doorway was suddenly blocked by a monstrous beast that looked like a black, horned beetle. It scored the ground with its talons and charged them like a bull. The beast was only feet away when, from one of the luminous pools, erupted a gigantic serpent. The green and brown horror wrapped its sinuous body around the beetle, constricting it until its carapace popped, and the creature's insides were splattered everywhere. The serpent moved with furious speed to encircle the women as they screamed in terror.

While dodging attacks from Aelis, Tieran tried casting life spells at the serpent. Everything he threw at the thing was ineffective, and at least once, he felt as though it were pushing back against his power in warning. The serpent continued to coil around and upward until it had completely surrounded the women, and then its skin began to change. Although it still bore the markings of the serpent, it became like a wooden carving of the creature. shaped into a snakelike domed structure from which sprouted twigs and leaves. He could still hear the women screaming from inside, so he knew they were alive.

Tieran pulled his gaze from the wooden structure just in time to see a mass of black balls, each the size of a peach pit, sailing straight for him. He dashed out of the way, but shouted in pain as his arm erupted into spasms. The skin around the place where the ball hit ached and blackened like a day-old bruise. Tieran had little *talent* in elemental magic, but he searched the cavern with his senses for anything else living. The only pulse of life he felt was from the snake-tree. He tested it, seeing if it was willing to cooperate. Aelis was preparing to cast another dark spell, and Tieran was forced to try before receiving an answer. He yanked at the being with a spell designed for plants, since that seemed to be what it was at that moment. A mass of stems shot toward the healer.

Aelis's eyes had turned black as ink, and he graced Tieran with a hateful snarl as he cast a spinning black disk that threatened to smash through the plant stems. The result of their meeting was not what Tieran expected. The stems and disk met in a powerful burst that rocked the cavern causing several of the stalactites to crash to the ground. A vine-like tendril snaked out to seize Tieran, but Aelis was thrown high to smash against the far wall before life-lessly tumbling to the ground.

20

After releasing the remaining three prisoners, Rezkin had joined the strikers in pushing back the swarm of cave creatures. Yserria stayed with the other two on the platform, gripping a long dagger that Rezkin had given to her. She was disoriented from her head wound, but she cut through those few beasts that managed to get past the others to attack the former captives. Individually, they were not so difficult to defeat.

Rezkin had just sliced through three little white creatures with one sweep of the black blade when something abruptly changed in their mannerisms. Their feral gazes became placid, and the incessant screeches and hoots gave way to sweet cooing sounds. They ceased their attacks and looked around at the slaughter. Many began to wail, a haunting cry of mourning, as they tugged at their fallen brethren. Those closest to the humans ran away in fear or cowered as they blinked up at them with tear-filled, crystal blue eyes as cold and bright as Rezkin's.

The strikers edged forward, and the little creatures scattered, clearing a way for the former captives to pass. As Rezkin stepped onto the path in front of the cave, the creatures' wanting gazes followed him. Those that had not fled inched closer, and when he did not strike them down, they bent as if suppli- cating themselves. Within minutes, he had dozens curled at his feet, like the Channerían cats, seeking solace. The cooing and wailing continued, and even the humans witnessing the strange phenomenon were stirred. Rezkin waded through the sea of white bodies, backing up the pathway that led to the surface. The creatures followed him with their pleading gazes, but eventually they turned and began gathering their dead, the haunting song of their sorrow echoing through the chasm.

Once everyone had regrouped at the surface, they took a head count. Everyone was accounted for, and only a few had sustained serious injury. Rezkin wanted to explore the cavern to see if anything pertinent could be found, but he was unwilling to wade into the nest so soon after the battle. While the enemy had been plentiful, they had been primitive, lacking in weapons, armor, or coordination. The creatures had been a distraction.

"We must return to the city quickly," he said.

～

Tieran watched in wonder as the tree-snake unwound itself, shrinking throughout the process until it resembled only a mild-mannered garter snake. It raised its head and spied him with yellow-orange eyes. Its tongue tasted the air, and then it slinked back into the pool from which it had arisen.

Frisha rushed over to Tieran. "Oh my! Are you okay? Look at this," she said, eyeing through his shredded sleeve the black mark that covered nearly his entire bicep. "We need to get you to a healer."

Tieran glanced back at Aelis who gazed at the ceiling with empty eyes.

He said, "A healer did this."

His gaze softened as he looked back at the women. Frisha was shaken but more concerned for his welfare. Shiela was absolutely distraught, crying and shaking as she hugged herself, and Ilanet seemed fairly well composed as she stared in the direction the snake had gone. He wondered if the girl was in shock.

"Are you well, Princess?" he asked.

She nodded absently. "Yes, I am well," she said but did not remove her gaze from the pool.

"Come," said Tieran. "Let us get back to the others. We know not how many others of these creatures are poised to attack."

As they headed toward the door, Frisha said, "Thank you, Tieran. You saved our lives. I think I underestimated you. I didn't know you had such *talent*."

Tieran glanced back at the dead mage, and said, "I do not. I may have guided it, but the power that struck down the demon was not my own. I believe we have that snake-tree thing to thank for that."

"Healer Aelis—do you think he was a demon?" Ilanet said.

Tieran shrugged as he begrudgingly wrapped an arm around the hysterical Shiela. "I do not know, but whatever it was, it was not Healer Aelis."

As they strode through the winding corridor, they saw few of the attackers. Tieran had not seen them up close earlier, but they no longer appeared to be the fearsome force that had somehow invaded the palace. Little white creatures cowered in corners, crying and shivering as they stared back at the humans with familiar topaz eyes.

"What is wrong with them?" Frisha asked.

Tieran said, "I do not know. Perhaps Aelis was controlling them somehow."

"That makes sense. He got us out of our room and down into the caves. He was probably using them as a distraction."

Ilanet added, "We do not know that he was working alone."

Tieran glanced at her and then griped his sword, anxiously awaiting attack. It was not long before they were set upon by someone who appeared as equally willing to kill them as Aelis had been.

"What, in the bloody Hells, are you doing out of your room? I go in there to make sure you are all secure, and what do I find? An empty chamber!"

Tieran said, "I apologize, Striker Kai. We were tricked into seeking refuge elsewhere, only to be confronted by what we presume was a demon in Healer Aelis's body."

Kai stared at Tieran. "What?"

Three and a half hours after the battle ended, Rezkin stood in the dawning light watching as everyone who was gathered in the courtyard filed into the palace. Kai had met them on the steps to inform him of the attack, although Rezkin bade him save the details for later. As his troops wearily dragged their feet through the doors, he stepped up behind Malcius and gripped his shoulder. Malcius jumped at the intrusion.

"What is it? Is something wrong? Shiela?" Malcius said with increasing alarm.

"Be calm. Everything is fine. Shiela is well." He waited for Malcius to release his pent breath and then said, "I need to speak with you alone for a moment."

Malcius nodded and followed Rezkin away from the crowd. Rezkin pulled a handful of crystals from the pouch at his waist. Three of them were colored and three were clear.

"Are those the fire crystals?" Malcius asked.

"More like life crystals," Rezkin said with displeasure. "Two did not take the flame because the demon hosts were already dead. One had turned blue but became clear again when the man died. This one"—he pulled a brilliant red gemstone tied to a black leather lace from the pile—"belongs to Yserria."

Malcius stared at it in awe. It was deeper than any ruby he had seen, yet brighter than a garnet, and he imagined he could see the fire trapped within its lustrous structure.

"I need you to carry it," Rezkin said.

"What? *Me*? Why?"

"Wesson believes it may be dangerous for Yserria to carry her own crystal. He says he has no idea what will happen, but it is conceivable that prolonged exposure to it could continue to drain her life force, thereby killing her. Conversely, it is possible that the life force may drain out of the crystal into her with the ritual attached. It might kill her or open her to a demon possession or both. We do not know. Until we figure out how to disconnect her from the ritual, someone will have to carry this for her."

"Why can we not just leave it in a vault somewhere?" Malcius said.

"That is even more complicated," Rezkin replied with a frown. "It is a sense that I got when I was inside the crystal, like it is alive. No, not alive, but *waiting* for life—or at least some kind of energy. Now that power fills it, the crystal needs to be fed."

"*Fed*?" Malcius exclaimed. "You mean it would feed off me?"

"No, I think it will use very little. The natural energy you release should be sufficient. If it is left without an energy source, though, the fire within will eventually burn out."

"Yserria will die," Malcius said.

"Yes, I believe so."

Malcius's face twisted with anguish. "Why *me*? I hate her. I want nothing to do with her *or* her life stone."

Rezkin looked at the crystal and then back to Malcius. "Wesson believes the spell linking the life forces to the ritual may become unstable if the crystals are separated from their donors for prolonged periods. As I said before, though, the victims cannot carry the crystals themselves. Wesson says that strong feelings for others, like love, create a bond between people that affects their energies. He thinks that if someone bearing this connection carries the stones, it will increase the chance of stabilizing the ritual spell. Wesson has studied much about life magic, so I am inclined to heed his concerns. I intend to give the other crystals to family members of the other donors. You and Yserria share a bond—"

"We most certainly do *not*," Malcius spat.

"It is a bond formed through your brother," Rezkin said, and Malcius's face dropped. "You continue to love him even though he is dead. Yserria did not know him long, but I think his loss has solidified her bond to him none-theless. Through him, through his memory, the two of you are already linked, but the strong emotions do not have to be good ones. Your hatred for her also links you."

Malcius met his gaze with fury. "If you know how I feel about her, why would you have *me* carry her life stone? I could crush it under my boot and kill her."

Rezkin shook his head and laid a hand on Malcius's shoulder. "You are a good man, Malcius. You are an honorable man. I trust that you will carry this burden with honor. Do it in Palis's name if you must."

Malcius fumed, his nostrils flaring as he inhaled air and exhaled anger. He snatched the stone from Rezkin's grasp and said, "Fine, but you had best find a way to destroy the link to the ritual quickly." He turned to leave, but Rezkin stopped him once more.

"Malcius, it is probably best that we not tell Yserria about this."

Malcius clenched his jaw and then huffed. "I have no desire to let that infu-riating woman know I am chauffeuring around her life stone."

Once Malcius stormed away, Rezkin was left alone in the yard—at least as alone as the strikers would allow. Shezar stood at the steps to the entrance, and Kai watched from the gate. Rezkin sighed. He needed some time alone, but he was not to get it. As soon as he stepped foot inside the door, Xa slinked out of the shadows to walk beside him.

"What do you want?" Rezkin said.

"I was helpful to you this night," Xa said.

Rezkin waved the strikers away. Once he was within the citadel, they begrudgingly gave him space.

He glanced at Xa as he felt the tingle of a mage ward surround them, but he continued walking. "Are you begging for appreciation? Desire for such sentiments seems beneath you."

Xa grinned. "I only wish for you to recognize that I protected you when you were vulnerable."

"I acknowledge the fact, but it will not diminish my vigilance."

Xa shook his head. "When you prove yourself to the Ong'ri, you will tell him that I served our cause?"

Rezkin abruptly stopped and captured the assassin in his icy gaze. "Need I prove myself? *I* do not serve the Order."

Xa stared at him knowing Rezkin was right but angry to admit it.

Rezkin said, "Why did you kill the girl?"

"What does it matter?" Xa said.

"I was poised to strike. Why did you kill her first? Was it to prove a point?"

Xa glanced down the corridor and then turned back to him with a grin. "Your lady would be upset if she heard that you killed a child."

Rezkin said, "The child was already dead."

"She would not understand," replied Xa.

"Why do you care?" asked Rezkin.

Xa bowed as he started backing away and said, "I serve the interests of the Riel'gesh."

The mage ward dropped, and the assassin disappeared around a corner.

When Rezkin arrived at his chamber, he wanted only to wash and rest. He found a horizontal prism that was low enough to the ground and then sat to shuck his boots. The little tortie crawled onto his lap and bumped his chin with her head.

"Is not the right place for the feline race," said a craggy voice.

Rezkin lifted his gaze to meet orange globes that were entirely too close. The cat hissed and then abruptly began purring as it rolled over languidly in his lap. Bilior lifted a twiggy appendage and dangled a leaf over the cat. It batted at the fluttering diversion before growing too lazy to continue.

The katerghen said, "In this palace of stone, with your crystal throne"—he slapped a branch against Rezkin's seat—"no cat should call home, in the forest they roam."

"I do not force it to stay here," Rezkin said. "It may leave at any time."

"It stays, as do you, and yet you are few," Bilior replied.

Rezkin glanced down at the cat. He had not considered that it might want more of its own kind or that it might feel out of place. It seemed happy enough. Was a cat capable of putting on a façade? Or was it just making do with what it had? He suddenly felt that he had more in common with the cat than the rest of the citadel's occupants.

"What do you want?" he asked.

"Daem'Ahn threatens sanctuary. A deal was struck. Here I must be."

"Yes," Rezkin said, "I was told of a strange serpent that turned into a tree. You helped to defeat the demon. How did it get here?"

Bilior stepped back and bent at the waist as if bowing but tilted his head up to look at Rezkin. "The Ahn'tep invites for the Daem'Ahn to call. The gates between realms are not open to all. On dead wood it traveled, across the sea, into the hall, amongst you all."

"You are saying that we brought it with us? How can that be? Why did you say nothing?"

Bilior blinked at him and rattled his branches. The sound of rushing wind and rain filled the room. Once it settled, the katerghen said, "Rheina and Nihko the Daem'Ahn be."

"I do not understand," Rezkin said.

"Powers of Rheina are ours and theirs, powers that fill this Ahn'tep palace. Daem'Ahn powers of Nihko we cannot see. Ahn'tep must find them."

Rezkin stood, the cat plopping to the ground unhappily. "You cannot sense the demons. That is why you need us—why you need me. You need an army that can find the demons. Once you knew where it was, why did you not kill it yourself? You obviously have the power."

Bilior rattled and said, "These Daem'Ahn, they were not *here*. Possession from afar. Human bodies held the power. Rules we must follow, to stay in this realm."

"So you could not interfere because humans were wielding the demons' power. We did not kill the demons, then. We only destroyed their hosts."

The katerghen was in his face again while hanging upside down from a stone spike. "Safety, a haven, a kingdom for an army."

"In case you did not notice, three of our people died," Rezkin said. "And I know, I must bring an army. I have told you that it will take time. Our kingdom is not yet secured, though. I must go to Gendishen to strike a deal with King Privoth. I do not know what he will want. Only after Cael is mine can I begin to concern myself with your army."

"Rezkin?" a soft voice said from behind him.

Rezkin turned to see Frisha standing in the doorway that he was sure had been closed.

"Yes?"

"Are you okay?" she asked with a pensive expression.

He finished removing his boot and said, "I am well. Why do you ask?"

"Because you are talking to a tree," she said.

Rezkin turned to see that Bilior had once again taken the form of a sapling.

She said, "Is that the tree you were asking about earlier?"

He glanced at it again and said, "Yes."

Frisha crossed her arms. "Yserria went missing, and you were worried about a tree that was in your room the whole time?" When he did not bother to respond, she huffed and said, "You didn't even come to check on us."

"Kai said you were well," he replied.

"But, didn't you want to see me? To see how I was?"

Rezkin furrowed his brow. "I knew how you were. Why would I need to see you?"

Frisha pursed her lips and then ran into Tam as she turned to leave.

"He's fine," she snapped and then stormed away.

Tam watched her retreating form and then looked to Rezkin. "What's wrong with her?"

Rezkin shook his head. "Nothing is wrong with her. It is I who does not belong."

End of Book Three

Rezkin will return in *Kingdoms and Chaos (King's Dark Tidings, Book Four)*

CHARACTERS

Rhesh Carinen – Second son of Lord Gresh Carinen; firemage

Gresh Carinen – Villainous lord who supports Caydean

Alon Gerrand – The second son of House Gerrand

Moroven – Swordmaster, Rhesh's instructor

Malcius Jebai – First son of Count Simeon Jebai, Rezkin's friend

Palis Jebai – Second son of Count Simeon Jebai, Rezkin's friend who died in Skutton

Frisha Souvain-Marcum – Rezkin's Girl Friend, General Marcum's niece.

Tieran Nirius – Heir to House Wellinven

Shiela Jebai – Daughter of Count Simeon Jebai

Brandt Gerrand – Heir of House Gerrand, friend of the Jebais

Tamarin Blackwater – Rezkin's best friend and apprentice

Wesson – battle mage

Reaylin de Voss – warrior/apprentice healer (Ashai)

Drom Nasque – Baron of Fendendril (Ashai)

Waylen Nasque – Drom Nasque's son

Jimson Bell – Ashaiian Army captain, friend of Rezkin

Drascon Listh – Second Lieutenant in the King's Army (Ashai)

Brell Millins – Sergeant in the King's Army (Ashai)

Zankai (Kai) Colguerun Tresdian – Ashaiian striker loyal to Rezkin

Merk Estadd – Captain of the *Stargazer*, the ship leaving Skutton

Bilior – Katerghen; wood nymph

Brendam LuDou – Captain of the Royal Guard for King Desbian of Torrel

Lord Gerresy – Middling Torreli lord; tournament ambassador

Colton – Tieran's man servant

Grebella – Brothel owner in Serret

Suras – Butcher in Serret

Urmel – Woman in brothel (Serret)

Tiani – Woman in brothel (Serret)

Count Mestison – Minister of Agriculture in Serret

Councilor Rebek – Member of the King's Council of Channería

King Ionius – King of Channería

Councilor Harid – Member of the King's Council of Channería

Councilor Onelle – Member of the King's Council of Channería

Ilanet – Daughter of King Ionius, Channería

Mables – Ilanet's nursemaid

Prince Nyan – Ilanet's betrothed, second son of King Vargos of Jerea

Ikaxayim (Xa) Jeng'ri – second in command of the Order in Channería (Lus)

Rella – Woman at brothel (Serret)

Hvelia – Ahn'an of wind

Uspiul – Ahn'an of water

Liti and Itli – Ahn'an of fire

Goragana – Ahn'an of earth

Commander Cosp – Guard in Serret

Collectiare Tiblot – Head of the Temple of the Maker in Channería

Dronnicus – Captain of the Channerían Royal Guard

Minder Barkal – Priest of the Maker in Channería

Elder Minder Thoran - Priest of the Maker in Channería

Minder Finwy - Priest of the Maker in Channería, Minder Barkal's assistant

Tami – Shiela's maid

Uratel – Assassin of the Black Hall

Hespion Mulnak – Duke Atressian's youngest son and heir

Fierdon Mulnak – Duke Atressian's eldest son

Adsden Vesti – Guildmaster of the Serpents (Justain)

Baelin Gale – Thirty-year-old wind and water elemental mage

Leyton Wuald– LeukCaptain, King's Army and former House Nirius Guard

Yserria Rey – Female commoner Swordmaster from Skutton

Yerlin Tomwell – Life mage

Marlis Tomwell – Ashaiian Knight of the Realm, Yerlin's brother

Tresq Abertine – Sandean Viscount who traveled to Cael as refugee

Jespia Lonneli – Healer from tournament

Nanessy Threll – Elemental mage, fire and water affinity

Aelis Cress – Healer

Regis Namm – Corporal, King's Army soldier, assisted the escape from Skutton

Grath Jaeg – Eastern Mountains man, Viergnacht Tribe

Prask Berly – Eastern Mountains man, Viergnacht Tribe

Gurrell Yuold – Eastern Mountains Chieftain of the Viergnacht Tribe

Myerin Ilgoth – Eastern Mountains Second, Viergnacht Tribe

Fedrin Malto – Young man from Torrel; brother of fallen Fifth Tier Swordmaster

Dennick Manding – Elemental water apprentice mage, Nirius house guard

King Desbian – King of Torrel

Opohl – Shielreyah of Caellurum

Elry – Shielreyah of Caellurum

Yeshri – Shielreyah of Caellurum

Groa – Half-Pruari guildmaster of the Diamond Claws thieves' guild in Kaibain

Breck – Guildmaster of the Razar Edge thieves' guild in Kaibain

Briesh – Master Assassin of the Black Hall

Cobb – A thief of the Justainian Serpent Guild

Simeon Jebai – Count of Glasbury; General Marcum's older brother

Manaua – Shielreyah of Caellurum

LeukSergeant Yail Stratus – Tournament official, former Third Tier champion

Gillis Cormack – Alternate identity for Striker Farson

Striker Farson – Rezkin's former trainer

Marcum Jebai – General of the Army of Ashai, Frisha's uncle

Pethela Jebai – Countess of Glasbury, Simeon's wife

Adelina Marcum – General Marcum's wife

Morgessa Freil – Elemental mage; earth and fire

Ondrus Hammel – Life mage

Aplin Guel – Apprentice life mage

DEFINITIONS

Definitions

Kingslayer – Sheyalin longsword

Bladesunder – Sheyalin shortsword

Jahartan Empire – Ancient foe of Ashai during King Coroleus's reign

vimara – Mage power, "water of life"

Stargazer – ship on which the refugees escaped from Skutton

marglow – a type of massive tree with large twisting roots

Keurg – an inedible animal known for violence

Katerghen – a fae creature; wood nymph

Ahn'an – fae (beings composed of the power of only two gods—Rheina and Mikayal)

Daem'Ahn – demon

H'khajnak –Daem'Ahn Realm

Rheina – Goddess of the Firmament, the Realm of Life

Nihko – Goddess of Death, the Afterlife

Mikayal – God of the Soul

Chiandre – the soul's connection between the physical vessel/body and Afterlife

Ahgre'an – Realm of the Ahn'an

Collectiare – head of the Temple of the Maker

Walcuttin Golden Ale – ale from Verril best served in the spring

The Order – Channerían assassin's guild (Riel'sheng)
Ong'ri – leader of the Order
Jeng'ri – second of the Order
Ahn'tep – (beings composed of the power of three gods)
Eihelvanan – name of the elven people
Darwaven – ancient race of elves
Argonts – ancient race of giants
Shielreyah – an eihelvanan warrior who gave up his spirit to guard the citadel
Drauglics – wild, vicious semi-intelligent creatures
"Leuk" – Prefix affixed to a military rank to indicate someone who finished his 5-year term and no longer serves (e.g. LeukSergeant)

ABOUT THE AUTHOR

Kel Kade lives in Texas and occasionally serves as an adjunct college faculty member, inspiring young minds and introducing them to the fascinating and very real world of geosciences. Thanks to Kade's enthusiastic readers and the success of the *King's Dark Tidings* series, Kade is now able to create universes spanning space and time, develop criminal empires, plot the downfall of tyrannous rulers, and dive into fantastical mysteries full time.

Growing up, Kade lived a military lifestyle of traveling to and living in new places. These experiences with distinctive cultures and geography instilled in Kade a sense of wanderlust and opened a young mind to the knowledge that the Earth is expansive and wild. A deep interest in science, ancient history, cultural anthropology, art, music, languages, and spirituality is evidenced by the diversity and richness of the places and cultures depicted in Kade's writing.

NOTE FROM THE AUTHOR

I hope you enjoyed reading this third book in the King's Dark Tidings (KDT) series. Please consider leaving a review or comments so that I can continue to improve and expand upon this ongoing series. Look for *Kingdoms and Chaos*, KDT Book Four! Sign up for my newsletter for updates and visit my website!

Printed in the USA
CPSIA information can be obtained
at www.ICGtesting.com
LVHW050846070923
757251LV00009B/253/J